THE
GENOCIDE
DIRECTIVE

a Novel
by

Arley Owens, Jr.

The Genocide Directive
Copyright © 2015 Arley Owens, Jr.

Cover Art: CL Owens

Editor: Pitman Sanders

First Printing March 2015
Printed in the U.S.A.

Soft Cover Edition
ISBN: 978-0-9896273-2-0

SHORTY MAE PRODUCTIONS
P.O. BOX 81102
MIDLAND, TEXAS 79708

To the memory of the millions
who died in
The Holocaust

Special Thanks to
Dylan J Morgan & Sue Smith

We hold these truths to be self-evident, that all men are created equal....
–Thomas Jefferson

"God is subtle but he is not malicious."

"Great spirits have often encountered violent opposition from weak minds."

"I know not with what weapons World War III will be fought, but World War IV will be fought with sticks and stones."

–Albert Einstein

Located within the Milky Way Galaxy two parsecs from the sun, Combria orbits a star the inhabitants call Life Giver. Forty-five percent larger than Mars, the planet's atmosphere and topography are remarkably similar to Earth's. Three humanoid races call it home: Combrians, Urths, and the spawn of interracial unions between the two—Mancombras. Technology has evolved to a point roughly equivalent to that of the United States circa 1970, but scientists have yet to split the atom.

ONE

THE NEWS REACHED DEATH CAMP 7 too late to save Drill's family: Prince Zane had succeeded in dethroning Gram Pillhigh and abolished the Genocide Directive. The edict called for the extermination of all Mancombras, their parents, and anyone assisting them. He'd been less than five feet from a gas chamber when the command came to desist and the soldiers released him.

Fearing the new regime would soon be overthrown by

supporters of the deposed king and another attempt would be made to eradicate his race, Drill had gone into hiding. The majority of Combrians and Urths weren't sympathetic so not many of his kind had survived Gram's evil decree, being so easily recognized. They'd viewed Mancombras with disdain for being half-breeds before Gram addressed the planet to explain his reasons for issuing the Genocide Directive. After that, most feared them.

Drill greatly admired Prince Zane, who'd started the revolution, but felt certain the self-titled warrior would soon be assassinated. This marked the first time in history an Urth ruled over the planet, and some militant Combrian was bound to make it a short reign. He'd traveled on foot to the south bend of the Opian River, the longest waterway on Combria. There were many abandoned homes in the area due to a devastating flood and he'd planned to hole up in one, but a black Urth woman named Polka had taken him in.

Sitting across from her in a shabby kitchen, Drill willed a steaming percolator to rise from the stove and fill two cups hovering beside it with kaffy, one of several beverages alleged to have originated with the Urths. According to ancient legend Urths came to Combria from another planet. Hardly anyone believed that anymore. Drill didn't either. It was merely a fable like Sacka Cloths—an immortal fat Urth who magically bestowed treasures to children the night before The Feast of the Annual Snow.

When the brown liquid almost reached the rims, he motioned the pot back to the stove as the cups teleported to his outstretched hands. Like all Mancombras, he'd inherited telekinesis and telepathy from a Combrian parent. Mancombras appeared pure Combrian in every respect: platinum hair, copper skin, purple eyes, and internal ears covered by tight membranes on the sides of their heads. But being eight feet tall, a genetic quirk shared by all half-breeds, made it impossible to hide their ethnicity. Rarely did a Combrian or Urth attain a height of even seven feet, and six was considered tall for both races.

"I wish I could do that," said Polka, watching him grasp the levitating handles. Most Urths spoke Anglish rather than Combrian and she was no exception.

"Why?" He handed her one of the cups and smiled. "It would tend to make you lazy like me."

The old woman laughed. "Oh I wouldn't mind, believe me."

Reading her thoughts, he saw what she really wished for was to be young again—his age—and have her mate back. She sipped kaffy and reflected on the day they met. Polka recalled things with remarkable clarity and retained even mundane details surrounding any event she deemed important. He felt her relive the anxiety of seeing a Mancombra standing by the riverbank. Not knowing King Gram had been dethroned, she had no idea the order to kill all half-breeds and anybody aiding one had been rescinded by Prince Zane.

"Sir, I live in that house over there—" she'd pointed at a small, weathered dwelling he'd thought was abandoned. "I have nothing against you people, but you can't loiter around here. If anyone spots you near my place they're liable to think I'm helping you and call for the authorities to take me to a death camp right along with you. So please, I'm begging you, move along."

He'd told her of the new regime and that he wasn't a fugitive, but she'd insisted on verifying the news for herself. Several days prior, a cyclone had cut a narrow path through the woods, barely missing her home. Unfortunately the power pole that energized her house had gotten knocked down and the company responsible for her area hadn't gotten round to repairing it. She'd been isolated from the outside world during the interim.

"That blasted wind blew the pole right on top of my wheeler," she'd explained. "The damn thing's stuck in a dent on the top and the vehicle won't budge, so I haven't been able to drive anywhere. My nearest neighbor lives a half hour walk from here but I'm going to go see her and confirm whether you're telling me the truth or not. I won't say anything about seeing you, but I advise you not to be here when I come back because my friend will be driving me, and she'll tell the authorities if she spots you."

After she'd walked off Drill had bent the metal pole back upright, freeing Polka's wheeler, assembled so long ago the brand was now obsolete. All current wheeler manufacturers produced vehicles with four wheels rather than three like hers. With the wheeler liberated and the dent forced back to its original shape, he'd then telekinetically fused her power lines back together with those dangling from a transformer on the full-current tower, reenergizing her abode. After spending almost an hour doing badly needed repairs around her small farm, he'd started down the river, hoping to find an abandoned structure of some sort to spend the night in. He hadn't gotten very far when a shiny new wheeler had pulled over near him and Polka got out.

"Well I never thought I'd see the day we'd have an Urth on the throne," she'd said as her friend motored off, "and I was elated to hear that evil beast Gram was killed. I feel so bad for your dead brethren. Nobody should be persecuted just because they're different than most. You must be so relieved to be free again."

He'd somberly nodded and said, "Yes, I'm free for now but your friend's mistaken. Gram Pillhigh isn't dead—he escaped the assault and went underground, and who knows how long the new government will last? Anyway, I have good news for you. I took the liberty of repairing your power pole while you were gone."

Polka's eyes had shot wide with elation and gratitude. "Oh how wonderful! In that case please come home with me and I'll make you a hot meal. Haven't cooked for a male since my mate passed away. I'm sorry I can't offer you a big, juicy sern steak, I had to go on assistance because I'm too old and feeble to work the land."

Her rail thin body and wrinkled face had voluminously testified to that fact. So while enjoying a large bowl of night lapper stew, he'd offered to get her farm functioning again in return for room and board. Polka had enthusiastically agreed.

Polka's thoughts suddenly became cloudy, but she didn't seem confused, which would normally be the case when he failed to receive a mental stream. It deeply puzzled him, he'd never had any trouble reading her mind before.

As if sensing his befuddlement—which she couldn't have, being an Urth—she gave him a knowing look. "Believe it or not I used to be a scientist."

Now he was totally mystified. "How did you wind up on a farm?"

"Our work. My mate was a scientist too. We were experimenting with something one of King Gram's spies got wind of. All of our documents were confiscated, our lab equipment destroyed, and we were given two choices: death or abandonment of our research. We managed to slip one journal past them that would have cost us our lives if they'd known its contents. We took what little of our savings we were allowed to keep and bought this farm."

Drill furrowed his brow, still unable to break through. Her conscious brain patterns remained hidden beneath a wafer of nonsensical meanderings, except when she spoke. "How did you keep them from knowing you were hiding the journal?"

"By what you're experiencing right now," she answered with a perceptive smile. "I could tell by your expression you were reading my mind. My mate developed a technique for resisting mind probes. Now watch this, in my brain that is. I'll shift gears every ten seconds."

Polka's thoughts began transmitting sharp and clear, only to turn hazy before becoming lucid again in the precise timing she'd announced.

He gasped with awe. "That's amazing!"

"I have my mate to thank for perfecting it, rest his soul. We escaped with our lives only because he did." Eyes glazing over with sadness, her thoughts became easily readable. She'd been incredibly lonely since losing her mate, and hated no longer being a part of the academic community in University City, where they'd been forced from their laboratory.

"But how were you able to deceive the authorities? Weren't they suspicious you'd learn to block them when they couldn't discern your thinking?"

"We didn't block them, we fooled them in a manner that I will demonstrate. I want you to concentrate on my thoughts as you listen to my words. Are you ready?"

He eagerly nodded and she began to speak. Though understanding the words he heard, while simultaneously receiving them from her thought patterns, the transmissions from the back of Polka's mind were incoherent gibberish.

"Okay, all done. All you could understand while scanning my brain were the same words I spoke aloud. Am I right?"

"You are!" he shouted, utterly dumbfounded. "How did you do it?"

"It's a very difficult thing to learn, because everyone's thoughts wander here and there to a degree, even when they're completely focused on something. I forced myself to think only of what I was telling you, allowing nothing else to slip through. My mate called it 'quieting the oblique mind.' After perfecting the art, we were able to almost think of nothing at all for up to forty minutes."

"Astounding. How long did it take you to master the technique?"

"Not long for my gifted mate, but it took me ninety days to keep my memory from creeping in after he taught me the basics." An image of her mate filled Polka's head: a wiry black Urth with a full beard, neatly trimmed, and a very engaging smile.

A wishful thought made his heart ache. "If only my father had learned your skill perhaps he could have prevented the soldiers from probing his mind and learning where the rest of my family and I were hiding."

Polka blew a sigh through her thick lips. Her breath carried the scent of kaffy and sweet wax. "It must have been devastating beyond belief to witness their execution."

"It will burn within my soul forever."

"And all because of Gram's paranoia."

Absorbing her statement, Drill looked down at his cup, thinking about the overthrown ruler. Due to Mancombras having triple the physical strength of Combrians and ten times their telekinetic power, King Gram saw them as a threat, fearing they'd one day form a coalition and attempt to overthrow his government. So he'd ordered their extinction, along with all the Urths and Combrians who'd conceived them—acting in haste out of fear that someone would come up with an antidote for Clodec, the only known substance capable of rendering Mancombras and Combrians as mentally powerless as Urths. Prince Zane—an exceptionally talented commander who excelled in military tactics—halted the nightmare, but not before Gram's soldiers had slaughtered ninety-five percent of the Mancombra race.

"Who was Combrian, your mom or dad?" asked Polka, snapping him from his thoughts.

"My mother, which means my family line will die with me." All male Mancombras conceived in a Combrian's womb were sterile. Had his mother been Urth and his father Combrian, he'd have had a slim chance of propagating. Regardless of which race sired them, about one in five females were fertile, but no two Mancombras could produce an offspring.

"I'm so sorry this nightmare had to happen, Drill. My mate and I knew it eventually would. When I watched Gram announce the Genocide Directive on my teleon I was so appalled I wanted to throw a chair into the screen. Thank The Spirit That Created All Things, Prince Zane ran the bastard out of the palace and abolished the directive. I wish for your sake he could have managed it sooner."

Watching her wrinkles deepen with disgust as she thought about the insane king, he wondered why some Urths were black, some white, some brown, and some yellow. Though similar in build and intellect to Combrians, they were all considered inferior because they had no mental powers other than processing thought—lacked the ability to jump their height or leap a distance triple it, and were generally not as strong. Their epidermises didn't have shiny copper sheens and their ears stuck out. Some males lost a goodly portion of their hair after reaching maturity, and though the color and texture of both sexes' varied from Urth to Urth, most turned gray in old age. A thick platinum mane covered the head of all Combrians, male or female, throughout life. The same was true of Mancombras.

Other than having protruding ears, the facial features of white and brown Urths were quite Combrian-like, while those of the black and yellow ones usually weren't. The majority of black Urths had large mouths with heavy lips, and rather wide noses. Yellow Urths had strange slanted eyes. A purple-eyed Urth was unheard of, though many of the white Urths had blue eyes.

His father had been a white Urth who'd fallen in love with a Combrian at a very young age. Despite being an extremely intelligent man who could have succeeded in numerous fields, he'd chosen the simple life of a farmer because he loved working the land. Drill strove to emulate the stalwart character of the one who'd taught him how to raise crops, hunt, play sports, and had put him through college. Now his cremated body, along with that of his loving wife and every child but one, lay in a rubbish heap along with the burnt corpses of the thousands asphyxiated under the order of a mad Combrian tyrant.

TWO

THEY REACHED THE FOOT OF Mount Opian a couple of hours before dusk. Spotting a cave beyond a thicket of colorful wild spurs, Hammer ordered his troops to set up camp while he went to explore it. A buck hopper scurried out of the dark green and bright yellow brush as he began his ascent. Long ears flattened on his back, the small bundle of fur fled to a thorn shrub, leaping gracefully like a flat stone throne across the surface of a lake.

Gram's directive had declared all Mancombras in the military dishonorably discharged and called for their immediate imprisonment to await execution by firing squad. Prince Zane had not only secured his release from the stockade after starting the uprising, he'd later promoted him to colonel, a position none of his kind had ever attained in the Urth Army. Hammer's half brother Arigot served King Gram at the rank of enforcer, the Combrian equivalent. Being a purebred, his elder sibling had been able to enlist in the far superior Combrian Forces, one of the many things he envied about Arigot. By law all Mancombras were named after tools or appliances, something Prince Zane vowed to change. He was grateful his father hadn't chosen to call him Crowbar as his step-grandmother had suggested. Arigot stemmed from the ancient Combrian word for *Cerebral,* about as far from a mindless hammer as one could get.

Arigot's mother had forgiven her mate when he'd confessed to impregnating an Urth, who'd died while giving birth to his illegitimate son. She had agreed to raise him, and though Hammer would always think of her as his only mother, she'd never permitted him to address her as such. His heart had smote him each time he'd heard Arigot call her Mom, Mama, or Mother. Ironically the terms originated with the Urths, from whom half his genetic makeup came. The many expressions for Father did as well, and before his had been killed by one of Gram's soldiers—who'd also taken his stepmother's life in a firefight—Hammer had used such endearments as freely as Arigot when speaking to his dad.

Since Urths were deemed inferior it had always puzzled him why so many Combrian traditions were obvious mimicries of their ways, such as military ranks. An Urth general wore four stars on his shoulders while a top-ranking officer of the Combrian Forces was garnished with four stones and called a universal. The descending Urth rankings for general—lieutenant, major, brigadier—were referred to as three-stone, two-stone, and one-stone universals in the Combrian Forces. And the copying went all the way down to the rank of private, called a personal.

The Urth Army had been a lesser subsidiary of the Combrian Forces until Prince Zane, then called General Zane, started the revolution, taking ninety percent of the Urth Army and a quarter of the Combrian Forces away from King Gram when the insane despot issued the Genocide Directive. Despite the death of his parents because of the decree to eradicate Mancombras and those who'd spawned them, Arigot had remained loyal to the king.

Rumor had it Gram had fled here after escaping the palace attack, and was hiding in a secret compound constructed inside Mount Opian thousands of double-years ago, thought by most to be nothing but a myth. Though siding with the majority on the matter, Prince Zane wanted it checked out. General Yonker said their leader had specified him to lead the expedition. Hammer didn't know whether to feel proud or insulted at being selected for this odd mission, but how sweet it would be to avenge the deaths of his father, stepmother, multi-thousand Mancombras, and their families if Gram *was* hiding in the mountain's bowels.

┼

Voola luxuriated in the rich steam gushing from a fissure on the rock floor, colliding with stalactites and slightly cooling before descending to her in a warm embracing cloud. The source of the vapors mystified her. She speculated an underground lake was being heated by a lava bed beneath, the molten ore separated from the water by some sort of mineral formation.

Lying naked on a thick blanket of white fur that once covered a night lapper, she watched the sparkling glimeralds spin in a circle, suspended in mid air by her thoughts. Their green hues became a blur as she willed them to move faster and faster. Then she sat up, relaxed her brain, and snatched each one from the air before it could fall to the ground.

"Redemption," she sighed while eyeing the seven jewels resting in her palms. She'd stolen them from King Gram's treasure chest when the mad hedonist fell asleep after pleasuring himself with her body. The queen openly despised her as she did all his mistresses, but Voola strongly suspected the high-and-mighty bitch merely feigned indignance, secretly relieved she didn't have to handle Gram's frequent lust surges alone. If a more unstable soul existed, she pitied those who had to put up with him. Gram's mood swings were more unpredictable than an unborn baby's personality, and anything could arouse or enrage him, depending on the sick bastard's twisted frame of mind.

Sometimes both emotions overwhelmed the demented tyrant simultaneously.

When Prince Zane raided the palace, Gram's sentinels had grabbed the chest, which the king always kept near his bed. They'd managed to escape with it while being fired upon, but the padlock got ruptured by a bullet. Any normal male would hardly have sex on his mind after narrowly escaping death and being forced to abandon his home, but not Gram Pillhigh. He'd ordered his valet to have her brought to his underground sleep chambers the very night he'd been dethroned. Voola had barely managed to hide her excitement upon spotting the maimed lock. She'd wanted to take more of the jewels but her vagina could only hold seven, and each mistress was always thoroughly searched when they left the king, who insisted they be gone before he awoke the next morning. For a few moments she'd toyed with the idea of hiding some stones in her mouth as well, but the possibility of being questioned by the guards had made it too risky. The notion of poking some up her anus had also been tossed aside. She wouldn't have been able to walk normally, which would have alerted them, resulting in a body cavity search and then her immediate death.

Instead of taking her place with the other members of Gram's harem, she'd cashed in a sexual favor with the guard who'd escorted her from the sleeping king's chambers, and he'd engineered her escape. Now safe within a cavern in Mount Opian, she'd wait until the revolution settled down some and then sell the glimeralds: each worth at least five thousand tibs, enough to live on for a double-year. Hopefully Prince Zane would succeed in his quest to execute Gram before the money ran out, for she dared not seek a job until then—the despot had spies everywhere.

The cave entrance darkened with the hulking figure of a Mancombra donned in Urth military garb. Voola quickly stashed the glimeralds in a slit in the night lapper hide she lay on, jumped to her feet, and started putting on her body suit—a one piece textile meant to show off a female's curves without revealing any skin. The half-breed made his way to her before she could get her breasts fully covered by the silver synthetic. Noting his purple eyes feasting on her cleavage, she slid the zipper from her mid-section up to her throat, unifying the tight garment. As their thoughts melded, she sensed his disappointment in her flesh being covered.

I'm Colonel Hammer, he transmitted. *What's your name and what are you doing here?*

"Voola," she said aloud. "I came here for sanctuary and was enjoying a steam bath until you interrupted me."

Pledge your allegiance to Prince Zane or prepare to die.

"I'm a runaway servant of King Gram, whom I despise. Long live Prince Zane, may he reign forever!"

His dark lips spread with a smile, creating shallow ripples on his tight copper cheeks. "I knew you were too pretty to be a foe."

"So you *can* speak," she said with a disdainful laugh, insulted the mongrel dared flirting with her, blocking his mind probe before he could discern it.

"Are you mated?"

She was beyond indignant at his impudence but managed to hide it for safety's sake. "No. I was one of Gram's mistresses."

"How long have you been hiding here?"

"Several days."

Two Urth soldiers appeared and started towards them. Colonel Hammer waved them off, addressing them in Anglish: "Wait outside. I'll join you in a few minutes."

They complied and he turned back to her, again speaking Combrian. "We've been dispatched to locate Gram. Do you know where he is?"

She shook her head, wishing she could betray the fiend's whereabouts and personally witness his long overdue execution.

"Where was he when you saw him last?"

"In a hidden bunker outside Juxbow, but you won't find him there. I escaped during the night and happen to know he was planning to move on the next morning. To where I wasn't informed." She telepathed the hideout's location, knowing he'd insist on relaying it to Prince Zane, and immediately blocked his probe.

He sniffed a breath through his nose and glanced around. "I was sent here to look for him because of the popular myth of a hidden compound within this mountain."

Wondering how a Mancombra managed to rise to the rank of colonel, she cinched her waist with both hands and allowed his mind to again search hers. "If such a configuration exists I am unaware of it. King Gram never spoke to me about such matters, but I doubt he believes it to be true any more than you or I."

For a lengthy moment he studied her from head to toe, expression revealing as much as his thoughts about what a superior female Combrian he found her to be. "You're welcome to join us if you like. I've been commissioned to either find the compound or verify it doesn't exist."

"I'd be honored." Besides being tired of eating nothing but wild berries and night lapper meat, she felt it wise to remain with armed soldiers opposed to Gram, who'd surely sent some thugs to find her.

†

His father was a mathematician, his mother an astronomer, and they'd named him after an old Urth legend concerning the advancement in both fields by two mythical men. Pythagoras Copernicus Zane they'd dubbed him. He'd grown up going by his initials. His flowing red hair, fair skin, and green eyes were traits neither of his parents shared. Though their blood coursed through his veins, he looked nothing like either of them.

Standing on a stone balcony attached to the third floor of the palace, he took in the lush greenery of the picturesque countryside for several moments before focusing on one of his officers assembling troops below.

"Brought you some kaffy, PC." His chief aide handed him a gleaming cup with steam rising from it.

He accepted the vessel. "Prince Zane to you, Lieutenant."

"There's no one around but us two Urths so don't get your dander up," quipped Free, grinning. "I don't know why you chose Prince as your title to begin with, it sounds inferior to King."

"For that very reason . . ." he took a sip of kaffy and grimaced. "How many times must I tell you to lighten up on the sweetener? Anyway, I want the people to know they have a benevolent leader for a change—someone who truly has their best interest at heart. Besides, to me it sounds a little less formal."

Free pursed his lips and frowned.

"Would you prefer I go back to being called General Zane?"

"Yes," said Free, "or choose some other title that denotes you as top night lapper. Prince sounds like you have someone over you."

"I do, old chum," he put a hand on Free's shoulder, "The Spirit That Created All Things. Long ago I learned there's an unseen power that permeates everything, and has a keen interest in seeing to it I choose right from wrong, humility over arrogance and pride. Invariably, every time I've allowed myself to indulge in a sense of self importance I soon get humbled by events surrounding me. General Zane sounds too military, would make the people think they have a rigid tight-ass soldier heading the government. Gram has made the term King synonymous with vulgarity in the minds of most, so I dismissed it right away. And the more I thought about it, I realized I wasn't really at the top anyway, the deity is. Ergo, being the leader of the people yet subservient to the invisible power, I chose prince—the rank beneath a king, which is the permeating spirit, but above the populace."

Pretending to be roving merchants, he and his troops had been able to carry on their current assignment with little resistance. Arigot knew that would change the more they succeeded. When Universal Quest gave him his new orders thirty days ago, he'd said Gram barely escaped the palace with his life. The king had been openly shamed and forced into hiding, but was still able to command through his universals, so Arigot couldn't understand why he'd ordered the army to retreat. Quest had answered the query only by saying Gram was hard at work on a retaliatory schematic and the war would commence again when this mission was completed.

Spreading rumors through his many spies that he'd fled to Mount Opian had been a clever move on King Gram's part, as he'd steadily traveled in the opposite direction to one of the royal bomb shelters, according to Quest. Besides the monarch, only Quest and two of the other three universals knew where they were located. Gram's family, harem, and servants had traveled there in massive windowless trailers, so even they had no idea where they'd been taken. The mobile quarters had been towed by commercial wheelers, each driven by a trusted universal. As instructed to do by Universal Quest, Arigot had told his troops the king was safely quartered at Serene Valley, a pure fabrication.

A Combrian had been added to the extermination list of the remaining half-breeds who'd been rescued by Zane's dissolution of the Genocide Directive. Assisted by a now dismembered guard, who'd claimed to be hauling garbage outside to the disposal, one of Gram's whores had escaped and the king was demanding her blood—but only after regaining the seven glimeralds she'd stolen from him. Seeing his half brother's name while scanning the death scroll, a mournful sigh escaped him, even though he knew it was on there. Arigot rolled up the document and inserted it into a cylinder, hoping that like his father and mother, Hammer would be felled by someone else's weapon rather than his.

THREE

DRILL SPOTTED A MALE NIGHT lapper nosing around the hicker pen. The frost-colored beast had to be at least nine feet tall. It laid down on its belly and began poking its long snout along the bottom of the wire-mesh fence, attempting to shove it up. The bipedal creatures had an amazing ability to force their bulky bodies through any opening they could get their heads through.

Trying to steal my eggs are you? We'll see about that. He willed a stone to come to him. Winding up to throw, he whistled to make the four-limbed omnivore look his way, and fired. The rock struck between the eyes, knocking the would be egg-sucker unconscious. Quickly covering the distance between them in a few rapid leaps, he grabbed the beast's head and jerked it in a three quarter circle, breaking its neck.

Hands in the pockets of his tattered coveralls, he hummed a tune while strolling to the house—the dead night lapper on one side of him, a bowl filled with eggs on the other, both hovering in the air.

Polka would be pleased to have such a generous supply of fresh meat. To avoid chaos Prince Zane left many governmental policies preceding his administration in force for the duration of the war, after which he planned to carefully examine each one to determine what alterations were needed. Consequently, Gram's relief program remained in effect. The paltry assistance Polka received from it in twenty-four installments throughout the double-year couldn't stretch far enough to buy much more than staple foods after the power company took its share and she fueled her wheeler.

For several days now they'd been getting their protein from eggs he'd gathered each morning and pinto beans. The legumes had a myth associated with them about not being native to Combria but brought here by the Urths who'd arrived from outer space. Drill liked them, but not enough to eat for supper every night. The hickers' dormant period loomed ahead. Once it hit, none of them would lay a single egg for at least ten days, and he'd have his hands full trying to protect them from a plethora of night lappers, whose behavior synchronously changed with theirs.

Someone had pulled the tent flap open and tied it back. Noting several soldiers gawking at her, not bothering to hide their lust, Voola scooped her body suit under the military blanket and wrestled her way into it. They quickly looked away and got on about their business when Hammer appeared.

"Good morning," he said with a polite smile, standing a few feet from the opening, thumbs hooked on his gun belt.

"Good morning to you, Colonel." She rose from the cot and spent several moments stretching her limbs before stepping outside.

A commercial wheeler with an odd looking machine chained to a flat cargo bed slowly pulled up, being directed to stop by one of the soldiers guarding the camp. An Urth in civilian garb climbed out. "I'm looking for Colonel Hammer."

Voola supposed Hammer being a Mancombra had prompted the driver to speak Combrian, since very few Urths used it as their mother tongue.

"That's me," said Hammer in Combrian. "I see you brought the borer I requisitioned."

"Yeah. Show me where to drill and I'll get started."

Hammer smiled at him. "No rush. Have some breakfast first."

Despite the fact he was a half-breed, Hammer had started to grow on her a little more each passing day. She'd misjudged him at the cave, he didn't have a presumptuous bone in his body. Though mannerly and unassuming, unlike any type of commander she'd ever been around, he kept his underlings firmly in line. For the first time in her life she found a Mancombra sexy, a verity she'd managed to keep hidden from his mind probes so far.

Eyes on his firm backside, she followed him and the civilian to the mess tent. Hammer grabbed a tray and handed it to her, insisting she and the machine hauler go before him down the chow line. Kaffy vessel filled, she carried her bounty to the head of a table so none of the soldiers could sit beside her. Hammer motioned for the civilian to join him there, and they perched to her left and right respectively.

The Urth seasoned his food while saying, "You don't really expect to find anything do you, Colonel?"

Hammer swallowed a bite of scrambled hicker eggs and shook his head. "Prince Zane's just being thorough."

"I'm surprised he's got your unit searching for Gram in a mythical stronghold, with his henchmen still trying to carry out the Genocide Directive. If it was up to me I'd have all my soldiers looking for those cold-blooded killers."

"My duty is to follow Prince Zane's orders, not question them," said Hammer. "He's on top of the raids and will put a halt to them soon."

Voola smeared booter on a toasted grain square and nibbled, wishing the Urth would close his mouth while he chewed.

He glanced her way. "Do you speak Anglish?"

Wondering why he would ask that, she shook her head, silently lying for she understood the language perfectly. Though Hammer always spoke to her in Combrian, he'd telepathically ascertained she not only comprehended Anglish, but could read and write it as well.

"Colonel," the Urth said in Anglish, "it appears you have only one female in your command, and she's not wearing a uniform. Anything I might be interested in knowing?"

Hammer frowned. "Such as?"

Monitoring the thought processes of both males, Voola saw the Urth hoped to hire her for sex, thinking Hammer had acquired a prostitute for this expedition because street walkers often wore body suits. The colonel knew this too— she'd sensed him also peeking inside the man's head.

"She's a real beauty, and if she's a pro I wonder if I could have a ride on the merry go round."

Not very bright is he, Hammer transmitted to her.

Please don't tell him I was Gram's mistress, it will only encourage him to try hustling me, and he could be one of the bastard's spies.

Perish the thought. "What is your name anyway?"

"Sam."

"Well, Sam, she's not a pro, and I'll thank you to keep your mind on your job if you want to keep it."

Radically surprised by Hammer's reprimand, the Urth seem to shrink in his chair as the bravado he'd been exuding dissipated. "My apologies, Colonel."

"Finish your breakfast and I'll get you lined out . . . ."

"Beautiful aren't they, PC," said Free.

He'd been gazing at the multi-colored wild spurs in full bloom, zooming past his window while Free drove. Since they were alone, he permitted the lieutenant to address him by name rather than title. An assault had taken place in a major metropolis—three Mancombras and several of their relatives had been murdered. Information gathered from numerous witnesses confirmed Enforcer Arigot had led the Combrian raid. Free was driving them to a mid-size town near the big city where a staff member's Mancombra friend was known to have gone. PC anticipated the enforcer would strike there next.

Two young night lappers, stealing sweet wax from a buzz hive constructed in the heart of a sour-berry bush, fled upon hearing their vehicle approach. The densely fruited lavender branches were still shaking when they whizzed by.

"Do you think Arigot knows where Gram is?" Free stupidly asked.

"Of course not, no one in his unit does. Gram may be crazy but he's no fool. He knows it's likely we'll capture some of them alive, so whatever information we coerce from them won't be his actual location but the lie they've been told. He's using one of his trusted universals as a liaison between himself and Arigot, I assure you."

After learning Prince Zane had seized the throne and revoked Gram's evil decree, he'd come out of hiding and received wonderful news from a Mancombra friend serving on Zane's staff: his half-sister had survived the death camp. The petite Urth was the most tender, caring, and guileless creature anyone could ever have the pleasure of knowing.

Jan's face beamed with a rapturous smile as she spotted him coming through the door of her clothing shop. She ran over and wrapped her frail arms around his waist.

"I've missed you so much, Jan," he lovingly declared. "They killed my mother and our father. Is your mother safe?"

The smile faded as tears filled her eyes. "They put her in a chamber two days before I got captured."

He probed her mind and reeled with the pain she felt. Something pierced his back and Jan's thoughts immediately vanished. Turning back, he saw four armed Combrians entering the store, one of whom had fired the Clodec dart. Though dressed as civilians, they were bound to be assassins loyal to Gram. His army friend had warned him to be on the lookout because the dethroned king had dispatched a band of killers to carry out the Genocide Directive. Not seeing any soldiers lurking around town without Prince Zane's insignia on their uniforms, he'd entered her shop with no concerns. *What a fool I was coming here—I've put Jan's life in danger again! Maybe they don't know she's a relative and will leave her alone if I give up voluntarily.*

Arigot holstered his service revolver. The half-breed lay

dead with a bloody hole between his unseeing eyes. "Bring in the Urth."

A weeping young Urth woman scrunched her eyes closed upon seeing the dead Mancombra littering the floor. She fell to her knees and grabbed her hair the instant the personals released her. "P-Please don't kill me! Please, I'll do anything you ask of me, but I beg you, please let me live—I don't want to die!"

Looking down at the trembling Urth, Arigot politely asked her name, to verify his disguised soldiers hadn't nabbed an innocent.

Almost convulsing with stark fear, she meekly uttered, "J-Jan."

Without hesitation he drew his weapon and put a bullet through the female's left eye, his aim a tad off. He'd meant to shoot the middle of her forehead. Gun once again riding his hip, he opened the canister, unrolled the paper within, and scratched a line through the names Screwdriver and Jan, the Mancombra's half sister.

Next on the list was a half-breed whose family had already been exterminated, named Drill.

FOUR

ENFORCER ARIGOT HAD GOTTEN THERE before them. His squadron was last seen heading down the thoroughfare leading to Juxbow, traveling in two merchant wheelers. PC looked around the modest clothing store, picturing the horror that must have seized Screwdriver and his half sister when Gram's merciless killers had barged in. A customer hiding behind a rack of coats witnessed their abduction.

"You've got to find King Gram and put an end to this senseless killing or anarchy is waiting around the corner," the Urth woman had warned him after reporting what she'd witnessed while peering between two sern-hide jackets.

Sergeant Brush, a member of his personal staff, came into the shop. The expression on the Mancombra's face grimly assured his friend was dead. "We found Screwdriver and Jan, Prince Zane. Permission to give them an honor burial, Sir?"

Blowing out a doleful sigh, he nodded.

Free shook his head remorsefully as the sergeant walked away. "What do we do now?"

"We're returning to the palace."

A confused frown pounced on his aide's face. "We're not going to Juxbow?"

"No."

"Why not?"

"Because neither is Arigot."

"What makes you think that?"

"Common sense, Lieutenant. No Mancombra or relative thereof in their right mind would seek refuge in that bigoted municipality, seeing as how its governors voted to ban all mixed races and mixed mated couples from residing there long before Gram issued the Genocide Directive. I'd guess ninety-nine percent of the inhabitants of Juxbow resent me and support Gram. The trail of blood Arigot's leaving verifies he's following orders to complete the death edict. When we get back I'll hold a press conference and urge all Mancombras and their kin to come to the palace, offering military escorts to ensure their safe travel. Not counting the hundred under my command, there're only forty Mancombras left alive. It's about time the vast residential areas of the palace were used to shelter somebody besides Gram's family, concubines, and servants."

Aware the Mancombra had been released from Death Camp 7 when Zane abolished the directive, Arigot went there and tried to put himself in the half-breed's frame of mind. If Drill left the place foolishly thinking his life was no longer in jeopardy he'd have no reason not to take the main road. That meant he'd traveled east or west. But Arigot had learned that on the day Zane came to power and the prisoners were released from the camp, they'd been offered transport to a holding area from which their friends or relatives could pick them up. One Mancombra, a male, had declined the offer and was last seen cutting a path through the woods towards the sparsely populated region near the south bend of the Opian River. Knowing he had no family left, Arigot suspected it was Drill and the half-breed was likely hiding in one of the dilapidated homes abandoned during the great flood. If not he'd still be able to scratch another Mancombra off his list once he caught whoever it was.

Zane was bound to have put the pieces together by now, so they could no longer afford to travel in broad daylight as merchants. Peering through the brush at two Urth sentinels guarding the gates of the camp that once again functioned as a regular military base, Arigot motioned for his troops to follow him back to the vehicles. They'd take a back road he knew of that wound through the forest, almost to the river. After that, they'd be on foot.

Hearing Needle enter his study, Wheelbarrow looked up from a differential equation he was wrestling with. She'd been tense since hearing Gram had ordered a strike force to carry out the Genocide Directive, but not this overwrought. "What's wrong?"

"I'm afraid we might be next in line for termination."

"We're definitely on the hit list, Needle, every Mancombra on the planet is."

"I think we should go to the palace like PC urged us to."

"No," he declared unequivocally.

The fearful look on her face shifted into exasperation. "No one will get suspicious, Wheelbarrow. It's not all that unusual for siblings to live together."

He dismissed the matter with a wave of his hand and went back to work.

"Don't turn away from me, Wheelbarrow! Why are you so worried? No one can expose us except you or I."

"I'm not worried about our relationship being discovered.

We can't risk PC being exposed. We're *not* moving into the palace and that's final."

He stood at the mouth of the tunnel Sam had bored into the side of Mount Opian. After penetrating top soil the Urth had chewed through thirty yards of solid rock before the machine refused to budge another inch. The drill being seven feet in diameter, Hammer had been forced to stoop while making his way all the way through and back out of the perfectly round corridor it had formed. He'd signed the invoice that morning and released Sam, whose machine couldn't penetrate a mysterious obstruction. According to the readings on the engineer's instruments, Sam's bore had collided with a mass of stainless steel at least two feet thick. X-rays couldn't penetrate it, so whoever constructed the wall had evidently sheathed its interior with lead.

Like himself, General Yonker had been flabbergasted to learn Mount Opian apparently did have a stronghold within it after all. Though convinced they wouldn't find Gram inside, Prince Zane had told the general to have him stay put, tell the engineer to calculate the safest way to blast through it, and find out what the enclosure had been built to protect.

Turning from the opening, he saw Life Giver had faded from its normal blazing yellow to a dark pink as it began to sink below the horizon. It would be dark soon and the colorful moons would appear. They'd be in full phase tonight and would remain that way for nine more days before waning.

The two orbs were beautiful to behold when full, but this

phase caused problems for farmers and ranchers. Every flying creature—fowl and insect—went into hibernation for the duration, causing pollination, sweet wax production, and egg-laying to cease. Night lappers, normally feeding only when Life Giver blazed in the sky, became nocturnal, creating havoc with unguarded livestock. The beasts were called night lappers because of the strange temporary alteration in their behavior: lapping up every drop of blood from their prey after devouring its entrails and musculature. When the moons weren't in full phase they preferred small aquatic creatures, berries, sweet wax, and eggs, all consumed in the light of day.

Bright green, Jealousy was twice the size of Anger, a brilliant glowing red. Their names originated with the Urths. For whatever reason the Combrian terms for the two moons had fallen by the wayside in antiquity. Life Giver owed its title to some ancient Combrian who'd dubbed it such, but the Urth translation had become popular so long ago, few people could state the name without looking it up in a dictionary.

Corporal Sills approached. Unlike most of the other troops who'd been assigned to this duty, the young Urth had volunteered. "Sir, the Combrian wants to talk to you."

He'd sealed off the area after discovering the steel wall. "Let her through."

Sills left and a few minutes later Voola came strolling up. The silver body suit she wore fit so snug it was like a second skin covering the contours of her voluptuous body and long shapely legs.

"Dinner was served an hour ago, Colonel. Aren't you going to eat?"

Her concern made his throat turn dry. Could she actually be starting to like him? He smiled and said, "Thought I'd catch a glimpse of Jealousy and Anger first."

The corners of her beautiful lips turned up. "They *are* so very lovely when in full phase. Mind if I watch with you?"

A noise in the nearby woods made Drill forget about the night lapper he'd spied lurking near the hicker pen, darkly illuminated by Jealousy and Anger in full glow. The sounds were too rhythmic and numerous to be hunters. Suspecting soldiers were approaching, he raced to the house.

Polka almost dropped her kaffy when he surprised her by bounding in the door. With no time to waste he transmitted, *I fear we're about to have visitors from King Gram. If you think you can fool them with your mental technique I'll hide in the attic. If not, I'll make a run for it.*

The news of late had been filled with surprise raids on Mancombras and their kin, and Polka's fearful mind played out the last murders they'd heard about. Those thoughts were intertwined with deep frustration. They'd planned to leave for the palace first thing in the morning after hearing Prince Zane implore all Mancombras to come there, and she wished they'd left immediately after hearing it so they wouldn't have to deal with this situation.

She inhaled a quick breath and nervously commanded, "Get to the attic—hurry!"

FIVE

ARIGOT EYED THE BLACK URTH suspiciously. Her nervous demeanor indicated she was lying, but her thoughts didn't verify that fact, or anything else he could discern. "When is the last time you saw a Mancombra?"

She cleared her throat. "To tell you the truth, Enforcer, it's been so long I can't remember."

Apparently her mental processes were so weak they had little range, so he stepped closer to her. The thoughts of a youthful Urth could be detected as far away as twenty feet, but the older they got the less distance their transmissions traveled. If she were Combrian or a half-breed she'd have the power to block him from reading her mind until he got within an arm's length of her. "You say your name is Polka?"

"That's right."

"I suppose you support Prince Zane."

"I would be lying if I said otherwise. Besides, you already know I do since you can detect my thoughts."

"That I do," he fibbed, not wanting her to know he still couldn't make any sense out of the claptrap emanating from her brain. It was almost like she wasn't thinking at all.

"Very well, I'll leave you now." He turned and started for the door but did an about face upon receiving a hopeful thought not his own. "Why are you planning to go to the palace tomorrow?"

Voola sat on a section of grassy slope staring at Jealousy and Anger, knees drawn to her chest, arms embracing her shins. She cut her eyes to Hammer sitting a few feet away, legs stretched out in front of him as he gazed into the night sky. "When we met, you asked if I was mated. Are you?"

"No," he answered, still looking skyward.

Again taking in the beauty of Combria's dual natural satellites, she said, "I almost mated but my lover got killed in a wheeler accident not long after we started college. That's how I wound up as part of Gram's harem as a matter of fact."

"What happened?"

Through her peripheral vision she discerned he was now eyeing her instead of the moons. "I was so despondent over my lover's death I dropped out of the university, started staying out all night, drinking heavily, became terribly promiscuous in the process, and wound up with the wrong crowd. I was at a party with my wild friends, who I didn't know were selling narcotics. It got raided by the authorities and I was incarcerated along with all of them, because no one believed I was ignorant of their illegal activities. A two stone universal came to the prison and set up a beauty contest. The winner got to serve out the remainder of her sentence in King Gram's palace as one of his mistresses, eating royal cuisine instead of prison swill, getting to bathe daily, pick out her own clothes from the royal commissary, and sleep in a comfortable bed. I'd have done anything to get out of that awful dungeon so I entered the competition and—all modesty aside—won it hands down."

Now Hammer was blatantly staring at her, she noted with pleasure while pretending to be absorbed with the moons.

"What was your sentence?"

"Two double-years. The day my time was served I went from the highest emotion—totally ecstatic at finally obtaining my freedom—to a depression you can't imagine when I learned Gram had no intentions of ever releasing me. I'd have never been able to escape from the palace, so you can understand my loyalty to Prince Zane. If he hadn't forced Gram to flee to his hideaway I'd still be enslaved to him. How is it you never mated?"

He rose to his feet and extended a hand to help her up. "I'll tell you on the way back to camp, I'm ready to have my dinner."

She walked beside him down a path the soldiers had cut through the dense brush. "Well? I'm waiting."

A self-recriminating frown draped his face as he inhaled a deep breath. "I'm not attracted to my own kind unfortunately. I don't mind tall females, but not as tall as me. Being a Mancombra borne by an Urth there's a slim chance I could sire a child. When I got tested I was told the odds were ten to one against my being able to reproduce. It would be unfair to ask a Combrian or Urth to spend her life with me, knowing she'd most likely never be impregnated, at least not if she remained faithful to me. So I just play the field."

His sensitivity to another's welfare, even at the cost of never having a mate to cook and clean for him, touched her. And it was good to hear he didn't mind tall females since she lacked only three inches being seven feet. "Not every female wants to raise kids, Colonel."

He stopped walking. "How about you?"

Continuing along the path, she blocked him out and thought about it before answering. "I'm not sure."

The old woman's eyes were almost bulging out of their

sockets as fear creased the contours of her face. "I've never been to the palace before and wanted to see it in person before I die," she finally answered.

Her trepidation should have made the Urth's mental stream course through his stronger rather than weaker, so the fuzziness in her mind made no sense. Arigot could only conclude this Urth who called herself Polka was on the verge of going senile. Nonetheless she could still communicate effectively, so he deployed a trap.

"I and the soldiers under my command hate this war and we're sick of killing unarmed civilians. When you get to the palace, would you please tell one of the guards you have a message for Prince Zane from Enforcer Arigot? He'll pass it on I guarantee you. Tell him we want to surrender, but will do so only to him and no one else. We're heading to Serene Valley from here and request that he meet us there in four days to take us into custody. We have only one condition, that he spare our lives. Tell him that I, Enforcer Arigot, will hold off on my mission to complete the Genocide Directive for that length of time but will have no choice but to resume hostile action if Prince Zane doesn't show. King Gram will order my death if I don't report another termination soon thereafter. I'd planned to send the message through a Mancombra I'd hoped to capture tonight, releasing him in the morning to deliver it as proof of my honest intent. But since I failed, time won't permit it, so I'm asking you to deliver it for me. Will you do it?"

The mentally deteriorating Urth nodded.

It didn't matter if she really meant it or not, Zane would see it as the ploy it was. But he hoped she'd tell her friends about this visit before leaving for the palace, and pass on that they'd left the area. He had no real intention of doing so until another name had been scratched off Gram's list. If the lie reached the half-breed he'd feel safe for the time being instead of fleeing to parts unknown.

Trembling in the attic almost directly above them, Drill wanted to probe the soldier's mind but didn't dare. In doing so he'd be melding thoughts with the Combrian, exposing himself. For the same reason he had to refrain from entering Polka's brain as well. He couldn't make out their conversation filtering through the ceiling, only muffled vocalizations.

His fear made him relive that horrifying day every member of his family had been put to death. Parents were the first to die, then the order went from youngest child to eldest. His father had boldly stepped into the gas chamber, as had his defiant mother, both of them brave to the end. But having to witness his younger brothers' and sisters' terrified screams—feeling their anguish as they cried out in desperation, asking why their lives had to end simply because of their genetic makeup—had tormented him more than knowing he'd be strapped to the chair next.

He'd been inundated with guilt as much as relief upon being released. The stilled body of his adolescent brother had been removed only moments before, and the guards were taking him to the chamber when a soldier rushed in to announce the Genocide Directive had been abolished and all prisoners were to be freed immediately.

"Tell me about your family," Voola requested while watching him eat, his huge Mancombra hand making the fork look like a child's toy.

Hammer swallowed and wiped his mouth. "As I told you, my mother was Urth. She died giving birth to me. My father was mated to a Combrian and already had an infant son when I was conceived. He confessed his adultery and told her he wanted to raise me. She agreed and I grew up in their home with my half brother Arigot."

Feeling pain in his thoughts over his sibling being with the enemy forces, Voola sensed him searching hers, discovering she'd seen an Enforcer Arigot at the palace once.

Drawing upon the mental image in her brain he transmitted, *The enforcer you're thinking of is indeed my half brother.*

Polka cooked night lapper sausage and toasted grain squares for breakfast. Eggs would have made both much more enjoyable. Watching her spread booter on her toast, Drill recalled his father teaching him how to make the fatty substance.

"Skim the cream off this whole sern malk," he'd instructed, "put it in the container and shake it until yellow globules form. Pour off the remaining liquid for booter malk. Then add water to the globules and gently shake it before draining it through the fine mesh, which keeps the booter globules in while the liquid pours out. Repeat the process until the water drains clear. After that, dump it on the pastry board and press it with a spoon to squeeze out any remaining booter malk. When you can't squeeze out any more, stuff the booter in the shaper and put it in the cooler."

According to legend, booter was unheard of on Combria until the Urths came.

"We need to get a malk sern—" he bit into a plat of sausage wedged between two squares "—then you won't have to buy booter, I'll make it for you."

"I don't want to talk about booter, Drill. Do you think it's possible Enforcer Arigot was telling the truth about wanting to surrender?"

He shook his head. The bitter disappointment enveloping Polka equaled his own, but circumstances couldn't be ignored. With Gram's soldiers roaming the countryside seeking to fulfill the mad king's Genocide Directive, it was far too risky to drive to the palace like they'd planned. She'd insisted he stay when he'd offered to leave for her sake earlier that morning. His presence endangered her and there was always the chance of a return visit by Arigot or some other goon under Gram's command.

A faint smile lightened the depression that had been clinging to Polka all morning. "Prince Zane said he'd send a military escort to any Mancombras who needed it. Why don't we contact the palace and request one?"

"No," he replied, sorry he couldn't answer otherwise. "I don't know how many soldiers Arigot has with him but my guess would be a lot. I doubt Prince Zane could spare more than a few of his to help us. If we were attacked in route and any of them were killed, their blood would be on my hands and I couldn't live with that. Were it not for your ability to prevent your mind being probed I wouldn't even consider staying here for the same reason. It's a shame you don't have a four-tired wheeler since Arigot wouldn't bother searching it with you driving. The spare cavity in yours is too small for me to hide in. Speaking of that, you need to come up with a reason why you changed your mind about going to the palace in case he sees your wheeler is still here."

PC stood on a terrace facing the entrance to the palace grounds, watching guards inspect each wheeler, verifying those within them were Mancombras or relatives thereof before allowing the vehicles through the gates. More than a dozen were lined up for inspection and there hadn't been any reports of an ambush yet.

He wished Needle could talk stubborn Wheelbarrow into coming to the palace. One of the first things he'd done after learning Gram planned to exterminate all Mancombras was procure a cabin in the country for the brother and sister. Following his advice they'd each taken a leave of absence from the university and moved there to wait out the storm. Arigot had no means to obtain their current address but they were vulnerable when coming and going, which both did regularly.

Gram had signed the Genocide Directive into law a mere four days afterwards. Their professional credentials, like that of all Mancombras, had been nullified the moment Gram issued the death decree. He'd restored their degrees but they were still in danger.

If it wouldn't rouse suspicion he'd station a dozen snipers near their temporary home to help protect them. The sharpshooters would wonder why he was so interested in guarding the lives of those particular Mancombras, and he couldn't afford for that curiosity to spread. It might reach the ears of one of Gram's innumerable spies.

The engineer entered the command tent and saluted.

"At ease, Captain," said Hammer from behind his field desk, noticing a greasy stray hair clinging to the Urth's forehead.

"Colonel, we'll need to support the tunnel with steel-reinforced concrete throughout before the directional explosives can be employed. My analysis of the natural formation leaves little doubt it will collapse otherwise."

Anxious to see what awaited on the other side of the metal wall, he hated to hear that, though he'd been expecting to. "How long will it take?"

Captain Wurz removed his hat and ran a hand over the few brown strands left atop his head, slicking the straggler back in the process. "A minimum of ten days, Sir, and that's with everything going without a hitch. It'll probably wind up taking twice that time if not a little longer."

"Pick out the personnel you need and get started."

Hammer heaved a sigh the moment Wurz left, thankful the captain couldn't read minds, as he'd been thinking of nothing but Voola all morning long. She'd seemed to be in the mood for romance last night and he'd managed to work up his courage while chatting with her over his dinner—yet the moment he'd committed to woo her, she'd shielded her thoughts and said goodnight, leaving him dumbfounded in the mess tent.

Most Combrian females were taller than Urth women, but he'd never seen one Voola's height. The top of her head almost reached his chin, the exact stature he'd always pictured the perfect female he'd never expected to find. He'd begun to think fate had brought them together when it became obvious she was interested in him. Why had she not wanted him to make a play? She'd blocked his mind probe after he'd asked if she wanted kids. Had she lied about not being sure? If so, perhaps she didn't want to chance falling in love with a male who couldn't provide her with them.

No, that wasn't it at all, Hammer.

Deeply embarrassed, he realized she must be standing outside the tent. He'd been so focused on her he hadn't felt her meld with his mind. No telling how long she'd been reading it. *Forgive me, Voola.*

No, forgive me for being invasive, and receive the answer to the mystery that troubles you.

"Ah," he said aloud, grinning after she transmitted the explanation. *So that's it. Not to worry, Voola, I understand your motivation perfectly.*

She blocked him out and entered the tent a moment later, wearing a bashful smile.

SIX

HARV ZANE SAT DOWN TO lunch, positioning himself at the table where he could view the teleon mounted on a wall of the kitchen in their living quarters. His faithful spouse Molly spooned pinto beans over a crumbled chunk of grain pone and handed him the plate.

"I wish we could go back home," she said wistfully.

"Bitch at your son about it, not me. He's the one who insisted we move here until he captures Gram and dismantles his army."

"I know PC's only looking out for our welfare." She swabbed booter on two surfaces of a halved triangle of pone. "I wish Wheelbarrow would stop being so paranoid. No one would be suspicious about them coming here since every Mancombra not serving in the military has been invited to seek sanctuary in the palace."

Stirring the legumes and baked grain into a unified mass, he thought about that day seventeen double-years ago when Wheelbarrow walked into his office and opened up to him.

The big Mancombra had drawn an edgy breath and said, "Harv, you wouldn't have been chosen as head of the mathematics department of the most prestigious university in all of Combria if you didn't have a level head on your shoulders and such an open mind. With your integrity, intellect, and tremendous work ethic I predict you'll be president of the university one day despite being an Urth. I've known you since I started teaching here. We met one thousand ninety-five days ago today—exactly three double-years and six Feasts of the Annual Snow have passed since.

When you work with somebody that long you develop a keen understanding of their character, especially when you can read their minds as I can yours.

"I said all that because there's something I need to tell you, and I'm counting on you getting past your initial reaction upon hearing it. What I'm about to say is going to shock you, but please hear me out. The day before I turned nine double-years my parents disowned me . . . and Needle."

Wheelbarrow had donned the strangest look, and as an awkward moment passed without him continuing, Harv had uneasily said, "Okay, so you were both in late adolescence. A lot of parents have problems with their kids when they go through that rebellious phase of their lives, though most don't disown them I must say."

"It wasn't due to us being unmanageable adolescents, Harv. It was because our father caught us making love."

Stunned, he'd reared back in his office chair so hard it had almost toppled to the floor. "You were having sex with your sister?!"

Wheelbarrow had shaken his head while emitting a heavy sigh. "If it had merely been that, my father would have forgiven us after a severe reprimand and a lecture on the evils of incest. We tried to explain to him that we were in love, and had been since Needle started developing her adult figure. I tried to make him understand that just as he'd followed his heart in choosing an Urth as his mate, which is frowned upon by society, I had to do the same even though Needle was my sister. Needle echoed my sentiments, my mother got involved in the argument, and when the dust settled our parents told us to leave and never contact them again."

"Why are you telling me all this?" he'd asked, wishing Wheelbarrow had picked someone else to confide the disgusting secret to.

The Mancombra had dragged a hand over his face and transmitted telepathically: *Needle and I trust you and Molly more than any mated couple we know. We've lived with the scourge of being different, being called names, looked down upon, having to out perform our Combrian and Urth colleagues two-to-one to get where we are in the academic world for the simple fact we're half Combrian and half Urth. If the truth about our relationship ever became public our lives would be ruined, all we worked so hard to accomplish would crumble to ash.*

Harv could still recall the anger he'd felt at that moment. He'd jumped to his feet and pointed a finger at the pervert. "How dare you make yourself a martyr over something you can control. You and Needle have no one but yourselves to blame if your incestuous lust ever becomes known. I sympathize with your plight of being called half-breeds, but your illegitimate relationship I cannot abide. I won't say a word to anyone about what you've told me—not even Molly—but I don't ever want to hear about it again, and we'll no longer associate with either of you in any social function. Now get out of my office."

Tears had pooled in Wheelbarrow's purple orbs as the giant leaned forward, forcing him back to the chair with a massive hand on each shoulder. "I didn't tell you all this because of Needle and I—"

His son's voice snapped him from the memory. PC was on the teleon saying:

"My fellow citizens of Combria, I'm pleased to report the safe arrival of twenty-six Mancombras and the surviving members of their families. Again I want to urge all civilian Mancombras to come to the palace and bring your loved ones. Call the number scrolling across the bottom of your screen if you want a military escort. Our soldiers are more than happy to assist you. We are here to protect and serve the citizens of this great planet whether they be Combrian, Urth of whatever color, or Mancombra. We will find King Gram and bring him and all who are assisting him to justice, rest assured. The Spirit That Created All Things bless you all."

†

"No one but a Pillhigh rules over Combria, you ungrateful piece of Urth shit!" Gram threw his metal chalice against the teleon screen, shattering it. Two maid servants immediately began cleaning up the mess. He rose from his chair and paced angrily back and forth, hands behind his back, cursing the day he'd ever laid eyes on PC Zane, wondering why the fool couldn't see Mancombras for the threat they were.

He'd approved the promotion of the ingrate's father to president of Combria University only days before receiving a request signed by the majority of officers in both the Combrian Forces and Urth Army that PC receive his fourth star, making him a full general. The soldier had never shown any indication of disloyalty, and all the universals were convinced the lower echelon of the armed forces couldn't have been in better hands than those of General Zane and the three Urths who ranked alongside him.

But the Genocide Directive had prompted Zane to declare war against him. Most of the Urth Army and a quarter of the Combrian Forces were now under the rebel's command. How a mere Urth could accomplish such a feat to begin with still astonished him, but PC being able to persuade so many troops to commit treason against the House of Pillhigh in such a short time was stupendously baffling.

Over seven hundred double-years had passed since someone besides a Pillhigh occupied the throne, and he wasn't about to let his reign be the last of the royal line. The House of Pillhigh had been victorious in all the many uprisings in history, but the great war his grandfather had endured—with over fifty percent of the populace rebelling against his rule—would have been lost without the invention of whirlys, missiles, and massive bombs. To ease tension afterwards his grandfather had allowed more personal freedoms, even for Mancombras, and initiated social programs to assist the poor. Gram's father had allowed those agendas to continue under his reign but increased military spending—quadrupling the number of troops in every branch of the Combrian Forces, including the Urth Army— and prepared for the possibility of having to fight a global war. The day the scepter passed to Gram, he'd learned from his deceased father's closest advisors that several elaborate bomb shelters had been constructed in strategic locations to keep the royal family safe should such an event occur. Now, besides himself, only three universals knew their locations.

Thankfully the trio had remained loyal to him and he could conduct his counter offensives without fear of being captured. One of the hideaways had been compromised when that thieving bitch Voola managed to escape, so he couldn't go back there, but he had four more besides the one he presently occupied. He'd ordered Universal Quest to take out all the civilian Mancombras who'd escaped execution, and Quest had chosen Enforcer Arigot to head the taskforce. The rest of his forces Gram planned to keep well hidden until being informed the only Mancombras remaining alive were those in Zane's army. Unfortunately PC had opened the palace to the half-breeds, and twenty-six of them were now secure behind its walls. He'd give the enforcer time to kill the fourteen remaining, hoping to receive word by then the spies commissioned to infiltrated the flying force would be able to steal back enough whirlys to provide decent air cover for the infantry. Of course if Nanzar and his fellow scientists completed their mission by then, conventional warfare would be totally unnecessary.

Gram Pillhigh's explanation for issuing the Genocide Directive had enthralled Stove. Though war had broken out soon afterwards and the death list included his name, he'd been thoroughly enticed with the possibility of Mancombras ruling Combria ever since hearing the king state his reasons for eliminating an entire race. He'd always wondered why Mancombras were looked down on when in reality they were in fact the superior species, but it had never occurred to him that if he and his fellow so called half-breeds were to unite in a common purpose of taking over Combria as Gram feared, they'd be undefeatable.

Combrians couldn't levitate or otherwise mentally manipulate anything weighing more than fifty pounds, whereas each of his kind could hoist over a quarter-ton with their minds. True, Mancombras had the same limitation as Combrians in not being able to sustain an object in the air longer than fifteen minutes if it had more girth than a thick book—but by uniting their efforts during such a time span, they could lift a fortification from its foundation, flip it sideways, and drop it on the soldiers within. They'd have the capability of turning wheelers, tanks, and warships over— spin an entire regiment towards each other and make them fire their weapons.

Now their numbers were so few if he couldn't convince the rest of the Mancombras serving in the military alongside him to unite, such a feat would be impossible. Stove hoped his civilian brethren still at large would make it to the palace like twenty-six of them already had. That would leave them one hundred and forty strong.

Females were only half as physically or telekinetically powerful as their masculine counterparts, but thankfully the number of surviving Mancombras comprised only thirty-two of them. Except for a notable astronomy professor the remainder of them all served Prince Zane in the military. Being easier to capture had resulted in fifty female civilians being gassed for every male. The military ratio killed by firing squad had wound up ten to one by the time Zane took control of all the forts. They stood as tall as males, but the hormones making them less muscular in build—curvy, with enlarged breasts—also compromised their battle capabilities. Still, they were stronger than Combrian or Urth males, and could certainly help the cause.

He'd enlisted in General Zane's army straightaway after his revolt against Gram, and was now a corporal in the Second Infantry, assigned to the palace since its takeover. Captain Morris had selected him along with forty-eight other soldiers to patrol the south bend of the Opian River. They were searching for Enforcer Arigot, reported to be in the area. Since the captain was filling in for Prince Zane, currently detained at the palace, he considered it a great honor to be included in this mission.

They'd stopped at a rundown house with an antiquated three-tired wheeler parked beside it. Captain Morris motioned for him and Sergeant Wrench to accompany him to the door, a smart move by the Urth in case Combrian hostiles lurked within. Besides himself, Wrench was the only

Mancombra in the search party.

An old black Urth opened the door. Checking out their shoulders and helmets, the woman smiled. Stove felt her mind fill with relief when she saw the red Zees thereon, denoting they were under Prince Zane's command. He also ascertained a Mancombra named Drill resided with her and had taken refuge in her hicker pen upon hearing them approach. His pulse quickened at knowing another brother would be saved from Gram's thugs. Hopefully he'd be receptive to the proposition of conquering Combria for themselves.

As I've told you repeatedly, Stove, it's a pipe dream, transmitted Wrench, who'd laughed him to scorn upon first hearing his proposal, never taking him seriously about it since. *It's high time you got your head out of the clouds and started channeling your energy towards something you* can *succeed at, like advancing to sergeant as I did.*

Well I can dream can't I? he answered lightheartedly.

Be careful your dream doesn't land you in front of a firing squad for treason, Corporal.

The navy didn't have Combrian equivalents for ranks, and it was the only branch of the military where Combrians and Urths were allowed to serve together under the House of Pillhigh. It wasn't due to any form of generosity towards the so called inferior race—the vast majority of service Combrians having no desire to spend long periods at sea had necessitated it. Being an Urth without such qualms, Baylor Denton and had spent most of his lengthy naval career on the water. Combria consisted of three large continents: Opian, Sorria, and Blancomet. An S-shaped body of seawater called the Sorrian Gulf ran north and south between Sorria and Blancomet, ranging in width from forty miles to a thousand. They were separated from Opian—which contained the government and most of the population—by the East and West Combrian oceans: further designated as the Upper East, Lower East, Upper West, Lower West Combrian Seas. Seeing the necessity for dethroning Gram, very few sailors had resisted Zane's takeover, and the seas were under the new ruler's total control. The WS Battle Fish, a missile equipped warship currently patrolling the Lower East Combrian Sea, was under Baylor's command—his fourth vessel to preside over as captain.

He'd been promoted to that rank shortly before a greenhorn Combrian named Arigot had been assigned to his boat as a basic seaman. Dutiful, respectful, and quite courageous, Seaman Arigot had worked his way to the rank of chief petty officer before Universal Quest transfered him to the army. Baylor had intuitively felt such a move wouldn't bode well for Arigot. Sadly, his suspicions proved correct. Not only had the former sailor refused to join the rebellion even after his parents were murdered as a result of Gram's madness, blind loyalty to the House of Pillhigh had turned him into a cold blooded killer.

When he'd heard vehicles approaching, Drill had told Polka he was making a run for the hicker shack, but he hadn't even slowed down once he got there. Still running, he leapt across a narrow stream and kept pumping his knees after landing on the other side.

He couldn't put her at risk any longer.

Hoping her probe blocking technique would get her off the hook once more, he fled for Mount Opian, planning to hide out in a cave he'd come across as a boy when his father had taken him hunting there. He'd feed off berries and wild game until some hunters, mountain climbers, campers, or sightseers loyal to Prince Zane happened by, then he'd beg a ride to the palace.

It would take two days to reach the mountain, but he had the dense forest to protect him from being spotted. Traveling to the palace on foot entailed a journey of many days, and he'd be traversing open fields for the greater part of it since he dared not chance the highway. If any of Gram's soldiers ventured into the area, they'd spot him easily.

An angry roar assaulted his ears, followed by another, soon joined by several more. Five rip howlers appeared on the far side of a clearing he'd entered. Gray fur stood on edge along their spines as long deadly talons emerged from their massive paws, signaling preparation for attack. The domesticated version of the ferocious carnivores, a fraction of the size, made for an affectionate pet that purred and whose appetite could be satisfied with a bowl of malk. Not so the wild breed. They were deadly hunters and ate only flesh killed by their enormous fangs and razor-sharp claws.

They had him surrounded in less than two seconds.

SEVEN

Because she'd taken in a Mancombra and risked her life for him, Captain Morris called his commander to inquire whether she might be given the consideration of a relative and be allowed sanctuary in the palace even though Drill wouldn't be coming too. Polka crossed her fingers.

The captain thanked the general he'd been talking to and lowered his field communicator, grinning wide. "Start packing your things, Polka, you're coming with us. I just got word the marauders we were looking for were seen by a farmer far north of here, and we've been ordered back to Opianapolis."

Overjoyed at the prospect of living a life of ease, if only for awhile since she'd be returning to the farm after Gram got captured or killed, she prayed The Spirit That Created All Things would keep Drill safe. He'd left for her sake and she loved him for it, but knew his chances for survival were slim to none if he didn't make it to the palace.

Drill turned slowly from beast to snarling beast, knowing that when the lead rip howler lunged at his throat the other four would immediately go for his legs. Because they were similar in size, each weighing about three hundred pounds, he couldn't identify the leader, who would initiate the attack.

Usually they traveled in packs with a noticeably larger alpha male in charge.

A hundred feet away the clearing ended. He'd have to make it to the trees in order to survive. Calculating his defensive moves, he waited for the attack—subtly bending his knees, preparing to act.

The rip howler to his immediate right went airborne, its hideous roar deafening. Drill jumped straight up, levitating the howling leader above him as the other four banged heads instead of sinking their fangs into his lower legs as instinct anticipated. Hurling the floating creature down on top of them with his mind, he somersaulted forward so as to clear the pile when he landed. The moment his feet touched ground he started leaping, heading for the trees as five ravenous, snarling tormentors regrouped and tore after him.

With the leader snapping at his heels, he willed a thick lower branch of the nearest tree to bend down while diving towards it. Relaxing his mental hold, the branch swung upwards and would have catapulted him into the higher boughs if he hadn't had his arms and legs wrapped tightly around it.

The infuriated rip howlers started jumping—swatting at him with their flesh-shredding claws, missing his forearms and calves by mere fractions of an inch. Heaving for breath, Drill focused on the leader and telekinetically sent it sailing back into the clearing where the beast uncannily landed on all four paws fifty feet away. As if sensing he couldn't manipulate it from that distance, the head rip howler paced left and right without moving forward—roaring its head off, long tail whipping the air like an angry viper.

Hissing and drooling, another hungry killer started up the tree, advancing by sinking its talons into the thick gray bark. Drill willed it towards the leader. Chunks of pulp sprayed from the trunk as the beast's grip failed and it flipped backwards. Now confused and afraid, the other three fled to their fellow pack members.

Drill dropped to the ground and faced them. Fingers curled into tight fists, he pounded his chest and flexed his arms while howling like an enraged lunatic, hoping the bluff would pay off.

It did. Thinking he was calling them out for another round of battle, the rip howlers disappeared into the forest opposite him.

†

Hammer told the proprietor to give him a dozen crimalot spurs, the loveliest and most expensive arrangement the petalist had in stock. *Voola will love them*, he mused with a smile that faded upon realizing he couldn't afford to have anyone see him give them to her. He pulled three paper tibs from his wallet, exchanged them for the scarlet blooms, and refused the change.

Guiding his open-air wheeler down the main road of the hamlet whose residents depended on tourists for survival, he spotted an eatery and devised a plan. He'd hide the crimalot spurs in the back cavity with the spare tire where the troops couldn't see them, bring Voola here for dinner, and present them to her then. He would leave Captain Wurz in charge during his absence, as he'd done while making this thirty-mile round trip from camp.

Smiling once again, he recalled her explanation as to why she'd withdrawn from him in the mess tent. *I was quite proper before my lover got killed and I became a tramp. I want to be that again, Hammer—for you. If you want an easy female, a low maintenance slut, look elsewhere. I'm very aware of how attracted you are to me, but I want love and commitment. If you can't give me that, then this is as far as our relationship will ever advance.*

Needle loved being in the observatory when Jealousy and Anger were in full phase. The many craters and what appeared to be dry riverbeds winding over their rocky terrains were crystal clear. Anger had a strange array of crystallized rocks on the side facing away from Combria at the moment. Neither had any appreciable atmosphere and both were desert globes without a trace of water, so life couldn't exist on the colorful moons.

Looking through the lens of a massive refracting telescope she'd helped develop, she peered past Combria's moons and gazed at a sector of white spirals stemming from the galaxy it inhabited called the Malky Way. Hundreds of billions of planets were known to exist within it. Many were bound to be orbiting their mother stars at the same life-sustainable distance as Combria did Life Giver. That meant the Urths *could* have come from the sky as legend contended.

She firmly believed they had. Many of her colleagues razzed her about it, especially scoffing at her notion that Urths were responsible for the rise in technology after so many unchanging double-years of Combrians hunting with clubs and spears. Not a single archeological find had ever provided any proof that Urths once dwelt in caves and consumed raw meat because they didn't know how to make fire. Virtually every ancient color cave painting depicted a copper-skinned hunter or warrior with platinum hair, and no ears could be seen on any sketches carved in stone where skin tone couldn't be known, denoting they too were images of Combrian savages.

The biggest argument against her supposition was that something had to have happened between the Urths landing here from outer space and the outcrop of the industrial age. Otherwise the current generation would be much further technologically advanced. They'd yet to put a single astronaut on their nearest moon, much less send a whole colony to a distant planet as the Urths had to have done if her assumption was correct.

Needle theorized the Urths either went to war against each other on a global scale, or some natural catastrophe wiped out most of their scientists and specialists, causing a degeneration of knowledge as the survivors proceeded onward, too worried about staying alive to bother accurately recording what happened. As the generations passed from the event, with its history being relayed only by word of mouth, the truth would have gotten diluted through embellishments and inaccurate memories, getting further twisted through the double-years by subjective opinions and superstitions, resulting in the Urths' arrival from space winding up a myth.

Nothing supported her theory archeologically, but other evidence strongly indicated Urths weren't indigenous to Combria. All modern tools and machines stemmed from rudimentary models invented by Urths, and were referred to by either an Urth word or a Combrian derivative of one. The Combrian armed forces had patterned its rank and file after the ancient Urth military. Many foods and beverages had a fable behind them of being brought to Combria by the Urths.

No one could prove a single Combrian ever invented any

useful device of a complicated nature, or created any type of functional social order that wasn't an outright copy of an Urth prototype. That disparagement would be impossible if both races had indeed evolved together in a shared environment.

The term double-year was another clue, and a major one she felt. Why would the ancient Combrians have coined Combria's orbit around Life Giver such an oddball term instead of simply dubbing it a year? She resolutely believed they hadn't, that the name was chosen by the Urths, who'd migrated here from another world—a planet that made a full circle around its star in half the time Combria did.

She speculated all the machines and computers and other technological devices the Urths either brought with them, or built after landing on Combria, got destroyed when the ancient civilization collapsed. The survivors had to revert back to forging simple tools and crude instruments. Because they possessed telepathy and telekinesis, Combrians then became the higher social order on what was once an uneven playing field with the technologically advanced Urths having the upper hand.

The two races had been sharply divided until an Urth invented the first steam engine, igniting the industrial revolution. Before then, a Mancombra was an extreme rarity as very few Combrians demeaned themselves socially by engaging with a lowly Urth in conversation, much less sex. Though bigotry still existed on both sides, technology had bridged the gap considerably.

It couldn't be denied Combrian genes were dominant over Urth genes, as all Mancombras looked like oversized Combrians, could read minds and levitate objects. Geneticists had yet to determine why the majority of them were infertile, or ascertain the reason Mancombras had never been known to make a baby amongst themselves.

Once again studying Jealousy's green landscape, Needle exhaled a deep sigh as Wheelbarrow entered her thoughts. Neither of them had chosen to unite hearts intentionally, but love didn't ask anyone whom they'd like to share it with.

It chose for them.

Arigot had abandoned the search for Drill the moment his spotter informed him fifty of Zane's troops were heading for the south bend of the Opian river. Universal Quest's orders explicitly forbade him to engage the enemy in combat, and concentrate on executing the Genocide Directive.

They'd snuck into University City shortly after nightfall. Two Mancombra siblings were next on the list after Drill: Wheelbarrow and Needle, professors at Combria University.

After stopping to pick up Voola outside camp, Hammer had given her the crimalot spurs while reciting a corny children's rhyme about the receiver being bound to the giver forever. Thoroughly delighted over the crimson blossoms, she'd then been flabbergasted when he'd taken her to a clothiers, from which they'd come to the restaurant. Civilians weren't allowed to wear military garb so he'd bought her some clothes so she'd have something to wear besides the garment she'd escaped in.

The waiter poured their wine and left them to enjoy their meal. Voola looked fabulous in a pink frock she'd selected for the occasion. He'd also purchased two additional body suits for her to wear around camp: dresses were hardly proper attire for bivouacking. The three items, plus two pairs of shoes, had set him back almost fifty tibs.

But she was worth it.

As she sliced off a juicy bite of barbecued sern steak, he heaved an exaggerated sigh, and intentionally being hoakie again said, "I bless the day I found you."

Grinning as she chewed, Voola transmitted, *Of course you do, I was naked.*

Actually, he telecasted back, *you managed to cover most of your beautiful body before I got close enough to fully savor it.*

Keep wining and dining me like this, Hammer, and you'll get to view it in full . . . as well as use it to your satisfaction.

He blew her a kiss in his mind. She caught it in hers and blew it back to him.

Wheelbarrow set the table for dinner and placed a candelabra on the center. Needle would be returning from the observatory soon, thinking she'd have to cook. Anticipating her pleasant surprise upon hearing her favorite cuisine waited in the oven, where it had been warming since he'd brought it home from a café in University City, he lit the candles and uncorked a bottle of vintage ale.

Hearing the door open, he went to greet her. Before he

could recoil from the shock of seeing a Combrian enforcer instead of Needle, the intruder opened fire with a machinegun. Hot lead riveted his upper body, burning its way through his internal organs, yet somehow missing his heart. Rapid flashes of pain crippling him, he dropped to the floor, discerning through a cloud of fearful astonishment that his killer's name was Arigot.

How did you find me? Wheelbarrow weakly transmitted, aware he'd be dead in seconds as blood poured from his many wounds, soaking the carpet beneath him. The agony brought on by the bullets was nothing compared to the horror of knowing his beloved Needle would soon suffer the same fate.

"You'd be surprised how many spies King Gram has working at the university," said Enforcer Arigot smugly, knowing he couldn't retaliate through telekinesis because his system had gone into shock. "It was unwise of you to tell the president where you'd moved."

He saw in the Combrian's mind that a janitor had rifled through Harv Zane's desk and found the address written on a slip of paper hidden beneath a stack of folders. The blurry mental image was a product of his murderer's imagination. Arigot didn't know the spy's identity, he'd been told about it from another source, who Wheelbarrow couldn't quite make out. Poor Harv would never forgive himself if he knew his failure to memorize the note and destroy it afterwards had cost him the lives of two very close friends, as Needle was bound to die this night as well.

Mentally witnessing Enforcer Arigot scratch his name off the death list, Wheelbarrow exhaled his last breath.

EIGHT

THE ENERGY CELL COULDN'T PRODUCE enough power to start the damn wheeler. Needle ran a hand through her hair and slapped the steering circle with frustration. The observatory lay eight miles out of University City, the final two a narrow winding road leading up the mountain upon whose peak it sat. Because Jealousy and Anger were in full phase she'd be able to navigate without lights. Not wanting to hear a lecture from Wheelbarrow over putting off getting her wheeler serviced, she decided against going back inside the observatory to call him. Instead, she yanked the torque lever into neutral and quickly turned the steering circle to get the rolling vehicle turned around so she wouldn't have to back all the way down. Once she got to the highway she'd flag someone down for a power boost.

King Gram's infamous worldwide speech had totally persuaded him Mancombras were a real threat to the security of the planet because sooner or later one of them would realize if they dared to unite in a common cause to control it, they'd be unstoppable. Arigot had viewed them as dangerous vermin ever since, except for his half-brother whom he dearly loved. Hammer had bested him in every childhood brawl, and if the Mancombra hadn't obeyed their father when they'd reached adolescence, promising never to playfully spar with anyone ever again because of not knowing his own strength, Arigot might not have made it to adulthood.

While waiting for the Mancombra's sister, whom he knew would be arriving any time, Arigot helped himself to the dead half-breed's dinner he'd found in the oven. Because of Wheelbarrow's overwhelming concern for her and his rapidly deteriorating metabolism, the professor hadn't been able to block his probe.

With his soldiers strategically hidden all around the isolated cabin, it would be impossible for Needle to escape should he miss. He'd wasted no time pulling the trigger when Wheelbarrow spotted him, for if he hadn't the Mancombra could have willed the machinegun from his hands or sent him flying through a window. Only one shot would be needed to take down his sister, and it would come from a pistol.

Disgust over discerning the two half-breeds were incestuous lovers had given way to stupefying amazement when he'd pried open a mental envelope containing a secret the dying Mancombra had desperately tried to hide. That secret would put at least one stone on each of his shoulders because King Gram would surely promote him to universal.

If Jealousy and Anger weren't in full phase, this time of night the forest would be filled with the sounds of moon fowl cooing as they hunted prey. With them hibernating, the woods held on to an eerie stillness. Willing the roasting carcass of a hopper to turn over, Drill inhaled the savory aroma as dripping fat excited the fire, causing streaks of flame to shoot up and lick the meat.

Able to leap a distance of five times their body length, hoppers came by their name honestly. The cute furry creatures fed on vegetation and seldom attained a weight of over ten pounds. Unfortunately for them they were very tasty, making hoppers the favorite meal of many carnivores. It had been a long time since he'd eaten one, and his growling stomach grew more impatient with each passing minute as the smell grew stronger, indicating the delectable vitamin-rich protein would soon be done.

He'd let the fire die down on its own after eating, using its warmth to ward of the chilly night air while he dozed off. Spears fashioned from tree limbs formed a vertical fence around his sleeping area, impaled deep in the soil close enough together to make it impossible for any nocturnal flesh-eater to slip through without waking him. They'd also serve as weapons should he be disturbed. Knowing he'd be stiff from sleeping on the ground, he already dreaded waking up in the morning. After he got to Mount Opian he'd hunt down a night lapper when the moons waned, and make a blanket from its hide. There wouldn't be any in the area until then because they'd be stalking farms, searching for unguarded livestock.

A painful memory tortured him as he thought of Opianapolis. He'd been to the capitol city several times but had never toured the palace, as Mancombras weren't allowed within its walls until Prince Zane took over. A beautiful Combrian he'd fallen in love with had told him of its magnificence. Her cruel unnecessary death would always haunt him, but at times it became almost overwhelming, like now. If he couldn't catch a ride there soon, he feared his own untimely demise would be forthcoming.

Hammer drove back to Mount Opian but parked in a secluded area on the opposite side of the mountain from camp. He stilled the engine and turned to Voola, who'd changed into a shiny black body-suit, using the female facilities at the restaurant as her dressing room. He didn't want any of his troops knowing they'd been on a date. Voola needed to appear hands off to everyone in the squadron, including him.

Releasing a deep sigh, she gripped the zipper at the base of her throat with a lithe index finger and thumb. "I hadn't planned to give in this soon, Hammer. I hope you believe that and won't lose respect for me."

Heart pounding, he pulled a latch and the backrest lowered to form a makeshift bed. "I wouldn't have lost any respect if you'd given in the night we were moon watching. I hope you believe me."

She nodded and unzipped the body suit. Before Voola could slither out of it, her large breasts sprang into view as if they were as eager for him to lay eyes on their exquisiteness as he was.

Polka gazed at the statues lining both sides of The Great Hall as they entered the palace. Each depicted a Combrian King going all the way back to the rise of The House of Pillhigh. When Captain Morris escorted her past Gram's life-size metal figure, she resisted an urge to spit on it.

Sergeant Wrench winked at her. "I too have trouble refraining, Polka. Only my desire is to piss on it."

"Shame on you for reading my mind, Sergeant," she giggled.

He laughed and put his enormous Mancombra hand on her back, guiding her down a corridor to the right.

Voola had never made love with a Mancombra before and would never do so again. Though Hammer had completely conquered her with his gentlemanly manner and generosity—thrilled her with his kisses and caressing hands—his gargantuan penis had felt like she'd been repeatedly rammed between the legs with a log.

To keep their date a secret, he had let her out a ways from camp at the same spot he'd picked her up. Voola wasn't sure she'd be able to walk all the way to her tent, the pain was still so severe.

It had broken her heart to feel his sadness as their minds melded and he'd sensed her torment. Hammer had tried to pull out but she'd locked her ankles together, demanding he finish because she'd never have the guts to do it again. *I want to please you, Hammer*—she'd yelled at him in her mind while screaming with agony—*don't stop until you climax!* Though it took only a few minutes from that point, the pain had made it feel like hours before he ejaculated.

Carrying a bag containing her crimalot spurs and new clothes, she waddled towards camp, crying because she couldn't hope to keep Hammer satisfied, and would therefore eventually lose him.

✝

Hammer took off his uniform and slid under the blanket of his cot, feeling depressed, frustrated, angry, and helpless. *What in blazes am I going to do? I've fallen in love with Voola, but she can't bear having sex with me.*

Voola's cries of anguish while mentally imploring him to continue, ran endlessly through his mind. Her willingness to suffer so that he might feel the pleasure of orgasm—if only for that one time—had moved him so deeply, torn at his heart so violently, she'd stolen his very soul. Having never been intimate with a female of his own kind, he didn't know if their vaginal canals were different than Combrians' or Urths'—but during boot camp, when all the buck privates had to shower together, he'd seen readily enough that like him, the five male Mancombras in his unit had genitals noticeably larger then a well endowed Combrian's, so he supposed females were probably proportionately deeper and wider than their Combrian counterparts.

Only a few of the many females he'd bedded down—Urth or Combrian—had found his penis too painful to handle, but none of them had been as tight as Voola, making him wonder if perhaps she was malformed. Either way, neither of them could do anything to change the size of their reproductive organs.

He turned over on his side muttering, "Voola, my love, there's got to be a way to work through this. I can't let you go."

A kind Urth man had finally stopped to help her after at least a dozen wheelers zoomed past, apparently unwilling to assist a Mancombra, even a female. Anger welled up in her upon seeing Wheelbarrow's vehicle parked near the cabin. Being an hour late should have caused him enough concern to look for her when she hadn't answered at the observatory.

Surely he at least called to check up on me, Needle fumed.

Slamming the front door behind her, more than ready to give him a piece of her mind, she heard a gunshot and instantaneously felt something sting her neck.

NINE

By JOGGING EVERY OTHER HOUR rather than walking, Drill figured to reach Mount Opian by nightfall, saving him another restless night in the forest. He hoped the cave still had steam rising in it because he'd woken up that morning chilled to the bone. Even if it didn't at least he wouldn't have to worry about the cold morning dew.

Needle woke to find herself in shackles, lying on the floor of a merchant trailer in motion. The shot she'd heard had obviously come from a tranquilizer gun. Managing to sit up she glanced around, looking for Wheelbarrow, but only saw two Combrian soldiers leaning against the wall across from her, both of them armed. "Where are you taking me?"

The one on the left brought a field communicator to his mouth. "Enforcer Arigot, the Mancombra's awake."

"What have you done with Wheelbarrow?" she demanded.

"Save your questions for Enforcer Arigot." His Combrian eyes were cold, his expression void of emotion.

Not sensing them probing her mind, she tried to mentally force the cuffs on her wrists to open but they wouldn't budge. *They must have pumped a dose of Clodec in my neck along with the sedative.* The drug had been developed long ago to keep Combrian and Mancombra prisoners in jail. Without it they could will the locks on their cell doors to open, manipulate an unsuspecting guard's weapon and the like. Since Mancombras could even levitate the guards, imprisoning one without the medication would be next to impossible. Depending on the dosage it could last for one hour up to forty. Being under its influence also meant she wouldn't be able to tell when her thoughts were being analyzed, or prevent anyone from doing so.

The door separating the cab and cargo area opened and a Combrian officer walked in. He instructed his underlings to go up front and close the door behind them. After they did so he turned to her. "Hello, Needle, my name is Enforcer Arigot."

"What have you done with Wheelbarrow?" she blurted out.

He stepped closer, gazing down at her with a haughty sneer. "Why he's been eliminated of course."

If she'd been thrown into a den of starving rip howlers, torn apart and disemboweled, the sensations couldn't have hurt any worse than those that seized her—shattering her insides like a mallet pounding a hicker egg. Her soul mate, lover, brother, best friend: her very reason for living had been taken from her. Crying so hard she had to gasp for breath, she screamed, "You filthy murdering bastards, you're all nothing but a bunch of animals! You had no right! You had no right! You—"

"Shut up!" yelled the enforcer, slapping her face with the back of his hand. "I'll do the talking here."

Glaring up at him, she spat on the murdering thug and received several more blows, this time from fists. Blood poured from her fractured nose and busted lips, but the pain meant nothing to her because she was drowning in an ocean of sorrow. "Why didn't you kill me?"

His handsome mouth spread with an arrogant grin. "I know your secret. Your brother and lover was unable to block me. You, Needle, are my ticket to the top of the Combrian Forces. Once General Zane learns we have you in custody he'll have no choice but to surrender."

Horrified to learn the Combrian had succeeded in probing Wheelbarrow's mind, she dropped her head, numbly watching blood and tears pepper her breasts.

"You and your brother are scientific wonders you know."

His haughty voice tortured her ears, but what the bastard said was true. "Who have you told?"

"Oh nobody of course. This fantastic news must be delivered to King Gram first hand. How do you account for it?"

Head still hung low, she groaned while wearily shaking it, refusing to answer. The beast lifted her chin, forcing her to look at him. A taunting smirk revealed he'd dug the information from her memory. Wheelbarrow thought their physiological makeup must have been an aberration, and being so genetically similar somehow enabled them to procreate despite both being Mancombra. He theorized that since Combrian genes are dominant over Urths', the combination of theirs was far too strong due to them being siblings, and they'd wiped each other out, leaving only their recessive Urth chromosomes able to unite. She cast Arigot a defiant look, fully expecting him to punch her out again. "You'll never get PC to surrender, you sorry bastard."

Instead of striking her, he laughed. "Oh I think we will. He knows the vast majority of the populace will refuse to allow a freak spawned through Mancombra incest to rule over them."

Now she laughed, and rather heartily. "You'll never be able to prove it."

"Oh no? We have some of his blood on hand. Every member of the armed forces is required to donate a pint when they enlist. It's safe and sound in a blood bank we still control. We'll have the most reputable geneticists on the planet examine it, along with your blood, and the truth will be known by all. Your son has only two choices: abdicate the throne voluntarily in order to keep all of Combria from knowing, or be forced off of it by revolt once all of Combria does. It's a victory for King Gram either way, and since I'm the one providing the opportunity, he'll reward me handsomely, so it's a win-win for me as well. Now then, tell me how you and Wheelbarrow convinced the brilliant Harv Zane of all people to agree to be your son's foster father?"

✝

"PC, I've got some very bad news."

His stomach twisted into an anxious knot because of the look on Free's face. "What is it?"

"I just received word that your Mancombra friend Wheelbarrow has been killed, and his sister is presumed dead too, though they've yet to find her body."

He took a step back as if recoiling from a physical blow—inundated with grief, and angry at Wheelbarrow for being so foolishly stubborn. His paranoia had not only cost him his life, but Needle's too in all likelihood. "Get out of here, I've got to be alone right now."

The moment Free left he slumped to his knees and broke down as a raging current of memories washed over him.

Combrian and Mancombra females possessed a primal instinct that made them immediately aware of conception taking place. When Needle told Wheelbarrow she was with child, he'd confided his incestuous relationship with his sister—and the shocking development stemming from it—to

Harv Zane: a strong supporter of a movement, eventually quashed by King Gram, to allow parents of Mancombras to name their children whatever they wanted.

Having no idea he'd conceived a son who would look like a purebred Urth, Wheelbarrow had wanted Harv to take the baby to raise, give it his surname, and tell the authorities the infant Mancombra had been left on his doorstep. Wheelbarrow's motivation hadn't been to keep his intimate relationship with Needle a secret, but to prevent his offspring from having to bear the scourge of not only being a half-breed but the end result of Mancombra incest. The government would have seized all three of them for scientific study since such a thing was deemed impossible.

Harv had initially refused, but finally agreed to the arrangement the day he was born. His natural parents had given him his first and middle name, Harv and Molly had preferred calling him by his initials. Eventually Wheelbarrow and Needle started calling him PC too.

He'd grown up knowing the truth, and had been forbidden to use the terms Mom or Dad to keep anyone probing his mind from detecting his love for the two Mancombras stemmed from the fact they were his natural parents. Since he looked like an Urth, Wheelbarrow and Needle never had to fear anyone growing suspicious that the child they babysat so often might be their own. However, the inflexible Wheelbarrow couldn't be convinced that if Needle and he moved into the palace like Harv and Molly, that suspicion wouldn't eventually arise.

Face drenched with tears, PC pleaded for The Spirit That Created All Things to protect Needle if she was still alive, bring Wheelbarrow's killer to justice, and give him the strength to carry on.

Hammer sat down at Voola's left to eat lunch. As always, she'd chosen to sit at the end of a table. She hadn't come into the mess tent during breakfast and looked as if she'd just woke up. Perceiving last night was still fresh on her mind as well, he telepathed, *I had a fitful night's sleep.*

Me too. I didn't fall soundly asleep until dawn.

Sensing she didn't want to discuss their physical incompatibility, he let the matter drop.

A moment later she vacillated. *I don't want to lose you, Hammer.*

Though very pleased to know that, he didn't see how they could proceed except as platonic friends. He'd wrestled with it all night long and hadn't been able to come up with a solution.

Reading his thoughts, she despondently transmitted: *I understand.*

Dammit, Voola, this is awful! I wish I was Combrian. Then I could give you pleasure rather than pain.

Or I a Mancombra.

If you were a Mancombra I wouldn't be attracted to you.

She ran her hands through her hair and sighed. *I think I'm falling in love with you, Hammer. If you can get me some pain killers maybe I'd be able to handle your girth then.*

I know I'm in love with you, but I couldn't ask you to do that. They're habit forming—it would be harmful to your health.

I don't know what else to try. Tears dribbled from the corners of her eyes. *I wish I could stand the pain, but I can't.*

He looked down and numbly gazed at a curl of steam

rising from his hicker soup. *I wouldn't want you to feel pain even if you* could *handle it. Sex must be enjoyable for both parties to be fulfilling.*

Captain Wurz took the seat across from him. The engineer would be greatly offended if he could read his mind. His annoyance at being interrupted had evoked some colorful names for his second in command. Voola had thought of a few choice words as well. They were both probing and simultaneously learned Wurz suspected they'd been together last night while he'd been left in charge. Hammer's irritation turned to a brief span of levity upon discerning the captain hoped he'd scored.

Thoughts now on his job, Wurz said, "We're making better time than I thought we would, Colonel. The tunnel should be completely reinforced in four or five days, six at the most barring any mishaps. I'm anxious to see what lurks on the other side of that steel."

Drill couldn't believe his good luck. A company of soldiers were encamped at the foot of Mount Opian on the same side as the cave he'd planned to use for shelter. Red Zees on their vehicles and tents designated them as part of Prince Zane's army. The camp was fenced in and behind a wire gate stood two uniformed Urths. Being a Mancombra made him obviously loyal to their leader, so he walked up to them without reservation and introduced himself.

"Why haven't you gone to the palace?" one of them asked. "Or haven't you heard that Prince Zane has asked for all civilian Mancombras to go there."

"Indeed I have heard that. I fled from a Combrian brigade at the south bend of the Opian River, and came here hoping to find someone to take me there."

"Come with me to see Colonel Hammer. He's one of you."

He followed the soldier to a tent with its flap open, through which he could see a Mancombra sitting behind a desk.

"Permission to enter, Colonel Hammer?" the guard requested.

The Mancombra looked very surprised to see a fellow half-breed, and grinned while saying, "By all means."

"This is Drill, Sir. He wants a ride to the palace."

A pleasure to meet you, Drill.

You have no idea what a pleasure it is to meet you, Colonel, he transmitted with a huge smile. *This is the first time I've felt truly safe since Gram issued the Genocide Directive.*

Fortunately for you, Drill, you showed up at dinnertime. I bet some food and kaffy might sound tempting.

Very much so, Colonel, thanks.

"Private, take Drill to the mess tent, then set up a cot for him in my quarters."

"Yes, Sir."

As he exited the tent, Drill sensed the colonel wanting to ask him about his sexual experience. There weren't any Mancombras in his command, so none of his troops could relate to his problem.

Universal Quest had told him via a field communicator to

head for his hidden command post in the heart of Juxbow. Idly staring at a bogus merchant pennant flapping in the breeze on one of the wheeler's antennas as the personal drove, Arigot daydreamed about his sure-to-come promotion to universal. He'd told Quest that he had stumbled onto something so important and sensitive he couldn't divulge it to anyone except Gram face to face, and that Needle had to remain alive for the time being because of it. When the universal had demanded he tell him what it was Arigot had said: "Sir, the king would have me shot if he wasn't first informed, and he'd likely put you before the firing squad with me for insisting I tell you."

"Very well," Quest had reluctantly acquiesced. *"Meet me at my post in Juxbow and I'll arrange for you and the Mancombra to be taken to Gram."*

TEN

PC HAD GONE TO HIS parent's cabin without escort, much to his aide's chagrin. "Look, I'm not going to argue with you, Free," he'd declared. "I need some time alone—time to grieve. Wheelbarrow was one of my dearest friends."

Staring at the blood stained carpet where his father had fallen, PC took a deep breath, sensing he was about to collect information.

A moment later the murder played out before him—not a fantasy produced by his mind, but the real thing. It was a gift he'd discovered as a child. Needle had told him it was only a form of daydreaming and he'd taken her word for it until a situation arose on a schoolyard before he'd reached puberty.

He'd watched a Combrian bully, showing off for his girlfriend, single out an Urth to make sport of. As it was a fair fight, none of the other children intervened. When the Combrian bloodied the Urth's nose the boy started crying and gave up, making the bully victorious. Feeling sorry for the lad he'd offered him a napkin from the lunch bag Molly had packed that morning before taking him to school.

"What's this for?" the boy had asked.

"So you can wipe the blood off your face."

"I have blood on my face? Where?"

Confused, he'd pointed at his nose. "There, from where that guy popped you with his fist."

"What guy?"

"That Combrian . . ." he'd turned to locate the bully but couldn't find him.

"What are you talking about?"

Suddenly seeing no blood on the Urth, and noticing his shirt was different than the one he'd worn during the fight, PC had gasped with confusion. "Wow! I could have sworn I just saw you and a Combrian fighting, and you gave up when he made your nose bleed."

The boy's face had dropped with shame. "Why are you making fun of me?"

"I'm not, I promise. I saw a Combrian boy provoke you into a fight so he could impress his girlfriend. Only you were wearing a different shirt than the one you have on now. It had blue and white stripes on it. I don't know how to explain it, but I thought it was real. Sorry you thought I was poking fun at you."

The kid had gawked at him with astonishment. "It *was* real . . . only it happened yesterday."

That marked his first lesson in learning not to get bigheaded. While bragging to all the children within earshot about magically seeing the fight, exulting in their admiration of his ability, the Combrian and his girlfriend had shown up. The bully used him to show off that time, achieving the same results. He'd run home crying with a black eye, vowing never to tell anyone about the ability again.

As he'd grown and witnessed other past events reenacting, the thoughts and emotions of the people involved were as clear to him as if he was inside each of them.

He possessed two other peculiar talents as well, abilities no one knew about.

Deep concern enveloped him as he witnessed Arigot probing Wheelbarrow's mind—the enforcer now knew the secret his father had so feared might surface if Needle and he were to move into the palace. The shock of sensing that caused him to lose the killer's previous thoughts. Only a vague image of an Urth man and a desk remained.

Wheelbarrow disappeared from his view as Needle walked in the door and angrily slammed it. Arigot rose from behind a chair and fired a tranquilizer pistol, putting a sedative dart laced with Clodec in her neck.

Experiencing the Combrian's cognitions, he knew Arigot planned to put Needle in the back of a merchant wheeler before contacting Universal Quest and demand to be taken to the king. It came as no surprise to learn the Enforcer didn't know where Gram was. PC had yet to find a room in the palace where he'd either spoken about, or thought of the location of his hideout. If only the despot had, Wheelbarrow would still be alive and the war would be over.

Harv Zane had spotted her while she was being taken to her quarters by Sergeant Wrench, and insisted she have dinner with Molly and him. She and her mate had been casual acquaintances with them back in the days they'd been part of an extended academic circle. Polka hadn't seen him since moving to the farm.

A dorm once used by King Gram's numerous concubines now housed several Urth women, all but her related in someway to a Mancombra. The Combrian females connected to Drill's kind were staying in a chamber next door, identical to this one. Gram's maid servants had slept in it, she'd been told. They weren't segregated because of race but so the roommates could understand each other when speaking. Everyone in her quarters spoke Anglish like her.

Polka had also heard that all but seven of the twenty-six

Mancombras that came to the palace enlisted in the army. The remaining were children, two of them toddlers. They and their families received their own suite of rooms within the palace like Harv and Molly.

A private showed her the way to Harv's apartment and Molly welcomed her inside.

"I hope you like sernloaf, Polka."

Her mouth watered at hearing that. "Oh I love it, Molly, and haven't had any in ages. You can't buy sern with assistance money. That and liquor is off limits to poor folks like me."

"PC will change that I'm sure," Molly forecasted, an optimistic smile guaranteeing it.

"I hope so. I'm not much of a drinker but I sure miss sern, it's my favorite meat."

The door opened and Harv walked in, looking pale and shaken. "Molly, the bastards got Wheelbarrow! He's dead and Needle's been taken hostage. PC told me they know—*they know*, Molly!"

Polka felt extremely awkward. She knew by their names the victims were Mancombras but had no idea what Harv meant by "They know." Judging by the look on Molly's face before she'd covered it with her hands, it would be inappropriate to ask. "Um, this is clearly a horrible tragedy for you two. I should go."

Molly wiped her eyes and signaled disagreement with a vigorous wave. At length she drew a deep breath and appeared to collect herself. "Wheelbarrow and Needle were very close friends of ours, and we feared this might happen. Obviously Harv and I don't have much appetite at the moment but please . . . stay and eat."

Manners dictated she should politely refuse and go to her dorm, but dammit she hadn't eaten sern of any kind for so long the wonderful smell emanating from the kitchen made that notion impossible. "If you'll show me where everything is I'll help myself and get out of your hair so you two can grieve in private. I'll bring your plate back tomorrow."

"I had an ulterior motive in asking you over," said Harv, wearing a peculiar expression of intense curiosity. "I didn't expect this bad news, but I still want to talk to you."

"About?"

"The research you were doing when the government seized your lab."

A few minutes after he'd sat down, Colonel Hammer entered the mess tent. Drill wasn't surprised to see where the Mancombra chose to eat. A stunning Combrian female perched at the end of a nearby table had blocked his probe, but not before he'd learned she and Hammer were lovers— at least they wanted to be. While anticipating the colonel joining her for the evening meal, she'd been musing on how to have sex with him without suffering excruciating pain. She was either a civilian or off duty, for she wore a body-suit rather than a uniform.

Drill sympathized with their plight because the same thing had happened to him and his Combrian sweetheart. They'd solved the dilemma and had planned to be mated before she got gassed to death for harboring her cousin, a female Mancombra.

How did you do it?! The words almost rattled his brain they'd hit so strong. The Combrian had entered his thoughts when Hammer telepathed to her his hope to get some advice from him. They'd transmitted the question simultaneously, and quite urgently.

Not bothering to look at them he washed down a mouthful of food he'd been chewing and lowered his kaffy vessel while informing: *She started douching with hicker fat and essence of valley fern. After that, she very much enjoyed having sex with me.*

Thinking it to be a joke Hammer transmitted, *Seriously, how did you conquer the problem?*

I am being serious.

How is it I've never heard of it? asked the Combrian, whom he now knew went by Voola.

My lover came up with it. She was a chemist and experimented with several different concoctions that failed before succeeding with that one.

How does it work? they asked in unison, the intensity of their thoughts almost giving him a headache.

It dilates the vagina and makes it secrete more lubricants than normal, allowing the membranes to stretch excessively without discomfort. Douche daily with a mix of one part hicker fat, three parts essence of valley fern, and four parts water. It serves as an aphrodisiac as well. Drill savored another bite of grain square covered with ground sern and gravy while enlightening them.

Colonel Hammer ordered an Urth captain named Wurz to take charge and hurried from the tent. Voola's mind began filling with erotic thoughts before she blocked him out.

Drill couldn't hold back a laugh.

The cargo doors of the windowless trailer opened to reveal a four star universal, a supervisor, and two personals standing outside. Needle eyed the supervisor, the Combrian equivalent of a sergeant: no Urth had ever worn such a uniform to her knowledge, yet this one did. Apparently those that hadn't joined PC in the revolution had been rewarded by having their rank and attire transferred to that of the Combrian Forces. She knew the universal and personals were bound to be probing her mind, but still under the influence of Clodec she couldn't do a thing to prevent it. So she kept her thoughts on astronomy—concentrating on her passion to keep anything else from being extracted.

"Universal Quest," said Arigot proudly, "this is renowned astronomer Professor Needle—our ticket to conquering General Zane."

PC entered the dormitory under the guise of inspecting it for possible booby-traps while its temporary occupants were supping in The Great Dining Hall. Feeling this would be the last place Gram Pillhigh would discuss his hideaway, he hadn't tried to pick up its location there before now. Standing in the center of the long room, beds lining the walls on either side, several brief scenarios reenacted before him—most consisting of female Combrians gossiping and making fun of their lover's inadequacies. Being such an egotistical hedonist, Gram would die of humiliation if he knew his whores only pretended to enjoy having sex with him in order to avoid his wrath.

An exceptionally tall Combrian with an incredible build

appeared. He witnessed a conversation between her and a less well-favored mistress that had taken place when they'd been alone in the dorm. The physically gifted female had recently learned that a promise given when she'd won a beauty contest that secured her release from prison had been broken by Gram. She spoke of a guard who said he'd help her escape if she'd have sex with him.

Her confidant shook her head. "He's lying to you, Voola. There's no escaping the palace. Gram would have you shot if he ever found out you cheated on him. Don't do it."

"It's too late I already have, but I made it quite clear that if he doesn't help me I'll tell Gram he raped me. That really frightened him because he knows I'm Gram's favorite slut."

The conversation halted when some Combrian soldiers burst in and grabbed the two concubines, saying they were taking them to a safe place because the palace was under attack. PC surmised this had happened the day he'd taken the throne away from Gram.

Unfortunately Voola hadn't known where they were taking her, so Gram's location still remained a frustrating mystery.

ELEVEN

Aʀɪɢᴏᴛ ᴅɪᴅɴ'ᴛ ᴋɴᴏᴡ ᴡʜᴀᴛ ᴅɪʀᴇᴄᴛɪᴏɴ they were heading or how long they'd be in transit. He'd been locked inside the cargo bay along with Needle and Quest's aides. The universal sat alone in the cab, driving the vehicle to a place no one else aboard knew the location of.

He'd ordered his second in command to continue trying to eliminate the half-breeds that hadn't gone to the palace. Lieutenant Enforcer Barrabon would be leading his troops until Arigot rejoined them, in the unlikely event King Gram didn't take him off the genocide detail after promoting him. Unquestionably he'd go down in history as a military hero and become a legend for defeating the only Urth to ever assume power over Combria.

Vern Yonker stood at a window in his office gazing at the Opian River, barely visible in the dusk. He wished the war was over so he could drop a hook in the water and nip at a jug of stout ale while awaiting a nibble. Its source lay thirty miles south of the northern edge of the continent, aligned with the meridian separating the East and West Combrian Oceans. From there the mighty stream cut a winding southern course past Juxbow—Combria's biggest metropolis—and flowed two hundred miles to Opianapolis, where a tributary fed Palace Lake. Then it continued further south past University City, the Army Command Center, and Mount Opian, before bending sharply to run three hundred miles northeast where it emptied into the Lower East Combrian Sea.

He'd been at the Army Command Center since PC vacated his post to become Prince Zane. The redheaded visionary had put together a secret sniper team to take down every officer opposed to him in the Urth Army, which included PC's three equals. After their elimination the newly titled prince had pinned a fourth star on him. Since the dawn of the industrial age four generals had commanded the Urth Army, answering first to the ruler of Combria and secondly to a quartet of universals leading the Combrian Forces. The east and west hemispheres were halved at the equator, dividing the planet into four military zones, and Mount Opian lay in his territory. Before the revolution Universal Quest had been the Combrian in charge of this quadrant. Now it was under Vern's sole jurisdiction, along with all the other zones since he currently held the temporary post of General of the Army, taking orders only from the new ruler of Combria. Such a title had always warranted a fifth star but PC decided that Vern alone would be a full general for duration of the war, making such a designation of his superior rank unnecessary. Until it ended, he'd be in charge of the navy and flying force as well.

In his last communiqué Colonel Hammer reported his engineer estimated it would only be a few more days before they'd know what lay beyond the mysterious expanse of stainless steel. He looked forward to receiving word that the wall had been breached.

The intercom squelched and his aide notified him that a sergeant requested entrance, having vital information he needed to hear at once.

Vern stepped to his desk and pushed the transmission button. "Send him in . . . ."

"You mean to tell me you got this over twenty days ago, Sergeant!" Vern threw the report on his desk and glowered at the young Urth who'd recently recovered from a serious bout of moon fowl virus.

"Yes, Sir. I wrote down exactly what Colonel Hammer told me and planned to give it to you immediately, but a sudden attack of nausea forced me to the flusher where I passed out. I was delusional with fever while I was in the infirmary and had forgotten about it until I came across it just now. The corporal who took my place filed it, not knowing you hadn't been informed. I'm so sorry, General Yonker."

"Damn that virus!" Vern growled while buzzing his aide.

"Yes, Sir?"

"Patch me through to the palace."

Hammer wanted to smash the glass counter when the clerk told him they were fresh out of essence of valley fern. He'd tried every other shop in town and none of them had any in stock either. Shoulders drooping, he made his way through the door, halfway thinking about kicking the damn thing down instead of opening it.

After dinner Drill had been taken to the colonel's tent. He sighed with pleasure upon seeing a blanket and pillow on an oversized cot designed for Mancombra soldiers. The moment the private left he took off his boots and threadbare coveralls, preparing to turn in for the night.

Before he'd gotten the blanket tucked beneath his chin, Colonel Hammer entered the tent carrying a container of hicker fat, and looked down at him with the semblance of a smile. "I really appreciate your help at the mess tent, Drill."

"Glad I could assist."

"I assume you've put two and two together?"

"Yes, it would have been hard not to. Congratulations, Colonel, Voola is a very beautiful female."

He held up the hicker fat and sighed. "That she is, my new friend. None of the troops know so please keep it to yourself. I purchased this at the first store I went to but not one of them in the whole damn town had any essence of valley fern. I need to tell her the bad news. I'll try not to disturb you when I get back."

As she always did first thing when returning to her tent, Voola checked the night lapper hide to make sure the glimeralds were still safely tucked within it. She eagerly awaited Hammer's return to camp, anxious to get the items blended and applied so they could sneak away and make love.

When he finally showed up her spirits dropped as she explored his mind.

PC ordered Free to gather Sergeant Brush, some techs, and ten snipers to accompany him to Juxbow. Vern Yonker had called the palace to say Colonel Hammer found a runaway mistress of Gram's hiding in a cave at Mount Opian. She'd escaped from a secret bomb shelter outside Juxbow where the king and his entourage had taken refuge. After telling Hammer she knew Gram was no longer there, she'd voluntarily divulged its location. If only the communication had gotten to him when Hammer intended, Wheelbarrow might still be alive. Unbeknownst to Vern, the vital intel had been sitting in a file cabinet for over twenty days.

Gram would have been thinking of little else other then his next move while at the hideaway. That meant there'd be plenty of signals for him to pick up. Perhaps the very ones he needed to save his mother.

Polka had stuffed herself with Molly's delectable sernloaf

while she and Harv only sipped kaffy, making her feel like a glutton. Now she was having her after dinner cup. They'd been discussing her ability to confound Combrian mind probing and she'd just told them what her mate had dubbed it.

"Quieting the oblique mind, huh," said Harv, frowning with interest. "You two were working in genetics, what prompted you to go that direction?"

"Fear of having what we'd stumbled across discovered by Gram. We knew his paranoia of Mancombras would eventually escalate to the point where he'd order their extermination. I still marvel so much time passed before he finally did. If he'd known what we found out, the Genocide Directive would have included every Urth on the planet as well."

Harv leaned forward, his age-drawn face crinkling further. "What did you stumble across, Polka?"

"Our technical journal documenting it is hidden in my attic at the farm. We wanted to determine why two fertile Mancombras couldn't make a baby, so we started experimenting, trying to fertilize an egg in vitro. As you know, every Mancombra has to be tested for fertility as a young adult, and we were able to secretly obtain a large quantity of healthy sperm and ova by volunteering at the University City birth control center. Using combinations of either Mancombra type—Urth mother, Combrian father and vice versa—we tried everything we knew of under every conceivable condition but failed to produce an embryo, and couldn't detect what was preventing fertilization.

"We were about to give up when it occurred to my mate there was one thing we hadn't tried: the sperm and egg of Mancombra siblings. The first experiment consisted of an ovum taken from a Mancombra sired by an Urth. Her brother's seed failed to take root. But when we injected the sperm from a Mancombra whose father was Combrian into his sister's egg, we succeeded in producing a living embryo, but couldn't pin down the reason why that particular combination worked while the others failed.

"It was what happened after the cells had multiplied over ten days that prompted us to find a way to prevent our minds from being read. The embryonic Mancombra's dominant genes weren't Combrian, which meant the child would have looked exactly like a purebred Urth. We conducted several more experiments using sperm and ova from other siblings with Combrian fathers and the results were the same. Four fifths of the injected eggs began multiplying, and the Urth genes were dominant in one hundred percent of them. Our artificial wombs couldn't keep them alive more than thirty days, but none of them self aborted before we terminated them."

She took a sip of kaffy and continued. "We had no way of knowing if they would have still inherited Combrian telepathy and telekinesis like all other Mancombras, or grow to be as tall and strong, but there was one thing we knew all too well—King Gram wouldn't take a chance on finding out. That paranoid bastard would never tolerate Mancombras who weren't readily identifiable as such polluting his planet. The only way Gram could make sure he'd gotten rid of all Mancombras would be to exterminate all the Urths along with them. And you know as well as I he'd have done just that if my mate and I hadn't been able to prevent the secret from getting out."

Instead of appearing to have his curiosity satisfied, Harv seemed to be analyzing something that really troubled him.

She asked what was wrong.

"Oh . . . nothing, Polka."

"Why did you want to talk to me about the research my mate and I were conducting?"

"I just wanted to know what got you two banished from your lab."

She could tell the old scholar was lying, but didn't inquire further—it would've been rude. Besides, she'd infringed on Molly's hospitality long enough. The poor woman needed to release her grief and obviously wasn't going to do so in front of her.

A winding country drive on the outskirts of Juxbow ended at the statue of a large bull sern, looming ghostlike in the light beams of PC's wheeler and the troop vehicle. The long horns jutting from its head encased energy receptacles tuned to an ultra high frequency. They couldn't be seen with the naked eye, being covered with the sculpted metal depicting the herbivore's only defense against natural enemies. One of the techs had discovered them while viewing the statue through an x-ray gun. Now firing a pulse transmitter at the horns, the tech finally found the proper wavelength and the statue began to rise. It kept doing so until the floor of an open elevator, big enough to hold a commercial wheeler, reached ground level. The residents of Juxbow had no idea the monument graciously erected for them a generation ago by the House of Pillhigh controlled the entrance to an underground shelter built for the royal family.

One tech stayed behind with Free, equipped with a field communicator in case the others couldn't figure out how to get them back up, and PC descended with the rest of the troops.

When the elevator touched down, he stepped off it and glanced around a vast open area, well illuminated by lights embedded in the cavern's ceiling. The floor consisted of packed dirt streaked with double tire tracks, indicating commercial wheelers had been driven off the elevator and back onto it. Trailing his soldiers, he passed a garbage incinerator while heading towards a concrete wall with a wide metal door, but halted when a tingling in his chest alerted him he was about to witness an event from the past.

His entourage vanished . . . The door opened and a rubbish cart covered with a tarp rolled out, being pushed by a Combrian bearing the marks of a palace guard. Reaching the incinerator, the guard hastily untied the tarp and another Combrian leapt from the cart: the female named Voola he'd seen at the palace.

Quick, get on the elevator! the jumpy guard urgently transmitted, pointing at the freight lift.

Voola ran to it, frantically telecasting, *Where will it take me?*

How would I know, I'm as clueless as you. Now go, this is all I can do for you.

Cutting his eyes to a control panel embedded in concrete near the metal door, the guard telekinetically pushed a series of buttons and the elevator rose. After it reached the top he waited only a few seconds before lowering it again. Relieved to see Voola had gotten off at the surface, he neatly folded the tarp, readying it to cover the next load when filled to capacity.

The guard was curious to see what Voola now witnessed—the location of the bunker—but couldn't satisfy that curiosity without giving himself away. Unbeknownst to Universal Quest or Gram, he'd been within range when the universal transmitted the elevator code to the king. But it required a pulse transmitter to operate the elevator from up above, so he wouldn't have been able to reenter the shelter. Being a palace guard, he had a tattoo of a crown on the back of each hand and the center of his forehead, making it impossible to prevent detection for long should he try to escape. That alone carried a death sentence, but to have his mind probed after getting caught would guarantee being drawn and quartered for having sex with one of Gram's mistresses. He rolled the cart back inside the shelter.

The vision faded and PC could see his soldiers again, waiting for the go ahead. "Carry on, Sergeant."

He impatiently waited by the garbage incinerator as Sergeant Brush and the snipers checked the interior.

"All clear, Prince Zane," said Brush when he emerged fifteen minutes later. "All the lights operate by motion detector so you'll have no problem finding your away around. The switches are all conveniently located if you want to override the detectors. You'd think Gram would have soldiers guarding this elaborate bomb shelter. Quite puzzling, Sir."

"Not at all," said PC. "Gram's escaped mistress rendered this hideout useless. Only Gram and a few Combrians who have his unquestioned loyalty knew the location of this shelter before the Combrian got away. You and the snipers wait here while I have a look around."

He didn't want to rouse any suspicions but feared he already had. After watching Voola's escape he'd noticed Sergeant Brush curiously eyeballing him. Thankfully he and the snipers had continued to the wall, leaving too great a distance for the Mancombra to read his mind during the vision—but Brush had apparently noticed his posture during it. Whatever empowered him to see reenactments of things passed, kept him paralyzed and mute during the process.

PC walked down a long corridor with open rooms mushrooming off both sides and many closed doors along the way. After crossing two similar hallways he discovered it ended at a naval hatch, behind which lay a cluster of teleons and every type of communication device known to science. It was Gram's tactical lair: a command center enabling him to administrate from the bomb shelter. As he'd surmised, the king had pondered his moves incessantly the short time he'd stayed here. There were five other underground sanctuaries identical to this one, but Gram's thoughts never revealed the exact location of any of them, only the general areas where they lay hidden. Whatever awaited Colonel Hammer beyond that mysterious steel wall inside Mount Opian wouldn't be anything Gram Pillhigh was aware of.

He searched all the sleeping quarters until finding where Gram had slept, whereupon he witnessed something totally unexpected: another vision of Voola.

"What's the king's pleasure tonight?" she said while stepping out of a silver body-suit at the foot of his bed.

Lying on his back, hands behind his head, drool oozed from the corners of Gram's black lips as he ogled her. "Surprise me, my tart."

Voola was blocking Gram's mind probe—partly to keep him from knowing how disgusting she found him, mostly because she'd spied a treasure chest with a broken lock and planned to ransack it after he dozed off.

"How long will we be staying here?"

"Only for the night, we'll be leaving in the morning," lied Gram. He'd been blocking her from knowing any of his strategies, so he didn't know she was doing the same to him. Combrians and Mancombras couldn't probe another mind while shielding their own. He had no plans to vacate the bunker, but didn't want anyone knowing that.

She climbed on top of him. Being so close to one another, either of them could now break through the other's probe block, but not without exposing their own thoughts. Neither of them did. After a rapid bout of sex Gram pushed Voola off him and fell asleep.

Waiting until confident he was truly slumbering and consequently unable to block her probe, she read his mind to confirm it, in the process learning how the lock got maimed. The palace assault was at the forefront of Gram's unconscious brain, overriding everything else within the mad king's psyche. Voola opened the chest. A mass of glittering jewels made her heart race, and she hated not being able to take the whole treasure. Worried about Gram's bedroom sentinels, she reluctantly settled for seven beautifully cut glimeralds.

PC winced in his mind when she began stuffing them up her vagina, and would have looked away if he could move his head or close his eyes. Holding one hand between her legs to keep the gems in place, she used the other to manipulate the body-suit as she struggled into it. Managing to get the fabric tight against her crotch, she freed her fingers, zipped up, and stepped through the door.

Despite wearing the tight-fitting outfit, which would have flagrantly bulged if anything but her wondrous body lay beneath the synthetic, she immediately got frisked the moment she entered the corridor. Voola concentrated on a tune to keep her secret safe. Being a catchy melody, her frisker began humming it aloud under his breath. Once finished, he nodded. Using a field communicator, the other sentinel called for an escort, as they weren't allowed to leave the king's quarters while he slept. A few minutes later Voola's ally showed up and led her away.

The scene switched to the next morning when Gram tore through his treasure chest after being informed of Voola's escape. He hadn't intended to leave this shelter any time soon but Voola had left him no choice, since she could tell his enemies how to find it.

Sergeant Wrench had informed Free that a black Urth woman was told by Arigot he wanted to surrender but would only do so at a certain place with the new ruler of Combria present. Being very familiar with the tactics of Gram's universals, PC knew none of them would divulge the deranged king's true whereabouts to the enforcer and his hit squad. Well aware of that fact himself, Arigot would have been instructed to give a bogus location to his troops in case they got captured. So what prompted the enforcer to pick the spot he'd lied to the Urth woman about surrendering at?

Gram Pillhigh had left this bomb shelter for one just like it hidden somewhere beneath the picturesque landscape of Serene Valley, the very place Arigot had named. Had the mad Combrian changed his mind while in route?

TWELVE

HARV WONDERED IF THERE WERE any other children on the planet spawned by incestuous Mancombras borne of a Combrian male and Urth female. There were bound to be very few, if any. Before Polka told him about her amazing discovery last night, he'd assumed some genetic fluke had made Wheelbarrow and Needle capable of reproducing. Wheelbarrow had carried the same assumption to his grave.

Academia was one of the few professions where Urths weren't looked down on by their Combrian colleagues. Even so, not many attained the position of president like he had. Back when he'd been head of the mathematics department Needle had taken a leave of absence from the university. Though the time she'd requested off coincided with the gestation period of Combrian and Mancombra females, until the day Wheelbarrow told him about the pregnancy and begged for his help it had never occurred to him she'd lied to the dean about having to care for her terminally ill grandmother. He'd vehemently refused to be the adoptive father of a Mancombra, knowing the stigma would hurt his career if not wreck it altogether.

"I'll keep your secret," he'd said to Wheelbarrow, "and I'll ask Molly to help Needle through labor since she can't risk going to the hospital when the time comes or she'll get fired for falsifying a request for an extended leave—but that's it, and that's my final word on the matter."

But when the baby came out looking like a purebred Urth, he'd had no choice but to reverse his position. Until the Genocide Directive Mancombras had the same rights as

Combrian and Urth citizens with three restrictions besides not being allowed in the palace: they could only serve in the Combrian Forces by enlisting in the Urth Army, they had to be tested for fertility after puberty, and Mancombras— though permitted to raise their own—weren't allowed to adopt children.

No one would have believed Needle bore PC without extensive blood tests proving she had. Such tests would have exposed her incestuous relationship with her brother, causing PC to be looked upon as a loathsome freak of nature, a scourge on the face of society. Like Wheelbarrow, Needle, and Molly, he'd assumed the baby would have Mancombra features and therefore hadn't planned to be a foster dad because there'd have been no suspicion a Mancombra sired Needle's child, since that was scientifically considered impossible. It would have been presumed by all that she'd been impregnated out of mate-lock by an Urth or Combrian, it didn't matter which—no Mancombra had ever sired or given birth to a baby that wasn't Mancombra through-and-through. Being illegitimate wouldn't have caused her offspring to be any more of an outcast than that already guaranteed by departing the womb a half-breed, and nothing could've been done about that. Therefore Needle could have raised her child without anyone raising an eyebrow as it would've been assumed Wheelbarrow had become an uncle rather than a father.

The infant coming into the world looking like an Urth hadn't been the only thing that forced a change of heart about sharing his surname, however. Like Molly, he'd fallen in love with the tot at first sight. So when the redheaded bundle of joy was weaned from Needle's breasts, Molly and he carried him to The Hall of Records and said the male Urth child had been left on their doorstep. After giving them permission to claim the boy as their own, the officer in charge had asked what name he should record on the birth register. Harv had kissed the forehead of the cuddly baby Molly lovingly held in her arms, and honoring the request of his natural parents answered, "Pythagoras Copernicus Zane."

The trailer stopped and remained motionless for several minutes. Then it rolled forward a short distance, quit moving again, and Needle felt the sensation of being lowered. When that motion ceased she heard the cargo doors being unlocked from the outside.

Arigot rose to his feet and helped her up. "Let's go. It's time to meet the king."

The powdered hicker eggs were overcooked, the kaffy too strong, but Drill couldn't complain. He'd gotten a good night's sleep on the army cot and felt completely refreshed. He walked out of the mess tent and gazed at a security fence standing about twenty yards above the foot of Mount Opian with a sign warning MILITARY ZONE NO TRESSPASSING.

"I wonder what's going on up there," he mused aloud.

"It's still a mystery, Drill, but we hope to solve it soon."

He turned to see Colonel Hammer strolling towards him. When he got within range the colonel transmitted a full explanation.

"So it's not just a myth after all?"

"We have no idea what we'll find, if anything, behind that steel. It was either treated with an unknown substance or forged in a manner we don't understand because a cutting torch won't even faze it. We're going to have to blast through it. But enough about that, tell me about yourself. What did you do for a living before the Genocide Directive?"

Drill blew out a sigh and shoved his hands in his pockets. "I wanted to go into archeology. I earned a college degree but wound up working on my father's farm because none of the reputable archeologists wanted a Mancombra on their team."

"How did you avoid being captured after Gram issued the directive?"

"I didn't. If Prince Zane's orders had reached the death camp any later than they did I'd have been killed like my whole family."

He felt deep empathy issue from the colonel.

So sorry for your loss. I too lost my father and stepmother because of Gram's madness, though they died resisting capture.

My sympathies for your loss as well, Colonel.

Hammer squinted towards the sky. "My half brother Arigot is an enforcer in Gram's army. I've been informed he was put in charge of completing the Genocide Directive while the rest of Gram's forces remain in hiding. It was most likely his regiment you fled from when you came here."

Drill cocked his head and grinned. "An Urth woman took me in after I left the death camp. I was hiding in her attic while an Enforcer Arigot spoke with her. It's a small world isn't it?"

"You were in the attic and Arigot didn't get that information from your friend?"

"No."

"Ah, she didn't know you were in the attic."

"Oh she knew all right," Drill answered with a chuckle. "Her name's Polka and she used to be a scientist. Along with her now deceased mate she learned how to control her mind in such a way you or I would only be able to understand what she speaks with her lips. After she told me about it I tried my best to defeat it and couldn't. Your half brother couldn't as well. It's all very natural, impossible to tell she's purposely misleading the probe."

The colonel hiked his brows. "You're saying this is a learnable skill—not a talent she was born with?"

He nodded.

"Well she needs to go to the palace and tell Prince Zane about this ability of hers. Every Urth soldier in our army needs to learn how to do it. I'll call General Yonker right now. Where can she be found?"

Vern's desk communicator sprang to life. He picked up the receiver and the notification buzzing stopped. "Yonker here."

"Colonel Hammer's on the line asking for you, Sir. He says it's urgent."

"Patch him through."

He heard a click, then a voice. *"General Yonker?"*

"You got him. What's up, Colonel?"

His pulse elevated at the information being passed on. When the sergeant said Hammer wanted to talk to him, Vern hoped the engineer had blasted through the steel ahead of schedule, but this was far more exciting than finally knowing what lurked inside Mount Opian. "This Drill said she lives at the south bend of the Opian River?"

"Yes, Sir."

"Captain Morris called me two days ago from that region requesting permission to have a black Urth woman treated as a relative of a Mancombra with that name. I told him he could take her to the palace. They should have gotten there some time yesterday. I'll check and see if she's the Urth we're looking for. This will give us a tremendous advantage if your Drill isn't exaggerating. If this technique really works, we can infiltrate Gram's forces by having some spies enlist in what's left of his Urth Army once they finally begin their counterattack. The Combrian bastards would never guess a lowly Urth could tune them out without them knowing it."

Polka was eating lunch in The Great Dining Hall. She'd selected her meal from a menu replete with rich foods and marvelous beverage choices. Such excellent cuisine would sorely be missed when she had to go back to the farm.

Sergeant Wrench walked up and put a hand on her shoulder, completely covering her right collarbone and bicep. "Polka, I've been instructed by Captain Morris to bring you to his office. It seems he got a call from General Yonker himself concerning you."

"Oh dear," she said while rising from the chair, unable to fathom the reason for such a request. "Am I in some kind of trouble?"

The sergeant laughed. "Should you be?"

"Well," she summoned a nervous grin, "unless I'm doing

something in my sleep that I can't remember, it's been a very long time since I've been a naughty girl."

"I wasn't told what this is about," said Wrench with a wink, "but you're in no trouble, I can tell you that much."

⸸

The Mancombra appeared to be about thirty double-years, which put her past menopause and at the last stage of middle-age. Severe facial bruises and a broken nose revealed she'd been slapped around. He told the guards to take her to a chair beyond transmission range and cut his eyes to Enforcer Arigot, who assured him the half-breed had been freshly injected with Clodec. Now using telepathy the enforcer excitedly revealed the details of why he'd kept her alive and the reason he'd refused to tell anyone else what he'd uncovered.

And she didn't bother denying this incredulous event that contradicts what science claims to be an absolute certainty?

No, Sire.

Gram scratched his chin while thinking everything over. *This has to be a trick.*

I'm confused as to what purpose such a trick would serve, My King.

Shocked that a Combrian with the aptitude to attain the rank of enforcer could be so imbecilic, he mentally shouted, *Why what it's already accomplished of course—to keep the half-breed alive! She and her brother could have come up with this idea as a protective device, carefully rehearsing it should either be killed. You told me her brother knew she'd be next to die, so he could have only been pretending when you sensed him trying to hide it, knowing you'd take it as the truth. If so, this great revelation you've presented me is nothing but a pile of sern shit. I'm not about to act on this at face value, I need some type of proof. I'll instruct Universal Quest to take you back to Juxbow where you'll immediately return to your command. Say nothing of this to anyone, it's no longer your concern.*

And the Mancombra, My King?

He sensed Arigot mentally reeling—trying to hide his anger, confusion, and extreme disappointment. The fool had thought this would garner him a promotion. *The half-breed stays with me until I get to the bottom of this.*

Needle couldn't read Arigot's mind but she didn't have to, the agony on his face told the whole story. Gram didn't buy it. Her spirits soared. Though she'd surely soon be put to death, PC's secret was safe.

At least for the time being.

Arigot was heatedly furious, and quit trying to subdue it the moment he got out of the king's mental range. Having been placed in a corner, the Mancombra who was supposed to be his ticket to glory was too far away to have picked up their transmissions even if she hadn't been doped up. He took one last look at her, knowing he'd never see her again. She appeared stoic, yet somehow serene.

He immediately blocked his mind when Universal Quest greeted him in the corridor.

"Well, Enforcer, I hope the king is pleased. Either way, now that he's been the first to hear your secret, I demand to be the second. What is going on with that Mancombra?"

Sergeant Wrench tapped on the door and cracked it open. "I have Polka with me, Sir. Permission to enter?"

"Yeah, bring her in."

She'd liked Captain Morris from the moment he'd introduced himself back at the farm. The Urth had fearless yet friendly eyes, dark wavy hair, a strong chin, and a tall, well developed body. If he'd been born black instead of white, and they were the same age, the captain would have gotten a serious run for his money had their paths crossed in her younger days before she'd met her mate. But since she was old enough to be his grandmother and unwilling to cross the color barrier, instilled in her by old fashioned parents, the young officer was safe.

He smiled at her from his desk. "Good to see you again, Polka. Please have a seat."

She chose a comfortable chair a few feet from the captain.

"That'll be all, Sergeant."

Instantly obeying, the Mancombra closed the door behind him and Captain Morris's smile broadened. "I've got good news. Your friend Drill wound up at Mount Opian where we've set up a temporary base under Colonel Hammer's command. He couldn't be in better hands."

Forgetting what being baptized with sheer joy felt like, she jumped to her feet and raised her hands in the air. "Praise The Spirit That Created All Things, Drill's still alive!"

The captain chuckled. "Don't be shy, Polka, show your enthusiasm."

She cackled and playfully slapped Morris's desk. "Captain, you have no idea what a burden your glad tidings have lifted off my shoulders. I've come to love that big Mancombra like my own son. I've been praying he'd be okay and you've just verified my prayers were answered. I was a little nervous about why you wanted to see me but oh my, you've really made my day."

He quit smiling and cleared his throat.

"Uh-oh, is there something else? Drill's not injured is he?"

"My understanding is that Drill's fine, but there is something else I wanted to talk to you about."

Frowning at him, she sat back down. "What is it?"

"Drill told Colonel Hammer you developed a technique which enables you to block the mind probes of Combrians and Mancombras. Is that true?"

Her entrails cramped with fear. She hadn't asked him not to say anything to anyone, but Drill should have known better. Now this Colonel Hammer and Captain Morris knew about it—two military officers who owed their livelihood to the government payroll. She supported Prince Zane, but if he lost the war and the mad king got the throne back, Gram would soon know about it too, and snuff out her life to keep others from learning the technique. Making a mental note to beg Harv and Molly not to tell anyone about it, she faked being confused and stood up. "I have no idea what you're talking about, Captain Morris."

THIRTEEN

Stove HATED GUARD DUTY AND wished another situation would come up requiring Captain Morris to leave the palace. Of course even if one did, he might not get picked again.

The number of Mancombra's had unfortunately dropped by one male with the murder of Professor Wheelbarrow. His sister was feared dead as well, leaving only a hundred and thirty-eight potential revolutionaries. His dream of planetary domination appeared doomed to failure. Not even one of the Mancombras he'd approached shared his vision. He'd only spoken to nine of them besides Sergeant Wrench, but their attitudes had been so similar to the sergeant's it seemed unlikely he'd be able to ignite the spark in many of his fellow half-breeds. Apparently he alone had the proper ambition every Mancombra should have been consumed by.

As he thought on that a fuzzy notion caused a prickling sensation to crawl all over him. It gained strength and boldly came into focus, turning him shivery with euphoria. All along he'd felt the top position among the ruling Mancombras should be his since the plan had been birthed by him. He'd been concerned about how to secure that leadership role but not anymore.

I've been so blind all this time! No wonder I'm the only one who can see the possibilities. Combria will never be ruled by a tribe of Mancombras because it's mine alone for the taking. I must instigate a Genocide Directive of my own, and once I succeed I'll be the strongest male on the planet.

"CSM Pliers reporting for duty, Sir." She stood stiffly erect, right hand chopping her forehead in salute, honored that her commander had chosen a Mancombra for this very special duty.

Returning her gesture, Captain Morris slid his chair back and rose from his desk. "At ease, Sergeant Major."

She lowered her arm and took note of the civilian she'd been assigned to protect.

"Polka, this is Command Sergeant Major Pliers, your new bodyguard. She'll be with you around the clock. She's skilled in every known form of hand-to-hand combat, is a crack shot, can throw a bayonet ninety yards with deadly aim, is a great cook, and tells a good joke on occasion."

Her commander's flattery made her feel proud yet humbly embarrassed. She hoped her cheeks were still copper and not red from blushing.

"I'll have one of my men give you a tour through the palace apartments that are available," the captain continued. "Choose the one you like best, Polka, because it'll be yours and CSM Pliers' home for the duration of the war. I'll give you a few days to determine what all you'll need to teach the troops, then we'll outfit a classroom for you."

The black Urth heaved a sigh and said, "Captain Morris, I hope I haven't made the biggest mistake of my life in letting you shame the truth out of me. How did you know I was lying anyway?"

"I didn't. I was merely being tactful in case you were."

At first the woman's thoughts were angry, but relief over not having to subsist on a paltry assistance allowance anymore soon transformed them. Wrinkled face reflecting her mood change, she grinned at Captain Morris. "You're a sly old night lapper, aren't you."

"I have my moments," he replied with a wink.

Still grinning, Polka turned to her. "I hope you can get along with me as well as the male Mancombra I took in did."

If not you can always request another bodyguard, Ma'am, she telepathically teased.

That brought a snicker and a pat on the arm from Polka, who then said, "Well at least I don't have to go back to the farm, even if you are bad company."

Captain Morris let out a short laugh and turned his eyes to her. "I had Polka demonstrate her ability to Sergeant Wrench and he was quite impressed. Now I want to see if she can do equally well with you . . . ."

⸸

Sitting on the trailer floor as it carried him from the bunker back to Juxbow where he'd be leaving Universal Quest's hidden post, supposedly to rejoin his troops, Arigot fumed over his stupidity he'd harshly awakened to. He'd stayed loyal to the king despite his parents pleading with him to see the Genocide Directive as the mandate of a psycho and resign his commission—and he'd remained committed even after they'd died as a result of it—but now he knew his parents and Hammer had been right.

Gram Pillhigh *was* insane.

After telling the universal he'd been forbidden by Gram to discuss the matter when his commander demanded to hear it, he'd asked for another audience with the king, and had been granted it.

Wheelbarrow's grief over knowing his sister would die soon after him couldn't have been a clever manipulation— he'd felt the half-breed's pain over it—no one could fake such a dreadful emotion. He'd tried to explain his reasoning, insisting that if Gram had been there and felt it too he'd know beyond doubt PC Zane really was the lovechild of the two siblings. But the king had refused to listen, angrily dismissing him instead, thinking him a gullible fool, even toying with the idea of demoting him because of it.

Arigot had felt all along that remaining in retreat until all civilian Mancombras were eliminated was a piss-poor strategy, only giving Zane more time to secure the entire planet. With the majority of the military force hiding in Juxbow, the rebels were no doubt fortifying their positions all over the globe, virtually unhindered. How many other idiotic notions did Gram entertain?

Continuing to block his mind so the two soldiers riding with him couldn't read it, he deeply regretted telling the old Urth woman he wanted to surrender. If she carried out his request, and he could only assume she had, PC knew it to be a strategic lie. And because of that the rebellious general would never believe he now really did.

Thankfully he had an ace up his sleeve.

A Mancombra guarding the entrance to the east wing saluted her bodyguard as they walked by, following an Urth private assigned to show them the available apartments. Polka thought she detected a flirtatious gleam in Pliers' eyes as the sergeant major saluted back.

You did indeed, Ma'am, telecasted Pliers, confirming it. *That's Corporal Stove. I've developed the biggest crush on him.*

Polka giggled and whispered, "Aren't you afraid he'll hear your thoughts?"

No, he can't at the moment because he's blocking my probe. Ah, I see you're wondering why I'd be interested in a male I outrank. Well it's not just because I think he's cute. Stove's extremely ambitious but has no desire for a military career. He has his eye on politics. Some time ago I caught him obsessing about becoming the ruler of Combria before he could block me out. Right now he's pretty much a dreamer, but he's very bright. With the proper guidance from this Mancombra, who doesn't want kids any more than he does, Stove could attain a high government office since all races are considered equal in Prince Zane's eyes.

The private stopped at a door with a plaque above it that read: Duke Kaleen of Lower Sorria. Polka followed him into a huge, lavishly furnished parlor, and gasped. "This room is five times the size of my entire house! This looks fit for the king himself to have lived in."

"One of King Gram's nephews used to reside here before being killed in the battle for the palace, Ma'am," said the private. "He was a confirmed bachelor. His cook and maid slept in the servants' quarters of the palace so this suite only has two sleep chambers—the one used by the duke and a guestroom—but they're quite luxurious."

He guided her to a spotless, gleaming kitchen that took her breath away. All the appliances were brand names only the rich could afford, and it had one of those newfangled wall ovens that heated food by microwave radiation.

When they entered the dining room its splendor made her eyebrows soar. The duke may have lived alone but he obviously enjoyed entertaining a large number of guests in fancy style. She counted thirty elegant chairs surrounding an exquisite stone-top dining table with intricately carved heartwood of melania legs, the rarest trees on Combria. "Private, if this apartment didn't have only two sleep chambers I wouldn't consider taking it—the parlor and dining room could handle the largest family with room to spare. As it is, I've seen enough. Pliers, if this place suits you, then I'll take it."

Beaming with excitement, her Mancombra bodyguard gushed, "I was hoping you would, Ma'am—I absolutely love it!"

Voola liked Drill except for one thing: the bright, mannerly Mancombra was a lazy coward. She couldn't believe he'd turned Hammer down, refusing to join the army under the guise of being a pacifist. Unemployed, his only possessions being a badly worn pair of boots and faded coveralls that were in shambles, he should have jumped at the chance. Instead, he'd be taken to the palace and mooch off Prince Zane's generosity. No doubt the loafer would be given new clothing as well. He'd refused to be escorted by soldiers at first—hoping to catch a ride to the palace with some tourists, hiding in the rear cavity of their wheeler since Gram's killers weren't harassing Urth or Combrian civilians unrelated to half-breeds. When Hammer explained he'd already called for an escort since he couldn't spare the personnel to take him, Drill had reluctantly agreed.

Watching him climb in back of the vehicle that looked like an armed version of a merchant wheeler, she suddenly felt guilty for being angry with him. If not for Drill there'd be no chance to make love with Hammer again. Of course they still weren't certain the concoction would work for her, as they hadn't been able to obtain any essence of valley fern to go with the hicker fat.

Drill had seen the palace interior numerous times but only on teleon, and those two dimensional images miserably failed to capture its true magnificence. The Grand Entrance was breathtaking: high arched ceilings of stone sculpted with majestic figures of ancient Combrian warlords engaged in battle hovered over polished fractured-rock floors assembled in dazzling arrays of colorful patterns, so intricate it must have taken numerous days just to perfect a square yard. Statues of each ruler of Combria belonging to the House of Pillhigh stood on either side of The Great Hall, the metal effigies so lifelike each one looked as if it might speak. The one depicting Gram flattered the despot immensely, at least according to how he appeared on camera.

Three hours after leaving Mount Opian the wheeler had stopped at a military base called Army Command Center, from which he'd been flown by whirly to the royal landing strip at the palace, covering a distance in only one hour that would have taken four by highway. Along the way he'd been given a new burden to bear besides being a half-breed: any adult male Mancombra seeking refuge in the palace capable of serving in the military was considered a coward if he didn't volunteer.

Every female Mancombra he'd ever met considered him a lady killer. How foolish he'd been in rejoicing that only a small percentage of surviving half-breeds weren't masculine. Stove now wished those proportions could be reversed. The ten he'd shared the vision with had all been males. He'd have to take them out first, one by one, leaving no trail that could be traced back to him. Meanwhile the females had to be seduced, convinced to join forces with him and become his Mancombra Queens when they succeeded in conquering Combria.

Pliers and the black Urth passed him again, presumably heading for The Great Dining Hall for dinner. This time he didn't block her out, but put his plan into action. *I wonder, Command Sergeant Major, if you'd have a drink with me when my shift ends?*

Feeling her turn giddy, his mind received: *I wish I could, Corporal, but I'm afraid this duty I've been assigned is around the clock for duration of the war.*

Allowing his disappointment to show, he kept everything else sealed. The CSM could tell he had hidden secrets, but not what they were. *How unfortunate. What is this duty?*

Guarding Polka, the Urth woman beside me.

Hmm . . . might I inquire why you've been ordered to do so?

No you may not.

She blocked him before he could pull it from her thoughts, but the blush on her face assured he'd be able to pry the reason out of her soon enough. The luscious Mancombra had a strong crush on him.

FOURTEEN

THE URTH INTRODUCED HIMSELF AS Captain Morris. Looking into his mind Drill learned the captain had been who he'd heard approaching when fleeing Polka's farm, and she'd returned to the palace with him. Relief and gladness warmed his insides. Not only was the old woman safe, she'd be residing in her own apartment for the duration of the war, treated like a VIP for agreeing to teach her probe-blocking skill to the Urth commandos.

Captain Morris told the Urth private who'd brought him to his office to wait outside. When the door closed he said, "I've been informed you've chosen not to enlist, Drill. Don't you want to help free your kind from Gram's oppression?"

He shoved his hands in his pockets, discovering the right one now had a hole worn through it. "Very much so, but it's not in me to physically harm another. I couldn't bear the guilt of taking a life unless it was King Gram's, and even then I'm not sure I could go through with it."

Morris raised an eyebrow, not believing it possible he'd have any reservations about killing Gram. "Not every soldier serves in the field of battle, Drill. There are a variety of duties I could assign you that wouldn't require you to bear arms. What's your educational background and employment history?"

"I graduated college with a degree in social science hoping to be an archeologist, but never made a tib from it because of my race. The only money I've ever earned was working on my father's farm."

An ironic smile crossed the captain's face. "My dad was a

cultivator too. I only joined the army to get off the farm, but soon discovered military life suited me fine. Anyway, I strongly advise you to enlist because otherwise you'll be blackballed, being the only able-bodied Mancombra who didn't out of those who've come here seeking refuge."

"I'm already acutely aware of that, Captain." The hole slightly expanded so he pulled his hand out and hooked his thumb on the pocket rim. "Perhaps I could assist Polka as a civilian. Forgive me for being intrusive but I know your plans for her."

Morris appeared unfazed. "Yeah, I figured you were reading my mind. Being in charge of that operation I could grant your request if Polka needs help, but only if you become a buck private. Otherwise everyone is going to view you as a freeloader during your stay here."

He frowned. "Why can't I help her as a civilian?"

"Because it's a military operation."

"Polka's not in the army."

"Oh yes she is, though I haven't told her yet. She'll be measured for uniforms tomorrow after I surprise her with the news. She became an honorary lieutenant upon accepting the post, and will be drawing the same pay as every other officer who had to earn that rank. Civilians with specialized skills enjoy that title and accompanying privileges for as long as they lend their expertise to the military. Those who assist such persons must be regular army. There's no such thing as an honorary private. Being aware of how fond she is of you, I'm sure she'd choose you over any of my soldiers if she requires an assistant, so I can almost guarantee the position if you'll sign up. I can't speak for Polka of course, and the choice would be hers alone."

Drill thought that over carefully before saying, "And if she doesn't need my help?"

"Then I'd speak with General Yonker and ask him to

assign you to Colonel Hammer. It can't hurt to have an archeologist on hand to have a look at whatever they find behind that steel wall."

"And if General Yonker says no?"

"Then I'd bring you back here to serve on the maintenance crew, unless of course you wind up changing your mind about combat by then."

"Bring me back from where?"

"From boot camp . . ." Morris donned a sly grin. "There's no way around that forty-two days of hell if you enlist. But I got through it and so can you."

Hearing boot camp would be forty-two days of hell solidified his original position. "Captain Morris, I appreciate you taking the time to encourage me to join the army but my mind's made up. If you can tell me where I'm supposed to go and how to get there, I'll let you get on with other business."

Looking frustrated and slightly angry, Captain Morris crossed the room and jerked the door open, startling the private guarding it. "Since Drill has no family he doesn't warrant his own apartment. Check with the young Mancombras' folks and see if any of them are willing to take him in. If not, put him in the barracks where Gram's male servants stayed."

Arigot knew PC made sure every set of guards included at least one Combrian or Mancombra on all his bases and outposts. Gram's soldiers could surrender at any of them, but not him. Being second only to Gram on Zane's most wanted list, broadcast hourly by every teleon network on the planet, he'd be shot on sight. No matter how clever his disguise the guards would see him as hostile if he blocked their probes. The moment they melded minds with him they'd know his true identity and open fire before he could prove his intentions.

He needed to be twenty-one inches taller or no one would believe he was a Mancombra. After leaving Universal Quest he'd bought the necessary items to do so, wearing bandages on his face so as not to be recognized. Since he'd look far too slight at eight feet to pose as a male, his purchase had included female enhancements to give him breasts and wider hips. Also hidden in the spare cavity of the open-air wheeler was a makeup kit with which to feminize his features. To keep anyone from seeing the adjustable stilts construction workers strapped to their feet when working on ceilings, he'd obtained a floor-length skirt.

Universal Quest wouldn't have a doubt he'd driven directly to his regiment to resume carrying out the Genocide Directive so that bought him valuable time. He'd contacted his second in command and after learning the company's whereabouts, had told Barrabon to stay put until he got there, not bothering to say how long he'd be in arriving.

Anyone trying to enter the palace, Combrian or Urth, would be thoroughly searched and have their identification verified to insure they were truly civilians and not one of Gram's spies. Mancombras on the other hand were welcomed inside with open arms. If his disguise could only get him past the guards where he could seek out someone in command, he'd announce his intention to surrender and declare he had vital information for Prince Zane that had to be delivered personally. He'd then tell the general that he knew his secret but wouldn't divulge it to anyone, and though his mother was alive when he left her with Gram, the mad king refused to believe she gave birth to him so she was almost certainly dead by now. Zane's true pedigree being exposed prohibited him from having a trusted Mancombra or Combrian probe his mind about it, and that was a shame. Because if one did, PC would know three things about him with absolute certainty: he wasn't lying about Needle, the desire to wear a red Z on his uniform was as sincere as his regret over killing innocents in the line of duty, and he would gladly face a firing squad after the war to pay for those murders if allowed to help win it.

Guilt over his parents flooding his mind, he thanked The Spirit That Created All Things that at least Hammer was still alive. Gram had so mesmerized him with fear of a Mancombra takeover he'd lost all objectivity. But seeing the king's mental deficiency first hand had opened his eyes. In reality he'd never heard of a Mancombra even organizing a street gang, much less an army. Like Combrians and Urths, some were more ill-tempered than others, but he'd yet to meet a single one he could call ruthlessly ambitious. By and large they were more docile and content than either of the other two races, and that was with them being looked down on. Under Zane they were declared equals with all society, so they'd be even more law abiding in the future.

He had blood on his hands that no detergent could wash off, but at least it lay within his power to apologize to his half brother.

If he could only succeed in entering the palace.

When Stove's shift ended he immediately went looking

for Sergeant Wrench and found him in The Great Dining Hall talking with the black Urth they'd brought to the castle after being called back from the south bend of the Opian River. Pliers smiled at him as he approached. Blocking his own thoughts, he couldn't read hers.

"Sergeant Wrench, could I have a word with you in private?"

The Mancombra frowned. "Can't you see I'm occupied, Corporal?"

"Yes, Sir, but I think there's something you need to see right away."

"What?"

"Um, it's rather sensitive, Sir."

Emitting an acquiescent breath, Wrench rose from the table and gave Polka a light nudge on the shoulder. "Allow me to congratulate you once again, I'm so happy for you."

She smiled broadly. "This has been such an amazing day. First I get told Drill is alive and well, and then I find myself being shown an apartment I would never dream I'd be living in. I'm really looking forward to seeing how comfortable the duke's bed is."

Wrench chuckled. "It'll beat the blazes out of mine I'm sure, so I envy you. Take care, hope we can talk again soon."

Stove led the sergeant outside the palace to The Royal Garden, continuing down a winding walkway shaded by immense fanleaf trees, planted equidistantly on both sides four generations ago when the original castle underwent its tenth refurbishment and expansion. Power poles interrupted the organic splendor, their lights enabling the paradisiacal setting to be enjoyed after nightfall, like now. When they entered The Vale of Hedges, Stove took him deep within the twelve-foot high maze.

"Where are we headed, Stove, and why are you blocking your mind?"

It had to be done in one move or his plans would fall to ruin. If Wrench got the chance to defend himself his superior combat skills guaranteed he'd win the fight and all would be lost. Stove wouldn't be able to prevent him from searching his brain at such close range, and after getting stomped by the sergeant he'd soon find himself in the stockade awaiting trial for treason, if Wrench didn't decide to empty his sidearm on him instead.

Still carrying the bayoneted rifle required for guard duty, he stopped walking and pointed at something he'd noticed on his first tour of the garden—a shiny strip of metal running a few feet along the bottom of a segment of hedge. "Sir, while I was on duty an Urth civilian walked by, thinking about where he'd hidden something he'd stolen. I recognized this location while scanning his thoughts and saw the metal. I have no idea what it is but I assume this is what the Urth stole."

As Stove hoped he would, Wrench squatted down to examine the stretch of silver. "Why this is nothing but a section of exposed conduit, Stove. Your Urth didn't put it here, it runs underground all the way to the palace maintenance center."

Quickly thrusting the bayonet in the back of Wrench's neck, just beneath the base of his skull, he twisted the rifle upward through the bone and shoved it into soft brain tissue, making sure those would be the sergeant's last words.

Withdrawing the blade, he took a few steps away from the corpse and released the rifle—levitating it level with his face, the barrel facing away from him. Gritting his teeth, he telekinetically made it fire a shot before willing the butt to ram the side of his head, knocking him out cold.

There weren't many patients left in the palace infirmary who were wounded in the final battle for the throne of Combria that caused Gram to flee for his life. Most were on medical leave convalescing at a relative's home, but some were already back on duty. Rope's career as a military nurse and had been disrupted when Gram issued the Genocide Directive. A regiment of soldier's led by Captain Hammer infiltrated the fort she'd been sent to after being dishonorably discharged for being a Mancombra, and the captain himself saved her life: gunning down every member of the firing squad as the Combrian soldiers were taking aim at her. He'd gotten promoted to colonel because of his bravery. She'd attended his promotion ceremony and had thrown herself at her rescuer, only to come away reeling with the horrid sting of rejection upon learning he didn't fancy Mancombras.

Ready for some kaffy, the moment the clock signaled break time Rope left her station and walked through the emergency bay, making for the nurse's lounge. The double doors flew open before she got there. Orderlies pushed two gurneys through them, each covered by a male Mancombra, one of whom appeared to be dead. The emergency ward doctor on duty entered, motioning for them to stop so he could examine them.

The Urth physician turned to her. "What happened, Lieutenant?"

"I don't know, Sir, you'll have to ask them." She pointed at the orderlies.

"Some guards found them in The Vale of Hedges after hearing gunfire," one replied, "but neither has been shot.

Their tags read Sergeant Wrench and Corporal Stove."

"Poor devil," said the doctor, feeling the sergeant's throat. "Take him to the morgue."

Tending to the corporal, he parted a mass of bloody hair while inspecting the wound. "Wheel this one to X-Ray. He took a nasty blow to the side of his head and might have a fractured skull."

Rope walked with them, looking down at Corporal Stove all the way. She'd never seen a more handsome face on a Mancombra.

†

PC felt it would be a waste of time to search every square mile of Serene Valley looking for another sern statue or something else containing hidden sensors to raise an underground elevator. Arigot choosing that location as bait made it extremely unlikely Gram hadn't changed his mind about going there. He'd decided to go after the enforcer instead.

He'd learned from Gram's signals back at the bomb shelter that most of his soldiers were hiding in Juxbow. Consequently, besides the troops PC had dispatched to govern the city the day he took the palace, he'd ordered twenty thousand more to surround it. Heavily armored and well equipped with missiles, they also had constant air cover for protection—whirlys patrolled the skies over the mega-metropolis day and night. Despite being reviled by most of its populace, they were still innocent civilians and he didn't want them slaughtered in crossfire, which would be the case should he try to flush the Combrian Forces out in the open.

Gram was probably still scratching his head over how he'd managed to gain control of the entire navy and flying force along with such a large portion of the Urth Army before declaring war against the king. The fool thought he'd decided to rebel only because of the Genocide Directive, but he'd secretly been hard at work long before that, collecting allies in strategic positions for one purpose: rid Combria of the bigoted House of Pillhigh forever. The Genocide Directive had forced him to act prematurely. His original plan called for an almost bloodless coup, and wasn't far from being perfected when Gram demanded the extermination of all Mancombras. To avoid a horrendous amount of civilian collateral damage, he couldn't afford to use bombs or missiles in the rebellion, and Gram had almost succeeded before he'd finally taken the palace—Mancombras were being gassed or shot to the deadly tune of one thousand a day.

The dethroned monarch couldn't hope to win the war, and if he wasn't insane he'd know that. With virtually every technical aspect of the military under rebel control, the Combrian Forces could only fight with infantry and a severely limited array of heavy artillery. Gram Pillhigh was a hopper taking on a rip howler.

Checking himself for feeling prideful about the conquest—the last thing he needed was chastisement from the unseen power to humble him—he told Free to stop the wheeler. A cluster of tents made from night lapper hides lay to their left. "That's their camp, I'd wager a hundred tibs on it. Their vehicles are bound to be hidden nearby."

"They quit pretending to be merchants it seems," said Free.

"Yeah, now they're disguised as Wanderers." Nomadic Combrians who shunned modern technology, Wanderers preferred to live like their ancestors. Rarely would a band of them be spotted in this area because they'd be trespassing on private land. They were allowed to roam preservation acreage set aside by the government because they killed only what they needed to survive, allowing the remaining wildlife and vegetation to flourish as intended by the statute. Since the beginning of modern times the House of Pillhigh had held nature in high esteem, something he couldn't help but admire in spite of his hatred for the royal line. It was a shame none of them occupying the throne had seen Mancombras in the same light.

FIFTEEN

Stove awoke with a severe headache. Gingerly touching the self-inflicted wound, he felt stitches beneath a bandage. He scanned the room and saw he'd been taken to the palace infirmary. Unlike Combrians, his kind had an instinctive and unbreakable mental block while unconscious that could only be breeched by administering Clodec. The mind of a sleeping Mancombra couldn't be probed. Since there wasn't a logical reason for him to be dosed, he had no fear the attractive half-breed standing by his bed knew he'd killed Sergeant Wrench.

She'd been checking his blood pressure when he first saw her and was now wearing a flirtatious smile as she released the band from his arm. "Glad to see you're waking up. I'm Lieutenant Rope. Can you understand me?"

"Y-Yes," he deliberately stammered.

"Please tell me your name, rank, and how many fingers I'm holding up?"

"Stove. Corporal. Four."

"Very good, looks like you're going to be fine."

"What happened?"

"You and Sergeant Wrench were assaulted."

He acted alarmed and tried to sit up, but his throbbing injury advised against it. "Is he okay?"

Her dark lips puckered as she shook her head. "I'm afraid another one of us has been taken, Corporal Stove."

Recognizing the look in her eyes, he quickly made himself think of wanting to have sex with her, because she'd soon be breaking through his block. Being so close he couldn't prevent it. When she entered his mind a fevered sigh streamed from her sexy mouth. Enthralled over his manufactured desire, the loose female didn't bother trying to pry open any secret compartments in his brain.

I want you too, Corporal, she transmitted while caressing his face.

Polka felt like she'd spent the night on a fluffy cloud, the enormous mattress was so comfortable. Forcing herself to leave Duke Kaleen's luxurious bed, she got dressed and soon discovered Pliers had already made breakfast.

"Captain Morris called awhile ago, Ma'am. He'll be dropping by shortly."

That dampened her spirits. "I can already see he's going to be a slave driver. He said he'd give me some time to get settled into the apartment, but I bet he's already got the classroom picked out and wants me to start today."

An air of humorous expectancy clung to Pliers—she obviously couldn't wait for her to find out what Morris's plans were.

"The cupboards were empty when we were shown the apartment yesterday, Pliers. When did you get groceries?"

"The captain had them delivered an hour ago, Ma'am."

Polka cheered up some when she tasted the food. "How about that, you *are* a good cook."

"Thank you, Ma'am. I was hoping you wouldn't mind me taking the liberty of being the first to use the kitchen facilities."

"Oh my, no," she laughed. "It wouldn't hurt my feelings

for you to do all the cooking, providing of course you can make something besides these delicious sern strips and grain cakes."

The door chime echoed through the apartment.

Pliers eagerly rose from the table. "That'll be Captain Morris, Ma'am. Keep enjoying your breakfast, I'll let him in."

The captain was grinning like a juvenile prankster when Pliers brought him to the dining room. "Polka, when you finish eating we're taking a trip to the commissary."

"Why? Pliers told me you had our food delivered."

"Oh we're not going there for food."

She frowned at him. "Then what?"

"To get you fitted for uniforms, *Lieutenant.*"

None of the family members of Mancombras too young to serve Prince Zane as soldiers would accept him, being a despicable coward in their eyes. He'd spent the night in Gram's male servants barracks, now used by the palace guards. Drill had been assigned a bunk at the end of a line of twelve. A dozen more occupied the opposing wall. Each had a footlocker, and the name attached to the one nearest him read Corporal Stove. Stove hadn't slept in his bed last night because he'd been attacked within the palace grounds along with his sergeant, also a Mancombra, named Wrench. He'd been taken to the infirmary and was expected to recover soon, but the sergeant hadn't survived. The bad news had been relayed to the off-duty soldiers shortly after Drill arrived.

The staff sergeant in charge of the barracks informed

him that if he wanted to eat he'd best accompany the troops to the mess hall for breakfast because he wasn't allowed to dine with the other palace guests in The Great Dining Hall. Instead of asking why, he read the Urth's mind and learned Captain Morris had placed that restriction on him. Following a line of soldiers, he entered a large canteen with no frills where Gram's servants must have taken their meals. A private doled out his food and he found a secluded spot, not wanting to offend anyone by daring to sit with them.

Unlike the powdered surplus he'd eaten at Colonel Hammer's camp, the scrambled hicker eggs were fresh and tasty. Whoever watched over the grocery inventory for the palace had apparently gathered a large store of them before Jealousy and Anger reached full phase. He hoped they'd stashed enough to feed the myriad appetites residing within the enormous compound for three more days. Hickers would start laying again then, at least those not eaten by ravenous night lappers. No doubt Polka's entire flock had been consumed by now with no one to guard them. But it was just as well, they'd have starved to death with their owner being a privileged palace guest.

He missed the old woman terribly but wouldn't be going to see her: it could mar Polka's reputation.

PC had told the Wanderers to move on because they were trespassing. Disappointment over finding them to be legitimate nomads instead of Arigot and his troops in disguise had made him rather sharp with the tribal chief. Now having slept on it, he wished he'd used a much gentler tone.

Other than having three strange talents, he'd been a typical youth with abundant good humor, but the solemn demands of his duty to free Combria from tyranny had all but turned him grim. A line from a play he'd seen as an adolescent frequently came back to him as it did now. Many generations had passed since an archeologist discovered the work, admitted within to be a copy of the original penned in antiquity. He couldn't remember the eloquent avowal in its entirety, but the ending had been permanently affixed to his memory: Some achieve greatness, some have greatness thrust upon them.

I am the latter, he thought with a twinge of sadness. *This awesome responsibility was thrust upon me by The Spirit That Created All Things.*

"We can blast tomorrow, Colonel," said Wurz while seating himself on the chair across from him rather than choosing the empty one at the end of the table. The captain correctly anticipated he expected Voola to eat her breakfast there. "The last of the concrete will have hardened enough to reach sufficient strength by then."

"Very good, Captain." Illuminating the tunnel required the bulk of their generator-powered lamps, but with the two moons making it possible to mix concrete themselves outside the tunnel at night, while commercial ready mix wheelers continued delivering it during daylight, the soldiers had volunteered to work in shifts around the clock. Their efforts had shaved three days off the engineer's latest estimate, which coincided with the last of Jealousy's and Anger's full phase.

Voola walked into the mess tent looking ravishing as always. Hammer was anxious to get through the wall and finish up this mission so he could take her to a big city where they could finally get their hands on some essence of valley fern. None of it had made its way to the tourist trap, and he'd been advised it would be a while before any did.

She sat down and unfolded a napkin while casting him a smile. "I wonder how Drill's first night at the palace went?"

Hammer chuckled. "Unless he changed his mind about enlisting, probably not very well."

"Why doesn't he want to serve Prince Zane?" questioned Wurz, frowning. "Being a persecuted Mancombra, you'd think he'd jump at the chance."

Voola made a sour face. "He claims to be a pacifist, but I think he's a coward."

"No he's not," Hammer defended, rather harshly. "Drill is merely following his convictions and I respect him for it."

Corporal Sills approached, holding a field communicator. "Colonel, one of the guards just informed me that a friend of yours would like to speak with you at—"

Hammer signaled him to be silent and lunged to his feet. "Never mind, Corporal, I read your thoughts. Captain Wurz, no one leaves camp until I get back."

Voola asked if she could come too.

"No, you stay here . . . ."

Fake breasts and made up face embarrassing him, Arigot

had tried to look nonchalant at the palace gates. Only one of the guards wasn't Urth, and the Mancombra being busy giving instructions over a field communicator to someone, he'd freed his mind to see if the Urths could unknowingly give him anything useful.

And they had indeed.

Not only had he learned PC wasn't in the palace, the Urths had been excited because they'd heard a report that Colonel Hammer would soon be breaking through a mysterious steel wall inside Mount Opian. Arigot had laboriously made his way back to where he'd hidden the wheeler, yanked off the damn stilts, and immediately headed for Hammer's camp. Exhausted after the long drive, he'd spent the night at a tourist trap fifteen miles from Mount Opian.

Now he stood inside a cave with steam filling the air around him, hoping the only surviving member of his family would hear him out and not tear him to pieces. The disguise lay on the damp floor—packed brassiere, hip pads, stilts, blouse, and skirt, along with the handkerchief he'd used to wipe the gunk off his face and lips. The civilian trousers and shirt he'd worn beneath them were now plainly visible, as were his boots. He hadn't bothered with any disguises beneath the feminine contrivances—the stilts would be a dead giveaway if a suspicious sentinel forced him to undress.

He'd approached Hammer's guards as a female Mancombra, and speaking in a falsetto voice had told the Urths: "My name is Crayon, I'm an old friend of Colonel Hammer's." He'd then pointed at the cave and said, "Would you please tell him I'd love to see him and ask him to meet me up there?"

"No need for that," one of the Urths had cheerfully stated. "Come with me, I'll take you to him."

"Oh no, I look a mess and would be too embarrassed to have everyone see me like this. It took all my nerve just to approach you. Please, just pass on the message. I'm going to the cave now and will wait for him there."

It had been very difficult making it up the slope in those stilts, but he'd succeeded and started stripping the moment he entered the smoky cavern, having no doubt Hammer would come.

Crayon was his half brother's imaginary childhood friend.

"You look like a true officer, Ma'am."

Posing in front of a full length mirror in the commissary, the black Urth giggled. "I look like what I am: an old woman in new army duds."

Pliers grinned and saluted her.

"Oh don't do that to me, Pliers . . . but I think I'll try it just this once, just to see how it feels."

She laughed when Polka saluted back.

"You'll need these before you can really look like an officer," said Captain Morris, opening a box containing silver bars. "Sergeant Major."

Pliers removed them and pinned one to each of Polka's shoulders and both sides of her collar, after which she saluted again.

"I've already fastened a bar to your hat, Lieutenant Polka." Captain Morris handed her the crowning touch of her dress uniform.

"My oh my . . ." Polka put it on and again checked herself in the mirror. "My mate would flip if he could see me in this getup, rest his soul."

One of the clerks, a female Mancombra who looked concerned about something, approached the captain. "Sir, have they found out who attacked Wrench and Stove yet?"

"Corporal Stove was attacked?" Pliers almost shouted. "When? Is he all right?"

"He'll pull through," Captain Morris assured before heaving a sigh. "But Sergeant Wrench is dead."

She felt sorry for the sergeant but had to hide her elation over Stove surviving. "What happened, Sir?"

"Stove couldn't tell us much. He'd asked the sergeant to check out something he saw in The Vale of Hedges that looked suspicious. It turned out to be nothing, but he'd leaned his rifle against the brush while he and Wrench were squatting down looking at it, and the next thing he knew he was waking up in the infirmary with stitches in the side of his head where he'd been butted with his own weapon. Whoever did it used Stove's bayonet on Sergeant Wrench. Neither of them were tranquilized so this killer is extremely confident and cunning. There weren't any prints on the weapon other than Stove's, so the only thing we know for certain is their attacker wore gloves."

"Why kill one and not the other?" Polka asked, squinting at the captain.

"The gun went off during the perpetration, so the killer had to flee before finishing off Stove, knowing the guards had been alerted. It was no doubt one of Gram's assassins. That blood-thirsty fiend is determined to complete the Genocide Directive."

Polka's heavy lips flattened with a sad frown. "I really liked Sergeant Wrench. This is awful . . . just awful."

"It is indeed," Captain Morris sadly agreed. "But at least Gram can't cross both of them off his list."

Pliers trembled with fear at the thought of how strong,

stealthy, and agile that Combrian had to be in order to subdue two Mancombra's without a tranquilizer gun. "Captain, do you think the killer is still in the palace?"

"No, he slipped in and out with the tourists—had to have. We've beefed up security. If another incident occurs we'll have to cancel the tours altogether."

Only three people knew about his imaginary friend Crayon, and two of them were dead: his father and stepmother. Whomever awaited him in the cave had been sent by Arigot. Hammer wasn't concerned about a trap because the entrance lay in plain view of the camp. It would be impossible to access it without being seen by the guards, and when he'd spoken to them before ascending the mount, they'd only seen the unarmed female Mancombra go inside.

Arigot had spared a Mancombra's life so she could deliver a message to him. That could mean only one thing, and the thought of it riveted him with jubilation:

His half brother wanted to surrender.

Praying he could somehow convince Prince Zane to spare Arigot's life, he stepped into the cave.

SIXTEEN

THERE WERE NO WINDOWS IN the dungeon, at least none Needle could see. If her suspicions were correct the whole compound didn't have any, for she felt certain it had been constructed underground. Gazing at the unoccupied cell across from hers, she briskly rubbed her sore wrists, relieved the shackles had finally been removed. She wondered why Gram was keeping her alive since he obviously hadn't believed Arigot's report.

Had the paranoid lunatic changed his mind?

Hammer entered the cave and stumbled with shock. "Arigot?!"

"It's so good to see you, brother. I beg your forgiveness for being blindsided by an insane oppressor . . . ."

The rapid information being telepathed brought tears to his eyes. Crying with joy, he grabbed Arigot and tightly embraced his only remaining flesh and blood.

"You'll break my spine, Hammer, lighten up!"

"Oh, sorry . . ." he released him, wiped his eyes, and looked down at the handsome face he hadn't seen since the revolution started. "When I was told someone named Crayon wanted to speak with me, I knew in my heart you'd decided to surrender, but I was certain I'd find a messenger rather than you here."

Arigot grinned. "You've always underestimated me."

"No, I've always been jealous of you," he corrected with a laugh, "but I have never underestimated your cunning. How fortunate you were able to learn of my mission here."

"Who is this Voola that haunts the back of your mind?"

"A Combrian I met in this very cave. She was one of Gram's mistresses but managed to escape from his hideout when he fled the palace."

A stunned frown leapt on Arigot's face. "And you've fallen in love with her?"

"You interpret my thoughts accurately, I have indeed."

"Did she tell you she stole some glimeralds from Gram before she got away?"

It troubled him Voola hadn't confided that to him, but only momentarily. He'd have been just as cautious in her situation. "Are you certain it was her that took them?"

"Beyond doubt. Gram said she'd been the last one in his sleep chamber when he discovered them missing. You've fallen for a thief."

"No, Voola's no thief. If she took them it was only so she could sell them to survive. Were I in her shoes I'd have done the same since she can't openly seek employment without risking being seen by one of Gram's spies."

Arigot gave that some thought and a laudatory smile appeared. "Congratulations, may the two of you find every happiness."

The sincerity in Arigot's mind warmed his heart immensely. Hammer pointed at the attire strewn on the dirt. "You need to put those back on. You'll have to pretend to be Crayon until I can speak with Prince Zane personally. I'm the only Mancombra in this unit and Voola's the only Combrian in camp. I trust her with my life, she'll keep our secret. How did you get here?"

"In a military open-air wheeler hidden on the other side of the mountain. I can't even sit down while wearing those stilts, I'd be exposed in no time trying to mingle with your troops."

Looking at the devices, he realized Arigot was right. "Okay, I'll sequester the cave, tell everyone it's off limits while my friend Crayon is camping in it, and supply you with food and drink. Be sure to wear the disguise when you venture outside because the guards will see you. I'll have to talk to Prince Zane in person, I'll never be able to persuade him otherwise. I can't go to the palace until my mission's finished here, and if we find something worthwhile behind that steel wall it's liable to be a long time before that happens. You'll go stir crazy if you don't get a glimpse of Life Giver occasionally."

Voola had tried to sneak after Hammer but the guards wouldn't let her pass. Unable to satisfy her curiosity, she'd gone back to the mess tent, thinking about how strongly Hammer's half brother had sprang to his mind when he'd heard the name Crayon.

Before she finished lunch Hammer returned and transmitted that Arigot was hiding in the cave where they'd met. Then he telegraphed, *Did you steal some jewels from Gram?*

If frightened her that the enforcer knew. Gram would only have divulged that to someone commissioned to exact his revenge. Hammer's half brother had no doubt been ordered to kill her. *I took seven glimeralds from his treasure chest. That's all I could slip past the sentinels with—I'd have stolen more if I could. They're tucked inside my night lapper hide. I'd planned to sell them so I'd have the means to stay in hiding, but right now I'd trade them all for some essence of valley fern.*

Hammer coughed out a raspy laugh and winked at her. *It serves the bastard right. After all, he stole your freedom.*

She caressed his genitals in her mind and smiled at his facial reaction. *Exactly the way I see it, my love.*

Arigot had succeeded in not letting his thoughts wander to Zane's secret. It would endanger Hammer if he knew, because a Mancombra or Combrian would eventually happen across the information inadvertently. His Voola would have found out in no time, leaving two minds for the truth about PC to be telepathically gathered from besides his own. And that information getting out would ruin him, so the general would have no choice but to silence them permanently for the good of his idyllic cause.

"Lieutenant Enforcer Barrabon speaking, Sir."

"Where's Enforcer Arigot?" said Universal Quest after a blast of static assaulted his ear.

"He hasn't arrived yet, Sir."

"What?! He should have been there by yesterday evening. You'd better still be at the location you told him, Lieutenant Enforcer, or I'll have you busted to personal!"

"We haven't moved an inch, Sir. I don't know what detained the enforcer. I hope he didn't get captured."

"He didn't. It would have made headline news and the whole planet would know about it. Have him call me the moment he gets there."

The field communicator went dead, the universal had hung up on him. Barrabon wiped his brow and handed the device to the supervisor, who drove the merchant wheeler which had been at rest since Arigot ordered them to wait for him. "I don't envy our enforcer having to deal directly with Quest. What an asshole."

Lieutenant Rope barged in while he'd been relieving himself, and practically tore off her uniform before lifting up his infirmary gown. The next thing Stove knew, they were having sex on the flusher.

When they finished she draped her garments over her arm instead of putting them on, teasing him with every sexy motion. Mouth slack with carnal fulfillment, the nurse put her lips to the side of his head and whispered, "Your dinner is waiting by the bed."

Gram told the guards to wait in the corridor and turned to the half-breed, sitting on the only piece of furniture in her cell: a metal shelf jutting from the wall, covered by a thin mattress. While waiting for them to get out of earshot he inquired her name.

"Needle."

"I already knew that of course."

"Of course you did," she said with contempt. "Why haven't you killed me yet?"

He raised his brows and snorted a dry laugh. "Oh have no fear, I will in good time, but enough about your insignificant fate. When did you and your brother concoct this wild fabrication you somehow made Enforcer Arigot believe?"

The excitement buzzing in her brain ricocheted through his. It wildly delighted her he thought it a contrivance. The fool thought he'd take the bait. "Very clever, trying to convince me it has to be true by faking joy over my thinking it to be a lie. But it won't save your life. Now tell me when you and Wheelbarrow came up with the idea."

"When our son was born."

Her arrogant prevarication grated on him, insulting his intelligence—but he'd wipe that smile off her face shortly. "Stop it, Zane's not your son. Were you and your brother really lovers?"

"We were," she proudly affirmed.

"Disgusting, but at least you answered truthfully this time. Is Harv Zane privy to this fantasy of yours?"

"He is. So is his mate Molly. The four of us were in it together. PC has all your whirlys, missiles, and most of your armored wheelers under his control. Why don't you give up peacefully? You can't possibly regain the throne."

The half-breed's insolence and sarcasm would make her death all the sweeter. "I have weapons he doesn't know of, and my soldiers outnumber his two-to-one."

Prideful, mocking laughter rumbled from her insolent throat. "But he has the Mancombras, my friend—those dreaded beasts you fear so. One of them is equal to ten of your soldiers. Face it, your reign is over, the House of Pillhigh is through. Long live Prince Zane!"

✝

Needle no longer tried to conceal anything, clearly seeing that tormenting Gram vocally kept him from focusing on her mind. Watching the twisted monarch cover his membranes as he screamed for her to shut up, she kept badgering and belittling him, confusing him with her contradictions. She didn't dare let up until succeeding in having him kill her, for once he did, no one could read her mind. Arigot's allegations would be worthless without proof, and after her body was incinerated there'd be no blood to test.

"You were right to fear us, for we are the superior race and Prince Zane knows it, that's why he protects us. Look deep inside me, you fanatical freak—see how much I despise you, how I loathe you, how you make my skin crawl! Down with the House of Pillhigh, long live Prince Zane, your conqueror! Oh, did I tell you the Clodec is wearing off? How silly of me not to warn your goons that my metabolism burns it off in half the time of most Mancombras. In a moment or two you'll be at my mercy. I'll have you bash your face against these bars until blood spurts out of it like a dozen fountains. How gratifying it will be to watch you die, Gram Pillhigh."

"Guards! Guards!" he yelled at the top of his lungs.

They came running.

"Empty your weapons on this half-breed shit!"

As her body convulsed with the onslaught of bullets being fired from two machineguns, she thought of Wheelbarrow and how they'd never be separated again. Then a torrent of memories raced through her mind in an instant's time: the night she and her brother had finally quit fighting the mounting temptation to make love, the astonishment she'd felt a few double-years afterwards when the impossible happened, the shocking surprise that awaited her after carrying that impossibility for ten months, the overwhelming joy of motherhood, how she'd so cherished the first few months of his life, the tears she'd cried when the time came to separate the suckling from her breasts, watching him grow into a man whose quest for justice was almost godlike, PC's incredible rise to power.

The roar of gunfire ceased and she heard Gram bark, "Take this lump of filth to the garbage incinerator and burn it!"

Needle managed one last smile.

SEVENTEEN

PC SPIED A VEHICLE AT rest behind a thicket. "Look over there. Why would a merchant wheeler be parked so far from the road?"

"No reason I can think of," said Free.

"Pull over." PC grabbed the field communicator and buzzed Sergeant Brush, riding behind them in the lead armored wheeler of the convoy. When the Mancombra answered he said, "Look to your left. Do you see that wheeler sitting behind the trees?"

"Yes, Sir."

"Direct all the drivers to surround it and warn the troops to be prepared for hostile action."

When the fleet swerved off the road, the merchant wheeler started moving.

"They've spotted us, Prince Zane."

"I do believe they have, Brush. Carry on . . ." he lowered the communicator.

One of the armored wheelers pulled in front of the merchant vehicle. It reversed directions but another managed to close in on the other side, forcing the driver to halt.

He watched as his troops emerged from their transports. Rifles aimed at the merchant wheeler, they proceeded cautiously towards it. Before long the cab and trailer emptied out. Twenty unarmed soldiers placed both hands atop their heads, signaling surrender.

"Drive me up there, Free. I want to have a little chat with Enforcer Arigot, then I'm going to put a bullet through his head."

✝

Barrabon had known PC for a long time but hadn't seen him up close since he'd become Prince Zane, exchanging the four stars on the shoulders of his uniform for a scarlet Z. His officers wore rank insignias affixed to their letters but PC's were barren. Only his readily identifiable face revealed him to be the new ruler of Combria, otherwise he'd be mistaken for a buck private without a hat. Long hair streaming behind him in the breeze like a red cape, he looked glorious yet humble, walking beside Free. What a pity he'd turned into an enemy.

"Where's Arigot, Barrabon?"

"I honestly don't know, PC."

"You'll address Prince Zane by his proper title, Barrabon!" Free indignantly snapped.

"Simmer down, Lieutenant," said Zane with a half grin. "We all go back a ways, let's be civil here. Barrabon, I'll have Sergeant Brush probe your mind. If you're lying, tell me now. If I have to hear it from him, you're a dead Combrian."

He inhaled a deep breath through his nose. "Probe away, I have no idea where Arigot is. He was supposed to rejoin us yesterday but no one's heard from him, not even our universal. The troops and I were only following orders, and as such I request imprisonment. None of us wanted this mission and neither did Arigot—we don't like attacking unarmed civilians."

PC looked skyward and sighed. "Having faithfully obeyed many a detested command myself, I understand. Sergeant

Brush! Check out the Lieutenant Enforcer, see if he's lying about Arigot."

The Mancombra ambled over, eyed him a few moments, then turned to Zane. "He's telling the truth, Sir. He last saw Enforcer Arigot when he left the unit with a female Mancombra to meet Universal Quest at a hidden post in Juxbow. They made the journey in a merchant wheeler similar to this one. A driver and two guards went with them. He's been concerned about the enforcer's welfare since the universal contacted him earlier today, wanting to speak to Arigot."

Seeing the general looked pleased he hadn't lied, Barrabon seized the opportunity to again plead for the lives of his comrades and himself.

Zane studied him for a long while before speaking. "Consider yourselves prisoners of war."

"And Enforcer Arigot?" he asked, hopefully.

"Arigot has yet to be captured, but when we catch him—and we will—he'll die at my hands."

Appetite depleted by nerves, Arigot forced himself to open a container of stew to keep up his strength. Hammer had brought it to him at dinnertime, along with water, kaffy, and a bedroll.

"I packed you some field rations," Hammer had said while lowering a backpack full. "I don't want the troops getting suspicious about why you won't come to the mess tent for meals, which they surely would, seeing me carrying a tray of food to this cave every meal time. I'll bring a canteen of water and thermos of kaffy daily, and re-supply your food stock when you run out."

While searching the cave earlier, he'd found a large recess with subtle air currents blowing through it, preventing steam from entering. Planning to spend most of his time there to keep from sweating to death, he'd pointed it out to Hammer. Unable to eat another bite he set the half-full container on a rock and unrolled the sleeping bag, preparing to spend his first night inside Mount Opian. He stretched out on it, thinking about his rash decision. Universal Quest most likely knew the score by now.

His trusted enforcer had become a traitor.

"Oh I should have known, I should have known!" Gram screamed at the teleon. The screen showed Quest grabbing his forehead, groaning with frustration. The universal's image was being transmitted from a camera in Juxbow. The consternation stemmed from realizing Enforcer Arigot had deserted.

"I've already abandoned the command post he's aware of and have instructed the other universals not to use the south expressway out of Juxbow anymore, so Arigot can't do any more damage than betray his last known location of the genocide squad, Sire."

"What kind of idiot are you, Quest?" he growled. "He can tell Zane where the bulk of the army's hidden."

"With all due respect, My King, General Zane is already well aware of that or he wouldn't have the city surrounded."

He thought that over and relaxed a little. "I knew he was

unstable when he brought the female Mancombra to me. I should have anticipated he'd defect when he didn't get promoted like he'd so hoped. Can you believe it, Quest? The gullible fool really thought I'd promote him."

Quest lowered his hand, revealing a frown. *"Sire, I have no idea what he told you, so I could hardly have an opinion on the matter."*

"And you still don't. Tell Lieutenant Enforcer Barrabon you'll promote him if he can finish the directive on the civilian half-breeds. If Zane doesn't capture him first through Arigot's treachery."

A heavy sigh left the universal. *"I'm afraid that's probably already happened. I can't get through to Barrabon—no one's answering the communicator."*

Seized with rage, Gram hurled a bowl of sweets. Dozens of sticky brown balls ricocheted off the wall amidst shards of broken glass.

Lieutenant Rope slid off his bed and finally put her uniform back on. Wearing a satisfied smile, she unlocked the door and headed for her living quarters. Her shift had ended at dinnertime, but having ulterior motives she'd volunteered to bring him his, surprising him in the flusher room. He wouldn't see her again until tomorrow.

Claiming his head ached far worse than it actually did, Stove had managed to finagle another night in the infirmary. Under the guise of wanting to know more about her he'd asked about her duties, subtly slipping in a question about the nurse's station and if he'd be able to sleep undisturbed.

She'd unknowingly provided two pieces of information which would enable him to take out three Mancombras, leaving only six alive of the ten he'd shared his vision with. No one would be checking on him again until the break of day, giving him the whole night to act—and nurses assigned to the station were allowed a ten minute kaffy break every three hours.

The robe he'd been issued had a hood with a facemask sewn in front, designed to prevent disfigured soldiers from being embarrassed when well enough to enjoy the patient's lounge. If everything went according to plan no one would see him anyway, but if anyone did, they'd only be able to testify to seeing an unknown Mancombra.

When break time finally arrived he peeked through the door and watched the nurse on duty leave for kaffy. He pulled off his gown, quickly donned the robe, and left the infirmary with his face covered.

Avoiding the elevators, he hurried down a stairwell and cracked open the exit door. Seeing no one, he crossed an expanse of smooth stone and quietly entered the palace maintenance center where he took off the robe. As anticipated, Sergeant Awl sat at the power monitor desk with his back to him. Careful to keep his mind blocked so as not to mentally alert Awl of his presence, he eased a long screwdriver from a tool belt hanging on the wall, and crept towards him as the sergeant enjoyed a teleon show while occasionally checking the gauges for power overloads.

Left hand poised and ready to latch onto a handful of platinum hair, he gripped the screwdriver tightly with his right. Mentally counting to three he acted—jerking Awl's head back and ramming the metal shaft through his right eye. The handle splattered the eyeball inside the socket. Pulling the bloody tool free, he wiped it off with the dead Mancombra's hair and went looking for Privates Eraser and

Sandpaper, who also worked this shift.

They were repairing a portable cooling unit, sitting atop a heavy duty steel table. Sandpaper stood in profile from his viewpoint while Eraser would have been able to see him if he looked up. Stove backed away from the open door, stepping to the side where he could keep an eye on them but wouldn't be spotted should either look towards the doorway. Searching the shelves, he tried to find something to assist him. The instant he willed anything to move they'd know it because he couldn't use telekinesis without unblocking his mind, so he'd have to act fast. A transformer lay on the floor awaiting repair. Stove estimated it weighed around two hundred pounds, about the same as the cooling unit they were working on. He took a deep breath and imposed his will with all his might.

The cooling unit flew into Eraser's face and knocked him flat on his back as the transformer crashed into the side of Sandpaper's head, hurling him against the wall. Lunging for the unconscious Mancombras, feeling an adrenaline rush he'd never known, he hastily stabbed each of them in both eyes. He drug the screwdriver back and forth across Sandpaper's shirt—leaving blood, eyeball and brain goo sticking to the cloth—then went to the flusher room to wash the weapon and himself. Carefully drying the screwdriver so it wouldn't reacquire any of the fingerprints he'd removed, he walked past Sergeant Awl—good eye appearing to be looking at him, the other oozing gunk from the pit of a gory socket—and slid it back in the tool belt. Tossing the towel, he put the robe back on, covered his face, and snuck back to the infirmary.

Four down, six to go, he thought with almost aphrodisiacal exhilaration.

Drill awoke to a commotion in the barracks. Three Mancombras had been found murdered in the maintenance center. King Gram evidently had an assassination squad lurking within the palace complex, somehow able to move about it freely. Captain Morris suspected they had to be posing as soldiers loyal to Prince Zane. Because of that, everyone had to give an account of their actions last night, which was then redundantly verified before they could leave for breakfast.

After the interrogating sergeant contacted Captain Morris to verify his statement of seeking refuge in the palace as a civilian, Drill was told to head for the mess hall.

They'd made love three times yesterday: once on the flusher, twice in Stove's bed. Rope felt guilty for savoring the memory—this was a time for grief, not sexual arousal. She dropped two pain tablets in a pill cup and went to his room. Jubilation coursed through her as she looked down at his handsome face. He had to be the sexiest male on the planet.

"Good morning, Lieutenant," Stove greeted with a smile. "I dreamed about you all night long."

The statement thrilled her, but to show respect for the dead she tried to appear solemn. "Gram took down three more of us, I'm so very sorry to say."

"Oh no . . .!" he sat upright and groaned into his palms.

"Those poor civilians couldn't make it to the palace I guess."

"No, it was three soldiers, and they were killed right here within the compound like Sergeant Wrench. That bastard Gram has infiltrated Prince Zane's army. Captain Morris is checking out every member of the military with palace duty, including close friends he's known for double-years. Even Mancombras aren't exempt, I was examined before I could start my shift. Of course like the other patients confined in the infirmary throughout the night, you won't have to go through the hassle."

He dropped his hands and glared at her as if she'd insulted him. "I wouldn't mind the hassle at all—they should leave no stone unturned."

"You're such a patriot, my darling . . . ."

EIGHTEEN

POLKA HAD BEEN ORDERED TO stay in her apartment until further notice. Captain Morris feared the killers were some of his own soldiers, and if so they might be aware of her probe blocking technique, making her a prime target.

Still visibly frightened, her bodyguard had been a nervous wreck since hearing about the last murders. Polka attempted to cheer her up with a stab at humor. "Don't worry, Pliers, I'll protect you. I may not look it but I can whip a rip howler if I get riled enough."

That at least provoked an edgy smile. "Oh Ma'am, I don't mean to be so morose but it looks like Gram's going to succeed in exterminating my race after all. These killers scare me more than anything I've ever been afraid of. Killing a lone Mancombra male is difficult enough, but to take out three without drugging them first with a tranquilizer gun is unthinkable. It really worries me they're not concerned about numbers. They attacked Sergeant Wrench and Corporal Stove when those two were together, then decided to go after three at the same time."

Polka blew out a sigh and tried to be reassuring. "But remember, Captain Morris said they were caught by surprise just like Wrench and Stove. Now everyone will be on alert at all times. It won't be long before they're captured."

✝

Captain Wurz detonated the charges and a fiery cloud erupted from the seven-foot diameter hole in the side of Mount Opian like the exhaust of a missile during liftoff. When the smoke cleared, Hammer started cursing loud enough to wake the dead.

The explosion had collapsed the tunnel.

"You're very fortunate the blow didn't break through bone, Corporal."

Stove lowered his eyes to the double silver bars on the doctor's uniform, mulling over what sort of decorations he should award himself when the time came. "Just proves how hardheaded I am, Sir."

The captain responded with a short laugh and said, "Well you're released. Report back here in four days to have the stitches removed. After that I don't want to see you back here again."

"I'll do my best to obey that order, Sir."

"Where the blazes did you get your degree, Wurz, Dumbass Academy?"

Wurz jerked his hat off and angrily swooped back a sprig of greasy hair from his forehead. "I attended Combria Military Academy, Colonel, as you well know. The structural failure wasn't due to any miscalculation on my part, it should have held up under the blast. The steel obviously didn't yield or the back pressure wouldn't have been so great."

Hammer dropped his jaw. "Are you telling me we didn't punch through that damn wall?"

"That's right, Sir. And that means either our instruments were off and it's a lot thicker than we thought, or it only appears to be stainless steel. We need to excavate the tunnel path, make an open ditch all the way to the wall. Not having to keep the tunnel intact, we won't be limited like before. We can use whatever amount of explosives we need to get the job done."

†

"Corporal Stove reporting for duty, Sir!" He saluted while standing at attention.

Captain Morris stepped towards him, eyeing the bandage. "I've got a cushy detail for you, Stove—a skate job. Remember Polka, the black Urth we brought back with us from the south bend of the Opian River?"

"Yes, Sir."

"I've provided her with an apartment. CSM Pliers is staying with her as bodyguard and I want you to do the same. You and Pliers work out your own schedules on this but the two of you can never be asleep at the same time. I want somebody watching over Polka constantly. Read me?"

"Yes, Sir."

"Head that way now, they're in Duke Kaleen's old quarters. I'll let them know you're coming and have the rest of your gear brought up."

Stove salivated. This would give him unlimited time to gain Pliers' trust, and once he unquestionably had it, he'd tell her of his plans and she'd be his alibi while he took out the rest of the male Mancombra's in the palace. In the interim he'd invite Rope over on occasion while Polka and Pliers slept, and win her over so completely she too would yearn to be a queen of King Stove. After that he'd seduce the shapely Mancombra who worked in the commissary.

They'd been taken to the stockade at Fort Pacific, named after a mythical ocean in Urth folklore. It served as the main base for the Urth Army when King Gram still controlled it. All Urths and Mancombras did their basic training there before the uprising. Barrabon didn't know if PC continued that tradition after becoming Prince Zane.

His ex-commander haunted his mind. Why had Arigot deserted—and why had he taken that female Mancombra to see the king? The two actions had to be related because he'd never known Arigot to be insubordinate in any fashion, and his old friend had become secretive and rather aloof after capturing her. He'd even injected Clodec into the guards and driver to prevent them from reading her mind before leaving for Juxbow. Why? What secrets did she keep in her head?

PC walked up to his cell. "I've been notified four Mancombras soldiers were murdered at the palace, Barrabon. I've got a proposition for you. I'll make your stay here comfortable and grant you amnesty after the war if you can tell me who Gram has posing as loyal to me within its walls."

That floored him. According to what he'd heard, Gram hadn't been able to slip a single spy past the palace gates. "Nobody that I know of."

"I'm about to go back there, and I'll find out who they are, but I'm giving an old friend one last chance to start anew. Are you sure you don't know?"

"Have your sergeant read my mind again if you don't believe me."

A scornful frown creased the corners of PC's sky-blue eyes. "Why can't you see that Mancombras are just like you and I or any other Combrians and Urths? How can you sleep at night knowing you've shed the blood of innocents who never desired anything more than to pursue a normal happy life like anyone else?"

The agony he'd buried in the line of duty resurfaced, sharper and more tormenting than before because of the reprimand. "PC, I don't like killing unarmed civilians, I've already told you that, but it hit home when Gram made that speech explaining the necessity of the Genocide Directive. If the Mancombras were to unite they'd be unstoppable, you've got to admit that. There were twenty-five thousand of them at the time, and the way social barriers were being crossed before the directive, the number of Combrians and Urths mating would have increased exponentially, producing more and more half-breeds if Gram hadn't made mingled-race mating illegal."

PC gave him a pitiful look, the kind of expression a parent casts upon a child for failing to understand a simple truth. "Barrabon, you are so blind. If Gram had succeeded in wiping them all out his paranoia would have turned towards the next perceived threat, probably Urths with superior intellect, out of fear they'd pool their resources and create a super weapon to take control of Combria. Even exceptionally strong Combrians like you might have wound up on a death list. Can't you see Gram Pillhigh is insane?"

The notion had crossed his mind more than once, but not because of the Genocide Directive. Barrabon couldn't understand Gram's strategy in hiding the Combrian Forces. PC had total control of the flying force from the onset, but Gram's order to retreat had resulted in most of the armored wheelers being captured by Zane's soldiers as well. The king claimed it would have been suicide to attempt a land war with the skies being controlled by his usurper, so he'd ordered his universals to hide the troops until a strategy could be developed to steal back enough whirlys to launch a counter offensive. Doing so had left Zane free to confiscate so many armored wheelers that fighting his soldiers on the ground now would indeed be suicidal.

So far Gram had been right about only one thing: PC not bombing the palace. However, it turned out the reason had nothing to do with preserving such a vital landmark of Combrian history—the rebellious general had intended to occupy it, and succeeded in doing so. All hope of conquering the revolutionaries rested in what might be nothing but mere propaganda to keep the hiding soldiers from being completely demoralized. Gram claimed to have scientists working on a secret weapon so powerful it could turn the entire city of Juxbow into an ash heap in only a few seconds.

Having Stove assigned to help her guard Polka brightened her day. Pliers had the handsome Mancombra all to herself and couldn't wait until their charge went to bed so they could be alone. They'd been chit-chatting telepathically in between snippets of verbal conversation with her concerning dinner.

"I'd like to have sernloaf," said Polka, "but you choose, Stove, since it'll be your first meal here."

"Sernloaf suits me fine, Lieutenant."

Polka glanced down at her uniform. "It sounds so funny to be called that. I can't believe Captain Morris wouldn't let me pick out some civilian clothes at the commissary after taking away my old rags I brought from the farm."

Pliers grinned at her and sang:

"You're in the army, Jane—

you'll never get out again.

No makeup or dress, you look quite a mess—

you're in the army, Jane."

Laughing, Polka gave her a love tap on the forearm. "I haven't heard that old jingle since I don't know when, and didn't know there was a female version. This is the first time I've heard it come out of non-Urth lips and that off key."

Flagrantly embarrassed, she slapped her hands over her face. "Was I really off key?"

"No, I was only teasing, you actually sounded pretty good. I didn't know the Urth Army still sang it."

"They don't, Lieutenant," said Stove. "At least this is the first time I've ever heard it."

"I didn't learn it in the army, Ma'am." She lowered her hands and took a quick glance at Stove, hoping the smile he wore while blocking his mind didn't stem from finding her impulsive action corny. "My father was an Urth. He taught it to me when I was little."

"Well it was fun hearing the tune after all these double-years, even with different lyrics." A sly grin crossed the old woman's weathered face. "I guess I should get started on the sernloaf unless, um . . . ."

Polka's overt manipulation made her laugh. "No fears, Ma'am, I'll make it."

Voola couldn't believe it. Hammer would be stuck at Mount Opian far longer than he'd anticipated. He wouldn't even hazard a guess at how long it would take to dig a canal up to the wall once the heavy machinery arrived. Then it would have to be blasted through, and the rest of his duty here would depend on what they discovered afterwards. She wanted him so badly. Why couldn't any of those shops in town have essence of valley fern? Fearing she'd be spotted by one of Gram's spies, he'd refused to let her use his wheeler to drive to the nearest big city and get some—but she did manage to talk him into letting her come along when he took Arigot some water and kaffy.

The enforcer looked as she remembered. About six inches shorter than her, he somewhat resembled Hammer in the face.

"Arigot, this is Voola."

"Pleased, I'm sure . . ." he took her hand and kissed the back of it.

She smiled. "I see you're a gentleman like your brother."

"We were raised properly by two wonderful parents."

"Indeed we were." A melancholy reminiscence clouded Hammer's face as he said it.

"You are very lovely, Voola—my brother is a most fortunate male."

"I'm the fortunate one, but thank you, Arigot. I saw you once at the palace, shortly before it got stormed by Prince

Zane."

His eyes lit up with recollection. "It was my only time to witness its grandeur from the inside. I was called there by my universal. I know I didn't see you because I'd never forget such a pretty face."

Feeling a blush warm her cheeks, she turned to Hammer. "I see you're not the only member of your family that knows how to charm a lady, my love."

Hammer laughed. "Should I be jealous?"

"Of course not. Arigot, Hammer and I met in this very cave."

"So he tells me."

"Well I'll leave you two alone so you can discuss whatever it is you males talk about when females aren't present. It was so very nice to meet you, Arigot."

"The pleasure was all mine."

When she exited the cave a rustling sound made her look left, towards the upper mountain. Life Giver was beginning to set, giving all the plant life a lovely romantic glow. Assuming some small animal made the noise, she admired the scenery for a moment. All at once a stone flew at her and she had to duck to keep it from hitting her head. Before she could rise to see who'd thrown it, an insect stung her shoulder and she passed out.

NINETEEN

VOOLA OPENED HER EYES TO find she'd succumbed to a sedative rather than an insect's venom, and had been abducted. Warily raising her head, she took in her surroundings. She lay on the gleaming white floor of a round room void of furniture, windows, or doors. The walls, composed of the same substance as the floor and ceiling, were embedded with blinking lights, buttons, and what appeared to be high-tech teleon screens, all of them blank.

Rising to her feet, she noticed her body didn't cast a shadow in the brightly lit enclosure, yet she couldn't locate the source of illumination. A nude statue without genitals stood several feet from her. Made of bluish-gray metal, it was slightly taller than her with the build of a male, but the face had no features, and the sides of the hairless head didn't have membranes or protruding ears.

"Hello?!" she shouted, turning full circle, voice reflecting her fear. "Where am I?!"

After a six hour visit with Arigot, Hammer returned to camp. Figuring she'd already gone to sleep, he didn't bother telling Voola goodnight. On the way to his tent he kept thinking about the new weapon his half brother had spoken of.

"According to what I was told," Arigot had said, "no one's seen it except the scientists. If they're not lying to Gram, or he isn't just making the whole thing up, if the prototype works, many bombs will be constructed. If misused they could wipe out all life on the surface of Combria."

✝

They were sitting in the parlor sharing a sofa, sipping kaffy. Polka had turned in for the night. Her sleep chambers were too far away for conversation to be overheard, so they chatted verbally rather than telepathically, as they'd done in her presence.

Pliers being the antithesis of the easy Rope, Stove knew he had to carefully bide his time. He had his mind blocked, and either out of respect for his privacy or due to protecting her own, she hadn't forced her way into his thoughts. "Incredible that we wound up with this duty, isn't it?"

"Very," said the lovely Mancombra, eyeing him with a smile. "When you asked me out I was so disappointed I couldn't accept. Now here we are."

"Yes, together at last. Call me foolish, but I think it was meant to be. It was our destiny to wind up with one another."

Seeing her blush, he knew romantic verbiage was the way to win her over.

✝

Word had gotten round that Prince Zane captured the team of assassins who'd been continuing the Genocide Directive on civilians. Still unwilling to join the army, and tired of everyone turning their noses up at him, Drill left the palace after eating dinner in the mess hall, despite being warned by Captain Morris that Gram would soon have another hit squad attempt to carry out the death edict. He'd had to get the captain's permission before the guards would let him leave, otherwise they wouldn't have spoken. Confessing he thought him to be an irresponsible coward, Morris had nonetheless furnished him with a sleeping bag, hunting knife, canteen, mess kit, and a military backpack to carry them in after learning his plans.

All property belonging to Mancombras and their relatives had been seized by the government under the Genocide Directive. When he'd gained power, Prince Zane ordered such assets to be restored to the rightful owners in what he had termed *Simple Cases.* But a Combrian had legally purchased his father's impounded farm before he'd been freed from the death camp, making his right to inherit it a *Special Case.* Those weren't going to be sorted through until Gram Pillhigh no longer posed a threat, so having no home to return to, Drill set out for a preservation lying south of University City, planning to live off the fat of the land until the war was over.

Sitting cross-legged on the floor crying, Voola wondered how long it would be before one of the teleons came on with Gram's ugly face on it, demanding to know what she'd done with his glimeralds. The strange room was bound to be part of his hideout. His soldiers must have crept into the camp and subdued it while she'd been in the cave. Hammer had no doubt walked into a trap after leaving Arigot to became another casualty of the Genocide Directive.

The sobs came harder.

Detecting motion from the corner of her eye she looked up to see the statue moving. "My galaxies, it's a robot!"

Voola gawked at the thing through a teary haze as it walked over to her—fluidly and silently as a living being—and extended a hand as if to help her up. Craning her neck back, she tried to meld with its mechanical mind but came up empty. Not knowing what else to do, she placed a palm in the artificial male's, surprised to find it pliable, almost flesh-like, as it lifted her to her feet. Apparently the outer covering only appeared metallic.

The robot led her to an opening that hadn't been there a few seconds ago. It gave access to a flusher compartment. Releasing her hand, the robot turned around, as if politely giving her privacy while she relieved herself, which she did immediately. Then it guided her to another section of wall, pushed a button, and the lower part slid out, revealing a streamlined chair somewhat resembling the pilot seat of a whirly. The robot pointed at it and she sat down. A teleon directly before her came on and a distinguished looking Urth man appeared, face filling the screen. He had gray hair swept back from a high forehead, pronounced nose, and a pointed chin-beard.

"Greetings," he said in Anglish. "Greetings," he repeated in Old Combrian. "If you are human, press the blue button at the bottom of the screen. If you're Combrian, press the red one." He spoke the first sentence in Anglish, the second in Old Combrian as the teleon showed him pointing to the buttons he'd described. The ancient language of her forbears being fatiguing, using several words when only one would do, she chose the human button, assuming the word was synonymous with being an Urth.

"Greetings, my Earth friend."

Voola frowned at the monitor. The man's words scrolled across the screen as he spoke, and she'd never seen Urth spelled that way. But inside she beamed with jubilation, for whatever was going on obviously didn't involve Gram, so Hammer hadn't been killed after all.

"My name is Doctor Ivan Goralov, and you are viewing this an undeterminable number of years after my death. The robot that brought you here was programmed for stealth. I couldn't take the chance of it being seen by anyone without receiving the education you're about to. My apologies for having you sedated, but by now you're alert and its effects have dissipated, or the robot wouldn't have you watching me.

"There are monitors to the right and left of the one you're presently viewing. Please turn them on by pressing the green button at the bottom of this screen." He again pointed at the button corresponding to his statement.

Jaw sagging with awe, she pushed it.

"The monitor to your left shows the solar system you occupy. Combria is the fourth planet you see revolving around your star, which Combrians presently call Eniah Ossappa. The one to your right shows Earth's solar system. Earth is the planet your forebears came from. It's the third one from the star we earthlings call the Sun. Both planetary systems are part of the Milky Way Galaxy.

"You're bound to be brimming with confusion and filled with questions. All will be answered in due time, but first I'll explain where you are and how you got here. The room you're in occupies the top of an underground spherical pyramid constructed of an impenetrable alloy. I won't instruct you on how to leave this room until you're further educated, and Charley—that's what I call the robot standing next to you—will prevent you from leaving the chair before that time except for a break that I'll announce, so please be patient. In a moment I'm going to sound a tone. If you can hear it turn to Charley and nod. If you can't, shake your head no at him. Ready? Here goes."

A very low hum reached her ears. She turned and nodded. The robot pushed a series of buttons. The Urth faded off the screen, then reappeared a second later.

"Charley has called up this video because you are Combrian listening to me speak English. Human ears can't detect a tone of that frequency."

Voola winced. Everyone on Combria spelled the word with an A instead of an E, and she'd never heard Anglish pronounced that way.

"Charley was programmed to ensure the apparently healthy adult he brought here can see and hear. Ergo I know you aren't blind or deaf. Now I must determine if you can read the words appearing on the screen when I speak. Please nod at Charley if you can, or shake your head if you can't. Do it at the tone."

Hearing a mid-frequency ding this time, she nodded at Charley and he again pushed a series of buttons which caused the teleon screen to go blank for a moment before Doctor Goralov reappeared.

"Very good, you can read. Since Charley has been activated I know someone has stumbled across the pyramid. It was constructed in the heart of a mountain and has sensors embedded throughout the outer walls. Someone, perhaps you who are viewing this, tried to blast through it. That's what prompted Charley to emerge and fire a sedative into the first adult human or Combrian he encountered that wasn't old, deaf, or blind, and appeared to have vitality. He brought you here while you were unconscious.

"Since the sensors were designed to filter out any type of primitive attempt to break through the outer walls, you are living in an age where technology has or is about to reach a critical point—the capability of nuclear fission and fusion. I'm a member of the last team of scientists, engineers, and construction specialists to land on Combria. My crew finished the pyramid, started many years before we arrived. We've been here for ten. When I complete the series of videos that you'll see along with this one, I'll be returning to Earth. The inhabitants of Combria at the time of my visitation are at a point of development similar to the midway point of Earth's Bronze Age, which you can learn all about in the electronic archives. I'll explain how to access them later.

"A hundred and fifty years ago probes sent to Combria transmitted data back to Earth, indicating its atmosphere and geography were very similar to ours, and the planet had abundant supplies of fresh water. We sent a team of astronauts here to determine if it was fit for a special program called Operation Noah's Ark. Discovering it was, we began sending specialists to construct the pyramid. An enormous ship is being assembled at a space station orbiting Earth. It will carry fifty members from each of our four basic races, which collectively form what we call the Human Race on Earth. The vessel will be loaded with the seeds of all the fruits and vegetables earthlings need to maintain adequate nutrition. Various species of animals, fowl, and fish used on Earth for food, dairy products, and textiles, will be sent as well.

"The ship will be piloted by robots because the humans aboard will be infants when they leave the space station. Half will be male, half female, genetically determined to have no risk of being infertile when they grow up. My crew and I traveled here, and will return to Earth, in a state of suspended animation like the livestock will, but the Earthlings to follow won't. They will land on Combria as young adults, and will have been specially educated and trained. They'll know Earth history, legend, and myth up to the point just preceding the dawn of the industrial age, and will be provided every tool congruous with that time. Religions not considered myths by those who currently practice them on Earth, we've chosen to keep out of their education, so that's the one concept of their past they'll know nothing about. Too many wars have been started by extremists in every branch of them. They will all speak, read, and write English.

"Why are we imposing such limits? To study their course and see how closely it follows that which occurred on Earth. Our sociologists theorize that having no ideological differences or language barriers will enable them to enjoy an almost Utopian existence and not destroy themselves after advancing technologically as we've almost done numerous times, and unfortunately will probably wind up ultimately doing. At the apex of this pyramid is a transmitter that sent a signal to Earth the moment Charley was activated. If we haven't destroyed our planet by the time the signal gets to Earth, and the program is still continuing, a team of astronauts will be sent to Combria to gather information about the current situation and send the data back to Earth before returning themselves, if they choose not to stay on Combria.

"The two hundred pilgrims we intend to send here will be taught that Combria is slightly smaller than Earth. They'll be instructed that Combrian days and nights are almost identical to Earth's, and that Combria orbits its star once for every two of our Earth years, yet goes through its four seasons twice during that time. They will also learn on their journey that time on earth is divided into millenniums, centuries, decades, years, months, weeks, days, hours, minutes, and seconds.

"They will know how to farm the land when they get here, and plant the large variety of seeds aboard their ship. To supplement their livestock supply they'll be taught which Combrian animals, fowl, and fish are beneficial to their needs—which ones to butcher for meat, which ones to milk, which hides to use for clothing and footwear. A large supply of coffee and tea will accompany them, and they'll know how to raise and process both by the time they land. The robots will teach them how to mine, extract metal from the ore, and forge it into whatever implements they need.

"Our two hundred pilgrims will be taught to be peaceful with the Combrians, use the superior weaponry they'll be supplied with only in self defense, and to share their technology with the natives. In return we anticipate the Combrians will show them things we've yet to learn about the planet. Once the robots have completed their tasks they'll board the shuttle used to bring supplies, livestock, and humans down to the planet in groups, return to the mother ship, and scuttle it after leaving Combrian space. The artificial intelligence guiding these specialized robots is so powerful that left unchecked it eventually becomes self motivated and extremely dangerous. Their destruction is necessitated because they would pass that critical point before getting back to Earth. That's why Charley doesn't possess such a processor.

"We on Earth originally designated your planet with an alpha-number. The first astronauts who came here learned the natives called themselves Combrians and the land Combria, so we adopted the title. Although several Combrians have observed our activities over the years in constructing this pyramid, they have no idea what it is, and none of the children who'll come here from Earth will be told of its existence. It is now completely sealed within the mountain. My crew is waiting for me on our ship as I speak. I'll have been the last person to be inside this structure until you arrived, assuming Charley didn't bring someone in who was disqualified. More about that later.

"At the tone you may get up and walk about—get your circulation flowing—but don't touch anything." The Urth smiled as he said it. "When the tone sounds again, please be seated or Charley will seat you, and you don't want that."

Voola stretched her limbs and walked around the room, marveling at all she'd been told, anxious to hear more. Charley stood motionless until the monitor signaled break time was over. He pointed at the chair and she scurried to it.

The robot pressed a button and Doctor Goralov reappeared.

"Good to have you back. Now then, we shall continue. In a moment a drawer will open and you'll see an indention of an open hand within it. Please place your right hand inside the indention and keep it there while I ask you a series of yes or no questions to test your psychological makeup, character, and intelligence. The hand print is a highly sophisticated sensor that will register either true or false in a computer. The computer is linked with Charley, and if you lie on any of the answers he'll know it, and you will automatically be disqualified. Alas, should that happen you'll have to be euthanized. The only chance you have of passing the test is to answer all questions honestly. If you fail the test Charley will have to find another who *is* qualified. That person will be told by the video Charley calls up that he or she isn't the first to be brought here. Charley will continue his mission until he succeeds in finding a qualified person. Keep your eyes on me during the test—don't look at Charley—he'll be watching your response. Nod your head for a yes answer, and shake it for a no answer. Let us begin . . . ."

TWENTY

"MUST HAVE WOKE UP RAVENOUS this morning," Hammer muttered with a chuckle as he peeked through the flap to find Voola's cot empty. He'd stopped by to escort her to breakfast.

When he didn't see her in the mess tent Hammer figured she'd gone to the latrine, but as time passed and she still hadn't shown up he got concerned. "Has anyone seen Voola?"

Nobody had.

"She didn't return to camp after going with you to the cave, Sir," said Corporal Sills, who'd been on guard duty last night. "At least not on my watch."

"Why didn't you tell me that when I came down from the cave?" he demanded.

"I assumed she'd stayed behind with your friend, Sir."

Hammer ran out of the mess tent and raced towards the cave, looking left and right, fearing Voola might have got bitten by a still viper, called that because their venom caused paralysis. Most victims recovered after a day or two, but some were stilled for life, never able to move a skeletal muscle again.

His world would shatter if such a fate had befallen her.

The doctor said "That concludes the test" and the teleon screen went blank. Voola's nerves were so frayed with anxiety her fingers had started twitching. She eyed the robot fearfully, having no idea if she'd passed or failed the grueling exam, only that she'd answered each question honestly. Charley pressed some buttons—the drawer with the hand print slid back inside a console flush with the wall, and another video of Ivan Goralov appeared.

"If you're watching this it means you've passed the test. Congratulations, you have met or exceeded the standards required, and no further examinations will be necessary. I'm also delighted to inform you that you are the first person Charley brought here, therefore no one had to be put to sleep, thank God. You are completely safe, so please relax as much as you can under what must seem to you a very bizarre situation."

Gushing out sobs of relief, she roughly wiped away the tears with her still trembling hands.

"A circle of red light will soon form on the floor in the center of the room. Please stand inside it with arms held at your sides. That section of floor will lower you to the next level of the pyramid. We'll speak again after you get there."

Rising from the chair, she saw a circular beam of crimson light appear from no apparent source. She stepped inside it. Anticipation laced with fear of the unknown almost intoxicating her, Voola stood like a statue in the manner Goralov prescribed.

As promised the floor beneath her feet moved downward. When her head cleared the inert floor, she looked down and saw she stood on a cylinder about three feet in diameter. She heard a *SWOOSH!* and looked up to see the hole in the floor above had been filled in without seams, making it impossible to distinguish that section from the rest of the shiny white ceiling.

The cylinder lowered her into another round room much larger than the one above. Only one blank teleon screen adorned its walls, but ninety degrees from it loomed a vertical row of buttons next to a shallow indention shaped like a hand with fingers spread. She glanced down and saw the circle of light had vanished, the area around her feet could no longer be demarcated, the floor appeared solid.

Doctor Goralov's voice pulled her eyes to the teleon. "Look around and you'll see comfortable furniture to relax on, a table where you can dine, and a food processor, which in all probability you've never seen the likes of before. It's the contraption on the wall with the hand print. I'll tell you how to operate it in a moment, but for now allow me to show you the septic amenities and water dispenser."

She heard another *SWOOSH!* and a section of wall slid open to reveal a flusher and bathing facilities behind it. A moment later it closed, leaving no visual clue of its existence.

"Simply walk towards that section of wall and it will open when you get within thirty inches of it, and close once you step inside. Do the same when you want to return to this room. The bedroom is behind the opposing wall and is accessed the same way."

The same swooshing sound made her turn to see a sleep chamber that disappeared a moment later when the wall closed.

"This monitor you're watching will automatically go into pause mode when you leave the room, and will turn off if you're gone longer than ten minutes. When you return it will turn back on. Don't sleep or nap in this room, or you'll miss vital information because the video will keep playing while you're slumbering. Now I'll show you how to work the food processor. Please push the top button beside the hand print."

Voola crossed the room and pressed it. A wide, thin slab

slid out from beneath the buttons, containing rows of depressions that held tiny pills of varying colors. Each depression had a title engraved above it in English and Old Combrian, and the rows were categorized as PROTEINS, LEGUMES, VEGETABLES, FRUITS, BREADS, DESSERTS, and BEVERAGES.

"As you can see, there are numerous items to choose from. Check the color code for the foods you want. For example all the dark-red tablets under the protein list are varieties of red meat, the white ones are fish, and so on. The processor will know the proper way to prepare each food choice according to your current nutritional needs. There are various beverages as well. A dark brown pill will produce coffee. Use a light brown one if you prefer tea. Containers of cream and sweetener will come with both. The hand print is a sensor that will determine the exact combination of nutrients your body needs at the moment. Please press your right hand against it now, and leave it there until a section of wall opens."

She palmed the print. A few seconds later a rectangular segment of wall slid sideways and a compartmentalized tray—with a drinking vessel and dining implements resting on a napkin—slid out of the opening.

"Each compartment on the tray is a different color corresponding to the foods you currently need. Please put the proper color tablet in each, and drop your beverage pill in the cup. Beverages are optional, but the processor will keep rejecting the tray until you put the proper colors in their corresponding sections. The confection compartment is located on the lower right. If it has an X on it, you won't be permitted dessert for this particular meal. Otherwise confections are also optional."

Voola saw her body presently required fish, vegetables, and bread. Having no idea what any of the many food varieties were, she selected them arbitrarily and chose coffee to drink, strongly suspecting it was really kaffy, since she now knew the legends about the Urths weren't myth after all. Though allowed a dessert, she didn't choose one.

"When you've finished loading the tray, take out the silverware and napkin, and press the second button from the top."

She complied. The tablet drawer disappeared into the wall as the food tray slid back into the compartment, whereupon the wall closed, then reopened almost immediately as the tray once again emerged. Steam rose from a hot meal of baked fish, three types of vegetables, and two toasted slices of what she'd call grain squares. A whiff of the coffee confirmed it was indeed kaffy.

"When your food is ready, gently lift the tray and it will detach automatically so you can carry it to the table. After you finish eating, press the third button from the top and another section of wall will open. Place the tray inside— including the cup, silverware, and napkin—and press the bottom button to close it. Don't worry if you have leftovers, they'll be taken care of by the processor. I'll give you half an hour to enjoy your meal, then we'll continue."

Hammer knew Voola hadn't left on her own accord because he'd found the seven glimeralds she'd stolen. Dropping the night lapper hide, he hissed a worried sigh. He'd searched a wide area all the way from the cave to camp but hadn't found her lying on the ground suffering from a viper bite as he'd feared. She'd obviously been abducted, and whoever did it had kept the guards from seeing them. That meant she had to have been captured very close to the cavern's entrance. Though Sills hadn't been instructed to watch the cave, its proximity to camp made it virtually impossible for one of the guards not to have noticed any type of action along the path, especially someone being kidnapped.

He went back to the cave and carefully examined the ground around the entrance. A trampled shrub caught his eye. Then he saw another one a few feet away. Placing his left foot on the first, he stepped to the second and looked around. Another one, then another, led towards the summit of Mount Opian.

Voola used the flusher before eating, and marveled at the technology that could make a wall act like a door without leaving any visible clues of its presence. The food and kaffy tasted fresh and savory, as if prepared conventionally after just being purchased. Apparently the nutrition tablets had an unlimited shelf life since they predated the arrival of the Urth colony the doctor spoke of. She deposited the tray and seated herself in a chair facing the teleon, waiting for Goralov to speak again.

Several minutes went by before he did.

"I hope you enjoyed your meal. Now I'll tell you the specifics of why you've been brought here and what is expected of you . . . ."

They'd left Fort Pacific after breakfast and were on their way to the palace. Once they got there PC would go immediately to the murder sites and hopefully receive a visual of what went down. Rarely did an event not reenact for him when he needed vital information. If he received it, he wouldn't be able to call the culprits by name with no apparent reason for doing so. He'd have to come up with something that seemed logical when he voiced his suspicion.

They passed a Mancombra walking along the side of the highway. He instructed Free to turn around and pull up beside him.

The male's face ignited with awe when he saw them drive up. PC didn't like being idolized, and that look assured the hitchhiker viewed him with far too much esteem. He got out of the wheeler and asked his name.

"Drill. What an honor to see you in person, Prince Zane."

"You're heading the wrong direction, my friend. The palace is that way." He pointed back down the road.

"I know, I came from there."

PC frowned. "Why did you leave?"

His big chest expanded and the Mancombra exhaled a deep sigh. "I didn't feel very welcome after refusing to join the army, so I decided to move on."

"You don't you want to join the army? For galaxies sake why? You're the very reason we started this war. You should feel privileged to have the opportunity to serve alongside your brothers and sisters."

He looked down and shrugged his massive shoulders. "I don't believe in fighting."

"Oh you don't?" He wanted to slap the coward. How dare

he seek safety in the palace without being willing to join the cause in liberating his own kind. Opening a flap on his belt, he pulled out a hypodermic containing a forty-hour dose of Clodec whose affects were immediate, and stabbed the ingrate's right thigh. "Well consider yourself drafted. Lieutenant Free! Got hold of Sergeant Brush and tell him to hold up. We're commandeering his wheeler while he uses ours to deliver a new recruit to Fort Pacific. And you, my fine Mancombra friend, will be shot for desertion if you try to get away from my sergeant while in route."

Free winced. "I haven't driven an armored wheeler in five double-years. I'm not sure I remember how."

"Then it's about time you knocked the rust off isn't it, Lieutenant."

The Mancombra sympathized with him after searching his brain as they sped down the highway for Fort Pacific, where he'd have to begin the forty-two days of hell Captain Morris told him about. Under the influence of Clodec, he wouldn't have known the sergeant had probed his thoughts if he hadn't been told. Drill liked Sergeant Brush, he was open minded like Colonel Hammer. He'd sensed Voola thought his pacifism to be an illusion he'd subconsciously created to shield himself from the harsh reality of being a slothful coward.

"Stop worrying about boot camp, Drill. You look to be in pretty good shape so you'll get used to the physicality in no time. Just remember not to speak unless spoken to and *never* volunteer for anything."

Stove was asleep, having insisted on taking the first watch when she'd grown fatigued last night. He'd turned in four hours ago after eating breakfast with them. She'd prepared fried sern strips and grain cakes at their charge's request. Polka, Pliers had learned, relished every part of a sern—even the liver, which she couldn't stand.

A chime rang out. Pliers answered the door and almost swallowed her tongue when she saw Prince Zane standing beside Captain Morris and Lieutenant Free.

The captain raised a finger to his nose, signaling her to be quiet while whispering, "Where's Corporal Stove?"

"He's asleep, Sir," she whispered back.

"Get Polka."

Seeing the lieutenant had a tranquilizer gun, she searched his mind as well as Prince Zane's. Knowing she'd be reprimanded if she asked, Pliers didn't say a word, but was deeply troubled—aching to know why the Urths thought Stove killed Sergeant Wrench and the Mancombras in the maintenance center.

Stepping back into the parlor she telepathed, *Please don't speak, Ma'am, until we're out of the apartment. Captain Morris is waiting for you outside the door with Prince Zane.*

"Prince Zane's at the door?" said Polka full throat, eyes wide with amazement.

Pliers grabbed an arm and hastily pulled her into the corridor, trying hard not to cry.

Captain Morris forced a frowning, bewildered Polka down the hall, taking her safely away should Stove manage to avoid the tranquilizer dart.

Lieutenant Free somberly whispered, "Take me to him."

Heart breaking, she sadly obeyed.

Stove being sound asleep, the lieutenant didn't have to worry about hitting a moving target. She closed her eyes when he took aim, and felt tears squeezing from them when he fired.

TWENTY
ONE

POLKA DEMANDED TO KNOW WHAT was going on but Captain Morris wouldn't utter a word as he urged her down the corridor.

"Dammit, Captain, why are you acting so weird, and what was Prince Zane doing at my apartment?"

Gritting his teeth, he angrily whispered, "Not here, I'll tell you when we get to my office!"

It finally dawned on her he didn't want any passersby to overhear, so she relented until they got to their destination.

Captain Morris closed the door, removed his hat, and wiped beads of sweat off his forehead. "Prince Zane thinks Stove killed the Mancombras."

"Stove . . .?!" her eyes nearly left their sockets.

"Yeah," he said with an unsteady breath. "And to think I had him guarding you. Thank The Spirit That Created All Things you're okay."

"Why would Stove kill Sergeant Wrench?"

"Prince Zane learned from an intelligence report that a Mancombra soldier had tried to convince ten other military Mancombras to join forces and attempt to take over the planet just as Gram warned. That list included Sergeants Wrench and Awl and the two dead privates, Sandpaper and Eraser. We contacted one of the six living Mancombras and he verified the allegation, naming Stove as the culprit.

Thinking him to be a harmless dreamer, none of them took Stove seriously and didn't want to get him in trouble, so nobody ever said anything. Apparently something happened that made Stove fear they would, and he set out to make sure they couldn't. Unfortunately he succeeded in silencing four of them. Lieutenant Free has him drugged by now with Pliers probing his mind. We'll soon know for certain if he's guilty."

The blindfold kept everyone from seeing the fear in his eyes, but his legs were trembling so hard he could barely stand. Stove couldn't imagine how he'd fallen under suspicion to begin with, much less what made Prince Zane so certain of his guilt, but with Clodec coursing through his veins he'd been unable to keep Pliers from learning the truth about everything. Another Mancombra, unacquainted with him, had then been ordered to probe his mind on the off chance Pliers might have a personal axe to grind in wanting to see him standing in front of a firing squad. If only the second mind-reader had been Rope, perhaps she could have telepathically convinced Pliers to lie like she'd have hopefully done in order to keep him alive. Instead, Prince Zane had called for his immediate execution.

He cursed King Gram for putting the idea into his head, his ambitious plan would cost him his life. Hearing the order to take aim, fear gripped him so tightly he couldn't control his bladder. Hot piss squirted down his leg, flooding his shaking boot. He'd reduced the number of Mancombras to a hundred and thirty-four. Any second now that tally would drop to one-thirty-three.

She'd been gone three days. Hammer couldn't eat or sleep for worry over Voola's welfare. The heavy machinery had gotten there that morning and he'd told Captain Wurz to take care of the matter. Standing inside her tent, once again admiring the filched jewels, how he wished he could see them draped around her pretty throat in a necklace. He stashed them back inside the night lapper hide and glumly carried it with him to his tent, along with a bag containing her clothes and crimalot spurs. Now void of petals, she must have kept the stems for sentimental reasons.

Hammer was so desperate to find her he'd even thought of deserting—but with no clue about where to look, he'd be throwing his career away in vain. Apparently a night lapper had made the tracks he'd followed from the cave, because the two-footed trail stopped at a large boulder with numerous depressions running past it, made by animals using four legs, which night lappers always resorted to when in flight. The ground being so heavily covered with grass and plants, he hadn't been able to find a footprint, only indiscernible dents and flattened shrubs.

He'd been totally morose since her disappearance, but one thing had forced him to laugh: the ridiculous way Arigot looked yesterday when he'd brought him water and kaffy. Seeing him standing outside the cave on stilts hidden by a skirt, he'd transmitted, *You've got to be the ugliest female Mancombra I've ever laid eyes on.*

Drill had survived his first day of boot camp and was midway through his second. His drill instructor, Sergeant Rake, had chastised him and a Combrian buck private for melding minds. Otherwise he'd dodged the Mancombra's wrath so far.

His unit had been taken to the firing range to have their marksmanship tested. Taught by his father to be proficient with a hunting rifle, Drill anticipated a pretty good score, but hadn't expected to achieve an accuracy level of ninety-four percent. No one else in his platoon even reached the eighties.

Sergeant Rake walked over to him, shouting, "Where'd you learn to shoot like that, larva?!"

"Hunting with my father, Sir."

"Let's see how you do with a moving target . . . ."

Drill stood at attention as Sergeant Rake showed their company commander his target tally. The Urth captain whistled through his teeth and looked up at him from his desk. "Can you handle long periods of isolation, larva?"

"Sir, yes Sir, Captain Landry!"

"Are you self motivating?"

"I'd say so, Captain Landry."

The captain rose to his feet and leered at him. "I didn't ask whether you'd say so, larva. Give me a yes or no answer. Are you self motivated or not?"

"Sir, yes Sir, Captain Landry!"

"Are you disciplined?"

"Sir, yes Sir, Captain Landry!"

He turned to Rake. "Sergeant, this larva is leaving for sniper school first thing in the morning. Dismissed."

TWENTY
TWO

AFTER FORTY DAYS OF SNIPER training Drill's uniform sported a chevron on each shoulder with an arc beneath, embellished by a rifle in the center. Now a Private First Class in Special Forces, his anger at Prince Zane had turned to gratitude: he felt pretty damn proud of the accomplishment. The corporal who'd driven him to Mount Opian dropped him off at his new post and headed for the tourist trap, hoping to score with one of the locals before returning to the base where sharp shooters were schooled.

An open mine had replaced the tunnel leading up to the mysterious wall. General Yonker wanted a team of snipers on hand because Prince Zane feared the structure must have been put there by aliens from another planet. If any were inside they might come out to defend it. A section ninety feet wide and forty feet high had been uncovered, but the curved sloping wall appeared to have no end.

Expecting his arrival the guards waved him through. He proceeded towards Colonel Hammer and Captain Wurz, conversing with a civilian apparently in charge of the crew operating excavation equipment.

Drill saluted.

Hammer saluted back. "Good to see you in a uniform, Drill. You look sharp."

"Thank you, Sir." He wanted Voola to see him in it so

she'd know he wasn't a coward after all. Drill still didn't think he could kill the enemy, and felt guilty about keeping that to himself in order to dodge regular boot camp. That disclosure would have disqualified him for sniper school. He'd certainly incapacitate any attacker however, and that soothed his conscience somewhat. "Is Voola still here?"

The Mancombra's face dropped. Hammer looked skyward and muttered, "She was kidnapped . . . I fear she's dead."

Taken aback by the horrific news, he started to telepath his reaction, but sensing Hammer had his mind blocked, Drill spoke instead. "How dreadful, Sir. I don't know what else to say."

Thanks for keeping my confidence, Hammer transmitted before once again shielding his thoughts.

He'd been thanked for not giving away the colonel's relationship with Voola, which the condolences he'd wanted to express would surely have betrayed. Using the excuse of satisfying his curiosity to change the subject he said, "Do you think aliens built the stronghold, Colonel?"

Hammer sighed. "We had some scientists examine the wall and their instruments read it as stainless steel the same as ours. But since no explosives can blast through it, those have to be false readings. They concluded that whatever the metal really is, it's not native to Combria. Prince Zane told General Yonker to uncover the whole thing."

"Only it's us that's stuck here doing it of course," Captain Wurz ragged while eyeing his shoulder. "Congratulations on making Special Forces."

"Thank you, Sir."

"What made you change your mind about enlisting?" asked Hammer.

"Nothing, Sir. I was personally drafted by Prince Zane."

The sad aura surrounding the colonel evaporated with a raspy laugh. Captain Wurz thought it humorous as well. But soon thereafter a gloomy shroud again enveloped Hammer.

Arigot had abandoned the steam cave after Hammer finally spoke with PC face to face when the ruler came to Mount Opian to view the mysterious wall in person after some scientists examined it. For the last ten days he'd been holed up in another one. Thankfully the moisture in his new cavern home consisted of a fresh water pond instead of hot clouds.

PC told Hammer that he'd learned of his desertion from Lieutenant Enforcer Barrabon, whom he had locked up in the stockade at Fort Pacific. Hammer had inquired whether his life could be spared if he were to surrender.

"My sincerest apologies," PC had replied according to Hammer, "but under no circumstances will I spare your half brother's life, any more than I would Gram Pillhigh's."

And so Hammer had brought him two backpacks filled with rations on what he'd said would be his final visit, and warned him to find another hiding place before PC learned of the Mancombra named Crayon and insisted on taking her back to the palace with him at the conclusion of his visit. Shortly after Hammer left he'd wandered off in broad daylight, wearing the stilts and floor-length skirt, discarding both upon reaching the hidden wheeler. He'd collected his weapons and climbed towards the top of the mountain.

Seeing some Urth civilians heading up the mount, he'd forced his way through the dense hedge and stumbled upon a narrow cleft in a boulder which led to the low-ceiling grotto he was stuck in now. The slender opening didn't allow much light to reach inside the cave, and with no ventilation he didn't dare make a fire, so he'd been forced to camp near the entrance.

Despite knowing he could never be free under any circumstances while PC and Gram remained commanders-in-chief of their respective armies, his allegiance lay with Zane. The Mancombra, whom everybody thought to be an Urth, was fighting for the right cause: equality, freedom, and justice for all. What a pity he'd awakened to that fact too late. PC didn't know it, but he needed all the help he could get. If Gram's scientists succeeded in splitting the atom, Combria was doomed, for that power would lie totally in the hands of a raving lunatic.

Polka enjoyed teaching, something she'd never done before. Captain Morris had chosen a conference chamber in the south wing of the palace to use as her classroom. In the beginning she'd insisted on no more than five students until determining which method proved most beneficial. After a few days she'd felt comfortable in doubling that number. The eight hour sessions were divided in half. Mornings were spent memorizing data, then being coached not to think about it by focusing on something mundane. Afternoons she had Pliers interrogate them while they tried to conceal the information. So far none of them could deceive the sergeant major. Tomorrow would mark thirty-eight days since she'd started working with the full class, and very little progress had been made. But one of the soldiers had begun making it a mild chore for Pliers to pick his brain.

"We're ready to test it, Sire," said Nanzar, who had the brightest mind of any Combrian on the planet. "We'll have to do it on some deserted island far from any land mass or Zane will immediately know about it."

Gram stroked his chin while eyeing the teleon screen. Nanzar's relativity theory maintained the power of the atom could be harnessed. Many physicists claimed he'd plagiarized Harv Zane's thesis, but Nanzar swore they'd merely coincidentally arrived at the same conclusions concerning the quantum relationships of time, space, and matter. "Get your team ready to travel."

Voola stepped through the opening and turned to see Charley vanish as the wall closed in front of him with a *SWOOSH!* Almost simultaneously a large boulder lowered, leaving no clue what lurked behind it. She headed down the slope and soon arrived at a point level with the cave where she'd last seen her beloved Hammer. The entrance lay a few feet to her right and she stood very near the spot where Charley had drugged her.

Horribly missing the big Mancombra, she hurried for the camp below.

PC hadn't had the heart to tell Colonel Hammer he knew Arigot was hiding in a cave above the camp. A scene had played out before him the moment he'd reached the guard station upon arriving at Mount Opian. A Mancombra calling herself Crayon had pointed towards the opening, saying she'd wait for her friend up there. He'd felt Arigot's nervousness about trekking up the slope on stilts hidden by a skirt. After reliving the event he'd ordered a dose of Clodec for the camp commander, using the excuse of having top secret information in his head, a tactic he often employed when uncertain of how much time he'd be in close proximity of non-Urths. It would have been impossible to mentally hide his excitement over locating the enforcer. He'd barely managed to keep a straight face when Hammer had asked if Arigot's voluntary surrender would avert his execution. Not wanting the colonel to witness his half brother's death, he'd secretly arranged to have Arigot tailed after Hammer warned him to flee. There'd be no reprimand for aiding the enemy because he'd have done the same for his own flesh and blood wanting to give himself up.

Knowing exactly what Hammer was up to when he'd left camp carrying two backpacks, PC had watched and waited until what appeared to be an extremely uncoordinated female Mancombra left the cave, carrying a sleeping bag and canteen along with the packs. A short while later he'd told Free he needed some alone time, and had ventured to the steam cave where he'd picked up strong signals regarding Arigot's plans and Needle's situation.

His mother had been alive when the enforcer last saw her in an underground throne room. She was bound to be dead by now because the deranged king hadn't believed Arigot's report. So much time had passed since, the absence of propaganda verified Gram hadn't changed his mind on the matter.

The burning desire to bring Wheelbarrow's killer to justice had grown stronger each minute that passed after his murder, but upon entering the cavern and picking up Arigot's thoughts, he'd been overwhelmed by the enforcer's repentant heart. Arigot yearned with every fiber of his being to fight alongside his half brother and put an end to the House of Pillhigh. Following orders to carry on the Genocide Directive, Arigot hadn't committed the atrocities merely out of duty but because he'd truly feared an eventual Mancombra takeover if they weren't eradicated. He'd forced himself to act as a heartless automaton in order to fulfill his mission, secretly loathing every minute of it. Upon discovering the king who'd instilled that trepidation in him was mad, objectivity had returned and he'd seen how groundless those fears were. PC felt it would be a crime against his own regime to destroy such a humble and adept soldier, whose drastic reformation caused by the rudest of awakenings had galvanized an unimpeachable loyalty to the right cause in the Combrian's heart and soul.

Nonetheless some type of punishment had to be meted, the blood of his parents and the other innocents demanded it. Standing on a palace balcony gazing at the stars, PC wondered what was going through Arigot's mind at the moment. Using binoculars Sergeant Brush had observed the renegade Combrian—watched him discard the disguise at a hidden wheeler and gather his weapons before climbing up the mountain to find a new hideout. When Brush delivered Arigot's location via field communicator, using the secret frequency, he'd ordered him and his men not to alert the enforcer of their presence until further notice. Ten days of being forced to live like a primitive savage after already having spent a good deal of time in the steam cave would serve as most of his sentence. Half an hour ago he'd given the order to capture Arigot and bring him to the palace via whirly.

Adrenaline flooding his veins Hammer threw his blanket off and leapt from his cot, praying the transmission hadn't been a dream. *Voola, is that really you?!*

Yes, my love, may I come in?

TWENTY THREE

THEY WERE BOTH CRYING, HOLDING each other as if their very lives depended on it. "I thought you'd been kidnapped by one of Gram's spies," Hammer sniffled out, "and had lost all hope you were still alive."

Voola gazed up at him, a fine mist clouding her striking eyes. "I'm so sorry I couldn't contact you and relieve your worries, Hammer. What happened is unbelievable. When I left you and Arigot, I'd barely stepped out of the cave when I thought an insect stung me and I passed out. But the sting came from a sedative fired by a robot, and I woke up to find he'd taken me inside the very structure you've been trying to blast your way into."

She drew a deep breath and let it out slowly. "The legends about the Urths are true. They *did* come from another planet a long, long time ago—bringing with them coffee which we call kaffy, butter which wound up being called booter in our times, and a variety of seeds, animals, fowl, insects, and tools. The myths about pinto beans and all the other foods alleged to have originated with them aren't myths at all. They came from a planet called Earth—E-A-R-T-H, not U-R-T-H—and were once referred to as earthlings, humans, and homosapien. They spoke Anglish like modern Urths but its proper name is English.

"A scientist named Ivan Goralov created a voluminous

library of teleon videos and left them behind for our benefit before he and his crew flew back to Earth. They were the last earthlings to visit Combria before a ship carrying two hundred colonists arrived, never to leave. Earthlings are composed of four different races and fifty members of each were sent here. That's why some Urths are white, some brown, some black, and some yellow. Yellow Urths stem from a race called Mongoloids. You owe half of your genes to Urths known as Caucasoid on Earth."

If he hadn't been able to probe Voola's mind while hearing such an incredible tale, he'd have been certain she'd lost it.

Aren't you glad you can read it then, my love, she transmitted with a teasing smile.

"Is that where you got those coveralls you're wearing?" he asked aloud.

She nodded and pulled them apart, making a tearing sound, yet the cloth didn't rip. Somehow a strip of fabric acting like a zipper held the outfit together. The body-suit she'd worn when he'd last seen her kept her glorious body from coming into view. She pointed at numerous bulges inside the coveralls and said, "I have devices in these inner pockets that Doctor Goralov taught me how to use through a teleon. We must go see Prince Zane at once. I know how to find Gram."

PC never used the throne room, preferring a modest office instead. Arigot looked frazzled, and being dosed with Clodec couldn't read his mind. Turning so he faced away from the captured enforcer, he winked at Sergeant Brush. "What do you think, Sergeant? Should we shoot him, burn him at the stake, hang him, or have this murderer drawn and quartered?"

Grinning, Brush replied, "I vote for barbequing him, Sir."

"Good choice. Make the arrangements."

Arigot gasped. "My galaxies, PC, be reasonable—I was following orders! Have Sergeant Brush probe my mind and you'll know I mean it when I say I'm willing to suffer whatever type of death you think I should, but *only* after you let me help you win this war. Gram claims to have a team of scientists working night and day to turn Doctor Nanzar's theory of a super bomb into reality. If they succeed all is lost. Please, let me talk to you alone, there's something I need to tell you. You have me in chains so I can't attack you."

He laughed. "Arigot, I wouldn't be afraid of you even if you weren't bound. Go make preparations for this animal's death, Sergeant Brush. Meanwhile I'll grant the enforcer's request for privacy."

When the door closed Arigot sucked in a deep breath and hastily relayed: "I know your secret—Professor Wheelbarrow was your father and his sister Needle gave birth to you. I took her to Gram and told him everything but he didn't believe me. Most likely he had her killed before I was transported from his hidden bomb shelter. If he did, her body was incinerated so there's no way her blood can be tested against yours for proof. I don't want this secret getting out any more than you do, but even if I were to spill my guts nobody would believe me. Please let me help you win this war. I swear by The Spirit That Created All Things that's all I want to do because nothing else matters. Your parents' blood mingles with that of my own mother and father in testimony against me. Like a fool I stayed loyal to Gram even after they lost their lives resisting capture, but now my eyes have been opened. I know now I was on the wrong side and I want to make amends. I'll serve as a buck private if I have to, but *please* let me join you."

PC folded his arms across his chest and steadied his eyes on Arigot. "The blood of every Mancombra and family member you killed testifies against you, Arigot. Tell me, did you enjoy watching my father die after you riddled him with bullets?"

Arigot's brow furrowed into four perfect rows of indented copper. "How did you know I took him down personally?"

"Wheelbarrow told me."

"What?"

"That's right, I can confer with the dead. Be thinking about what you want for your last meal. You'll be burned at the stake at star-rise." A long night of agonizing over perishing by flame would wrap up Arigot's punishment. Careful to keep his expression stern and unyielding, PC held back the laugh his future colonel's fearful demeanor induced. By this time tomorrow Arigot would have a red Z with a silver hunter fowl pinned to it on each shoulder.

Voola's tale being so unbelievable, Hammer decided they should keep it to themselves until Prince Zane was informed. When he put Wurz in charge, the captain's unspoken thoughts were that he was only taking leave in order to screw Voola. Hicker fat stashed in the spare cavity of his wheeler, he prayed the first town they came to after the tourist trap would have essence of valley fern because they'd be stopping at an inn to break up the long trip to the palace.

Drill had given him a knowing grin when they'd passed him at the guard's station.

Locked up in the palace dungeon, Arigot couldn't summon any tears for his fate. He wept solely because of the innocent lives he'd taken in the line of duty. Death by conflagration wasn't nearly severe enough, but dammit to blazes if PC would only stop and think about it he'd realize that having an enforcer of Gram's on his side would greatly help his cause. Praying to The Spirit That Created All Things, he vowed to light the fire himself if only the unseen deity would make PC let him fight Gram's forces until the end of the war.

Pliers couldn't go back to sleep. She'd been startled awake by a vivid dream of Stove's execution, an event she hadn't witnessed in real life. The painful memory of reading his thoughts and seeing how he'd manipulated an amoral nurse in the infirmary raced across her brain. He'd been plotting a course to become dictator over all Combria by using her, Lieutenant Rope, and every other female Mancombra to help him achieve that end. The first stage of his sick plan had called for the deaths of all Mancombra males, leaving him the only one on the planet. Thankfully Prince Zane had gotten wise to him before he'd tallied a fifth victim.

Captain Morris didn't assign Polka another bodyguard after Stove since it turned out Gram hadn't infiltrated the palace with some of his assassins after all. There'd been a big hubbub after dinner when news spread that Enforcer Arigot, the most notorious of them, had been captured. Not only would she like to witness that evil Combrian standing before the firing squad, she'd eagerly volunteer to be one of the gunners if her present duty didn't prevent it.

They'd stopped at an inn to sleep before continuing on to the palace in the morning—and nocturnal rest was *all* they'd be getting. Frustrated more than she'd ever been in her life, furious over the improbability of such a thing occurring, Voola wanted to scream. Not one of the numerous shops they'd checked along their journey had any essence of valley fern.

Molly kissed him goodnight and went to their sleep chamber. Harv resumed watching a movie about two Combrian hunters lost in the Sorrian mountains. Having seen it before, he knew they'd survive in the end, yet their plight still gripped him.

Five minutes before the conclusion the door chime rang.

He muted the teleon and answered the door.

PC entered the apartment looking troubled and didn't waste time explaining why:

"Arigot told me Nanzar's working on the super weapon. I know you don't think he stole your ideas for his relativity theory, but the vast majority of the scientific community wouldn't have accused him of doing so if he didn't. I side with them, but if it *is* possible to make a bomb capable of killing thousands, is he smart enough to do it?"

Drawing a harried breath, Harv looked into the clear green eyes of the noblest soul he'd ever known. "PC, such a bomb correctly equipped with the right radioactive isotope would destroy millions if dropped into the heart of a major metropolis, and the fallout would cause many more to die of radiation poisoning. It's not a question of whether such a weapon is possible because it definitely is. The problems Nanzar will have to overcome are finding the right isotope, figuring out the best way to trigger it, and safely assembling all the necessary components."

"How problematic would such a task be?"

"Not enough to guarantee he won't succeed. Now let me ask you something. When is Arigot getting his just due?"

"Tomorrow at star-rise, he thinks."

"He thinks?! What's going on here, son?"

"I'm having him translated from enforcer to colonel."

"What?! Have you lost your mind?"

PC tossed him his aggravating I'm-not-going-to-budge-an-inch grin. "I'm sure most will think so but I know what I'm doing. Arigot deserted Gram because of rudely awakening to the fact he'd been fighting for an evil cause. He wanted to surrender but didn't out of fear I'd have him put to death. That Combrian wants to bring Gram to justice as much as I do, and though he doesn't know where Gram's hiding, his knowledge of the universals' tactics since the psycho king went underground will be very useful."

Speechless from shock, he could only gawk at his son—unable to comprehend him not only allowing that Combrian viper to live, but to actually serve in the revolutionary army.

"Wipe that look off your face, Harv, I know he killed Wheelbarrow. And since Needle's bound to be dead as well, that too falls squarely on him. He told Gram our secret but the fool didn't believe him. No one else knows except him, and I'm confident he won't tell anyone. Even if he wanted to, as he pointed out to me, with no way to prove the allegation everyone would think him mad. When the war's over I'm going to announce the truth in a press conference anyway."

That only confused him further. "Why, for galaxies sakes?"

"Because I've got too damn many secrets. The people have a right to know all about the man watching over them. Since I can't tell them everything it's the least I can do."

"What are you talking about? You don't have any secrets other than being a Mancombra who looks like an Urth."

PC donned a refuting smirk that made him feel uneasy. "Or do you?"

"Harv, I not only contradicted medical science by being conceived and looking the way I do, I was also born with some odd . . . talents. When I first experienced one of them I told Needle about it. She dismissed it as wishful thinking—idle daydreaming—and basically chastised me by saying a sharp mind like I'd been blessed with should never waste a moment entertaining such foolish notions. Seeing how much it troubled her I never said anything when I later found out she was wrong. Because of my position I can't afford for anyone to know what they are, and I don't want you to say anything to Molly about them. This is as much as I'm going to divulge. I hate that I don't have any peers to freely discuss them with."

Amazed and perplexed about his son's *talents,* Harv shook his head.

"What's that supposed to mean?" PC asked, frowning.

"If you announce you're a Mancombra to the world you're liable to find out you do have peers, son. Polka, the black Urth Captain Morris has teaching the probe blocking technique, is an old acquaintance of mine and I had her over for dinner one night. She was taught how to do it by her spouse in order to keep something secret they learned while experimenting with genetics. She told Molly and me all about it."

"Oh? Where is Molly anyway?"

"She turned in for the night an hour ago."

PC checked the time. "It's late, you should be in bed as well. I'll drop by again tomorrow night if duty permits and hear about this research. Before I go, are you telling me I wasn't just a fluke, and other Mancombras can reproduce in spite of what science has said all this time?"

"Yes. According to what Polka and her mate discovered, two Mancombras *can* make a baby but only if they're brother and sister sired by a Combrian."

Hearing boot heels marching down the stone floor of the dungeon, Arigot summoned his courage, preparing to face death. Life Giver had risen, it was time to die.

Keys clanked together as a guard unlocked the cell door. After receiving another clodec injection even though the forty-hour dose he'd been given at Mount Opian was still active, Arigot turned around with hands behind his back to be handcuffed. A circle of steel clamped shut over each wrist. He turned again and two Urth corporals led him away. Trying to keep the image of flames engulfing him out of his mind, he thought of Hammer and prayed his half brother would find another to take Voola's place. Losing her had completely devastated the poor soul.

TWENTY FOUR

THEY'D LEFT THE INN WELL before dawn and arrived at the palace at breakfast time. Hammer curled an arm around Voola's waist as they traversed The Great Hall.

It feels spooky being here again, she transmitted.

He looked up at the opulent ceiling and sighed. *I think it's beautiful—I never tire of its grandeur. But then this is only my fifth time here.*

She winced. *If you were one of Gram's slaves like I was, you'd see all this splendor through a vulgar lens the way I do.*

Giving her a love pat on the hip, he withdrew his arm as they turned a corner and proceeded down the corridor leading to Prince Zane's office. Hammer wished his commander would use the throne room because he'd only been inside the royal chamber once. Its magnificence was breathtaking.

The door sentinel motioned for them to halt.

⸸

Arigot had been standing in the same spot for over an

hour—still handcuffed and utterly baffled. He should have been nothing but a pile of ashes by now. The guards handed him over to Sergeant Brush at the dungeon gates and the Mancombra had brought him here: PC's office. He'd asked what was going on but Brush wouldn't speak. Apparently they were waiting for PC, but he had no idea why.

Strolling towards his office PC immediately recognized the Combrian as Voola, Gram's escaped mistress. "Colonel Hammer, why wasn't I notified you were coming to the palace?"

Hammer saluted. "Sir, this is Voola—she's who told me about Gram's bunker outside Juxbow. Last night she relayed something to me of such tremendous importance I had no choice but to deliver her to you in person. I didn't notify anyone of my intentions because it involves the edifice inside Mount Opian and a means to expose Gram's location."

Relishing the serendipity, and anxious to hear what Voola had to offer, PC kept his distance so the surprise couldn't be picked up telepathically. "Well since you've come with such significant intel, I'll give you the honor of pinning the hunter fowls I'm carrying in this box on a new colonel."

Hammer's confused frown made it all the grander.

"The two of you go on inside, I'll be right behind you."

Seeing Prince Zane in person had been a shock, but Voola gasped and brought her hands to the base of her throat when she saw Arigot. His face reflected the same surprise as Hammer's.

"W-When—"

"When did we catch him, Colonel?" asked Prince Zane, grinning like a child on the morn of The Feast of the Annual Snow. "Yesterday. And you, Enforcer Arigot, are wondering why you're still alive, are you not?"

Apparently stunned speechless, Arigot merely nodded, mouth ajar as a Mancombra sergeant released him from handcuffs.

Prince Zane handed Hammer a narrow box he'd been holding. "Colonel, your brother has just been drafted into our army. Accompany Sergeant Brush to the commissary and when Arigot puts on one of our uniforms after bathing, decorate him with his new rank of colonel, then report back here. Any objections, Enforcer Arigot?"

Tears rolling down his copper cheeks, a huge smile stretching his dark Combrian lips almost to his hearing membranes, Arigot saluted. "With all due respect, Prince Zane, from now on it's *Colonel* Arigot."

Prince Zane turned to her. "Make yourself comfortable, Voola. I'll have some breakfast brought in and you can tell me this revelation Colonel Hammer spoke of. Not a word until we're alone."

The brothers embraced one another and left with Sergeant Brush. Prince Zane sat down behind his desk, pushed a button, and ordered breakfast for two. He then folded his hands together and leaned forward. "Okay, Voola, I'm all ears."

Pulling the Velcro apart, a term she'd learned from Ivan Goralov, she removed a rectangular device from the top left inner pocket of the coveralls she'd received from Charley.

Placing it on the desk where Prince Zane could see the doctor's face on the tiny teleon screen she said, "This was given to me while I was inside a pyramid constructed eons ago within Mount Opian. Control the volume with that slider on the side."

She turned it on. Goralov appeared and started speaking. "This recording will instruct you on how to activate the data transmitter placed on your smaller moon by our last advance team. Besides giving you the ability to locate any person, place, or thing on the surface of the entire side of the planet facing the transmitter at the time, it will enable you to find anything you're looking for subterranean or beneath the sea waves.

"Your fishermen won't have to waste time searching for schools of fish, the transmitter will pinpoint the exact spots where they're gathered in abundance. You'll no longer have to worry about wasting resources drilling a dry hole when searching for fossil fuels, or digging a useless mine for coal, salt, minerals, metals, precious stones, and the like. You'll be able to tell precisely where to drill and dig. It can inform you exactly what's needed to fertilize barren lands to enable crops to grow with minimum need for water, and much more. The moon rotates at half the speed of your planet, therefore you'll be able to access the transmitter for twenty-four hours—seeing what lies on and within each hemisphere facing it for twelve. Then it will be inaccessible for the same period of time until it again looks down on Combria."

She leaned over and turned it off. "With this, Prince Zane, you can easily find out where Gram Pillhigh is hiding."

The prince looked very skeptical. "Where did you say you got this?"

"From inside Mount Opian. Um, it occurs to me you might want to have your sergeant, or some other Mancombra or Combrian probe my mind before I go any further. You'll likely think me delusional otherwise."

Drill had been on guard duty last night when Voola entered the camp. She'd transmitted something so farfetched he'd never have believed it if her mind meld hadn't confirmed the truth of her amazing tale. Prince Zane had been correct in thinking aliens constructed the stronghold, but the Urth was in for an incredible surprise. According to Voola it had been built by members of the ruler's own race. He'd telepathically begged her to tarry and tell him more but she'd been too anxious to see Hammer. Having once been in love himself, he'd completely understood.

Voola's brain had been extremely hyper, but her strange experience within the mountain hadn't been able to override a fierce irritation over failing to obtain any essence of valley fern. When they had left for the palace he'd prayed they would find some along the way.

Gram clutched the slut's tits when orgasm neared, then shoved her off him immediately after achieving it. A little sex before lunch always whetted his appetite. Unlike her he hadn't undressed. Securing his penis within his trousers, he stepped out of his sleep chamber. The sentinels saluted. Ignoring them, he made his way down the corridor, past the royal underground dining room where his queen Releen and their children were taking victuals. He'd have his brought to the command center.

Passing the common eating hall, he saw his harem gathered around a long table. One chair sat empty, awaiting the young Combrian who'd just pleasured him. She wouldn't be arriving until the guards got through searching her.

Nanzar and his team had put to sea under guard at dawn and would be arriving at the designated island before nightfall. They expected to have everything set up within three days and test the device on the fourth. If the bomb worked, Combria would soon have its rightful king back on the throne. If it didn't he'd have the scientist put to death. Being very much aware of that fact, Nanzar would be giving his all.

Universal Quest appeared on the teleon. *"Happy midday to you, Sire."*

"Yeah, yeah. Have you got the new unit ready?"

"I have, Your Highness. Principal Nobb left Juxbow with ten troops two hours ago, posing as a power pole repair team. The Genocide Directive is once again underway. I also have other news. One of our spies informed me that Colonel Hammer and a Combrian female spent last night at his inn and learned they were heading for the palace. He has all the rooms equipped with hidden listening devices, and though they mostly communicated telepathically, he was able to determine Hammer has been stationed at the base of Mount Opian for a good while. Arigot had been hiding in a cave near Hammer's camp with the colonel's blessing but had to flee when General Zane paid a visit. There's something going on inside the mountain but our spy wasn't able to find out what. I thought you'd be interested to know the female's name is Voola and she fits the description of the one who stole your glimeralds."

Rage seizing him, he threw his head back and roared. "That stealing bitch is cheating on me with a half-breed?!"

"It appears so, My King."

"Oh . . ." he rubbed his hands together and lunged forward, face a mere inch from Quest's on the screen. "How I'd love to slice that whore apart—flay her alive with a heated blade. I want her captured, Quest! I don't care how you do it, but bring that sleazy piece of shit to me so I can mete out the justice she so richly deserves!"

Knowing PC had been facetious in saying he conversed with the dead, Arigot assumed Barrabon must have given him the details about how his father died. While relishing the first hot bath he'd had since deserting, he kept pondering what made the general change his mind about executing him. Whatever it was, he thanked The Spirit That Created All Things PC had. Quest's hidden post in Juxbow would be the second secret he'd betray, Gram's super bomb having been the first. Unfortunately, since Quest knew he'd deserted, the universal would have abandoned it for another location by now.

Washing over forty days of residual filth off his skin, he wished the same could be done to the guilt tainting his soul. He couldn't bring a single one of those innocent civilians back to life, but at least he had the chance to lay his own on the line to bring Gram's Genocide Directive to a permanent halt. The poor Urth girl Jan who'd pled for mercy filled his mind. All she'd been guilty of was loving her Mancombra half brother the same as he did Hammer. Tears blurring his vision, he tried to shake off the horrible memory of blood spurting from her eye when the bullet obliterated it, but couldn't.

✝

Hammer wondered if Arigot planned to make a career out of that bath. He'd been at it almost an hour. Then a chuckle escaped him as he recalled his disappointment in learning the inn only had shower stalls. If he had the chance to soak his limbs in a tub full of sudsy warm water instead of having to use the camp shower, he'd be reluctant to leave it too.

Voola turning up alive had been so amazingly wonderful Hammer had thought he'd never live to see such a joyous moment again. But now Prince Zane had not only spared his half brother's life, he didn't even have to fret about Arigot being a prisoner of war. It just couldn't get any better than this.

Until he finally latched onto some essence of valley fern that is.

TWENTY FIVE

TUNING OUT THE WHINE OF the whirly's engines, PC gazed at the distant peak of Mount Opian, its rocky apex kissing the sky like an artist's painted rendering. Within it lay the only hope for a handful of survivors if Gram succeeded in using Nanzar's super weapon. He'd had Hammer and Voola flown to the Army Command Center earlier. From there they'd be driven to the colonel's camp. Sergeant Brush wouldn't be arriving for several hours, having been ordered to drive the colonel's wheeler back.

Still under the influence of Clodec, Arigot sat next to him, wearing his new uniform. They were heading for University City. After the eighteen minute flight from the palace, they'd be chauffeured by Free to the observatory.

PC wished he could chat with Ivan Goralov. He found the scientist very intriguing, hearing him explain how to activate the transmitter placed on Anger so long ago Goralov hadn't been aware it would eventually be given an Earth name.

✝

Hammer got out of the wheeler, told the Urth corporal who'd driven them to help himself to the mess tent, and assisted Voola as she dismounted the vehicle. Seeing Captain Wurz at the excavation site, he headed straight for him.

"We've been ordered to reverse directions, Captain. Have those machine operators cover the wall back up . . . ."

"No, Private Ling, you may not leave class early today." Polka stood with hands on hips, frowning at the yellow Urth. She'd been far too lax and some of her students had begun taking advantage of her good nature. For nearly five minutes Pliers had been unable to break through and verbally tell her what Ling had memorized that morning. Praising the Urth for starting to get the hang of the technique had prompted his request for early dismissal as a reward. Though careful not to show it, Polka was very excited. Until Ling's accomplishment, no one had been able to resist the Mancombra's probe for longer than thirty seconds.

She called a corporal to the front of the class. The white Urth took the chair and Pliers stepped to him. Before long the sergeant major vocalized everything he'd memorized during the morning session. The next three soldiers faired no better.

Polka heaved a sigh. "All right, class is dismissed. I'll see you boneheads in the morning."

Harv had invited her over for dinner again. Pliers would be supping alone tonight because he'd gotten permission from Captain Morris for her to be relieved of a bodyguard during the visit. The sergeant major would escort her to Harv's apartment and be called back when she was ready leave.

The lights of camp illuminated most of the path to the steam cave but grew dim near the entrance. Seeing bushes move in the vicinity of the opening, Drill raised his weapon. Colonel Hammer had informed him that although Prince Zane no longer worried about any aliens coming out of the stronghold, word had spread too far about the wall found inside Mount Opian to chance Gram's forces not hearing about it. His duty now was to be on the lookout for enemy spies posing as vacationers.

He'd started to tell his fellow guard to cover him while he went to investigate but a hopper emerged from the thick brush—long ears standing at alert, nose bobbing for hostile scents, pink eyes warily surveying the area. Being dinnertime he wished he had the plump furry animal roasting on a spit. He hated having to eat a meal late because of guard duty: not only the wait, but the taste of food left in warming vats too long.

Harv chuckled inside while watching Polka savor another mouthful of Molly's scrumptious filet of prime sern. The old scientist had such a robust appetite he wondered how she stayed so skinny. "The percentage of Mancombra embryos you succeeded in producing was pretty high as I recall."

"Mm hmm," she hummed before swallowing. "Eighty percent of the eggs taken from Mancombras borne by Urth mothers achieved conception when injected with healthy sperm from their brothers."

"And none of them self aborted, right?"

"Right. Molly, you're a marvelous cook. This meat is just wonderful."

He sliced off a wedge of his and followed it with a bite of baked starch-root, which he washed down with dinner ale. "I don't suppose you have any way of knowing what other strange occurrences might have developed besides them all having dominant Urth genes, do you?"

"What do you mean?"

"Whether they'd have abilities other Mancombras don't."

She shook her head. "There was no way to tell. Telekinesis and telepathy aren't revealed in genes. No one knows why Combrians have those capabilities while Urths don't. Just as we don't know why Mancombras, who inherit both from a Combrian parent, have much stronger powers of telekinesis yet virtually the same telepathic range."

He'd been ceaselessly pondering PC's statement about having hidden talents. The look on his face revealed they were very special, whatever those gifts were. "What do you suppose the odds are that some people we'd all swear are pure Urth are really the offspring of Mancombra siblings with Urth mothers?"

Frowning, Polka put her utensils down and crossed her arms beneath her tiny breasts. "Why are you so curious about that, Harv?"

"Because he's really a Mancombra and scared to death someone will find out," Molly butted in with a nervous laugh.

Polka cackled. "Well how strange, so am I."

Molly giggled and turned up her ale.

"Now tell me the real reason, Harv . . ." Polka went back to work on her filet.

"Oh can't we talk about something else?" urged Molly, edgily. "Sperm and embryos hardly make for good dinner conversation. How are your classes going, Polka?"

"Tedious. But I have one student named Ling who's starting to come along real well. Harv, do you know someone who claims to have Mancombra parents?"

He started to lie but changed his mind. PC was going to announce it to the whole world eventually anyway, and he trusted Polka would keep his confidence. "Don't panic, Molly, but I'm going to tell her our little secret."

"Don't you dare!" she shouted, eyes almost doubling in size.

"Relax, everybody will be hearing it on the news someday—hopefully soon—because PC's going to tell it all in a planetary address when the war's over. Polka, remember us telling you about our colleagues Wheelbarrow and Needle being brother and sister?"

Polka's black face almost turned pale. "Are you telling me Prince Zane is their biological son?!"

He nodded and took a deep pull of ale. "And last night he mentioned having some hidden talents, but wouldn't say what they were. I know he wasn't referring to telekinesis or telepathy because he didn't inherit either one."

"Prince Zane is a Mancombra." Polka seemed to be in a daze, speaking to herself.

"Did you hear what I just said . . .?" he snapped his fingers in front of her nose.

"Yeah," she rejoined, gazing into space, "he has hidden talents. Maybe that's why he's such a brilliant military commander."

"Polka, please," begged Molly, looking as if she might faint, "whatever you do don't tell anybody."

"Nobody would believe me even if I did—they'd say I was crazy. Harv, are you certain of this?"

"Unequivocally. Molly helped Needle through labor. We were all completely stupefied when PC came out looking the way he did."

She put her elbows on the table and leaned into her fingertips, leathery forehead indenting behind each one. "I know he didn't inherit the Mancombra height since he's barely six feet if that, but does he have the physical strength of one?"

"No. Until last night I thought he had the same limits as any other pure Urth man like myself."

"I wonder why he won't tell you what his hidden talents are?"

"He said he can't afford for anyone to know because of his position."

When he neared the telescope PC received a clear image of Needle peering through it. Now seeing through her eyes, he beheld Jealousy and Anger in full phase while she pondered the evolution of Urths and Combrians. Undoubtedly it had been her last time in the observatory. Thankfully the vision had been a short one because he came out of it to find Arigot looking at him curiously—most likely wondering why he'd stopped in his tracks. He'd brought him along because Arigot knew how to operate the sophisticated telescope and possessed enough technical skill to hook up an apparatus Goralov had instructed Voola to take with her.

"Is something wrong, General?"

They were alone so he didn't take offense over Arigot addressing him by his old rank. Free and two other soldiers were in the lobby with the custodian, making sure no one entered the room. "Just a jolt of sentiment, that's all. Needle loved peering at the stars from here."

A painful glower of guilt and remorse clutched Arigot's face like an ancient Combrian death mask.

"Enough self reprimand for the moment, Colonel. It's time for you to do your stuff."

TWENTY

SIX

ACCORDING TO THE READINGS ON Goralov's device it would be 9 hours, 53 minutes, and 13.2 seconds before Anger rotated enough for the transmitter to reach proper alignment for activation. It then gave the coordinates needed to aim the telescope precisely. PC read them off and his new colonel made the adjustments.

"Well we have a long wait before we can turn it on, Arigot, but at least this will give Voola plenty of time to assemble the other components she left the pyramid with."

Arigot rose from the telescope and stretched his back. "This is unbelievable, PC—um Prince Zane, forgive me. How ironic that one of Gram's mistresses was chosen to receive such an incredible revelation. It will likely be the thing that does him in."

Hammer marveled at the gadgets chained together atop his desk with energy cords. Each had a small teleon screen at the top of a tiny keyboard, the letters and symbols so minute

Voola had to use the tip of a writing implement to press them.

"There," she said after manipulating the last one. "They're all turned on and waiting."

He glanced at the bulky coveralls laying across his cot, no longer hiding her figure. She'd taken them off in order to pull the mechanisms from its many inner pockets. The bodysuit she wore perfectly conformed to her beautiful curves and bulges, hiding only the magnificence of her nakedness.

Sensing him ogling her, she gave him a sad smile. *What a shame we don't have any essence of valley fern because all we can do now is wait for Anger to turn the transmitter towards us.*

Inhaling a deep breath he telepathed, *I'd kill for some, Voola, I really would.*

As would I, my love.

The military hadn't released the identity of the Mancombra executed for the four murders committed within the palace walls until that morning. Now she knew why Stove hadn't come to call as promised. When Rope got off duty she wanted only two things: to get drunk and laid. Inebriation would ease the pain of learning Stove had used her and betrayed his own race. Sex, she merely craved. She donned her military uniform and drove to the officer's club located at the Royal Army Base near the palace. The place appeared packed with only Urths and Combrians, whose penises weren't large enough to satisfy her, but after getting served at the bar she spotted a Mancombra with double bars on his collar, sitting alone with a bottle of ale. The same brand she'd chosen.

"May I join you?" she asked while undressing him with her eyes.

He looked up with a smile. "Sure, have a seat, Lieutenant."

"Thank you, Captain. I'm Rope."

"Pick . . ." he extended a hand.

She shook it and sat down. "Pleased to meet you, Pick. Did you have the displeasure as I did of knowing Corporal Stove, the one who killed four of us?"

His dark lips turned down with a mournful scowl. "No, I didn't know him, but I heard he'd told the victims a long time before he killed them that we all needed to unify and take the planet for ourselves. Talk about having a screw loose."

Hearing him say *screw* made her want him all the more. "Um, I wonder if you'd be interested in going back to my place. I hate crowds."

At first she feared rejection because he looked offended at her directness, but then a wanton smile slowly spread across his eye-catching face.

"You don't believe in wasting time, do you, Lieutenant."

"Mm mm."

"Where are you quartered?"

"At the palace in the medical apartment complex. I'm a nurse."

"I've had enough of the military for one day so let's make it my place. I have a cottage by the lake."

She accepted his arm and he took her to his wheeler.

When they got to his house some Combrians were tending to a power pole, something she'd never seen done at night. The captain frowned while peering at them and said, "Something's not right about this."

While nervously transmitting her agreement, she saw

several males jump out of the back of the utility truck. Before she could blink Pick's windshield exploded with machinegun fire.

Nobb scratched Pick off the death list and told an underling to read the female's military tags. He couldn't believe he'd been fortunate enough to get a bonus kill.

"Lieutenant Rope, Principal Nobb."

Scanning the page he located the name and scrawled a line through it. He'd have to slay all the civilian half-breeds to make it to enforcer, but Universal Quest had promised him a step up in rank towards that end for each military Mancombra he bagged. Pick's demise would have put him at chief but the bonus death meant he'd be awarded the insignias of lieutenant enforcer even if he accomplished nothing else.

Drill recognized the Mancombra pulling up to the guard station. "Good to see you again, Sergeant Brush."

Purple eyes scanning his sleeve, the sergeant grinned. "Well look at you, Drill, you made Special Forces."

Corporal Sills walked up with a sniper at his side. "You're relieved, Private. Go fetch yourself some victuals and get some sack time."

"Thank you, Sir."

"Let me park Colonel Hammer's wheeler," said Brush, "and I'll join you in the mess tent. I'm famished after that long drive from the palace."

Dinnertime having passed four hours ago, Drill related very well with the sergeant. He went to the quarters he shared with three other privates, deposited his rifle, and made for the mess tent.

Voola spotted him and waved him over, wearing a big smile. She sat at the end of a table with Colonel Hammer to her left. Both were having kaffy rather than dining.

It had warmed his insides that she'd been so proud to see him in a uniform last night. Taking the chair beside the colonel, he quickly started in on the main course. "You know, I used to really love ground sern with gravy over toasted grain squares, but now I know why the Urths call it shit on a shingle."

"Don't talk with your mouth full, Drill," Voola chastised, an acerbic scowl broadcasting her disgust. "It's ill-mannered and gross."

"Sorry," he said before swallowing, which caused her to wince again. He glanced at the chow station and saw Sergeant Brush heading his way with a loaded tray.

The Mancombra seated himself across from Hammer. "Your wheeler needs the steering adjusted, Colonel. It's pulling to the right."

"Yeah, it started doing that not long after we left camp last night."

The field communicator on Brush's hip buzzed. He pulled it to the side of his head. "Sergeant Brush here . . . Oh no! When? . . . So sorry to hear that, Captain Morris . . . Yes, I'll pass it on, Sir."

"What was that all about?" asked Hammer as the sergeant lowered the device.

Brush contorted his lips is if he'd just taken a bite of spoiled meat. "Two Mancombras were gunned down— Captain Pick and Lieutenant Rope, a female. Gram didn't waste much time replacing Arigot's unit."

"Dammit it to blazes . . .!" Hammer grabbed his forehead, stretching the skin so taut his naturally arching eyebrows formed a straight line. "How many of us does that leave now?"

The sergeant gazed at his food as if feeling guilty for being hungry at such a time. "After Professor Wheelbarrow's death there were thirteen civilians who hadn't come to the palace, including Drill who finally did. Then he got drafted, dropping that number to twelve. Assuming Professor Needle's dead and the eleven other civilians are still alive, we numbered one hundred thirty-three after that imbecile Stove's execution—a hundred and two males, thirty-one females. So the murders of Captain Pick and Lieutenant Rope make it one-oh-one and thirty. Only a hundred and thirty-one Mancombras left on the whole planet."

"How dreadful . . ." Voola closed her eyes.

Drill had to ward off images of the death camp.

"I wonder why the eleven haven't come to the palace?"

"Probably pacifists like Drill," Hammer answered Voola.

"That can't be the reason," Brush enlightened. "They wouldn't know they were expected to enlist until after they got there."

"That's right," said Drill. "Prince Zane is a crafty Urth. I wouldn't have known beforehand if I hadn't been taken to the palace by soldiers. Speaking of that, how are you going to get back there, Sergeant Brush?"

"I'm not, at least for awhile. Prince Zane has me stationed here until further notice."

"I bet we can squeeze one more cot in the tent I'm staying in, Sir."

Hammer discharged a humorless laugh. "Brush is a member of Prince Zane's personal staff, Drill. He'll be staying in the VIP tent."

A newscast reported two military Mancombras had been found shot to death near Palace Lake, a male captain and female lieutenant. Shoehorn smiled at his eleven comrades. There were two less half-breeds standing in their way. They'd come to this uncharted island two double-years before Gram issued the Genocide Directive, spending the entire time preparing for the very thing the king feared: planetary control.

He didn't share the telepathic and telekinetic skills of his fellow Mancombras, nor their appearance. But he was their leader nonetheless. His mother had chosen a half-breed name for him before birth, having no idea he would look like a purebred Urth. To avoid a death sentence for appearing to defy the adoption prohibition, she'd been forced to tell the authorities she'd happened upon an infant Urth who'd apparently been abandoned. He'd been raised in an orphanage and the Urth woman who ran the institution had given him the name Daniel Smith. When he became a free adult she'd been legally bound to reveal the identity of the person who'd brought him there. He'd gone to see the female Mancombra and learned the truth.

She'd planned to call him Shoehorn and he'd gone by that name since coming to the island. A Combrian father's abuse and drunken Urth mother's selfish indifference had turned her older brothers viciously mean, while completely demoralizing her. After being raped by her eldest sibling, she'd found herself with child and he was born ten months later.

A strong believer in fate, Shoehorn hadn't been surprised to learn what the Combrians who'd landed on the island were up to. The scientists and soldiers thought it was uninhabited, having no idea a dozen Mancombras called it home. They hadn't been able to see him as he'd watched them come ashore from the comfort of his subterranean home. Luckily they'd set up camp near one of the many hidden monitoring devices strategically placed all around the island to alert him of intruders. Hearing instructions being given to a crew of builders, he'd learned they'd come here to test an atomic bomb.

Quartered in a deep cavern converted into a luxurious haven, he and his cohorts would wait underground until the scientists assembled the bomb. Then they'd wipe them out before it got annihilated in a test.

There'd be no way of knowing if the weapon worked, but Gram wouldn't have the capability of building another once they eliminated Nanzar. Only one other genius on the planet currently understood the concepts necessary for nuclear fission: Harv Zane, whom many thought Nanzar plagiarized. Harv had been head of the mathematics department at Combria University when Shoehorn received his doctorate in psychiatry there, and he well knew the benevolent professor thought such a weapon should never be built.

A very lucrative position at a renowned asylum, coupled with some creative bookkeeping, had enabled him to retire early and concentrate on fulfilling his secret ambition of ruling Combria.

Now it was only a mater of time.

Unlike most psychiatrists, Urth or Combrian, he'd allowed Mancombras to join his staff. Of the fifteen who'd worked for him, only four resisted recruitment, and had been promptly disposed of. Each death had been legally deemed an unfortunate accident, a hazard all who worked with the criminally insane knowingly risked.

Having no doubt Gram would eventually try to rid the planet of all half-breeds, Shoehorn had gathered his eleven and sailed to the island, hoping the king would succeed because only an organized band of Mancombras could thwart his plans. Unfortunately Gram had been usurped by PC Zane, Harv's adopted son, who championed the cause of the downtrodden race. Though Gram obviously hadn't given up his quest to kill them all, having to do it in secret had slowed the death toll down to a miserable crawl. Shoehorn had planned to wait until the only Mancombras on Combria were those on his island before initiating the planetary takeover, but now he'd have to finish what Pillhigh started if the fool took much longer.

TWENTY
SEVEN

THE APPARATUS BEGAN TO BEEP, warning a sixty-second countdown had just commenced. Finger on the blinking button per Goralov's instructions, PC watched the glowing digits decrease until the numerical light read zero. He pressed it, saw the screen flash ACTIVATED, and turned to Arigot—standing beside the telescope. "Let's hope it still works after all this time."

Voola frowned at the small monitors arranged on Hammer's desk. Eight long minutes had passed since the start time Prince Zane had given ten hours earlier by field communicator, and six of those eight had rolled by after he'd called again from the observatory to say the device indicated successful activation. The screens should have been filled with data coming from Anger, but instead they all read: WAITING FOR RECEPTION.

"This is horrible, Hammer—the transmitter must be broken."

Despite understanding the necessity for both, Harv hated being escorted to the university by guards almost as much as he detested the military presence on campus. He also didn't like having to get up so early to make the ninety minute drive from the palace to University City. Welcoming the solitude of his office, he went to his desk and immediately dove into a long equation, savoring a temporary escape from the tangled mess of the real world into the beautiful precision of quantum physics.

His mental paradise collapsed when the door opened. He looked up to see PC walk in with a worried look on his face and an odd contraption in his hand. "What's that you're carrying, son?"

He handed it to him. "A lot has happened since we last talked, Harv, but before we get into all that, can you tell me if this thing is malfunctioning?"

Harv examined the rectangular box. It looked quite futuristic with its tiny teleon screen and a large glass button amidst solid minute ones. Electrical terminals on either side indicated it wasn't battery operated. "I've never seen anything like this, PC."

"No, you wouldn't have," he answered with a sad smile. "It came from a planet called Earth, spelled E-A-R-T-H . . . ."

Major Pick being the only half-breed soldier that didn't

live in army housing had made him an easy choice. If he hadn't lucked out, Lieutenant Rope would have remained beyond his reach. Nobb would love to bag another military Mancombra but any further attempts would be suicidal, so he'd begun looking for the civilians who hadn't gone to the palace. Gram's spies hadn't managed to infiltrate the palace but one of them at the university had provided excellent intel. Nobb had been given the names and resumes of all eleven.

Going through the reports he'd picked up at a location pointed out by the anonymous spy, he noticed an odd singularity: at one time or another each of them had worked at the same mental asylum during the administration of a Dr. Daniel Smith, now retired, whereabouts unknown.

A few miles outside University City, perched atop a steep hill, stood a massive edifice surrounded by high concrete walls to keep inmates from escaping. The maximum security institution housed the criminally insane. Nobb produced his bogus credentials as an energy inspector, and the guards let the power company wheeler through the gates.

According to the university spy, none of the half-breeds who'd worked here still lived at the addresses recorded on their employment files. Shovel was the name of the last Mancombra to leave.

After viewing his fake license, the Combrian working the reception desk called for an orderly to take him to the maintenance room.

A male Urth soon appeared and said, "Follow me."

Nobb pretended to make small talk while checking the voltage meters. "Worked here long?"

"Longer than I like to admit."

"A Mancombra friend of mine used to work here back when Daniel Smith ran this place."

The Urth smiled. "Oh yeah, who?"

"A male named Shovel."

"Yeah, I remember Shovel. He was Smith's chief assistant until the doctor retired."

"Haven't seen him since forever," lied Nobb. "Have any idea where he lives these days?"

"Last I heard he decided to give up modern life and joined a tribe of Wanderers on the Greater Opian Range."

He jotted down the readings of the power input panel and turned to the orderly. "Well, that does it. I don't suppose you were around when my buddy Handle was here were you?"

"Handle? No, he must have left before I started—never heard of him."

"I wonder if some of your coworkers might know him."

"Not likely. I'm the longest tenured employee here."

Handle was the last Mancombra to resign before Shovel, so inquiring about the others would be pointless. His hope of making enforcer had taken a severe blow. The eleven half-breeds could be anywhere on the planet.

Shoehorn sat at the monitors watching soldiers construct a tower to place the bomb on. Once they got the device in place the whole crew would board ship and sail a safe distance to activate it by remote control.

So they thought.

Dr. Nanzar's dictations were so explicit and redundant, Shoehorn didn't have to worry about piecing together the meaning of any ambiguous remarks. If one of his Mancombras had read the scientist's mind and relayed the information to him, Nanzar's intentions couldn't have been any clearer.

The device hadn't been assembled by screws or rivets—the top and bottom sections snapped together, Harv finally figured out. The capacitors, diodes, and resistors weren't all that different from their Combrian counterparts, though built on a much smaller scale. The layout of the circuit board was similar as well. But several tiny crystals soldered into the board completely baffled him. He had no idea what they were. Pointing at one of them with a test meter lead he said, "There appears to be a short right here, PC, but I don't know that it's not supposed to be blocking current because of that crystal. It might act as a power gate, an on-and-off switch if you will. That's the only flaw I can find in the circuitry."

PC leaned over the desk and peered down at it. "Can you bypass it?"

"Well yeah," he snickered out. "But not having a clue what that thing is, I can't tell you what will happen. It's liable to burn out the board for all I know. Arigot didn't get the wires crossed when he hooked up the power did he?"

"No, I watched him do it. Ivan Goralov said the red terminal was positive and the white one was negative. The screen even showed an image of him pointing to them while he said it so there'd be no confusion. Before he attached them, Arigot checked the polarity of both wires twice just to be safe."

"Maybe the voltage was wrong."

PC shook his head and stood upright. "Goralov said it

didn't matter what voltage was hooked up to it because an internal transformer would automatically adjust it to the correct current needed. The only caution he gave was not to use a source stronger than what a household appliance required."

"Hmm . . ." Harv pursed his lips while rubbing his chin. "Well since you said it appeared to work correctly, my guess is the transmitter's malfunctioning. Maybe a meteor hit it."

"It's buried far beneath the surface for that very reason. Goralov said it's designed to read our planet and transmit the data through numerous sensors on the surface though, so maybe all of them got banged up."

Still pinching himself over all he'd been told, Harv rose from his desk and blew out a worried sigh. "Galaxies I hope not. If that device can really show you where Gram's hiding, not being able to use it will be the biggest tragedy since the Genocide Directive."

To be certain she'd followed them correctly, Voola painstakingly went over the instructions Ivan Goralov had given her. Exhausted, she gave up for the night and crawled into Hammer's cot, as her tent was now being used by Drill and the other three snipers. Hammer had turned in hours ago, bunking with Sergeant Brush in the VIP tent.

She'd rehearsed each step in the assembly again and was cursing under her breath. There'd definitely been no error on her part. Eyeing the battery of monitors once more before turning off the bed lamp, she thought back on the doctor's explanation of why she'd been brought inside the pyramid.

"At the bottom of this conical structure lies a spacecraft," he'd said. "Two deactivated robots are sitting at the controls. They've been programmed to fly the ship to Earth unless a continuous signal from there has quit reaching the pyramid. If that signal has stopped, it means Earth's no longer inhabitable, and you'll be taken to a planet so far from Combria the journey will take centuries. Don't worry, the pilot robots don't have the specialized artificial intelligence processors installed in the teachers of Operation Noah's Ark, so they can't become self aware. At present we lack the technology to travel the speed of light, and all indications are such a feat is impossible for anything corporeal. The craft within the pyramid is equipped to fly a third that velocity, the fastest speed attainable to date. Rockets will propel the ship through the Combrian stratosphere and then it'll be powered by an endless supply of cosmic radiation, continually reenergizing its solar engines. It can carry up to seventy passengers but only has fifty suspended animation chambers.

"The ship must be used only in the event of global nuclear war because there's every possibility as you're viewing this that life on Earth no longer exists. And although we think the other planet can support humanoid life, we aren't one hundred percent certain. You've been chosen to prevent the necessity of the spacecraft ever being boarded. For several days you'll remain here, receiving special instructions and learning how to use equipment you'll be provided when Charley escorts you back outside the mountain. You won't be permitted to leave until you pass an exam I'll be giving you at the conclusion of your special education. Should you fail, Charley will recall the videos of the particular areas you didn't grasp initially, and this will be repeated until you completely understand them. He'll remain in the room above you until it's time for your comprehension to be tested.

"When you leave the pyramid, Charley will hand you what appears to be a marble. Guard it with your life. Should nuclear war breakout or some other catastrophe threatens to destroy the planet, go to the boulder you'll see lowering after your exit, and press the marble against it with your palm until the artificial stone sucks it from your hand. It will then rise to give you access to the pyramid. You can only do this once so be certain it's your last alternative. When the boulder rises you'll see Charley waiting to take you to the ship where the pilot robots will have been activated along with a device that will blow a hole through the mountain for the vessel to fly through. Choose your fellow passengers wisely because you'll be stuck with them for the rest of your life if the ship doesn't take you back to Earth. In the hope of spawning future generations, make sure to include humans and Combrians of both sexes. Once you're aboard the craft I'll appear on one of the monitors and instruct you on how to use the suspended animation chambers. Now we'll begin your first session.

"The root cause of war is one faction trying to impose its will on another, usually because it wants something the other has. You're about to learn of a technology that can abundantly provide every necessity for all the inhabitants of your planet. In the right hands it can guarantee a high standard of living for all. In the wrong hands, it can be a tyrannical weapon. By passing the character assessment of the test you were given in the floor above, I know you don't have the traits of a tyrant. And the intelligence portion of the exam assures me you're smart enough not to divulge the technology to anyone who'd be tempted to abuse it. Whatever governing body you're under, seek out the highest member you trust won't be corrupted by it, and share all you're about to learn."

Tears filled her eyes. Prince Zane was perfect for the job but the damn transmitter wouldn't transmit.

TWENTY

EIGHT

"THAT FOURTH STAR LOOKS GOOD on you, Sir." Vern Yonker had been a lieutenant general when he'd last seen him before PC ignited the revolution.

The salty Urth cracked a smile. "Does, doesn't it. Those hunter fowls look damn odd on you, Enforcer."

Arigot laughed. "Respectfully, General, I'm a colonel now."

"So I've been informed. All right, Colonel Arigot, what brings you to me?"

"Prince Zane's orders. I've been debriefed about my knowledge of the universals' tactics after Gram fled the palace, and since he no longer needs me to hook up the device and aim the telescope, I'm at your disposal."

"So the damn thing won't work, huh?"

"No, unfortunately. He took the gadget to his father, hoping he can figure out if it's broken. Our only hope is that the problem lies with it and not the transmitter for obvious reasons."

A big sigh escaped Vern. "I still can't believe my ancestors really came from another planet. If anyone but PC had told me I'd have strongly advised them to have their head examined. Who else knows about this?"

"Voola—the Combrian who was taken inside the mountain—Lieutenant Free, Sergeant Brush, Hammer,

Captain Wurz, and the Mancombra sniper Drill you sent to Mount Opian. The rest of Hammer's command have no idea what's inside the stronghold."

"Have a seat." Vern pushed a button on his desk and said, "Haul in two cups of kaffy, Sergeant."

He chose a chair facing the general.

"Where do you think the slime ball is hiding, Arigot?"

"Gram? Not a clue except I know it's nowhere in Serene Valley because that was the lie Quest ordered me to tell my troops."

An Urth sergeant came in and handed Vern a steaming cup before presenting him one. Arigot blew across the hot surface and took a sip. "Mmm, this sure isn't military issue."

"Perks of the rank," Vern quipped with a grin. "I'm glad you came to your senses—if only the rest of the Combrian Forces would. Gram's a damn hypnotist, isn't he? I've never seen anybody with such powers of persuasion. When he made that speech announcing the Genocide Directive he almost convinced *me* it was necessary in order to protect Combria."

Painfully recalling how that infamous planetary address affected him, Arigot glumly replied: "I wish I could say *almost*, Sir. Unfortunately I bought into it heart and soul, despite my half brother being a Mancombra."

"Tragic," said Vern, raising his cup, "but at least you changed your mind. Why did you, pray tell?"

Soul-crippling guilt wrenched his entrails as a hideously vivid image of Needle's bruised face and broken nose—both afflictions cruelly administered by him—tortured his mind. "Witnessing Gram's insanity first hand made me realize I'd been acting like a trained animal. I'll never forgive myself . . . never."

"A soldier can't afford a conscience," Vern reprimanded. "You're under my command now, Arigot, and my first order for you is to clear yours and keep your mind on your duty for the cause. Got any idea who replaced your unit after Barrabon and the rest of your troops were captured?"

"Principal Nobb begged for the duty before Quest ordered me to do it. My guess is I was replaced by him. He's very resourceful but has a major flaw, his—"

"Yeah I remember Nobb. You're talking about that over inflated ego of his."

"Yes, Sir, he's blinded by ambition. Quest knows that too of course, so I'm wagering he offered to promote him if he can fulfill the Genocide Directive on the civilians that didn't go to the palace."

"I'm puzzled none of them have. Wonder if they're still alive."

Relieved their blood didn't tip the scales of justice against him, Arigot shrugged his shoulders. "If they're not, it wasn't my doing."

Chisel brought the indefatigable brain trust a glass of malk and a plate of sour-berry tarts. "You've been sitting in front of those monitors for six hours straight. Enjoy a snack and let me take over for awhile."

Shoehorn stretched his arms and rose from the chair. "Believe I'll take you up on that offer, Chisel. I'm about to go cross-eyed."

Handing his leader the refreshments, Chisel reflected on the amazement he'd felt that day at the asylum upon discovering Daniel Smith wasn't lying. Probing the doctor's mind, he'd discerned a Mancombra really had given birth to him and planned to call him Shoehorn until he came out looking like an Urth instead of a half-breed. But a greater shock followed when his employer explained the reason for confiding the secret. Ruling the planet had never entered his mind before that, and Chisel knew it wouldn't have done so in even the remotest abstract terms if Dr. Smith hadn't chosen to share his vision with him.

Now nothing else mattered.

PC stood with arms folded, gazing at Anger, dangling like a fractured red jewel in the night sky, oblivious to the fact astronauts from a planet called Earth had equipped it with a means to locate every valuable commodity and undesirable inhabitant on Combria. No longer in full phase, it appeared to have lost three quarters of its mass, as did Jealousy.

After examining Goralov's device, Harv had begged to know what his special talents were. "I'm not going to tell you," he'd resolutely affirmed, "and I'd appreciate you not asking again. You haven't told Molly have you?"

The answer had enraged him: not only had Harv told Molly, he'd also betrayed the secret—along with the truth about his heritage—to his old colleague Polka.

Harv's intellectual brilliance sometimes muddled his common sense. Upon hearing the reasons for telling Polka, and being assured she'd keep the secret, he'd transferred his anger to himself, where it squarely belonged. He never should have mentioned his intention to announce his true race to the populace. If he hadn't, Harv wouldn't have told Polka about his pedigree.

But that didn't matter at the moment. For three days he'd been agonizing over whether or not to have Harv bypass the crystal and reattach the gadget to the telescope. He had to make the toughest decision of his life. If it worked, he'd be able to capture Gram and Nanzar, bringing total peace to the planet, along with incredible prosperity. If it burned out the circuit board, Nanzar might well succeed in perfecting the super weapon, and that would sound Combria's death knell.

Not long after discovering events sometimes reoccurred for him, he'd started having peculiar dreams about being in two places at the same time. One night he awoke in the middle of one to find himself sitting on the flusher, yet still lying in his bed. Each location appeared as tangible as the other. On instinct he'd simultaneously turned on the hand-washing tap in the flusher room and tossed his pillow on the floor of his sleep chamber. Then he'd gone to the hall from both locations but neither self could see the other. He'd walked back to his bed in two bodies. When he'd woken up in only one, the pillow lay on the floor and Molly warned him not to leave the water running when he had to use the flusher at night.

Like viewing the past, he had no control over becoming two people: it commenced and halted of its own volition, and started happening while he was fully conscious when he neared adulthood. He'd soon discovered that whatever locality he suddenly found himself in, no one could see or hear his second persona. Able to function normally from both bodies during the phenomenon, he'd never had to worry about anyone finding out. Most times it lasted only a few minutes, but occasionally continued longer. Once he'd been in his palace office conversing with Free while his emerged self wandered around Fort Pacific for almost an hour with no one at the army base aware of his presence. That had been the lengthiest duration to date.

It was happening again now. While standing on a balcony eyeing the red moon, his other self had manifested in a palace apartment whose residents, Polka and CSM Pliers, were asleep. There appeared to be no reason for the surroundings he'd find himself in during the occurrences, but he kept hoping to appear in Gram's current hideout so he could blow the insane tyrant away. He always wore his gun belt for just such an event, even when sleeping.

During the lengthy manifestation at Fort Pacific, he'd experimented. A Combrian sergeant was entertaining an Urth private by juggling balls through telekinesis. PC poked the back of the private's neck with his index finger. The skin sank in but the private couldn't feel it. Then he injected the Combrian with a Clodec hypo. The sergeant had been unaware of the action, but frowned with bewilderment when the balls suddenly fell to the ground. Since the drug had been effective, a bullet fired from his pistol would have similar results.

Polka's parlor faded from view and he was no longer two people. PC wished he could meet another Mancombra like him so he could verify whether his three unique talents were inherited, or divinely bestowed. While they might be merely an element of his genetic makeup, he suspected they were a gift from The Spirit That Created All Things—especially the third one, because it entailed a radical transformation of his body and whatever he happened to be wearing or holding at the time. He could utilize that ability at will, but fearing the omniscient deity might take it away if employed frivolously, he summoned the incredible endowment only when absolutely necessary. Unfortunately Gram always had armed guards nearby, which prevented him from using the power against him before he'd escaped. To do so would have been suicidal, and cast the revolution into chaos. Once the mad dictator went underground he'd lost that option, and would regain it only when Gram was no longer incommunicado.

✝

Pliers focused with all her mental might but couldn't fathom anything except the private's vocalized answers to her questions. "His thoughts aren't coherent, Ma'am. Private Ling has successfully blocked me out."

"Are you absolutely certain?"

"Yes, Ma'am. I've been giving it my all for the last fifteen minutes."

"Congratulations, Ling!" Polka clapped her hands and motioned for everyone else to do likewise. "You got the hang of it in half the time it took me to learn the technique. This time I *am* going to reward you. Class, you have the private to thank for early dismissal today."

The applause grew louder.

Polka seemed to float to the adjoining room where they kept kaffy and snacks. Pliers smiled with happiness for her charge's success. As the soldiers filed out she noticed a handsome Mancombra standing in the hall. A patch on his sleeve marked him as a member of Special Forces which meant he was either a sniper, demolition expert, or aqua commando. She stepped to the door, noticing a rifle in the center of his PFC insignia, denoting him a sharpshooter. "Something I can do for you, Private?"

"I'm looking for Polka."

She gripped the handles of her pistols—one fired Clodec darts, the other bullets—giving him a firm look of warning in the process. He might have gotten past the guards because of his race, but after Stove she wasn't taking any chances, and he was blocking her probe. "Who are you and what business do you have with the lieutenant?"

"Drill!" shouted Polka from behind her.

She turned to see her charge hastily place a cup of kaffy on one of the school desks and run to him.

He entered the room and scooped her up in his arms. "Polka, it's so great to finally see you again!"

"Oh, you too, you too! Now put me down before you crack my ribs. When did you join the army?"

A timid smile, hinting of embarrassment, crossed his face while lowering Polka to her feet. Pliers found the look boyish and engaging.

"Prince Zane drafted me and I wound up a sniper."

"I was so happy when I heard you were alive, but then I wanted to cut your head off after Captain Morris said you'd told Colonel Hammer about my mate's mind blocking technique. Now I can't thank you enough. Look at us, will ya? Both in the army now. Are you stationed here?"

"No, Mount Opian. My colonel gave me a three day pass because I hadn't gotten a single break since being forced into the military. I'd made it to the palace before I got drafted, and learned you were here from Captain Morris. I was despised for not joining the army so I didn't seek you out for fear it might tarnish your status. Since I'm no longer stigmatized I hitched a ride on a whirly just to come see you. Very strange how things turned out, isn't it?"

"Sure is," Polka replied while pointing at her. "Drill, this is my bodyguard, assistant instructor, and personal friend Command Sergeant Major Pliers. She's heard all about you."

"That I have." She extended a hand which he shook. "And all of it good, rest assured."

"I see you've been lying about me, Polka, shame on you. Very glad to make your acquaintance, Sergeant Major."

"Same here." Sensing his shield falter as he visually

examined her, she melded minds with him. Exhilaration propelled an excited smile at what she discovered. *Seldom have I been so immediately attracted to a member of the opposite sex. I'm flattered you feel the same, Drill.*

You caught me off guard, he telepathed, smiling back. *I meant to block the emotion but now I'm glad I failed to do so.*

Polka grinned and put her hands on her hips. "Well you two sure hit it off. There's enough energy in this room to light up Juxbow. Come on, Drill, I'm dying to show you my apartment. You'll be our honored guest . . . ."

Adrenaline racing through him, Gram eyed Nanzar on the teleon screen. He'd just been told the bomb had been placed and the scientist was about to board ship and move a safe distance to test it. "I want to know the results immediately, do you hear?"

"Yes, Sire."

Not bothering with a departing salutation, he hurried from the command center for his sleep chamber. A quick piece of ass would help calm his excitement. While trying to decide which mistress to gratify, Voola rudely sprang to his mind. Thinking about the conniving bitch threw him into a wild rage, compounding his sexual lust with the burning need for raw guttural violence. That narrowed the choice down to two aging sluts he'd been planning to replace. He'd have one strapped to the wall face-forward. While the other kneeled before her king giving him oral satisfaction, he'd flog the bound female with a barbed lash, fantasizing that every bleeding laceration was being ripped across the stealing whore's bare back. Then at the moment of climax he'd strangle the female on her knees with the whip before wrapping it around the other's throat, pretending that each satisfying death was Voola's.

Shovel, Key, and Level had taken the ship, telekinetically forcing each soldier to fire at his nearest comrade before willing their bodies overboard. His other eight Mancombras had done likewise with the troops on land, sparing only Dr. Nanzar's life. They'd brought the physicist aboard and Shoehorn forced him to contact Gram, directing him to tell the mad Combrian his treasured bomb had been a smashing success. He'd insisted the pun be used.

"I'm still shaken by the power of the explosion, My King," Nanzar answered Gram's demand to know why he was acting so nervous. "The lenses on all our monitoring equipment were destroyed—it was frightening to behold."

The eleven Mancombras stood outside camera range with rifles pointed at the fear-gripped scientist. Shoehorn had to stifle a laugh at Gram's giddy squeals of elation.

Abruptly the king signed off without a goodbye, and Nanzar turned to him. "What's to become of me?"

Shoehorn folded his arms across his chest. "I had intended to kill you but have changed my mind. If your weapon works we'll help you build more, but it can't be tested on our island. We're going to move it to another one and test it there. If it fails to detonate, you're dead, being of no other use to us.

"Stapler—you, Handle, Doorknob, and Hoe dismantle the tower and bring it aboard, along with the bomb of course. Doctor, through eavesdropping on you and your colleagues discussing the bomb, I'm of the opinion you think this is merely a first step to an even more powerful weapon."

Nanzar glanced about, eyes wide with fear.

"Explain it to me," Shoehorn demanded.

"W-What we constructed is a . . . fission bomb."

"Yes, go on."

"Its, its purpose is to split r-radioactive isotopes of heavy el-elements into smaller atoms. If successful the explosive energy released will be as-astronomically greater than the most p-powerful bomb ever built. It would level every building and annihilate every resident of Juxbow."

"Marvelous. Now tell me more." Several seconds went by with Nanzar fidgeting, fearfully eyeing the Mancombras aboard. "You're trying my patience, Doctor. Start talking."

"If, if you were to take two atoms of the lightest element and, and fuse them together to create one atom of the second lightest element . . . the uh, the explosive force would be at least ten megatons greater than, than the bomb you're about to test."

"My galaxies!" Shoehorn ejaculated, salivating at the possibility of having such power at his disposal. "Sounds like it wouldn't take many of those to blow Combria to smithereens."

The scientist ran a hand over his face and cleared his throat. "They wouldn't incinerate the planet itself, but if they were ever used in a global war Combria would be incapable of supporting life as we know it for ages."

If the completed device worked he'd get Nanzar started on developing a fusion bomb immediately after building another fission weapon to replace the one destroyed in the test. "What is Gram expecting you to do next?"

"Go back to my factory laboratory and start building more weapons."

"And where is this factory of yours?"

"Hidden beneath on office building in Juxbow."

"Hmm . . ." he contemplatively tapped his chin with his right index finger. "Tell me what you need to replicate it. We've got a huge underground warehouse in a cavern on the island. If your bomb works, we'll build more there."

Nanzar inhaled an anxious breath. "That won't do. I need a technical team to help me. You killed my whole staff."

"I chose my fellow revolutionaries carefully, Doctor. They'll have your tower up on the other island in time to really test the bomb today. If it works, you'll be instructing them on how to build another. They grasp new concepts very quickly if correctly taught. If you can't do that you're of no use to me. So can you teach them or not?"

Wiping sweat off his forehead, Nanzar claimed he could.

"I'll soon know if you're bluffing so I wouldn't advise it. Can you really teach them what they need to know?"

"Yes, but only if they're as bright as you say."

Shoehorn grinned. "Oh they are, Doctor Nanzar—each of them holds a degree in psychiatry."

TWENTY NINE

TOGO'S GRANDFATHER HAD GIVEN UP modern life and resorted back to the old ways after discovering this uncharted island while serving in the Combrian Forces. Upon fulfilling his military commitment he'd convinced a tribe of Wanderers to join him and they'd come here on hand-built boats, propelled by oars. So happy were they living here, they'd made him chief when the old one died.

Staring across the waters from the shore, the wise Combrian's aged face looked solemn and fearful. "Togo, during my days on a warship I served with a crew that tested sophisticated explosive devices far at sea, but all of them were like children's fireworks compared to that one."

Forming an immense dark umbrella high in the sky only seconds after the explosion, smoke continued to rise from a neighboring isle sixty miles away, blocking out Life Giver's rays like a billowing cluster of storm clouds.

Drill thanked The Spirit That Created All Things for

bringing Piers into his life. He hadn't hoped to fall in love again after losing his sweetheart, at least not as deeply. Only the unseen deity could have arranged this incredible circumstance. "Three days wasn't nearly enough time to spend with you lovely ladies. I wish I didn't have to leave the two of you."

Polka snickered and pointed a bony finger at him. "Bunk on that, you lying night lapper. You just wish you didn't have to leave Pliers."

He bent down and kissed the old woman's cheek. "That I do, but I don't want to leave you either."

When will I see you again? transmitted the lovely sergeant major.

As soon as I get another pass.

That won't be soon enough.

The urgency in her thoughts made him sigh. *No, Pliers, it certainly won't.*

Free stepped into his office with a pale look of fear frozen on his face. "Captain Denton, skipper of the WS Battle Fish, just reported a gargantuan mushroom cloud rising to the upper reaches of the atmosphere from an archipelago in quadrant six of the Lower East Combrian Sea. He's certain it wasn't a volcanic eruption."

PC sprang to his feet, heart racing with such alarm he could feel his temples pulsating. "My galaxies, that's what Harv predicted would happen after an atomic explosion! Nanzar succeeded in perfecting the doomsday weapon. Was Denton's warship damaged?"

"No, he was forty-three nautical miles away from the blast. Vern ordered him to stay put until you were informed."

He exhaled a doleful breath and looked to the ceiling. "Nanzar has made my decision for me. We don't have any choice but to try bypassing the crystal now. Let's hope he doesn't already have a stockpile of bombs ready to use at Gram's command. Tell Vern to deploy more warships in that area and try to capture Nanzar. I'll get Harv to bypass the crystal and we'll set out for University City."

"What's wrong, Colonel?"

Hammer numbly held the field communicator at his thigh, not wanting to believe what Vern Yonker had told him. Captain Wurz's query left no doubt his reaction upon hearing it showed on his face. "Apparently Gram has perfected the bomb. Prince Zane is going to have his father bypass the crystal. If that fails, we may all be doomed. General Yonker is sending us more troops to beef up security. We can't afford for Mount Opian to fall into Gram's hands."

Vern had ordered him to lead a regiment to Mount Opian whereupon he, like the accompanying soldiers, would be under Hammer's command. Arigot knew he would have received a good razzing about it from his half brother if the circumstances weren't so dire. It appeared the mad king now had the whole planet at his mercy.

Some ancient Combrians had witnessed the construction of the pyramid but the truth became a fable as time passed after the earthlings sealed it within the mount. Arigot prayed Ivan Goralov's mission hadn't been accomplished in vain.

THIRTY

Voola paced back and forth in Hammer's tent, praying the monitors would soon show something besides WAITING FOR RECEPTION. He stood beside her, nervously toying with the field communicator, awaiting Prince Zane's call from the observatory.

The communicator buzzed and Hammer hastily brought it to the side of his head.

Gram was beside himself with elation. Nanzar still looked frightened at not being able to offer proof of the bomb's success. Little did he know the guards would have riddled him with bullets if it hadn't exploded. He'd promised the doctor a second attempt if the first one failed, but had never intended to keep his word. Nanzar's cameras might have been destroyed by the blast but proof of it had surfaced anyway. He resisted an urge to taunt the frail scientist. "The news is filled with reports of a mysterious cloud of smoke rising from the Lower East Combrian Sea. PC is lying to the press by calling it a volcano but the bastard knows exactly what it is. As soon as I hear you've got some more bombs assembled I'll cover the entire planet with the real facts of the matter and force that shit-eating usurper to his knees. Now get back to work. Contact me tomorrow at the usual time."

He switched off the teleon and hollered for his valet.

York soon appeared. "Yes, Sire?"

"Get a bitch to my sleep chamber immediately."

"Um, whom do you desire, My King?"

"I don't care, you choose."

Harv had long dreaded the possibility of an atom being split for the sole purpose of destruction. He'd published his thesis hoping to inspire research in nuclear energy to replace the need for fossil fuels which would eventually be depleted. Most of his colleagues thought Nanzar had plagiarized him, but feeling otherwise he'd denounced that as nonsense. If he or Nanzar hadn't presented their findings to the scientific community another physicist would have done so sooner or later after arriving at the same conclusions the two of them had. But it most likely would have been at least another generation before that happened. Nanzar's research being funded by Gram had left the scientist no choice but to aim it towards military ends.

Now he'd been asked to do likewise. The circuit board wasn't damaged after bypassing the crystal, but the alien device still wouldn't activate the transmitter on Anger.

PC felt their only recourse was to fight fire with fire.

Aiming his weapon, Drill yelled for the thing to stop but it kept descending the slope of Mount Opian from the direction of the steam cave. The blue-gray being had to be the robot Voola told him about, and he feared it must be malfunctioning since she had said the only way she'd ever see it again was if the world ended.

"I have to get Voola!" he shouted to his fellow guard, also drawing a bead on the approaching machine. "Don't do anything until I get back."

Drill hurried to the colonel's tent which she now occupied. He barged in uninvited as she lay sleeping. "Wake up, Voola—the robot is heading towards camp!"

"Huh?" she mumbled, squinting against the brightness of his hand-light.

"The robot is on its way to the camp, you must come quickly!"

"Charley?"

Voola closed her eyes after muttering the name, so he yanked the blanket away to fully rouse her but immediately spun around. She was naked. "I'm so sorry, Voola. Please, you must get dressed and come with me."

Hearing the quick ruffling of her body suit, he knew she'd finally become alert. A moment later she ran from the tent and he followed.

The robot was a mere twenty feet from the guard station when they got there. Its featureless face turned instantly towards Voola and the robot stopped while extending an arm, some sort of gadget resting in the palm of its hand. When she got near, it pointed at the apparatus with a finger of the other.

She grabbed it, the robot turned, and went back up the mountain. An excited smile came to Voola as she examined the object. "It's a mini-video player! Charley must have somehow known we couldn't activate the transmitter."

"What transmitter?" asked the Urth guard, complexion pasty white from seeing the robot.

Frowning at Voola, Drill raised a finger to the tip of his nose. "The information is sensitive, remember?"

Not bothering to respond, she ran back to the colonel's tent, which had become hers for the time being.

✝

Voola set down at Hammer's desk and turned the video on. Ivan Goralov's face appeared.

"We've got to stop meeting like this," he quipped with a smile. "Sorry, just a bit of levity to lift your spirits because if you're viewing this Charley had to hunt you down, and that means you've failed to activate the transmitter. If you're wondering how he managed to find you wherever you are at the moment, I'll explain. When you passed the test an indelible imprint of your essence registered in his memory chips. That's how he differentiated you from anyone else. Within his robotic mind lies a three dimensional map of the whole planet. Wherever you go a blinking light reveals your exact location. Now then, back to the transmitter.

"A complete schematic of the circuitry of the activation device will appear at the end of this video. As a safety precaution you weren't given it when leaving the pyramid so Charley could verify you were still alive and well if the transmitter wasn't activated within a certain time frame. Had you not been, Charley would have destroyed this video, returned to the pyramid, and initiated its self destruction to prevent what I'd have to assume to be your killer from using the ship. It wasn't built to preserve self-serving malevolence.

"I'll carefully explain the function of each component—how to test its functionality, and how to repair it if it's not working properly. My terminology may differ from yours but by telling you how a capacitor works for instance, anyone with a working knowledge of electronics will figure out what to replace it with because I'll give the specifics—ohms, wattages, amperes, etcetera—of each component, and painstakingly explain what I mean by ohm and so on. Alas, if the problem lies with the transmitter there's nothing I can do to assist you further. Good luck and may God be with you."

She turned the video off and ran to the VIP tent.

Hammer, we have to go back to the palace right away!

Harv blessed Ivan Goralov. The crystal he'd bypassed wasn't an on-off switch but a micro-processor, as were the others on the circuit board. It had automatically shut down to prevent being burnt out by an overload. Per Goralov's instructions he carefully removed the electronic marvel and placed it in his top desk drawer where it would remain for the next twenty-four hours, during which time it would reset and be good as new.

Smiling broadly, within and without, he called it a day—a wonderfully productive day—a day which might well go down in history as the beginning of Combria's salvation.

He dutifully cleaned the president's office before snooping through Harv Zane's drawers. An odd piece of glass caught his eye. It had tiny metal protuberances signifying it as some sort of technical gizmo. Having never seen anything like it before, he figured better safe than sorry, and pocketed it.

THIRTY

ONE

CARRYING GORALOV'S ACTIVATION DEVICE INTO his office, Harv whistled a tune while removing his jacket. He rolled up his sleeves on the way to his desk and plugged in the soldering iron. Carefully extracting the circuit board, he positioned it on a heat-resistant pad and slid the top drawer open. Panicked, he pulled it all the way out and dumped the contents on his desk . . . but still couldn't find the processor.

⚔

Arigot placed his tray on a table and sat down for breakfast. Before he'd taken his first bite Hammer came in, carrying a field communicator and wearing a frown.

Hammer had been irritable and moody over being unable to accompany Voola to the palace yesterday. He couldn't leave his post for the time being so he'd ordered Sergeant Brush to drive her to the Army Command Center to be flown there. He held out the communicator and said, "Prince Zane wants to talk to you."

Accepting it, Arigot greeted his supreme commander,

who answered:

"Do you know if Gram has any spies at Combria University?"

Slapping a hand over his eyes, Arigot groaned. In the flurry of excitement the transmitter had generated, he'd neglected to pass on that crucial information. "Forgive me, Prince Zane, for not thinking to tell you he in fact does. A spy who wouldn't reveal his name contacted me to relay Wheelbarrow's address which he said he got from a janitor who works there. I wasn't told the janitor's name but the spy said he found the address in Harv Zane's desk. There's also a female Combrian who works in the cafeteria under Gram's thumb, but I don't know her name either. Those are the only two I know about, but I've heard there are several more. I have no idea if the spy I talked to works there or not. Please accept my deepest, sincerest apology, Sir. It was a negligent oversight on my part and I feel horrible about not thinking to tell you."

He heard an angry sigh before PC said, *"I hope your oversight doesn't cause us to lose this damn war, Arigot!"*

"Prince Zane, I—"

The communicator went dead.

Wanting to throw a chair through the window, PC brusquely asked Harv to leave his own office.

"Why, son?"

"I just want to be alone for a few minutes, okay!"

"Okay!" he shouted with a bared-tooth scowl. "You don't have to bite my head off."

"Sorry, Harv. I'm just distraught over the chip missing, that's all. Please, give me a few minutes to unwind a little."

As Harv slammed the door behind him, he drew a deep breath and mentally begged the unseen power for a reenactment of the crystal being stolen.

A moment later the door opened, but it wasn't Harv that entered the office. He watched an Urth man wearing a name tag that read Duel Jones tidy up the place, then start snooping through Harv's desk drawers. The crystal caught his eye and he took it—not knowing if he should or shouldn't, just not wanting to take a chance of being reprimanded for not doing so. The vision ended without the janitor thinking anything further about the processor.

PC mumbled through gritted teeth: "Jones, you'd better be able to produce that crystal or you won't be allowed the dignity of death by firing squad like the spy in the cafeteria, most likely in custody by now."

Nobb again examined the diode he'd been given last night. He'd never seen one like it but figured that's what it had to be. Professor Beal, the spy who'd supplied him with the information on the eleven civilian Mancombras, had been given it by a janitor, also secretly on Gram's payroll. Ironically the duplicitous professor taught ethics. He'd refused to divulge his identity over the field communicator when he'd made contact to pass on the Mancombras names and tell him where to pick up the files on them—but feeling he might have stumbled onto something very important, Beal took the risk of revealing himself so King Gram would give him proper credit.

"I saw Prince Zane carrying a strange looking contraption into Harv Zane's office several days ago," the Combrian had said while handing him the diode. "I've got a hunch this came out of it."

Giving it one last look, Nobb placed it in a compartment of his tool box and shut the lid, making a mental note to pass it on to Universal Quest when next he saw his commander. Not knowing where else to look for the eleven Mancombras, he decided to head for the Greater Opian Range, hoping to find one of them in a tribe of Wanderers.

"According to the news it was merely a volcano, Doctor Nanzar," Shoehorn informed the overwrought scientist. "How unfortunate the whole of Combria doesn't know your bomb was a *smashing* success. Needn't worry though, we'll make sure you're accredited for the next explosion."

Nanzar had coughing fit. When he finally caught his breath he said, "How did you get that vertical-takeoff whirly down here?"

He grinned at the perplexed physicist. "Allow me to give you a little backdrop, Doctor. The warehouse has a sliding dome. The topsoil moves right along with it because it's really a synthetic turf that rolls up when the dome opens, and unfurls as it closes. The workers I hired to build it were promised two million tibs for the materials and their labor. I had a crooked banker handle the escrow account which guaranteed they'd be paid upon completing the job. It really didn't have any money in it, and I'm afraid they were never compensated nor were their creditors ever reimbursed. Their corpses must be mere bones by now, what with so many scavengers dwelling on the sea bottom and all. Shovel over there willed the banker to jump off the top of his multi-level office building. Actually he threw him off telekinetically, but you get the picture I'm sure. Miter took care of the architect in similar fashion. Anyway, since you brought up the whirly—tell me how to equip it to carry your bomb when it's ready."

PC had called for Voola to be brought from the palace. There were many Combrians unquestionably loyal to him who worked at the university, but he didn't want any of them knowing about the crystal. After having to lie yet again about receiving an intelligence report, two guards had brought Duel Jones to Harv's office an hour ago. It took all his resolve not to punch out the spying bastard. The Urth janitor was tied to an armless chair with his hands cuffed behind it, the sickly pastiness of his terrified face mutely testifying he knew Life Giver would rise without him tomorrow.

They were alone, just the two of them, until the pretty Combrian was brought in.

"Probe his mind, Voola . . . ."

Lecturing his students on the evils of situational ethics, Beal turned his head towards the door when it flew open. Lieutenant Free shot him in the shoulder with a Clodec dart, and Prince Zane entered the classroom.

Two hours later he was pleading for his life on a gallows in the palace dungeon, a rope cinched around his neck. Duel Jones dangled beneath it, having been hung first.

†

Pliers strolled beside her charge and Private Ling. The door sentinel saluted and granted them admittance to Captain Morris's office.

"So this is your first graduate," said the captain to Polka. "Are you sure he's ready?"

"Absolutely," she answered with a proud smile. "Neither Pliers, the Mancombra at the commissary, nor two Combrian clerks could mentally extract any information from him. He's almost reached my level, and that's quite an achievement considering it took me longer to get there. His limit is twenty minutes, after that the technique becomes too fatiguing."

"What's yours?"

"Thirty to forty."

Relax, Private, Pliers telepathed to Ling, nervously shifting from one foot to the other.

He cut his eyes to her and grinned, trying to still his happy feet.

Captain Morris looked him over. "Private Ling, you were selected for Lieutenant Polka's first class because of your aptitude, as were your fellow students. You'll be spending the next ninety days training for SIS, established surreptitiously by Prince Zane before the revolution started. Are you aware of what the initials stand for?"

"Yes, Sir. Secret Intelligence Service."

"If you pass the final exam you'll be promoted to specialist and inducted into it. It's my duty to inform you that once you're a secret agent there's no leaving the service until retirement. I'll grant you the right to back out, but only this once. What'll it be, son?"

"Captain, I'm honored to be given this opportunity and hope to qualify for enlistment into SIS."

Polka elbowed him in the ribs. "Ling, you just want to get away from me and you know it."

The private laughed. "Not true, Ma'am."

"Captain, Pliers and I are throwing a celebration party at my apartment tonight for Private Ling. All my students will be there and we'd love to have you join us."

"I wish I could but I'll be spending the evening in University City. Prince Zane caught three of Gram's spies at Combria University earlier today, and ordered me to help interrogate all the employees after office hours. I'll be lucky to hit the sack before dawn."

Releen impatiently paced back and forth in her boudoir, hating it had no windows to look out of. She always felt so romantic viewing the stars while waiting for her lover. Her revolting mate hadn't touched her since impregnating her with their youngest child four double-years ago, a neglect she felt extremely grateful for. She hated having to fake jealousy over his whores but it was essential she do so. Because Gram always kept his mind blocked, she never had to worry about him probing hers and learning his trusted valet pleasured her every night as soon as the mad king dismissed him for the day.

The door opened and in walked York. He locked it, bowed before his queen, disrobed, and approached her. She willed the sash of her royal bathrobe to loosen, and the silky fabric flew off her body. Shaking her naked breasts invitingly, savoring the hungry look on the Combrian's face, she lowered her eyes to his rigid penis.

After beating the bitch to a bloody pulp, he set fire to her hair, took a step back, and poured fuel oil all over her naked body. Voola screamed in terror and pain as she burned. Standing in his sleep chamber Gram opened his eyes while ejaculating in his concubine's mouth, completing the fantasy by pulling a hidden knife from his sleeve and slicing her throat.

Shock frozen in her purple eyes, Hanna gurgled for breath as blood spurted between her fingers reflex had forced to her severed neck—pouring down her breasts, saturating the pillow shielding her knees from the hard floor. Raising his right foot to her thorax, he kicked the slut onto her back, hearing a bone crack in the process. She'd been one of his favorites, but the complexity of the intense arousal he'd been feeling since learning the bomb worked had demanded this type of release. Mere sex with two concubines earlier just hadn't done the trick.

Free held back a laugh. His deep yawn had apparently been contagious because it triggered one from Captain Morris. They were sitting in the professors' lounge drinking kaffy. PC and his Combrian mind reader Voola were still at it. The employees, high and low, of Combria University had been divided into thirds. He'd completed his interrogations and hadn't uncovered any spies. Captain Morris and the Combrian officer assigned to help him had exposed four, who'd be shot at star-rise. The captain knew nothing about the missing crystal, nor the device it came from. PC trusted Morris completely, but being in charge of palace security put him around a slew of Combrians and Mancombras, making it impossible for the secret to remain safely tucked away in his head. Free had been careful to keep his mind solely on the job at hand while querying the professors, administrators, maintenance, and cafeteria personnel so his Combrian helper would remain ignorant of the transmitter. But he'd been doubly vigilant to keep suspicions about his old friend from mentally surfacing during the interrogations.

For some time now he'd been aware PC was acting on nonexistent intelligence reports, and hadn't a clue he knew the secret intel to be a crop of lies. He couldn't figure out how his old friend really obtained the information until exhausting every other possibility. PC possessed a most amazing gift, one he'd only seen imitated by charlatans: clairvoyance. Why he didn't want anyone to know was beyond him.

THIRTY TWO

Voola ROSE AT NOON. SHE'D assisted Prince Zane last night and hadn't gotten to bed until the first rays of Life Giver crept over the horizon. They'd uncovered seven spies: four exposed by Captain Morris, the janitor who'd stolen the crystal, a cook, and the ethics professor—who may have sealed Combria's fate by passing the micro-processor on to a principal whose location no one knew. Combria University had been purged.

She had probed Prince Zane's mind on several occasions throughout the night, marveling at the precision and decisiveness of his thought processes. Never had she witnessed such dedication to duty—the Urth seemed incapable of any form of self indulgence. His insides also revealed an unshakable belief in The Spirit That Created All Things, and he severely chastised himself for all failures to live up to the unseen power's expectations for him. Long ago he'd abandoned sex and inwardly vowed never to take a mate so nothing would dilute his undying effort to bring all of Combria under an umbrella of true equality and justice. To him, government should exist only to protect and serve the people rather than be exalted above them.

How wonderful the future would have been under such a splendid ruler. But having no idea where Principal Nobb went after leaving University City, the prince's chances of finding Gram were nil, and he secretly thought Dr. Nanzar would escape capture as well, so more bombs would be coming and he'd have no choice but to capitulate to the mad king to keep Combria from being destroyed: he'd asked his father to develop a similar weapon but Harv Zane refused, explaining such an arms race would ensure the eventual extermination of all intelligent life on Combria.

She rose from the bed in Prince Zane's guestroom and went to the kitchen for kaffy. The small apartment had been used by Gram's valet York when she'd been stuck in the palace. The new ruler of Combria choosing to occupy it instead of Gram's exorbitantly luxurious rooms, all presently empty, was indicative of his humble nature. Voola halted at the entrance when she saw the prince standing stiff as a tree trunk with his back to her, arms dangling at his side. She entered his mind and stifled a gasp of incredulity.

"Captain Denton can't approach the island because of massive radiation readings, Sir. He didn't spot any vessels leaving the area."

Eyeing his sergeant who'd read the telegraphed communiqué, Vern expelled a frustrated sigh. "Nanzar's probably back in his hidden lab by now."

"What do you want me to tell Captain Denton, General?"

He massaged his chin a moment and lowered his hand. "Tell him to break up the convoy and have each ship search the waters throughout the archipelago. We've got to find that son-of-a-bitch."

✝

"What sort of boat is that coming from that big one you called a warship, Grandfather?"

"It's a power shuttle, Togo. I haven't seen one in fifteen double-years."

The craft moved incredibly fast, leaving beautiful foamy-white furls in its wake. Togo watched it halt near the shore, and several armed sailors waded towards them, led by an Urth male. The visible ears, along with the color of his skin, hair, and eyes, fascinated him.

"What's your name?" the Urth asked Grandfather.

"I go by Chief, I'm a Wanderer. This is my grandson Togo. You're trespassing on my island, sailor. I filed a legal claim to it when I retired from the Combrian Forces."

The Urth glanced towards the village. "So you're a vet. Have you seen any ships in this area?"

"No. I assume you're here because of the explosion?"

A grim nod followed. "You witnessed it, Chief?"

"I did. Frightening. Your cursed technology is going to doom the planet."

"Wasn't our doing. That bomb was detonated by order of the House of Pillhigh, our sworn enemy."

"I can see that ship you came from belongs to the Combrian Forces. Are you pirates?"

"No, we serve Prince Zane."

"Prince who?"

Disbelieving laughter blasted through the Urth's peculiarly colored lips. "You must have broke all contact with the outside world or you'd know who Prince Zane is. Gram Pillhigh is a fugitive from justice. Prince Zane, formerly known as General Zane of the Urth Army, is the new ruler of Combria."

Grandfather looked more shocked than he'd ever seen him—eyes bulging like hicker eggs, mouth gaping wide enough for a moon foul to enter. "Gram was only a small lad when I retired, I didn't know his father had passed away. Why was a Combrian serving in the Urth Army?"

"Prince Zane is an Urth, Chief."

The old Combrian's eyes widened even further. "An Urth rules?! . . . My galaxies how the world has changed, I never thought that would happen."

"We have to search this island," said the sailor. "Are you going to give us any trouble?"

Crossing his arms over his paps, Grandfather shook his head, but sternly warned: "Just don't harass my tribe."

The vision stopped and PC turned to see Voola gawking at him. "How long have you been standing there?"

"Long enough," she answered in an awe-struck voice.

I've been exposed! Raging alarm flooded his mind and spirit.

"That you have, Prince Zane, but I won't tell anyone, I swear. How long have you had this ability?"

He listlessly made for the percolator to finish what he'd intended to do before the past event paralyzed him, pour a cup of kaffy. Completing the task, he turned to Voola and said, "It started happening when I was a child. Take this and I'll fetch another for myself."

She accepted the kaffy and seated herself at the table.

"I should have known better than to let you stay here."

"You were worried someone would probe my thoughts and learn about the transmitter, remember?"

"Yeah . . ." he took a sip of kaffy and discovered he'd used too much sweetener. It tasted like a cup prepared by Free.

"What other secrets are you keeping?"

The question further rattled him. "What makes you say that?"

"A section of your mind is worried about someone finding out about them. It wasn't there last night but it's easily discernable now."

Though irritated she'd been poking around in his psyche during last night's interrogations, he wasn't at all surprised to learn she had. "You Combrians are the nosiest damn race, you know that?"

She laughed and raised her cup. "You're not as angry with me as I thought you would be."

"No, but you do realize I'll have to kill you."

"I know."

"I'm serious."

"No you're not, you like me. I remind you a bit of a childhood friend."

"So you do . . . This is a touchy predicament I find myself in. I can't afford for an enemy to find out about these bouts of paralysis. I'm afraid you're stuck with me until the war's over, or we're all blasted by Nanzar's doomsday weapon. From this moment on you're an honorary lieutenant and will serve as one of my aides. You'll quarter in my guestroom. I know you and Hammer will hate the arrangement but nothing can be done to change it."

Voola's features contorted with shock. She held that look for several seconds, then narrowed her eyes as her surprise-slackened lips stretched into a smile. "How did you know about Hammer and me? Can you read minds as well as see things that happened in the past?"

"You don't have to be a mind reader to sense the chemistry between you and the colonel. I'll order us some food, then have Lieutenant Free take you to the commissary to be outfitted for uniforms."

A funny look came over her. "Um, the commissary wouldn't happen to carry essence of valley fern, would it?"

Free couldn't believe PC had made Voola a lieutenant. He had to hold his temper since she was present, but couldn't help venting. "You won't promote me, yet you'll give a civilian the same rank. What gives, Prince Zane?"

"I'm not in the mood to have my orders questioned, Free. You know why I won't promote you."

Biting his lip, he guided Voola out the door.

"Why won't he promote you?" she asked.

He concentrated on the chore at hand to keep her from telepathically learning the answer to her question.

"Too late," she laughed. "That's a silly reason to hold you back, Lieutenant."

"Agreed, but PC Zane doesn't think so. He's a brilliant military commander but holds a grudge like a child."

Pirating a bulk carrier, which now lay at the bottom of the ocean with its slaughtered crew, they'd obtained the ore from which Nanzar would extract his heavy-element isotope. Shoehorn laughed at the scientist's amazement of how quickly his Mancombras set up the equipment and knew exactly what to do with very little verbal instruction from him. "They simply read your mind, Doctor. I told you they grasp new concepts very quickly."

"I can read minds too," said Nanzar, "but I never would have understood such intricacies without first learning the precepts that led to my discovering them."

Shoehorn cut his eyes to Saw, inserting fins on the rear of the bomb, preparing to weld them in place. "What's the key component we need to make your fusion device, Doctor?"

The Combrian grew more ill at ease. "Droggen. You Urths call it hydrogen. I'd think long and hard before creating a thermonuclear bomb if I were you, it could easily wind up turning Combria into a ghost planet. Prince Zane will have no choice but to convince his father to form a team and produce such weapons for retaliatory purposes, and believe me Harv Zane can do it. His expertise in quantum mechanics equals mine . . . perhaps exceeds it."

"I'm aware of Harv's genius, Doctor Nanzar. I also know of his hatred of scientists using their talents to create superior weaponry. He'll never agree to it—we'll have it all to ourselves. You'd better get to the two-way teleon, Gram expects you to contact him in five minutes. I want that psycho fat, dumb, and happy until we take over Combria."

Professor Beal had given Principal Nobb the micro-processor at an appointed meeting place on the outskirts of

University City. Voola had sensed great humiliation within Lieutenant Free at being left behind, fearing she'd replaced him as chief aide. The emotion was groundless but she couldn't tell him why. Prince Zane hoped to relive the event and learn where Nobb planned to go from there. It had been a very strange day, starting with her stumbling across his secret ability. The stiffness of the new uniform added to her feelings of disorientation.

Disappointment had greeted her at the commissary when she'd been told they didn't sell essence of valley fern. Though she didn't know how long it would be until she'd see Hammer again, she'd desperately hoped they could make love when that time came. Hands on the steering circle, Voola followed the armored wheeler escorting them. Another one tailed their rear. She glanced at Prince Zane, sitting a short distance to her right. "I probed Lieutenant Free's mind and learned why you won't promote him. Why won't you relent? After all, you were both very young and in boot camp at the time."

"I didn't know Free was a gambling sharp." Looking straight ahead, he appeared indifferent to the matter, but his voice had an angry edge to it. "After losing fifty tibs to him I had to leave the table because I couldn't cover the next ante. By the time one of the other buck private's discovered he was cheating, he'd put all his winnings in the pot which he had to forfeit, and couldn't pay me back. I warned him I'd never forget and it would come back to haunt him one day. He's lucky I didn't demote him when I took charge."

"But he eventually reimbursed you, didn't he?"

"Doesn't matter. It was the principal of the thing, not the money."

His refusal to forgive Free after all this time puzzled her. "Why did you make him your chief aide then?"

"Because he's my best friend."

She couldn't keep from giggling over his absurd stubbornness. "All the more reason to let bygones be bygones."

"This is none of your business, Voola, and there'll be no further discussions on the matter."

†

PC watched Professor Beal get in his wheeler and drive away. Nobb planned to give the micro-processor to Universal Quest but didn't make it his first priority, having no idea what it was. The principal planned to leave for the Greater Opian Range the next morning, hoping to find a Mancombra nestled in a tribe of Wanderers.

The scene vanished.

He contacted Colonel Hammer by field communicator and told him to get Arigot on the horn. The Combrian colonel greeted him a few minutes later.

"Nobb's posing as an energy inspector. Take your regiment to the Greater Opian Range, I'm going to have surveillance whirlys scan the area. You're looking for a power company wheeler. The crystal's inside it so don't fire at the vehicle under any circumstances."

THIRTY
THREE

OPEN FIELDS BETWEEN CLUSTERS OF fanleaf trees were filled with lush valley fern and spiral vines peppered with wild spurs of diverse colors. Moon fowl diving for insects in the dense flora looked like feathered missiles while descending with wings locked to their sides. An occasional night lapper could be seen, hoping to raid a hive filled with sweet wax. Arigot viewed the beautiful scenery from the cab of an armored wheeler. One of the surveillance whirlys had spotted a power company wheeler parked near a tribe of Wanderers. Only a few miles from the location, he smiled inside at how shocked Nobb would be to see the red Zees on his shoulders.

Prince Zane had three lunches brought to his office. While Lieutenant Free imbibed his, Voola discerned he strongly suspected his superior was clairvoyant. She dug through his memory and saw he'd seen the prince in a trance-like state several times. Prince Zane had convinced him he sometimes got so deep in thought he so thoroughly tuned everything else out he couldn't even blink his eyes. Free had no idea those states were due to him being miraculously pulled into past events.

Looking into the prince's brain, Voola's brows lurched as a gulp of astonishment lodged in her throat. Though he sat not four feet from her in his palace office, he was also standing on a beach of golden sand at a place he'd never seen before.

Neither had she.

Turning from the ocean waves, PC headed towards a village composed of hide-covered tents. The tribal chief and a prepubescent Combrian male, oblivious to his presence, were discussing a visit by some sailors who'd searched their island. They were relieved the intruders had left peacefully after being satisfied the enemy they'd been looking for wasn't on it. A pillar of smoke, that had to be the aftermath of Nanzar's bomb, also entered their conversation. While eavesdropping, his primary self still in his office grimaced as he caught Voola giving him the evil eye.

He should have dosed her with Clodec because now she knew he was in two places at the same time.

Nobb's hunch to wear his real uniform had paid off. He climbed into the cab and told his driver to move on. "There're no half-breeds in that tribe. As I suspected, none of them know King Gram's been usurped, which means the other tribes most likely won't either. That'll make the search much easier. Since they still fear the Combrian Forces we'll get full cooperation from them all—they won't risk covering for a hiding Mancombra. What the . . .?"

An armored wheeler pulled to a stop and two dozen soldiers poured out of it. Watching an officer get out of the front, Nobb reared his head back with rude surprise. "My galaxies, that's Arigot!"

"What should I do, Sir?" inquired the advanced personal holding the steering circle.

Pulling his sidearm from its holster, Nobb shot him in the face and immediately dropped the weapon to signify his surrender before drawing fire, motioning for Arigot to take note. He then stepped out of the cab and put his hands on top of his head, hollering for his troops in the back of the wheeler to do likewise.

Nobb had rehearsed the lie repeatedly until he almost believed it himself, knowing he might be captured when Universal Quest gave him this assignment. Welcoming Arigot's mind probe he said, "I'm one of General Yonker's spies. My driver was about to open fire on you, Enforcer."

Arigot donned a knowing grin. "You're no more a spy of Vern's than I am, Nobb—and for your information I'm a colonel now, proud to serve Prince Zane."

Nonplused he replied, "General Yonker would agree with you, but only because there's a liaison between him and me—an Urth sergeant. The noncom will verify I'm telling the truth."

Arigot stabbed a hypodermic in Nobb's shoulder to render him incapable of telepathy and telekinesis, then ordered his troops to do the same with the principal's soldiers, and shackle them. He grabbed the Combrian's arm and tugged him to the power company wheeler. "I know you're lying to buy time. There's no need for such theatrics, Nobb. Give me what I want and you live. Try to deceive me about it, you die."

"What is it you want?" he smugly asked, doing a great job clinging to his spy façade.

"The crystal Professor Beal gave you."

Nobb's confident demeanor turned fearful. "How did you know about that?"

"Prince Zane went through the whole university staff and caught all of Gram's spies working there. A Combrian probed Professor Beal's mind before he was hung for treason."

"But how did you know to look for me here? I never mentioned my plans to Beal."

"You must have. How could Prince Zane have known about it otherwise?"

Unfeigned confusion gripped Nobb's mind. "I didn't say anything to Beal except that I would tell Universal Quest that he gave me the diode as he requested."

That puzzled Arigot . . . Nobb was telling the truth.

Free walked into his office broadcasting a big smile. "Just got word from General Yonker that Arigot retrieved the crystal, PC."

Though tremendously relieved to hear that, he frowned at his aide for calling him by name in front of Voola, who still looked amazed that for several minutes he'd been on an unknown island while sitting near her. The moment Free had left to resume his duties a short while ago, he'd warned her to keep it to herself.

Recoiling from the visual reproof, Free cleared his throat. "Sorry, Prince Zane. Old habits are hard to break, Sir."

"And you wonder why I won't promote you. Tell Vern to have Arigot bring the micro-processor to the university so Harv can reinstall it. Then I want the colonel to take it to the observatory and hook up the device. He knows how to operate the activator, having watched me do it." Turning to Voola, he donned a sly grin and winked. "I'm sure you'll be greatly disappointed to hear you and I are on our way to Mount Opian. It'll be horrible having to put up with Colonel Hammer again, won't it?"

It must be wonderful to be in love, he mused, taking in her beaming face. He turned his attention to Free. "Were there any casualties in Arigot's unit?"

"No, Sir. None in Nobb's either, except for his driver. Nobb shot him to keep him from firing at Arigot. They surrendered without a fight."

"In that case they're prisoners of war. See to it they're taken to the stockade at Fort Pacific. Have Arigot's second in command do it, the colonel needs to head straight to University City. Get hold of General Yonker right now and pass everything on—time is not our friend at the moment. Nanzar may already have more bombs ready to deploy."

Barrabon easily understood why Universal Quest had chosen Nobb to carry out the Genocide Directive after his team had been captured. The principal should have been picked first to begin with, since killing unarmed civilians didn't faze him at all. Now he had to share his cell with the cold-blooded bastard, who'd been brought in an hour ago.

"I'm serious, Barrabon, there's no way he could have gotten the information from Professor Beal because I didn't tell him I was planning on going to the Greater Opian Range." Nobb had been ranting about Zane having some sort of new surveillance technology, and they somehow had to get word to Universal Quest about it.

I wonder why they don't have the equipment Doctor Goralov gave Voola brought to the palace instead of using it here, telepathed Drill, chewing a mouthful of sernloaf.

Hammer swallowed a sip of kaffy and lowered his vessel. *Because the transmitter beams information to the pyramid, and the equipment has to be within a mile radius of the mountain to receive it.*

Then why can't it be turned on from here as well? Drill asked.

It could if we had a big telescope to hook it up to, like the one at University City Observatory, transmitted Hammer while chewing a bite of potted sern liver. *Goralov told Voola that once the transmitter's turned on it can't be turned off, so if the activation device will work just once, we won't need it again.*

Drill shot him a puzzled frown. *If that's the case it seems illogical that Goralov didn't activate it before returning to Earth.*

He couldn't afford to do that, Drill, since he had no way of knowing how long it would be before someone discovered the pyramid. The transmitter won't work indefinitely and likely would have reached the end of its life expectancy by now. Goralov said it should remain operable for a thousand Earth years. According to what he told Voola, that makes five hundred of our double-years.

Looking more bewildered, Drill telepathed: *With such high technology, it seems to me he could have activated the transmitter from the pyramid simultaneously with that robot. Wonder why he didn't?*

Hammer shrugged. *You're asking the wrong person. Only Ivan Goralov can answer that, and he's not available for comment.*

Her lover lay next to her, naked skin sensuously touching hers. York had a concerned look on his face. "Gram is getting out of control, My Queen. He's slain five concubines since we came to this shelter. Usually he only murders a couple of them over the course of a double-year."

Releen ran a hand over his strong upper arm and sighed. "He's angry over losing Voola. There'll be more deaths to come until he exacts his revenge on her. Where is he anyway?"

"At the command center. He told me not to disturb him for an hour because he and Universal Quest were going to have a conference with all the universals. I'd better go in case he cuts it short."

She sighed again. "Yes, you should. It was very risky for you to come here before he retired for the evening, but oh how I enjoyed it. How clever of you to pretend you were bringing me an after-dinner desert, my love."

Gram was stretched out on his stomach, relishing the new slut's massaging fingers on his back. The beautiful Combrian had been brought to him by Quest that morning along with four others to replenish his stable. The universal's choices had so pleased him he'd insisted Quest join him for dinner and spend the night before returning to his new hideout in Juxbow.

"Does the king not wish to have sex with me?"

Eyes closed, he laughed at the puzzlement in her voice. "I wish nothing more, but I was anxious to partake of your skill the moment I learned you were a masseuse. I've been working too hard lately and have gotten all tensed up. Your magic hands relax me well."

Kneading the base of his neck she said, "I'm supremely glad to hear that. It's such an honor to be part of your harem, Sire. I so look forward to living in the palace if you ever regain the throne from Prince Zane."

Enflamed with wrath, he spun over, causing her to tumble off the bed, then dove on top of her. Hands squeezing her throat, thumbs collapsing her larynx, he savored the wild expression of fear and alarm in her gaping eyes. While choking her he repeatedly banged the slut's head against the unyielding floor until the fearful purple orbs glazed over, never to blink again.

"If I regain the throne indeed!"

Arigot had notified Prince Zane, who waited with Voola in Hammer's tent at Mount Opian. The sixty-second countdown would commence in fifteen minutes. Harv, who'd ridden to the observatory with him, nervously paced back and forth.

WAITING FOR RECEPTION filled each monitor. Voola was explaining why she'd needed a picture of Gram. "All these devices are highly sophisticated computers, Prince Zane. The one with the tray attached is a sensor. If we wanted to find a glimerald deposit, for example, we could either put a real gem in the tray or a photograph of one. The other computers would then filter out all data being sent from the transmitter not related to glimeralds. The teleon screens would give the locations of the richest deposits, what their depth is, and what sort of natural formation we'd have to dig through to reach them. Alternatively, I can also type in a description of whatever or whomever we're looking for on the keyboard, but it wouldn't be as accurate, so we'd have to wade through a lot of extraneous data. When a picture of a person is placed facedown in the tray, the sensor instantly identifies minute superficial qualities unique to that individual and will give the exact coordinates of their location anywhere on or within the side of the planet facing Anger."

PC shook his head with wonderment. "Incredible."

"Yeah . . . let's just hope the activation device works this time."

He checked his timepiece. "We're about to find out. Arigot should be calling any second."

"I wish you'd reconsider forcing me to be an aide, Prince Zane. I won't tell anyone your secrets, and you're at far greater risk of having them slip out to a Combrian or Mancombra than I am, since you don't have the power to block their probes."

The field communicator buzzed before he could tell her he'd think on it. "Tell me something good, Arigot."

"The gadget says the transmitter's been activated."

Glancing at the monitors he shouted with elation at seeing data scrolling down each screen. "It worked! Praise The Spirit That Created All Things the transmitter has been turned on!"

Voola started dancing a jig, waving her arms in the air as she shouted, "Gram, you filthy murdering bastard, prepare to meet your fate!"

THIRTY
FOUR

PC LEFT VOOLA AT MOUNT Opian, but not because of her logic in arguing the reason she should be relieved as an aide. She was the only one who knew how to read the data being sent from Anger. Combria needed her to bring on a new age of incredible prosperity. He'd instructed his hover whirly pilot to fly him to a meeting point near a historical monument erected midway between the Army Command Center and Serene Valley. The memorial stood directly over the bomb shelter Gram Pillhigh presently occupied. Vern Yonker already had a regiment equipped with several techs heading that way.

Hammer's camp wouldn't consist of a group of tents much longer. Soon a maximally secured army base named Fort Goralov would be erected at the foot of Mount Opian, where Voola could use her equipment in a comfortable office with all the amenities. Her love-smitten colonel would remain in command as a brigadier general. He hadn't divulged his plans to either of them. Hammer richly deserved the promotion for discovering the metal wall which resulted in Voola being told of the transmitter's existence and taught how to interpret its data. Captain Wurz warranted a step up in rank too, since he'd engineered the explosives that activated the robot, setting everything in motion.

Bowing his head, he silently thanked The Spirit That Created All Things for the mighty blessing the eternal being had brought to the tiny portion of its universe called Combria.

Quest trembled with alarm as he pulled to the side of the road. Thankfully he was wearing civilian clothes, so Zane's soldiers wouldn't recognize him unless they got a good look at his face. Unlike the civilian commercial wheeler he drove—using it to secure Gram's new mistresses in the locked trailer when delivering them to the king yesterday— those repeatedly passing him were armored, and marked with red Zees. He reached for the field communicator to warn Gram not to surface for his daily routine of enjoying a half hour of Life Giver's rays, but before he could turn it on he saw a hatless commando with no rank insignia on his uniform walking towards him. The communicator slipped from Quest's hand as a spray of machinegun fire shattered the windshield. Unable to believe his dying eyes, he figured it must have been a shock-induced hallucination.

The soldier looked like General Zane.

PC called for some troops to investigate Quest's trailer, and entered the cab. The universal lay sprawled across the seat in a pool of blood. "Your days of kissing Gram Pillhigh's ass and fulfilling his whims are over, you night lapper sucking son-of-a-bitch. I hope Wheelbarrow and Needle are watching this from on high, along with all the other Mancombras you killed. You were quite efficient in running the death camps weren't you, you slimy piece of scum—and did an excellent job of continuing the Genocide Directive after I took the palace, didn't you."

As he'd hoped, Quest's last moments played out before him: the universal had tried to warn Gram but failed, thank the unseen power. PC smiled with satisfaction at the astonishment Quest had felt in seeing him stroll calmly towards him carrying the machinegun. "You died in raw, naked fear as you should have, Quest. It's your king's turn next, but I solemnly swear his won't be an easy death like yours."

Viewing the area around the monument from a camera hidden within it, Gram was pleased to see no one around. He switched off the teleon and left the command center, heading for the elevator to exult in a few minutes of daylight.

The monument started rising.

Grinning as he peered through the scope of his rifle, PC prepared to squeeze the trigger. Having discerned through Quest's desire to warn Gram not to surface, that the king did so daily, he'd ordered his troops to wait behind him. Meanwhile he'd positioned himself on the edge of a ridge facing the monument, lying on his belly so he wouldn't be spotted by a monitoring device like the one they'd found in the bull sern statue outside Juxbow.

Since Gram couldn't afford to have even one guard know the whereabouts of the hideout, PC knew he'd be coming up alone. When the freight elevator stopped moving skyward, he fired the tranquilizer gun and dropped the insane dictator. "Okay, soldiers, you know what to do!"

Polka thanked the private who'd been sent by Captain Morris, and eagerly hurried back into the classroom. "You boneheads listen up. You get to leave early today, and I seriously doubt this course will be continued. Prince Zane captured Gram Pillhigh and is bringing him to the palace for execution. The war is over!"

In unison with the students Pliers jumped to her feet clapping and shouting, acting like a spastic fool. Polka laughed over how silly the sergeant major looked, but couldn't help joining her.

Shoehorn sat stunned in front of the teleon, marveling at this radical turn of events. Zane had captured Gram Pillhigh and had him on display at the promenade of the palace entrance, bound in chains and gagged. Every broadcast system on the planet had cameras aimed at the two of them.

He turned up the volume to hear Zane's speech.

". . . we've secured the bunker and everyone inside who didn't resist us has been taken into custody. Citizens of Juxbow, be warned. The majority of Gram's soldiers are hiding in your midst, a fact I know a great number of you are already aware of. Leave the city as soon as possible because tomorrow at dawn my troops are going to flush each one of them out, using whatever means necessary. Don't try to avoid the inspection stations or you'll be shot for treason. Anyone caught assisting hostile commandos in any form or fashion will suffer the same fate without exception.

"I now speak to the soldiers who oppose me. Universal Quest is dead, and Gram's three other four-stone universals will also be shot on sight. However, I'll spare the lives of any of the rest of you who peacefully surrender before Life Giver rises tomorrow. You'll be treated as prisoners of war. If and when deemed worthy of repatriation you'll be freed. This offer ends at daybreak, so act quickly if you want to live.

"And now I address all citizens of Combria. At noon tomorrow this monster you see kneeling at my feet will be burned at the stake—a death far too merciful for one who has shed an ocean of innocent blood. His ashes will be glued to his statue in The Great Hall to stand as a shameful reminder of an evil tyrant who called for the extermination of an entire race. All who visit the palace are encouraged to spit on it. For as long as I serve you in my present capacity, the statue of Gram Pillhigh will never be cleaned. As time passes it will grow moldy and grotesque to look upon, reflecting the true image of the beast it was constructed to represent.

"Because many of you were uncertain of how the war would end, I held off instituting some changes that will become effective as of now. From this moment forth Mancombras will not be forced to have their fertility tested, and can legally adopt children. Future Mancombras will be given whatever name their parents desire, and those of you who wish to change yours may legally do so. The ban against mixed-race mating is now officially abolished, and no municipality can prevent mix-raced couples or Mancombras from residing within their city limits. Any attempt by city governors or anyone else to do so will result in their immediate execution. Bigotry will no longer be tolerated anywhere on the planet. I have another announcement concerning this matter, but will wait until Gram's forces have been completely gutted and the war is officially over before sharing it with you. A new day has dawned for Combria: peace and great prosperity lies ahead. The Spirit That Created All Things bless you all."

Pulse quickening, Shoehorn turned to Nanzar. "I want that bomb ready by dawn. Zane will have his focus on Juxbow tomorrow so we should be able to fly over University City unimpeded."

The Combrian's face paled. "Why University City?"

"To destroy our only competition. We can't take the chance that you might be right and me wrong about Harv Zane. He must die. We'll kill two fowls with one stone—take out the professor and show Zane that he must surrender to us after we explain that the atomic bomb we dropped on the city is nothing compared to the destructive force of our thermonuclear weapons. Of course we won't tell him we haven't completed any of them yet."

"Harv doesn't live in University City anymore," said Nanzar, voice hoarse with fear. "Gram has spies in the university, and they reported Zane moved him into the palace."

Shoehorn brought a finger to his chin and started tapping it. "I wasn't thinking. Harv will want to witness Gram's execution first hand, so he wouldn't have been in University City tomorrow anyway."

Nanzar nervously cleared his throat. "You said you've been planning to take over Combria for a long time. May I ask how you intended to accomplish such a feat before capturing me?"

The scientist's bewildered expression made him chuckle. "You may indeed, good Doctor. While waiting for Gram to wipe out all the Mancombras, I've been training my co-conspirators to pool their resources to act as one mind, thus increasing their telekinetic power eleven-fold. Together they can levitate objects weighing as much as a hundred-ten-thousand pounds for almost an hour."

Skepticism manifested in a jumpy frown before Nanzar voiced it. "That's not possible. They could only lift a twentieth of that weight acting in unison, and couldn't sustain it in the air for longer than a quarter of an hour."

"Oh yes it is," he assured with another laugh. "Allow me to explain. While at the asylum I spent a good deal of time trying to find an antidote for Clodec, thinking that if I couldn't, my aspirations to take over Combria would never come to fruition. Lathe over there was my assistant at the time, and as there was nothing in any of the medications I came up with that could harm his health, he allowed me to test them on him. I failed time after time, but in the process stumbled onto a mixture whose results totally surprised me. It didn't neutralize the Clodec at all, but after the hour's dosage wore off we discovered my serum had radically increased his power, range, and endurance—similarly enhancing his telepathic abilities as well. When I achieved the same results by injecting Level, Stapler, and Miter, I realized I no longer needed an army of Mancombras to enact my plan, as few as ten would do. As a safety measure I'd hoped to raise that number to fifteen, but wound up with the eleven you see here.

"Aviation has always fascinated me. I became a licensed pilot before finishing my courses at Combria University. It had only been a passionate hobby until I came up with the serum and realized if my eleven comrades were able to fly they'd be impossible to beat in air combat, especially with me flying with them as commander. Their range is such they can tear the wings off a whirly from half a mile away. So I altered my plan of storming the palace with hundreds of Clodec-proof Mancombras and made the eleven who'd joined me take aviation classes. Now they're all exceptional pilots like myself.

"We'd planned to take over the flying force, knowing a large percentage of the soldiers there would join us rather than face certain death upon witnessing such immense power. But I wasn't going to risk it until there weren't enough Mancombras left alive to unite against us. You see, my serum has one serious drawback, which thankfully we learned early on. If a dosed Mancombra battles an untreated one, the latter somehow absorbs the same increase in mental abilities. I've yet to determine the cause of the paradox and am therefore helpless to remedy it.

"I plotted a means to steal one whirly at a time until we had a dozen with which to conquer the flying force, but fate intervened, much like it did with you choosing our island to test your weapon. Did you happen to hear the news about a mini-carrier sinking in a violent sea storm? It happened shortly before Gram issued the Genocide Directive."

The doctor gave him a tense nod.

"My associates crept aboard it that stormy night after

doing away with the crew, and managed to sail it here despite the raging waves. It's hidden in an alcove on the other side of the island where we keep a boat used to get supplies from the mainland. We flew one whirly to the warehouse for emergency use, but there are nineteen others aboard. Did Gram's spies say whether or not Harv is continuing his duties as president?"

Nanzar closed his gaping mouth and swallowed hard before responding. "He's escorted to the campus by guards and returns to the palace the same way."

"Excellent." Shoehorn eyed the whirly. "We'll drop the bomb on the university before classes conclude day after tomorrow. Get to work, Doctor."

THIRTY
FIVE

Releen had never seen the dungeon before: it was the one area of the palace she'd avoided since being crowned queen eight double-years ago. Now she stood behind a wall of bars, bitterly weeping. She didn't know where her five children had been taken, but hoped they weren't locked up in a dank cell like her. Gram's mad reign was over—she'd been told the bloodthirsty sex maniac would die in flames tomorrow. The sorrow pervading her had nothing to do with the perverted hedonist getting what he so overabundantly deserved. York had been killed in crossfire when Zane's soldiers invaded the underground compound.

His office door opened and Free walked in looking very perturbed.

"What's wrong?"

"Having Gram's brain probed helped a lot, PC, but didn't give us Nanzar. I just got word he wasn't in the hidden lab, and neither were any of the other scientists. All the universals are dead though, and the checkpoints are glutted with surrendering soldiers."

Devastated to hear that, he bolted from his chair. "Dammit, he deceived Gram then! Nanzar claimed to be there when he last made contact, and was told to remain in the lab until he got another weapon completed. That means he's gone rogue and may have already constructed more bombs. Get a picture of him miniaturized immediately—we need to get it to Voola. Tell Captain Morris it's top priority."

The Great Dining Hall reverberated with the sounds of celebration. Captain Morris had given her a seven day pass and Pliers would be leaving for Mount Opian tomorrow afternoon. Prince Zane wanted the classes to continue but she'd be serving only as an assistant since Polka no longer required a bodyguard. Nonetheless the kind black Urth had insisted she stay in the apartment anyway.

Anxious to see Drill again, she would have skipped the celebration dinner and already be on her way if not for the execution. She wasn't about to miss the sight of Gram Pillhigh engulfed in flames—crying out in agony, suffering but a minute fraction of the torture he'd inflicted on her race.

"Uh-oh," muttered Polka, looking to her left. "Something tells me we're not going to like what we're about to hear."

She turned to see an approaching Urth private, whose serious expression sorely contrasted with all the jubilant faces in the enormous chamber. He saluted her and said, "Sergeant Major, Captain Morris wants to speak with you right away."

Pliers rose from the table and followed him, desperately hoping her pass hadn't been revoked.

The walk to his office seemed to take forever.

Captain Morris handed her a tiny photograph of renowned physicist Dr. Nanzar. "Take this to Mount Opian with you and give it to Colonel Hammer."

Immensely relieved, she saluted with a big smile. "Yes, Sir. Permission to rejoin the celebration?"

"Denied. You got picked for this detail because you were going to Mount Opian anyway. Pack your bags and get to the palace landing strip quick as you can. You're being flown there by hover whirly. Sorry you'll have to miss Gram's execution but this is urgent. I wasn't informed why it's so important, only that I was to give it top priority. Enjoy your leave."

Head hung low, Gram looked past his shackled wrists. Zane wouldn't permit the guards to take off his cuffs after they'd put him in this cell several hours ago.

"You'll be wearing them until they fall off your burning bones tomorrow," the arrogant usurper had said while pulling a pouch from his pocket. He'd then thrust it through the bars and emptied its contents on the cell floor. "I was told these belong to you. Voola sends her regret at not being able to watch you die."

The pompous, arrogant bastard had then scornfully laughed at him while walking away.

Still glaring at the seven glimeralds she'd stolen from him, he knew even the fires of death wouldn't match the white-hot rage burning within his breast. His vengeance would go unrequited and that cruel injustice caused him to howl like a wounded night lapper. Then, stark reality descended upon him like a weighted fishnet and his raving abruptly ceased. Terror churned through his cramping entrails—relentlessly flooding his insides while outwardly entrapping him in a thick, suffocating blanket.

Tears pouring down his cheeks, he pressed his face between two bars and screamed, "I don't want to die! Please, someone help me! Guards, guards, I have seven glimeralds to give you for my release! I'm the wealthiest person on Combria and can make your wildest dreams come true if you'll get me out of here! Is anyone listening?! Is anyone there?! Help! Help! Help . . .!"

"Shut up, you cowardly fool!" shouted Releen, hearing Gram pleading for mercy down the echoing corridor. She couldn't see him, but there was no mistaking that grating voice.

"Releen, is that you, my love?!"

"I'm not your love, you murdering psychopath. How long I've wished I could tell you what a pitiful lover you are, and that my jealousy over your whores was fake, but I knew you'd kill me if I did. Of course you're not male enough to take on a member of your own gender, are you. You never satisfied me, not one time did you even come close. Ah but your trusted valet did. York and I have been lovers since I last gave birth. He pleasured me nightly, totally fulfilling all my sexual and emotional needs."

She laughed as he screamed endlessly about what he would do to her.

". . . I'll slice off your breasts and make you eat them! I'll gouge out your eyes and smear them across your face! I'll—"

"Ha! You'll do nothing but burn tomorrow, do you hear? Now shut up and let me get some sleep."

Arigot spat on Gram's statue as he walked past, and joined the celebration in The Great Dining Hall. He'd had the pleasure of taking out two of the universals personally. The third got bagged by a sergeant under his command. Tomorrow at dawn he'd lead his regiment to Juxbow, a task he wished could be put off until after the execution.

Since the activation device would no longer be needed, Harv had taken it with him after the transmitter started sending information from Anger. The professor hoped to figure out how the micro-processors worked, and in doing so take a quantum leap in technology, making for an even brighter future than that already presenting itself. However, if they didn't catch Nanzar soon, there might not be a future.

Feeling a hand on her shoulder, Voola opened her eyes. "Hammer?"

"The picture of Nanzar arrived."

She rose from the cot and put on her uniform, savoring his lustful gaze, hating she couldn't quench his fire, as well as her own.

"A female Mancombra brought it. Sorry to inconvenience you but you'll have to share the tent. She'll be sleeping in here for the next six nights."

"Oh well . . ." Voola zipped the starchy trousers, then started buttoning a shirt with lieutenant bars on the collar and shoulders. "What's her name?"

"Pliers. She's the command sergeant major Drill has been going on about since he came back from the palace."

"Oh really? Well in that case you should give him another pass and let them rent a room at the tourist trap."

He chuckled. "Since she's on leave I could do that."

"I certainly would." She pulled his face to hers and kissed him. "Then maybe we could make love vicariously through them."

Another laugh escaped Hammer, tinged with frustration.

Baylor Denton barked the coordinates to his navigator and the ship set sail for an island forty nautical miles southwest of the nuclear blast site. General Yonker had assured the communications officer Dr. Nanzar would be on it, but hadn't divulged how he'd gathered the intelligence.

Seaman Arnold, a fellow Urth, had awakened him with the news, wisely extending a mug of kaffy while doing so. Life Giver wouldn't rise for another two hours and he was sipping his third cup, standing on the bridge.

He'd been captain of another warship before being sent to

this one to commit mutiny under Prince Zane's orders at the onset of the revolution. The Battle Fish's former skipper had been thrown in the brig after Baylor convinced the crew it was their duty to rebel against a mad king, claiming the Genocide Directive as proof of Gram's insanity. The Combrian admiral he'd usurped had committed suicide in a stockade after being brought ashore in bonds. Baylor knew if he captured Nanzar he'd most likely be promoted to that rank, but that didn't motivate him.

Survival of the planet did.

Hearing a warning buzz, Stapler turned to the radar screen situated left of the monitors. He activated the alarm to wake everyone up, and jabbed the transmit button on the intercom: "Vessel approaching at eighteen knots, heading for the bay where we anchored Nanzar's ship. Expected arrival is twenty minutes."

Captain Denton had dispatched four shuttles to the island. Ensign Craig hoped the machinegun mounted on the bow wouldn't be needed, but deeply feared it would. He held a tense finger on the trigger, ready to fire at Gram's soldiers, who'd reportedly brought Dr. Nanzar to the uncharted isle. Apprehension kept his nerves on edge because there had to be another super bomb or Nanzar would've returned to the mainland to build more after testing the prototype. Craig hoped to blazes the damn thing wouldn't be accidentally discharged by a stray bullet and vaporize them all.

The shuttle commander fired a flare and the shore lit up before them. Thank The Spirit That Created All Things there was nothing but an expanse of white sand beneath the soaring flame.

"Okay, have you got it?"

All eleven Mancombras assured him they did.

"Good." Shoehorn put a hand on Nanzar's back. "Let's you and I have some breakfast while we watch the monitors, Doctor. This won't take long."

Craig saw some Mancombras appear on the sand just before a flare shot from another shuttle fizzled out. The next thing he knew an invisible force flung him around, gluing his hands to the machinegun, forcing him to shoot all the sailors aboard. Then his fingers released the weapon as if they had a will of their own and he felt himself being plunged into the cold dark water. Though the surface lay a mere three feet above, he couldn't rise from the bottom: the telekinetic power holding his body down was far stronger than him. From the moment he'd seen the Mancombras until forced to take his dying breath—sucking in bitter seawater instead of life-giving air—he feared Gram Pillhigh might have been right about the half-breeds after all.

Shoehorn helped himself to another cup of kaffy and grinned at Nanzar. The shocked Combrian was gaping at the monitors. Cameras outfitted with infrared lenses transmitted images of four empty shuttles resting on the seashore where the Mancombras had levitated them. Each vessel had carried twenty sailors planning to storm the beach. Now they were all dead. "My comrades will have reached the mother vessel by now and should be returning to us shortly. Life Giver is going to rise in a few minutes. I anticipate a lovely day."

"We can't raise any of them on the secret frequency, Skipper," said Commander Dorph. "Should we try another?"

"No." Baylor tilted his hat back and swabbed his forehead. "They're either in a compromised position, captured, or dead. We can't risk Gram's soldiers being alerted to their presence if it's neither of the last two possibilities."

Oh they're all quite dead, Captain.

Baylor glanced all around but couldn't spot the Combrian who'd telepathed the chilling message.

Oh do relax, Captain Denton, it's not one of your sailors communicating with you. My name is Chisel, and I'm about fifteen hundred feet off your starboard side. Amazing isn't it, that I can reach you from such a distance? Allow me to show you what else I can do from here. Say goodbye to your second in command.

Before he could say a word Dorph pulled out his sidearm and shot himself in the head.

"Dorph . . .!"

Staring at the warship gleaming in the dawn's early light a safe distance away, Chisel killed the outboard motor. "Now that we've eliminated the captain and crew, it's time to scuttle their ship, my fellow future rulers of Combria."

The WS Battle Fish fired a barrage of missiles that launched at a forty-five degree angle and arced gracefully backwards, each vapor trail forming an almost perfect circle before striking the ship and exploding on impact.

THIRTY
SIX

AFTER LOSING CONTACT WITH THE Battle Fish, Vern ordered the other warships closest to the area to hold their positions until the CS Storm, an aircraft carrier, reached the archipelago so reconnaissance whirlys could find out what in blazes happened to Captain Denton and his crew. Gram's brain had been thoroughly probed, revealing thirty soldiers were assigned to guard Nanzar's scientific team, and they'd sailed to the island in a civilian vessel carrying only their infantry weapons, making it impossible for them to sink a warship. He knew the Battle Fish hadn't been destroyed by an atomic explosion as none of the other vessels reported seeing a mushroom cloud like that produced by the test bomb.

In three hours Gram's funeral pyre would be ignited and the evil Combrian would justly be burned alive. Vern hated he'd have to watch the execution on teleon like most of Combria instead of getting to see it up close. The vast majority of Gram's forces had surrendered or been killed, but the war wouldn't really be over until Nanzar's capture. Therefore he couldn't leave his command post.

The Combrian reading her mind chuckled aloud. Releen couldn't imagine what the handsome male found so humorous since her thoughts were nothing but a dark cloud of gloom: fear over her children's fate as well as her own, sorrow over losing York. Clodec made it impossible to probe his brain for the reason.

Arigot had returned to the palace from Juxbow via hover whirly. With the situation well under control before Life Giver had shone for two hours, he'd contacted Lieutenant Free by field communicator and asked to speak with Prince Zane. PC had granted his request to let his second in command take over so he could see the execution, but ordered him to meld with Queen Releen's mind beforehand to ascertain her intentions if allowed to go free.

He'd been amazed to learn the beautiful Combrian had been carrying on behind Gram's back with his valet, and deeply mourned her lover's death. Uncovering deep feelings of satisfaction that her mate was about to be brought to justice, he'd snickered aloud before receiving a major surprise which had quickly sobered him: despite her current plight, the female he'd always admired from afar found him attractive.

Arigot vividly recalled watching the royal mating on teleon as an adolescent, and hoping he might one day win the hand of one so gracious and lovely. The flattery he felt over her attraction was so intoxicating he found it difficult to concentrate on his assignment. "Suppose Prince Zane were to release you, what would your plans be? Remember, your mind is open to me so I'll know if you lie."

Her pretty face took on an air of hope. "Why I hadn't even thought of that possibility. Are you telling me such a one exists?"

"I'll make the inquiries here and you'll answer. Pretend you've just been set free and given an endowment to provide for your needs until you can be self-supportive. What are your plans now?"

"Does this fantasy include my children as well?" she asked.

"Yes, but only the ones who fully understand how evil their father is, and how justice calls for his demise. If any of them don't, they'll be confined for life. Otherwise desire for vengeance might lead them to organize a revolt against this regime when they reach adulthood."

The queen frowned with thought. "If the endowment permits, I'd finish my education and pursue a career as a news reporter." An un-vocalized statement followed that she tried to dismiss so he wouldn't be able to sense it. If spoken aloud she'd have concluded with: "and hope to mate with a male like you."

"I can plainly discern you see the king for the insane beast he is," he said stoically to conceal the headiness her unspoken words had evoked. "You thought he was wise and considerate while he was courting you, only to discover soon after the mating that you'd become the bondslave of a monster."

Sadness clouded her exquisite eyes. "My entire family was put to death because I confided that truth to them. Gram ordered that fire set and lied to the press afterwards. That's why I'm so happy about the mode of death Prince Zane chose for the bastard."

That shocked him more than learning of her attraction. He'd never doubted Gram's truthfulness when the king had so sadly explained the accident to the world, saying, "The power pole fell against the house and set it on fire while my in-laws were sleeping in their chambers. Tragically, none of them survived the inferno. Please keep your grieving queen in your thoughts and prayers during this time of her bereavement."

"Prince Zane is undoubtedly trying to find Nanzar. More ships are sure to follow and they'll have air support. Are you certain you can carry on the job without him, Chisel?"

The Mancombra smiled confidently. "My mind has totally absorbed all his thoughts and theories on nuclear fusion."

"In that case we must give Zane what he wants." Shoehorn turned to the terrified physicist. "Having fled the mainland when Gram issued the Genocide Directive, Shovel was hiding on an island near the area you chose for a test site, Doctor Nanzar, having no idea the directive had been abolished. He boated out to sea to do some fishing and found you floating, helpless and injured. Being the kindhearted soul that he his, Shovel took you aboard. You explained to him that the Battle Fish exploded after Gram's soldiers boarded it and a fight broke out. You were being held under guard aboard a shuttle, and got injured by flying debris from the disintegrating ship.

"When the next vessel draws near here from Zane's forces they'll find a persecuted Mancombra and a dead scientist on a motorboat. Alas, I'm afraid you'll have drawn your last breath before being rescued. But don't be troubled, Shovel will tell them everything. I'll have hypnotized him so he'll believe every word I've just told you really happened, which will easily evade the truth coming out in a mind probe. When we leave him with your corpse he'll think you just died after conversing with him, never knowing I planted it all in his mind. He, of course, will tell his rescuers that he wishes to return to his island home. Once he gets back here, I'll restore his normal memory."

Nanzar fell to his knees, hands raised like a beggar. "Don't do it! You'll be making a big mistake by killing me—Chisel may think he knows all that I do but he doesn't—he can't possibly! Please don't do this, I've given you my complete cooperation and will continue to do so!"

Shoehorn blew out a bored sigh. "I can't have Zane turning over every rock to find you or he might uncover our hideaway, Doctor, surely you can understand that. Lathe, place the remote detonation equipment where it can be easily located. I want Zane's sailors to find it. Once they do they'll have no reason to come back here. Hoe, you and Saw sail Nanzar's ship out to where the Battle Fish was destroyed and sink it. Miter will follow and bring you back. Key, make certain the camouflage over the entrance to the alcove hasn't been compromised, they must not spot the carrier."

To Drill's amazement Colonel Hammer had given him another pass, this one twice as long as the previous. What a pity his relationship with Pliers hadn't reached the stage of sexual intimacy, though it certainly would eventually. He'd received the furlough in the mess tent while eating breakfast with her that morning. They were there now, along with everyone else in camp except the guards on duty. It was nearing lunchtime, but the gathering had nothing to do with food. The colonel purchased a portable teleon at the tourist trap and had just set it up.

Gram Pillhigh would be on the screen in a few minutes, and no one wanted to miss it.

Sitting beside Arigot on the bleachers' first row, Free gazed at a six-foot pyramid of fuel-soaked kindling with a metal pole jutting through the center. A portable ramp looming in front of the pile would be removed after guards marched Gram up it and shackled him to the stake.

Every non-Urth had to receive a Clodec injection before being allowed in the open arena, allowing Polka to beat the crowd and find a good seat midway up the stands. After they were filled to capacity a trumpet sounded and the dungeon gates opened. Two helmeted soldiers wearing body armor emerged, forcing an hysterical tyrant to stay on his feet. Along with the rest of the spectators, she cheered and clapped as the weeping despot was coerced down a long concrete path leading to the pyre. If not for a line of military police preventing an angry mob from climbing over the fence surrounding the execution grounds, Gram Pillhigh would have been torn to pieces.

Good thing the sentinels wore protection because a torrent of items were being hurled at their prisoner—rotten eggs, spoiled fruit, and all manner of debris accompanied stones. Gram was a garbage-dripping, bruised, bleeding mess by the time they got him chained to the death pole. They walked down the incline and one of them shouted, "Stop throwing things, Prince Zane is about to come out!"

The barrage ceased immediately. As they rolled the ramp away from the soaked wood, a military band began playing an ominous dirge, prompting even more fear to rise on the face of Combria's nemesis. A drum roll commenced when the song concluded, followed by the steady beat of an ancient cadence Combrians used eons ago while advancing towards an enemy in a time when wars were fought with swords and spears.

"How fitting!" yelled Polka. A prepubescent Mancombra stepped through the gates carrying a burning torch. The male marched proudly in rhythm to the pounding drums. Captain Morris walked behind the torch bearer, followed by Prince Zane.

They halted in front of the wood pile. The Mancombra handed the torch to Captain Morris and hurried for the waiting arms of his Combrian mother, standing with the soldiers who'd escorted Gram to his fate. The captain passed it to Prince Zane then faced the weeping murderer, now pleading for mercy, begging for his life.

Holding it high above his head, the new ruler of Combria looked to the stands. "Are all the cameras in place?"

Numerous affirmations followed the prince's amplified voice.

"Very well." He turned around. "Gram Pillhigh, I send you to the eternal damnation The Spirit That Created All Things surely has prepared for the likes of you. Painful though your death will be, justice will not nearly be served by it alone. Die, you evil perverted beast, and may you suffer for eternity!"

Prince Zane threw the torch into the midst of the pile and in seconds the wailing dethroned king was trapped in the center of an inferno.

"Nooooooo!" he howled.

The stench of burning Combrian flesh, hair, entrails, fuel-soaked wood, and clothing saturated with rotten substances, filled the air with a rancid odor she'd have found intolerable under any other circumstance. But watching the dark silhouette behind the flames shuddering on the pole with violent intensity—screeching, squealing, screaming in the throes of fire-meted justice—made it the most satisfying aroma Polka had ever smelt.

THIRTY SEVEN

FOUR DAYS AFTER GRAM'S EXECUTION an amazing thing happened. Dr. Nanzar had been discovered floating on a piece of wreckage out at sea by a Mancombra named Shovel, one of the eleven civilians who hadn't gone to the palace. Though elated Nanzar couldn't build any more bombs, the WS Battle Fish puzzled Vern.

Shovel had piloted his motorboat to the area planning to fish, and spotted Nanzar. Seeing the CS Storm on the horizon, he'd pulled the physicist aboard and motored towards it. Nanzar died of a head wound before the Mancombra could get him to the vessel for treatment. He'd been debriefed and released, preferring to return to the island home he'd made for himself rather than rejoin the civilization he'd fled from because of the Genocide Directive.

Nanzar had been wounded when the Battle Fish got scuttled while Gram's soldiers were fighting the sailors aboard. None of the combatants on either side survived. Two Combrians guarding Nanzar in a civilian craft a ways from the ship had been killed by the same barrage of shrapnel that struck his head and sank their boat. The physician aboard the Storm verified the cause of death.

Nanzar had given Shovel only sketchy detail about how

the soldiers who'd forced him to carry out Gram's order to construct and test an atomic bomb managed to board Captain Denton's ship under the guise of giving themselves up. Vern couldn't imagine Baylor Denton being outsmarted like that, but mind probes verified the Mancombra had recounted Nanzar's tale exactly the way he remembered hearing it. With Nanzar having nothing to gain by lying to Shovel, enemy subterfuge had been recorded as the official reason the Battle Fish sank, leaving no survivors.

A reconnaissance crew had combed the island pointed out as Nanzar's location by the transmitter on Anger and found no other bombs, only the equipment used to remotely detonate the prototype. Nanzar's death had brought the war to an official end.

The revolution was over.

When the hover whirly landed at the palace, Hammer immediately unfastened his seatbelt, stood up, and stretched. Voola did likewise. They'd been flown there under order of Prince Zane. He had no idea why.

"Amazing, isn't it?" said Voola. "Only days ago the locations of Gram Pillhigh and Nanzar were unknown. Now both have been found and the war is really over."

He smiled at her. "And we have you to thank for it, my love."

"No, Ivan Goralov saved our planet, I just happened to be the one Charley captured. Wonder why Prince Zane wants to see us in person."

"Whatever the reason, we're about to find out."

She heaved a belligerent sigh and pouted like an angry child. "I don't understand why we had to be given a twelve-hour dose of Clodec for the occasion."

"That makes two of us." Hand behind her back, he guided Voola to the hatch.

✝

Arigot asked for the keys.

The Urth corporal furrowed his brow. "May I ask why, Sir?"

"Because I want to do it alone."

Keys in hand, he started down the corridor for Releen's cell. Sadly, unable to grasp the reality of their father's true nature, her children had nothing but hatred for Prince Zane. He hadn't spoken to her since fulfilling the order to probe her mind the day of Gram's execution, but she hadn't left his since. It struck him as very ironic that his half brother had fallen in love with Gram's mistress and he was heavily drawn to the dead king's widow.

After hearing what he'd learned from exploring Releen's thoughts and memories, PC had sought the opinions of Lieutenant Free and Captain Morris. It wouldn't have been necessary if her offspring had shared her view of Gram. Maternal instincts being what they are had complicated things. While he'd been searching Releen's psyche, another Combrian officer had tended to the children's, and they'd given their reports shortly after Gram's demise. PC had told Free and Morris to deliberate four days on the matter of releasing Releen or keeping her in custody. They'd given their conclusions forty minutes ago and Arigot had been granted permission to inform the queen of her fate.

The lovely Combrian stood with delicate fingers wrapped around cell bars when he approached.

He unlocked the door and opened it.

"Where are you taking me?" she asked, eyes widening with trepidation.

"To a halfway house. It's a place where certain prisoners about to be freed or paroled spend some time getting re-acclimated to society."

A momentary expression of relief turned to concern. "How long will I be there?"

"For quite awhile I'm afraid. But it won't be anything like the dungeon, you'll have similar comforts and freedoms as if being under house arrest."

She smiled. "Will I see you again after you take me there?"

The hope that she would reverberating through his brain from hers, he couldn't keep from smiling back. "I could pay you a visit from time to time if you'd like."

"I'd like that very much. May I ask your name?"

"Arigot."

"Ah," she sighed, "Old Combrian for *Cerebral.* Releen means *Beautiful and Sensual.*"

The name suited her perfectly. "I know."

"And my children?"

"I regret to say they won't be joining you. They'll be sent to a juvenile detention center in Juxbow."

Tears pooled in her stunning orbs as her sorrow filled his head. He cleared his throat. "I'm very sorry it has to be this way, but they're extremely hostile to Prince Zane."

She gazed at him with self blame torturing her mind. "I shielded them from the truth about their father. Please ask Prince Zane if I might be permitted to speak with them and explain why Gram deserved to die."

"No need. You'll be allowed maternal visits every sixty days, in which time you'll all be quartered in an apartment under guard for forty-eight hours."

That brightened her spirits a little. "When you questioned me, how much did you dig from my thoughts?"

Embarrassed, he looked away.

"You know I'm attracted to you, don't you."

He nodded.

"I wish I could probe your mind and learn how you view me."

Again clearing his throat, he turned back to her. "I requested the job of escorting you to the halfway house, so that should give you some idea."

A glowing smile rose on her beautiful face.

PC paced back and forth, hands behind his back, pretending to be concerned about something. Hammer and Voola sat near his desk, expressions curious and slightly anxious. He kept up the farce until Free showed up with the box and handed it to him.

"Thank you, Lieutenant, that'll be all."

As his old friend left the room, he turned to his visitors while tapping his left palm with the narrow container. "Colonel, I've commissioned a base to be built at the site your camp currently occupies. I've chosen to call it Fort Goralov—a brigadier general will oversee operations there. Voola, you're going to have a top of the line office to work in, and gracious living quarters at the fort. As we speak a specialized desk is being constructed for your monitoring equipment. As of this moment you're officially drafted into the army." He handed her the box. "Since you're no longer an honorary lieutenant you can be promoted and will be. Those are your captain bars you're holding. Captain Wurz will be promoted to major and stationed wherever General Yonker decides. As for you, Colonel Hammer . . . well I've been pondering that issue. How do you think you'd best serve our military in peace time? Juxbow perhaps? I could use another Mancombra officer there to show those bigots I mean business about not tolerating racial barriers."

Gross disappointment showed on Hammer's visage but he didn't speak, clearly geared up to dutifully accept whatever assignment got handed to him.

"Well, Colonel, what do you think?"

"It's your opinion that matters, Prince Zane, not mine. I'm a soldier . . . I obey orders."

"Well let's hear your opinion anyway."

"With all due respect, Prince Zane, I'd like to serve at the new base at Mount Opian."

"Oh? Might I inquire why? Seems to me you'd be sick of the place by now."

The love-struck Mancombra had such a strained look in his eyes he found it very hard not to laugh. Voola, on the other hand, appeared quite suspicious, knowing he was aware of their relationship. She obviously hadn't confided it to Hammer or he wouldn't be so befuddled.

"You seemed perturbed, Colonel."

On cue, Free opened the door where he'd been told to eavesdrop. "Permission to enter, Sir?"

"Granted."

Hammer squinted at him as he accepted another box from his aide. "Well what have we here?" He opened it and feigned surprise. "Why, it's a set of silver stars. Lieutenant Free, whom did you have in mind for this promotion?"

"Me, Sir."

"Now, Free, we've been over that. Pick someone besides yourself."

Breathing out a fake sigh of disappointment, Free pointed at Hammer. "If you're not going to pin them on me then I chose the colonel."

"Why, what has he done to deserve them?"

"What has he done?!" Free slammed a hand over his heart. "Only discover the pyramid that led to the salvation of Combria, Prince Zane!"

"Hmm, I suppose you have a point there." No longer able to restrain himself, he started laughing and shook his head. "I had the two of you drugged so you wouldn't catch on, but I didn't think you'd be this dense. Brigadier General Hammer, stand and receive your stars. You'll be in charge of Fort Goralov the remainder of your career. I decided to promote you when Voola located Gram. Forgive me the indulgence of this charade, but having very little time for entertainment, I sometimes create my own."

The joy on Hammer's face and the rapture on Voola's made him wish he didn't have such awesome responsibilities. But his life belonged to the people of Combria, he couldn't risk love clouding his judgment. "Contact General Yonker for further details on the new base, then the rest of the day is yours to do as you wish. Head back to Mount Opian tomorrow and send Sergeant Brush back to me when you get there. Lieutenant Free will give you Captain Wurz's new insignias so you can promote him. Now if you'll excuse me, I have a teleon address to prepare for."

Shoehorn made himself comfortable before the teleon. Prince Zane had scheduled a planetary address and he was eager to hear the details about Nanzar which would surely be forthcoming. As always, Lieutenant Free spoke first, welcoming the viewers before presenting Zane.

Red hair parted down the middle and falling behind his shoulders, the green-eyed Urth stepped up to the podium. "My fellow citizens, it is with the utmost pleasure that I announce the end of the battle to liberate Combria from the tyrant that was Gram Pillhigh. The war is officially over."

Cheers and applause rose from the palace audience.

"Doctor Nanzar has been found and I regret to say he's dead. Now I know a lot of you, perhaps the majority of you, feel as I do that he should be that way, but I promised my father I'd say a few words on the doctor's behalf. But first I want you to know that his death wasn't ordered by me. He died of injuries sustained during a sea battle while being held captive by some of Gram's soldiers. So to Nanzar's credit, his attempt to build the doomsday weapon was coerced by Gram. His only contemporary, my father Harv Zane, has asked me to tell the world that he firmly believes Doctor Nanzar's relativity theory was an original thesis, not a plagiarized edition of Harv's research. Harv considered Nanzar a friend. Now having fulfilled that obligation, I'll go on to other matters.

"If you'll recall, when I announced the abolishment of fertility testing for Mancombras, I mentioned having more to say on the matter. Well tonight I'll inform you what that is. You look at me and see an Urth man. While it is true that I have Urth blood in my veins, it mingles with that of Combrian. Fellow citizens, your leader is a Mancombra."

A wild uproar rose from the palace audience—most of it laughter—the majority thinking he must have been joking. Shoehorn lurched forward, gaping at the screen. *So there* is *another like me!*

It took ten minutes for the crowd to settle down enough for Zane to continue. "If I'm a Mancombra, how is it I look totally Urth-like, you may well ask. Because, despite what medical science has declared impossible, both of my natural parents were Mancombras. I spent most of last night speaking with a geneticist who discovered long ago that under the right conditions two Mancombras can in fact reproduce. According to her research, if fertile male and female Mancombra siblings—conceived by a Combrian father and Urth mother—have sex, there's an eighty percent probability of producing a baby if a healthy sperm reaches the egg before one of the barren seeds seals it—which unfortunately comprises the majority of spermatozoa in even the most fertile Mancombra males—and that child will always appear to be pure Urth. My natural parents are dead, killed as a result of Gram's madness. It's no secret that Harv and Molly Zane adopted me as an infant. What has been a secret until now is that Professors Wheelbarrow and Needle of Combria University spawned me.

"Though I'm the offspring of two Mancombras, I'm like any other Urth in respect to telekinesis and telepathy. I'm capable of neither. I call out to any of you who've lived with the same secret I have. Please come to the palace so I can meet you. This invitation includes anyone who only suspects they may be like me. Any Mancombra who looks like an Urth came from Mancombra siblings conceived by a male Combrian and a female Urth. No other combination of Mancombras will result in pregnancy. Regular blood tests will show you to be an Urth, but the geneticist I spoke of can verify it through a special test, so don't rely on any physician to determine if you're a rarity like me. Before I'll meet with you, you'll have undergone such a test to verify you're truly a Mancombra. If the test proves you're not you'll be sent away, so don't waste your time if you're merely wanting to meet me in person."

Shoehorn muted the teleon and turned to Chisel. "Get the boat ready, I'm heading for the mainland to buy a whirly ticket and fly to the palace."

Chisel frowned. "Do you think that's wise?"

"No one can connect me to Nanzar, I'm an innocent civilian."

"But they'll probe your mind, Shoehorn, and learn our plans."

"No they won't—learn our plans that is. You forget how well I control my thought processes. I simply won't allow myself to think anything damaging while in Opianapolis. There's bound to be very few of my kind, perhaps I'm the only one other than Zane. Either way he'll feel a special kinship with me because of it, and if I can befriend him we may not need a thermonuclear bomb to conquer Combria. Harv Zane and I are old acquaintances, so that gives Zane another reason to like me from the start. Being attacked forced us to sacrifice Nanzar which delayed my plans of bombing University City, otherwise Harv would be dead. Fate has blessed us once again."

THIRTY EIGHT

Pliers ENTERED THE APARTMENT TO find Prince Zane and his father in the parlor conversing with Polka, who looked up with a smile. "Did you have fun at Mount Opian?"

Uncertain of proper procedure when being in the presence of Combria's new ruler in an informal setting, she meekly nodded.

Prince Zane rose from his chair and stepped towards her. "We didn't get properly acquainted when I was here last because of the situation with Corporal Stove. Your name's Pliers, right?"

"Yes, Prince Zane."

"Did you catch my address earlier this evening?"

"I regret I didn't, Sir. I was on a whirly, flying back from Colonel Hammer's camp."

"Polka will fill you in then." He glanced at his father. "Well, Harv, I guess we should be going so the sergeant major can get some rest."

Harv patted her on the back while walking past. "Good seeing you again, Pliers."

"Likewise, Doctor Zane."

"You'd better sit down for this, Pliers," said Polka the moment they left. "You're not going to believe it."

"I'm going to ask once more, and this time you'd better give me a different answer!"

The market clerk laughed and shrugged her Combrian shoulders. "I wouldn't lie to you, miss. I'm sorry it upsets you so much, but we don't carry essence of valley fern."

Voola bit her lip to keep from screaming. She could tell Hammer wanted to pitch a fit as well.

Polka started cutting up a fried hicker egg. "I hated having to cook my own breakfast while you were away. You've really spoiled me, Pliers."

The sweet Combrian grinned. "Glad to do so, Ma'am."

"So did you and Drill consummate your relationship while you were at his camp?"

"Ma'am!"

She giggled. "You're blushing, Sergeant Major. Come on and tell me—we're like family you, Drill, and I. I'm dying to know."

"Colonel Hammer gave him a six day pass and let us borrow his wheeler and um . . . we got a room at an inn night before last. I've never felt this way about a male before. Drill and I are soul mates."

"So have you two set a date yet . . .?" she bit off an end of a sern strip.

Pliers smiled. "We're to be mated this coming Feast of the

Annual Snow."

Polka bemoaned their sterility: such strong character traits should be passed on. "Thanks to Prince Zane you guys can adopt kids if you want, since you won't be able to have any of your own."

"That's right, Ma'am, but as I've told you, I don't want children. Thankfully, neither does Drill. He said having a child running around would remind him of his young siblings and constantly bring back the horrid memories of losing them at the death camp."

"That's a shame, the two of you would make wonderful parents."

"Speaking of that, Ma'am, are you sure Prince Zane is really a Mancombra?"

"Mm hmm, no doubt about it. You should have seen the audience at the palace when he made the announcement— talk about pandemonium. I have to go to the infirmary after breakfast so I can test anyone claiming to be like him. I'll be stuck there all day and I'll bet not one person that shows will be the real deal. It's very possible Prince Zane's the only one on the planet."

Free chewed off a corner of toasted grain square coated with swabbed egg yolk and looked across PC's desk, currently serving as a breakfast table. "Being a Mancombra isn't the only secret you've carried all your life."

"What makes you say that . . .?" PC covered a stack of grain cakes with sweetened fanleaf sap.

"I've been playing dumb long enough. I'm on to you, old

pal—I know you're clairvoyant. All those bogus intelligence reports didn't fool me."

PC grimaced as if he'd taken a bullet in the gut. "Have you told anyone about this?"

"No. Since you didn't divulge it to me, I knew you wouldn't want anyone to know. Why are you so intent on keeping it secret?"

Two unblinking green eyes stared a hole through him for several long moments, then a deep sigh vacated PC's lungs. "I'm not clairvoyant . . . I had to use intelligence reports as a cover to keep anyone from knowing how I really found out the information. It's a talent I was born with, and that's all I'm going to say on the matter."

"Sure sounds like clairvoyance to me."

"Call it that if you want but the term is incorrect. You'd better keep this to yourself, Free."

"Don't worry. You know you can trust me."

"Yeah . . . except at cards."

He looked to the ceiling and groaned. "How long are you going to hold that against me for galaxies sake?"

The intercom buzzed. PC hit the button. "Yes?"

"Morris here, Prince Zane. Polka's ready to start testing."

"Very good, Captain. Let me know if she finds a live one."

"Will do, Sir."

Vern couldn't shake a suspicion that grew stronger each time he mulled over the sinking of the Battle Fish. Baylor Denton had earned his rank the hard way, through an education obtained by rugged experience. He didn't enter the service as a second lieutenant fresh out of the naval academy like most naval officers did, but started from the bottom as a basic seaman. Streetwise, full of common sense, extremely savvy, the captain wouldn't have taken the word of Gram's soldiers at face value that they wanted to surrender. So how had they fooled him? And how had they managed to engage in combat without arms? Denton would have made damn sure each of them were weaponless before taking them aboard.

Something very irregular went down on the Battle Fish and he was determined to get to the bottom of it.

Polka had tested over fifty Urths, mostly giggly adolescent girls hoping to meet Prince Zane in person. How any of them fancied getting past the protocol was beyond her. Fifteen minutes remained before she could call it a day, and not a single analysis had turned up positive.

An orderly stepped into the lab, escorting an Urth she recognized right away. "Doctor Smith! My galaxies it seems like a lifetime since I last saw you."

His face contorted with immense surprise. "Polka?"

"The one and only."

"When Prince Zane mentioned the geneticist on teleon last night I wouldn't have thought it was you in a million double-years. I thought you'd retired to a farm."

She lowered her chin and raised her brows. "How about exiled from the academic community by Gram's thugs."

"Oh, that kind of retirement. My sympathies."

"Well I know you really retired. Where are you living

these days, Daniel?"

He shrugged. "I'm enjoying the life of a vagabond, never staying anywhere for long."

"So what brings you here?"

"Prince Zane isn't the only Mancombra cloaked in Urthdom, dear. When I left the orphanage as a young man I met my real mother—a Mancombra. I'm the result of her being raped by one of her brothers. As a matter of fact I'm now going by Shoehorn, the name she'd planned to give me before having to take me to the orphanage when I was born without copper skin and purple eyes."

Disappointment gnawing at him, PC impatiently paced the floor. He'd hoped at least one other being on the planet was like him so they could compare notes and he'd finally know if his gifts were genetic or spiritually bestowed. He thanked the unseen power for Polka. Her ability to verify his breed of Mancombra would weed out any pretenders. The old woman had no idea she'd soon be standing beside him at the podium with all of Combrian watching as he hung the Combrian Medal of Honor for Scientific Achievement around her neck. With Nanzar dead, she'd join Harv as the only living recipient on the planet. Ironically Gram Pillhigh had bestowed it on his father shortly before the revolution began. The tyrant had revoked it soon afterwards, but like Wheelbarrow's and Needle's professorships, it had been restored when he came to power.

Her lieutenant bars would be taken from her and so would her honorary enlistment. In the near future she'd be working in a laboratory built to her specifications, receiving a handsome salary from the government. She needed to continue her research in genetics after training someone to take her place teaching the probe blocking technique. Though unnecessary now, it could prove invaluable if a revolt broke out. He'd let her remain in the duke's old apartment or have the government build her a fine home if she preferred.

The intercom sounded. He hurried to his desk and pushed the button.

"Polka verified one, Prince Zane," Captain Morris enthusiastically reported. "He's a retired psychiatrist named Daniel Smith and is being escorted to your office as we speak."

Excitement washing over him, he thanked the captain and started walking the floor again, feet now motivated by anticipation.

Fifteen minutes later Daniel Smith stepped into his office.

"It's an honor to meet you, Prince Zane."

He examined the psychiatrist's features: black hair graying at the temples of an aging face, dark eyes hinting of a vast intellect looming behind them, stature a tad shorter than his, and the physique of a man unacquainted with athletics or physical labor, much like Harv's.

"Tell me about yourself, Daniel . . . ."

Drill raised his brows when his commander and Voola pulled up to the guard station—the colonel had a star on each shoulder. He saluted. "Congratulations on your promotion, General."

Each of them looked frustrated about something and their minds were blocked. Hammer gave him a cursory thank you and pulled into camp. They'd driven from the Army Command Center after being flown there from the palace, so he surmised they were just tired from the trip.

Pliers had returned to the palace only yesterday, but it already seemed like she'd been gone a double-year. He'd felt lonesome eating breakfast without her that morning after doing so six times in a row. He loved they'd gotten to see Gram's execution together. She'd started crying when he broke down as the screaming king brought back horrid memories of his last day at the death camp. Gram had evoked something else within him as well. Had he been the child carrying that torch, Captain Morris would never have gotten his hands on it. He'd have been unable to resist setting the fire himself.

He had dinner brought to his office when Daniel finished relaying his life story. The psychiatrist sat down and began eating heartily. Merely picking at his meal, PC dug for the information he coveted. "Do you have telekinetic or telepathic powers, Daniel?"

"No. I thought it interesting while listening to you last night that you don't either."

After considering several approaches, he finally settled on one least likely to give anything away. "How about weird dreams?"

"What do you mean . . .?" his guest took a bite of baked

hicker.

"I have recurring dreams about being in two places at the same time. Very strange."

"Unusual dreams aren't unique to any race, Prince Zane. Everyone's susceptible to them."

"Have you ever had one like that?"

"No, but I've had my share of nightmares like anyone else."

He let a few moments of silence roll by, pretending to be interested in his food. "I have other peculiar dreams as well. In those I'm paralyzed—can't move a muscle or even blink my eyes—and a historic event plays out before me in intricate detail. I can sense the thoughts and emotions of all the people involved."

Daniel took a swig of light ale and resumed eating. "Never dreamed anything like that either."

"Ever experience anything similar in real life?"

"Of course not," he laughed, mouth full of mashed starch-roots. The white tubers were the most consumed vegetable on Combria—fried, baked, or boiled.

Endeavoring to conceal his exhilaration over learning his gifts *did* evidently extend from the unseen power, he ate a small bite of hicker breast before saying, "I've always thought I had those dreams because of my parentage. Since they're alien to you, I see I was wrong."

The psychiatrist frowned inquisitively. "You think some of those dreams really happened, don't you."

"No." He tried to sound matter of fact because he'd clearly roused the doctor's psychoanalytic side. It was time to change the subject. "Where do you live?"

"I'm never at the same place for any appreciable length of time. I've become a world traveler since I retired. How many more of us do you suppose exists?"

"That's something I hope to find out. So you go by

Shoehorn now, huh?"

"Mm hmm. As I told you, it was the name my mother planned to call me."

"I guess I should quit calling you Daniel then."

"Whichever you prefer, Prince Zane. I've grown used to being called both. Polka didn't switch when I explained it to her. She still calls me Daniel or Doctor Smith like she used to."

"So you two know each other?"

"Yeah, Polka and I go way back."

The night he'd been at her apartment while at the same time standing on a palace balcony came to mind. It struck him very odd that she'd wound up playing such an important role in his life after the event. Had the unseen power caused him to go there in order to begin cluing him in on why such manifestations occurred? If so, being sent to that island and witnessing the tribal chief conversing with his grandchild about the sailors must be important. But with Nanzar no longer a threat, he reckoned it didn't matter now.

THIRTY NINE

ARIGOT LEFT THE HALFWAY HOUSE with a lump in his throat. He'd taken Releen there yesterday and had just concluded his first visit. It would likely be awhile before his return. Vern Yonker wanted to see him about something and he could tell by the general's tone some type of mission awaited him. With so many surrendered soldiers to be processed, he supposed Fort Pacific or one of the other bases with large stockades would be his ultimate destination. But he couldn't complain since he'd dodged being reduced to ashes like Gram Pillhigh.

Hammer had his troops at attention. "A construction crew will be arriving soon to break ground on a new base to be named Fort Goralov. Voola is no longer an honorary lieutenant. Prince Zane has dubbed her a full-fledged captain and she'll be treated as such. The sniper team will be reduced by one, but the rest of you will remain under my command, with the exception of Captain Wurz and Sergeant

Brush. Corporal Sills, drive the sergeant and PFC Drill to the palace in my wheeler and report back here in two days. The three of you are dismissed."

As they broke ranks, he opened the box Lieutenant Free had given him. "Captain Wurz, these insignias are for you. I've been given the honor of promoting you to major."

Wurz removed his hat and slicked back the few sprigs of hair on his head while stepping towards him, smiling wide. "Where am I headed, Sir?"

"To General Yonker's office to receive your new orders."

The drone of the boat's twin engines filling his ears, Shoehorn gazed across the glistening sea. Zane had been too inscrutable not to be hiding something. He wasn't looking for kinsmanship with Mancombras spawned by Mancombras, the usurper wanted to find out if they shared what he kept hidden about himself. Their friendship would never advance past the cordial stage because he'd discerned PC Zane was a Type C Personality: one who kept everyone at arms' length. Ergo the atomic bomb would have to be dropped after all.

He'd hoped such a strong bond would be forged between them due to their unique pedigree that Zane would invite him to reside in the palace. In only a matter of days he'd have been able to scout out the defense systems and learn the number of soldiers within the grounds. Then, disguised as tourists, his eleven Mancombras could have taken it over. At that point he'd have announced to all of Combria they'd garnered Nanzar's technology for the doomsday device, had the capability of destroying all their cities, and would start doing so one by one if not recognized as supreme rulers of the planet by every citizen.

The island appeared on the horizon. A moment later a gull landed on the bow, head cocked with curiosity. Shoehorn grinned at the fowl. "Hi there, big fella. Sorry but I don't have any fish aboard."

As if understanding him, the gull took flight, but quickly disappeared.

He sucked in a terrified breath and slapped his palms over his face. "Oh no, not again!"

A swarm of gulls descended on him, tearing his shirt off with their clawed feet, pecking his skin away, eating through his bleeding fingers to reach his eyes. Several attacked his gonads, piercing through his trousers with their sharp beaks, while others tore out his rectum. He screamed in pain for several minutes before they evaporated, leaving him unscathed . . . physically. Hyperventilating, sweat pouring from every duct in his body, he lowered his shuddering hands and saw the alcove nearing.

Two days and only one like him had come to the palace. PC had decided there most likely weren't any more on the planet. Sitting at his desk, thinking about Daniel 'Shoehorn' Smith, he found himself envying the doctor's drifter lifestyle. How wonderful it must be to have no responsibilities, no longer have to earn a living—go wherever, do whatever one wanted.

BZZZZZZ!

"Yes?"

"Polka said another one passed the test, Prince Zane. She's on her way now."

"Polka?"

"No, Sir. The Mancombra."

"Thank you, Captain."

He got up and started pacing, marveling at the coincidence of meeting a second peer near the same time of day Daniel Smith arrived yesterday. Since Smith didn't have his abilities he didn't expect the female would either, but he'd query her in similar fashion to be certain. Thinking about odd talents brought Harv's superior comprehension of physics to the forefront of his mind, along with a wave of irritation over the genius's hardheadedness in refusing to admit that a Combrian scientist stole his ideas. He suspected Harv knew Nanzar's relativity theory was a thinly veiled proliferation of his thesis. Wheelbarrow and Needle had certainly thought so, even though they'd always admired Dr. Nanzar. He'd announced his adoptive father's belief in Nanzar's integrity begrudgingly, at Harv's insistence.

The guard announced the Mancombra's arrival and PC told him to let her in. A jolt of astonishment immobilizing him, he had to force his mouth closed as she strolled into the room. He'd never been so impacted by a woman. She had wavy blonde hair, almost Combrian platinum, the prettiest face he'd ever seen, and a shockingly voluptuous figure, covered by a silk body-suit.

"I can't believe I'm actually getting to meet you, Prince Zane. You have no idea what this means to me."

Her voice electrified him. "What's your name?"

"Stellar Allure."

Well of course it is! "Um, won't you please have a seat?"

She gracefully eased into an armchair and frowned.

"Is something wrong?" he asked.

"I was just wondering why you're wearing a weapon when

the war is over?"

"If it offends you, I'll take it off."

Her cheeks turned bright pink as she smiled at him. "You'd do that for me?"

I think I could probably do a double-back flip if you asked me too, he chuckled to himself. "I don't want to make you feel uncomfortable that's all."

"It's okay. I'm very flattered by the offer though."

Maneuvering to the edge of his desk, he sat down on it while folding his arms across his chest, trying to act nonchalant—having a very hard time doing so. "Tell me about your parents."

"It's very bizarre, but also quite romantic. Their parents separated when they were toddlers. My grandfather took my dad with him, my grandmother raised my mom. They met at a party and started dating, having no idea they were brother and sister. They mated, and of course never used birth control since it was supposedly impossible for two Mancombras to procreate. Because of the law they had to pretend they'd found me abandoned after keeping me hidden until I was old enough to leave my mother's breast. They approached my grandmother to see if she'd take me in, and the moment she saw my father she suspected he was her long lost son. My dad took her to his father's house and it was confirmed. Seeing each other again after such a long time, my grandparents' love for each other was rekindled. They re-mated and adopted me. I wasn't told the truth until you confessed your ethnicity. Up until three days ago I thought I was a pure-bred Urth adopted by a Combrian father and an Urth mother."

✝

Polka groaned while easing into a luxurious armchair, and heaved a weary sigh as she propped her feet on a footstool.

"Tough day, Ma'am?"

"I've run over a hundred tests these last two days and only two were legitimate. How stupid can people be, Pliers?"

"The sky's the limit on that, I'm afraid."

"Isn't that the truth. You know what's strange? The two real Mancombras were the last ones I tested before leaving the lab—my old colleague I told you about last night, and a female named Stellar Allure today. And oh she's such a pretty thing, Pliers. I'll bet Prince Zane had to pick his jaw up off the floor after he first saw her."

Pliers giggled. "Don't let her anywhere near my Drill then."

"Drill only has eyes for you now, dear."

Vern told Arigot to have a seat. "Been to dinner?"

"I ate on the way here, Sir."

He locked his fingers together and started rotating his thumbs. "As I recall, you spent your first double-years as a sailor after you enlisted."

"Yes, Sir. I made it to chief petty officer before Universal Quest ordered me to the infantry and promoted me to lieutenant principal."

"Funny how the House of Pillhigh chose ancient Urth ranks for the navy isn't it? I suppose it would have been too demeaning to come up with Combrian equivalents with Urths and Combrians serving on the same boats. Anyway, you knew Baylor Denton pretty well, didn't you?"

"Yes, Sir. I served under him as a matter of fact."

Unclasping his hands, he leaned forward and brought them back together atop his desk. "Let me tell you what allegedly happened on the Battle Fish, and see if it squares with your logic, Colonel . . . ."

⸆

PC had taken Stellar to his quarters and ordered dinner from there so she wouldn't have to eat at his desk. They were sitting at the kitchen table, sipping kaffy.

She'd given him a brief synopsis of her life. After obtaining her degree at Combria University five double-years ago, she'd gone to work as a veterinarian at a big clinic in University City, where she'd remained since. An Urth had won her heart but she'd broken off their engagement upon discovering he was unfaithful. He'd winced inside upon hearing that. Males of every race could be foolish at times, but he'd never encountered one that stupid.

Her pretty lips puckered over the rim of her cup, held by long slender fingers with polished nails. She took a dainty nip of kaffy and fixed her arresting cerulean eyes on him. "The lady that drew my blood told me I was only the second one to test positive."

"That's right. A retired psychiatrist named Daniel Smith came to the palace yesterday. He was born as a result of incestual rape. That makes three of us so far."

"How many more do you think there'll be?"

"Our numbers can't be very high for obvious reasons. You, Doctor Smith, and I may be the only ones. Of course there's always the possibility that a few are ashamed to admit their parents were siblings. Some may not want the world to know they're really Mancombras, and some may have been adopted as infants by parents who've never told them the truth. I'm sure most of the populace thinks I'm mistaken and can't possibly have been bred by two Mancombras. Otherwise there'd be a lot more flack aimed at me than what has been since the announcement.

"Anyway, I'd like to ask you a few questions. I queried Doctor Smith too, but he didn't share any of my quirks. I grew up thinking they were unique to me because of my parents being Mancombras."

Her eyes widened. "You've always known where you really came from?"

"Mm hmm."

She lowered them and sighed. "I wish I had. When my grandmother—who I grew up thinking was my adopted mom—told me the truth after watching you on teleon the other night, I've concluded that's why I have such unusual endowments. I didn't inherit my parents' mental powers but I think they passed some things on to me that either lie dormant in their genes, or their telekinetic and telepathic facilities got jumbled up in me at conception."

Disappointment blasted him like a strong dry wind—his gifts weren't bestowed by the unseen spirit after all. Certain of what she'd say, he numbly asked what unusual endowments she possessed.

"I doubt you'll believe me, Prince Zane."

"Oh you'd be surprised at my open mindedness on the unusual. Tell me."

She grinned like a little girl caught in an embarrassing situation. "I can communicate with animals—and I don't mean like an animal trainer does—I really carry on a conversation with them. I have to speak to them vocally, but they answer me in my mind. My grandmother thought I was making it up until I proved it to her by telling my pet hopper to paw the floor each time she blinked. It almost gave the poor woman a heart attack. She's Urth of course, or my parents wouldn't have been able to conceive me, according to the geneticist you spoke of in your planetary address. I was a small child at the time and when my dad—sorry, my grandfather—saw I could really do it, it frightened him and he warned me to keep my talent to myself or the government would take me away and force me to help the military. You're the only person besides them I've ever told."

Stunned to hear her talent differed from the three he possessed, he realized his abilities must have passed to him the same way: his parents' mental powers getting tangled up in a unique combination in his chromosomes. He suspected none of his kind would have the same capabilities because the genetic dice of telekinesis and telepathy obviously hadn't landed on the same numbers in Stellar and him at conception. Apparently the mix sometimes came up dormant and no peculiar capacities were passed on, since Daniel Smith didn't have any. Unless, of course, the doctor had lied to him.

Discovering his gifts hadn't been bestowed by The Spirit That Created All Things after all made him feel empty inside, but he forced a smile. "I would imagine that greatly helps in your line of work."

"Oh yes, significantly. That's why I studied veterinary medicine in the first place. You don't really believe me, do you."

"Of course I do," he firmly declared.

Stellar narrowed her eyes. "Why? Because you can do the same per chance?"

"That's not the reason."

"Why then?"

"Because of my quirks I spoke of. Though I can't socialize with animals, I inherited some unusual endowments as well."

"Did Doctor Smith?"

"No . . . at least he claims not to have any."

She leaned towards him, face aglow with anticipation. "What talents did you inherit? I'm dying to hear."

"If I didn't have the burden of leadership bearing down on me I'd gladly tell you. Unfortunately I do, and can't risk anyone knowing what they are. But please, tell me what other abilities you inherited."

"Uh-uh. If you won't tell me yours then I won't tell you the other strange knack I inherited."

The flirtatious way she spoke it made him realize she'd picked up on his immense attraction for her. Faking an angry scowl, he steeled his jaw as if finding her refusal impossible to tolerate. "I don't like to flaunt my power but I think I'm going to have you beheaded for refusing to cooperate."

She gasped and clutched her hair. "Oh I beg you, Prince Zane, don't do it—I'll tell you, I'll tell you!"

Her unexpected reaction floored him and he burst out laughing. "Galaxies, I was only teasing, Stellar, I'd never do anything like that."

He was still shivering through the aftereffects. Chisel brought him a glass of ale to calm his nerves. "Here you go, Shoehorn."

"Thank you . . ." he downed half of it.

"What happened during this spell?"

"Gulls tried to eat me."

Chisel shook his head sympathetically. "I'm so sorry you have these episodes."

A painful air pocket formed in his esophagus as he emptied the glass. He burped it out and ran a hand over his wet lips. "I'm convinced Prince Zane suffers some type of torment as well. He pumped me about it, using the disguise of strange dreams, but I think he may have inherited something else besides these hallucinogenic spells I suffer periodically."

"Aren't you glad you didn't."

"I'm speaking of some sort of power, Chisel, not another psychosomatic syndrome. Whatever it is, I think he used it to sway all the soldiers that sided with him when he mutinied."

Chisel frowned. "That seems unlikely since you didn't inherit anything like that."

He held the glass out for a refill. "Not really. My kind would be as diverse as yours, Combrians, or Urths. Children from the same parents inherit different capabilities as well as deficiencies. I suspect Zane was genetically gifted with something very unique. Something that enabled him to assume the rule over Combria."

FORTY

TRUE TO HIS WORD, COLONEL Arigot had paid her a visit earlier in the day which thrilled Releen. Unfortunately he didn't know when his duties would permit him to come see her again. When he'd brought her here yesterday the handsome Combrian had been able to probe her mind, but today he'd been given a shot of Clodec at the entry gates like any other visitor. They'd been allowed to stroll the grounds, but she couldn't set foot past the wire fence surrounding the minimum security halfway house.

Dinner had been served two hours ago and she'd been watching teleon with some other inmates since then. They were granted that privilege until bedtime arrived at ten. The show now airing may or may not have been entertaining, she didn't know. Though idly viewing the screen, her thoughts were absorbed by the colonel.

He'd finally gotten Stellar's nerves settled and apologized once more for not realizing his sense of humor wouldn't be appreciated. She poured a generous portion of sweetener into a fresh cup of kaffy, stirred it, and held the vessel with both hands while sipping.

"You didn't really think I was serious did you?"

"What else was I to think, I've never seen how you deal

with such matters. You really frightened me, Prince Zane."

He'd memorized her splendor in order to pull the breathtaking image from his vault of treasured memories from time to time. This special night he'd never forget, and he planned to savor every moment with her, for their paths must never cross again. Stellar Allure induced in him an irresistible distraction from duty that had to be avoided at all costs.

The corners of her pretty lips turned up. "I'll tell you what my other ability is if you'll answer a personal question."

It dawned on him he'd been blatantly staring. He lowered his eyes to his cup while slipping a finger through the handle. "What is it you want to know?"

"How is it you never mated?"

"I am mated—" he looked up "—to my mission."

She squinted at him with a cute expression that made her gorgeousness less intimidating, giving her an air of approachability her typical appearance belied. "But you've completed it. Don't you want someone to share your life with?"

That hit him square in the gut, but he refused to allow his reaction to show. "You were allowed one question, not two. What's your other talent?"

"I feel ill all of a sudden . . ." Stellar fell to the floor and rolled over on her back. Eyes clenched shut from obvious pain, large breasts undulating with rapid shallow breaths, she coughed once and her chest quit heaving as her lovely complexion turned a putrid gray.

Immediately dropping to one knee, he felt the side of her neck and couldn't detect a pulse. "My galaxies she's dead!"

"Wrong." Death-tainted skin regaining its vibrant fair tones, she opened her eyes and grinned. "You asked what my other ability was, well this is it. I can perfectly simulate death."

He gawked at her stupidly as she stood up, dusted herself off, and sat back down at the table, giggling all the while.

"You're not the only one with a sense of humor, Prince Zane."

Arigot lay on a bunk in his temporary quarters, pondering what Vern had told him last night about the Battle Fish. He'd been obsessing about it before finally drifting off to sleep and woke up fifteen minutes ago still thinking about it. Like the general, he didn't believe Baylor Denton had been fooled by Gram's soldiers' false surrender in the manner Nanzar had said. The venerable captain would never have fallen for such a stunt. He'd have had some sailors shuttle back and forth between Gram's ship and his vessel, carrying a few soldiers at a time—each dosed with Clodec and taken aboard the ship in bonds. Since mind probes proved the Mancombra had relayed Nanzar's tale accurately, the scientist must have lied about it.

But what had he hoped to gain by doing so?

A private set their breakfast trays on PC's desk and vacated the office. Combria's chief administrator seemed preoccupied. Free still hadn't fully come to grips with his old chum being a Mancombra, but now understood why

Wheelbarrow and Needle had been so dear to him. Having visited with two of his own kind, Free supposed PC's thoughts were revolving around that. He'd met Daniel Smith, but official business with the palace press corps had kept him away from the office yesterday afternoon, so he hadn't gotten acquainted with the second visitor. He bootered a toasted grain square, set it back on the tray, sliced up a trio of fried hicker eggs, and stuck his fork into a link of hopper sausage. "Sorry I didn't get to meet the Mancombra yesterday evening. How did it go?"

PC quit staring into space and looked at him blankly. "I'm not sure."

"Something bothers you about him?"

"Not him, her."

"Oh, the Mancombra's a female, huh." He sampled the sausage, finding it deliciously spicy. "Aren't you going to eat?"

"I don't have much of an appetite this morning."

Free washed down the bite and scooped some egg into his mouth. "What's the matter, PC?"

"You apparently weren't taught not to talk with your mouth full any more than you were to mind your own business." The vinegary sneer he wore while berating him mellowed into a sympathetic frown. "I'm sorry, Free, you didn't deserve that. I just don't want to discuss it, that's all."

Having arrived at the palace last night near midnight, Drill had slept in the guards' barracks, not wanting to wake Pliers and Polka. He'd eaten breakfast at the mess hall before going to Captain Morris's office to receive his new orders.

An aide showed him in and he saluted.

Morris smiled at him from behind his desk. "I'm proud of you, Drill. At ease."

"Thank you, Sir."

"General Yonker has placed you under my command. I'm waiting for Polka and CSM Pliers to get here so I won't have to repeat myself."

"My new duty involves the two of them, Sir?" he asked hopefully.

"It does. Ah, here they are now."

Pliers beamed at him while saluting the captain. *What a fantastic surprise! How long have you been here, Drill?*

I arrived with Sergeant Brush last night, he transmitted with a smile. *It was late so I didn't want to disturb you, my love.*

Polka walked over and leaned into him with a hug. "Well I didn't expect to see you again so soon, Drill, but it's sure great to do so."

"The same goes for me, Lieutenant." He gently patted her on the back.

She raised her chin and glared at him. "Don't you ever address me formally again, it sounds vulgar. I'm like your mama, boy."

"As far as I'm concerned you are my mother, *Lieutenant.*" He received a slap on the hip for emphasizing his defiance, but she laughed while doing it.

Captain Morris cleared his throat to get everyone's attention. "You're a civilian again, Polka. Prince Zane wants to meet with you this afternoon to discuss building a laboratory for you where you'll resume your research in genetics. While it's being constructed I need you to pick out a successor and instruct them how to teach your probe blocking technique."

"Whoop!" cried Polka before covering her mouth. Her face blazed with jubilation when she finally lowered her hands. "My oh my! Captain, do you realize if you hadn't happened by my house that day I'd still be stuck on that damn farm instead of having my career resurrected? This is unbelievable."

Morris grinned. "That's not quite true. If Drill hadn't told Hammer about your ability, you'd have been sent back there when Doctor Nanzar's corpse turned up, bringing the war to its official end."

"That's what sons are for, Ma'am," said Pliers, also grinning. "Congratulations."

"This feels like a dream come true!" Polka hooted after a joyful sigh. "I've really missed working with microscopes, test tubes, and beakers. If only my mate could be here to work with me."

Captain Morris gave her a wistful smile. "I can't raise the dead, but since you're so fond of Drill and he has a college degree, I'm assigning him as envoy to keep me posted and to assist you in whatever means he's capable. CSM Pliers will be at your disposal too. You'll be choosing your own assistants from the scientific community as well, of course."

Polka sobered. "Um, will I still get to stay in the duke's apartment?"

"For the time being. Prince Zane will talk to you about future arrangements, along with your pay structure and all the other peripheral matters concerning your new position."

Drill raised his hand to speak.

"PFC?"

"Sir, where am I being quartered?"

Frowning with indignance Polka snapped, "Well you'll sleep on that super-long couch of Duke Kaleen's, like you did when you paid me that surprise visit."

"If that suits you, Drill, you may quarter there for now,"

said Captain Morris.

From the corner of his eye Drill saw Pliers assume a knowing smile which both warmed and excited him. "That suits me exceptionally well, Sir."

Polka winked at him, humorously thinking about how he wouldn't really be sleeping on that couch anymore.

I'm glad you're not offended at the idea of me sharing Pliers' bed. She agreed to be my mate and we're officially engaged.

"I know, she told me."

Confused by Polka's statement, Captain Morris cocked his head.

Pliers telecasted a message to express her joy, but it could be as easily detected by the look on her face.

Vern sat down at a table reserved for him when he took meals in the mess hall instead of his quarters. Arigot joined him for a late breakfast. All the hungry soldiers had filled their gullets and were now on duty, busy with their routines.

The pensive Combrian poured a dabble of malk into a bowl of malted grain and blended it in. "Sir, after giving it much careful thought I've come to the conclusion the Mancombra lied. I just can't fathom a reason for Nanzar purposely misrepresenting what really happened to the Battle Fish. I'm at a loss to explain how Shovel avoided being exposed by the mind probes, but I'm convinced he somehow did."

"What motive would he have, Arigot?" He dissolved a lump of sweetener in his kaffy and laid the spoon on a saucer.

A glint of fear rose in the colonel's worried eyes. "I think Nanzar must have constructed more bombs besides the one he tested, and Shovel somehow took possession of them. He'd need help to overcome Gram's thirty troops. I suspect he got that help from the other ten civilian Mancombras that remain unaccounted for. I think they boarded the Battle Fish by pretending to be refugees, wiped out the entire crew by combining their telekinetic powers, and sank the ship."

The cup Vern had raised to his lips slipped from his hand and splattered on the table.

FORTY
ONE

GENERAL YONKER HAD CONTACTED THE palace to voice concern over a possibility Colonel Arigot had laid out: that the Mancombra who'd allegedly tried to save Nanzar had in reality killed him and fabricated the details surrounding the Battle Fish to conceal the fact he'd gotten his hands on at least one atomic bomb.

"We know Polka learned how to deceive mind probes," said the general, *"so it's not impossible that Mancombra discovered how to do likewise. If Arigot's suspicions are correct we've got to find Shovel and the other ten civilians."*

Free blustered a troubled sigh into the communicator. "I'll pass it on to Prince Zane immediately, General."

"See that you do, Lieutenant...."

PC scoured the information Free had been provided concerning the eleven civilian Mancombras who hadn't come to the palace. Besides Shovel—who'd appeared to be truthful about finding Nanzar floating on a piece of wreckage in the Lower East Combrian Sea—their names were Handle, Doorknob, Key, Hoe, Level, Stapler, Miter, Lathe, Saw, and Chisel. He didn't like what he'd read about them. Arigot's apprehension might indeed be warranted. Vern had contacted SIS immediately after calling Free two hours ago. The Secret Intelligence Service hadn't been able to procure their current addresses or obtain a picture of any of them, so Ivan Goralov's computers were of no help at the moment.

He closed the folder and leaned back in his chair. "It's possible they may all know each other all right, Free. Each one's resume includes a stint at the mental asylum Daniel Smith once presided over, though only a few of them were there at the same time, according to this report. Have Vern keep the other warships at the archipelago. All of the Mancombras may be on the island Shovel claims to have lived on since the Genocide Directive was issued. Tell SIS we need a photograph of a psychiatrist named Daniel Smith who once ran the asylum for the criminally insane outside University City. He was in charge of the place when each of them worked there and might have kept in touch with some of them."

Free headed for the door, paused, and turned back to him. "What do you want me to do if they can't come up with one?"

"Tell Vern to have Arigot hunt down the doctor."

"Why Colonel Arigot?"

"Because he's very adept at finding people, and a Combrian. I need someone who can probe the psychiatrist's mind. If Smith is close to any of them he might lie about knowing their whereabouts, since he'll likely assume they're in some kind of trouble. If we can get a picture of him to Voola, I'll have Sergeant Brush run him down after she locates him."

The memory of appearing on that Wanderer's island and

feeling the chief's anxiety over a colossal explosion he'd witnessed across the waters flooded his mind. Morbidly disturbed, PC feared it might be a portent of things to come.

Shoehorn eyed the device lovingly. Attached to the vertical takeoff whirly, looking like a stubby missile, the fission bomb would be the last of its kind. The thermonuclear prototype engineered to fuse two droggen atoms into laneel was ready to test. He'd called the elements hydrogen and helium before switching to Combrian as his first language upon learning his true race. Chisel assured him the prototype would be successful so two others had been constructed to the same specifications. They'd stolen enough droggen to build four more.

The theft had been a breeze due to his Mancombras' incredible telekinetic powers. Driving a stolen commercial wheeler behind a cargo vessel on its way to a medical research facility at nighttime, Handle had levitated several canisters from it. Miter had then transferred their contents into specialized containers constructed for the transaction, and sent the originals back. No one would ever know the gas hadn't leaked out through faulty seals. Nanzar had been petrified when the Mancombras returned with the stuff, along with other vital components they'd stolen.

Instead of dropping the fission bomb on a desert island to alert Zane of the power he and his comrades possessed, Shoehorn had decided it would be best to prove straightaway he wasn't bluffing. He'd selected a harbor town nestled on the eastern edge of Serene Valley as the worthy recipient. It would surely work since Nanzar had overseen ninety-five percent of its construction and all of the atomic assembly. Two hundred thousand residents were scheduled to die in little more than a blink of an eye. He'd then contact Prince Zane and inform him that Combria would now be controlled by him and his eleven Mancombras. If the fool resisted, they'd drop the droggen prototype on the center of a densely populated section of Opian's lower east coast, where a conglomeration of eight metropolises were clustered near each other. Faced with the grim possibility of having no one left alive to govern, the rebel prince would have no choice but to surrender his reign.

He'd changed his mind about destroying University City because of a fact pointed out to him by Chisel, derived from having absorbed Nanzar's expertise on the matter. Being only ninety miles from Opianapolis, radioactive fallout might render the palace uninhabitable, and he certainly couldn't have that since he planned to spend the rest of his life there, occupying the throne.

Harv Zane would have to be eradicated by much subtler means.

Harv squinted into the microscope, studying the interior of a crystal extracted from the activation device. Applying subtle bursts of current to one side of the processor, he noted power left the other end as a series of rapid, systematic pulses that varied in only one sense. "Binary! That's how it's sending the information. It converts the energy received into binary code—short intervals equaling zero, the longer pulsations signaling one. Oh what pure genius, Doctor Goralov. Of course you chose binary, it's the fastest way for your computers to communicate with each other—a fraction of the time any other code would take."

Grabbing a writing implement, he jotted down his findings and quickly glued his eye to the microscope again, excitement racing through him as if he too had energy wires attached to him like the micro-processor, only conducting a much higher voltage.

Releen had been in the halfway house for three days. She'd get to visit her children in fifty-seven more, but felt ashamed for having a stronger desire to see Arigot again. The colonel had unknowingly purged her feelings for York. She no longer even mourned his death, compounding the sense of guilt. *What kind of female am I? Did Gram corrupt me?*

He certainly had in some ways. Before meeting the monarch she'd been generally well-rounded and far less self centered. The indulgences of living a royal life spoiling her—having to put up with his sexual inadequacies, cruelty, and eventual indifference desensitizing her—she'd turned into a person who only pretended to care about others, while in reality being consumed with her own wants and needs. Viewing her affair with York from a fresh perspective, she realized it had been the delicious illicitness of cheating on Gram she'd fallen in love with rather than the mad king's valet. The sensual pleasures had been exquisitely real, but she'd basically used poor York to masturbate—a cold dark fact she could no longer deny. But then, how could she have ever really loved a male whose life revolved around the menial task of tending to the whims of the one she so vehemently despised?

Colonel Arigot hated Gram with a passion akin to her own, and had rebelled against the bastard upon seeing what his king was really made of. She couldn't help wondering what life would have been like if they'd met before Gram had spotted her touring the palace with her family.

Her parents had taken her there as a birthday gift the day she'd turned nine double-years. It had been none other than York who'd approached her in The Great Dining Hall to extend an invitation to dine with the king in his royal rooms. Her father being a male of modest means, she'd allowed Gram to woo her in order to lift her family into a higher economic strata. Though partially an act of selflessness on her part, the real motivation had come from a desire to live in luxurious splendor. When the maneuver eventually resulted in their deaths, guilt had driven her deeper inside herself.

In the beginning Gram appeared to be the ultimate judicious intellectual, but she'd never been attracted to him physically. During her last pregnancy he'd confessed he no longer found her desirable. Though the words had hurt, they'd inflicted no more pain than she'd have felt if a stranger had said them to her. In truth, the tears she'd shed that day had been brought on by tremendous relief of not having to go through the counterfeit motions of being sexually pleased by him anymore. Upon discovering he wanted her again after obvious indifference to him had somehow sparked a new interest in her, she'd started pretending to be jealous of his mistresses. The fakery had worked—if she wanted him, he had no craving for her, just one of his many idiosyncrasies. So she'd vigilantly continued the ruse until telling him the truth in the dungeon.

Of course she'd also feigned being jealous in order to sooth his ego as an act of self preservation. Having supreme power, he'd been able to order anyone's death on a whim. Only the necessity of maintaining a spurious public persona had prevented him from killing a multitude of people who'd angered him. The House of Pillhigh had been rebelled against many times, and the last insurrection before Prince Zane's revolt had almost resulted in its collapse. That motivated Gram to sway popular opinion his way through propaganda. In carefully explaining the need for the Genocide Directive, he'd convinced the vast majority of Combrians and a large portion of the Urths that a malignant cancer was growing in their midst and must be surgically removed. His eloquent speech on the matter had persuaded her as well . . . for a time.

If she'd met Arigot before that fateful palace tour, their mutual attraction might have led to them being mated, and her children wouldn't be doomed to live as prisoners the rest of their lives. Gazing at a field of wild spurs stretching beyond the wire fence encircling the grounds, she began to weep.

He'd worked as a street vendor for the last three double-years, selling useless items to the tourists Mount Opian drew to the area. However, the bulk of his income had secretly come from the House of Pillhigh. Left with no king to spy for, that revenue stream had ceased. Motoring northeasterly across Serene Valley towards Marigold, he thought about his failure to live up to the name his parents had given him. Enidat meant *Truthful* in Old Combrian. But it did fit him in some ways, especially concerning his feelings for Borella.

She'd survived the attack when Prince Zane routed Gram's bomb shelter. A teleon reporter said she'd been enticed to serve as one of the king's mistresses the day before his capture. Universal Quest had communicated an offer through a spy working in the Marigold Halfway House where she'd been serving the last portion of a double-year sentence. She'd foolishly opted to become a whore rather than wait out her last ninety days. The spy being the warden, he'd had no trouble spiriting her to the universal. Thankfully, according to what she'd told the reporters, Gram hadn't gotten round to having sex with her. Despite giving up the warden, now dead from bullets administered by firing squad, she'd been sent back to the halfway house to finish doing time for embezzlement. He couldn't wait to see her.

After locating Gram, Voola had placed one of his glimeralds on the sensor before giving them to Prince Zane, requesting he humiliate the beast with the ill gotten jewels. There were rich deposits all over the globe, unfortunately most were under leagues of seawater.

Since time immemorial the bulk of the population had resided on fertile Opian, the continents of Sorria and Blancomet being mostly desert wastelands until the industrial revolution, due to their lack of rivers and lakes. Some underground streams, reservoirs, and aqueducts had been discovered on both, but the vast majority of their lands remained uncultivated, and therefore uninhabited. Goralov's equipment would soon change that. Data showed countless acres of subterranean fresh water at reachable depths beneath their surfaces, just waiting to be tapped.

She didn't understand how the computers continued receiving data when Opian faced away from Anger, but they somehow did. For now they were inactive, waiting for the red moon to rotate the transmitter back towards Combria. The picture she'd been given of a psychiatrist named Daniel Smith wouldn't be able to reveal his whereabouts for 18 hours, 42 minutes, and 6.3 seconds.

FORTY TWO

Chisel notified him the mini-carrier's radar indicated empty waters ahead. Shoehorn calculated his Mancombras were close enough to fly to Opian's upper middle-east coast after having sailed towards it for the last fifteen hours at thirty knots. They'd draw straws to determine who'd pilot the whirly with the fission bomb and which four would remain on the carrier to assist in takeoffs and landings. The other six would fly escort—three on either side of the bomber's whirly—taking out any aircraft sent to deter them if detected. It was possible they wouldn't be since the nearest military base lay two hundred miles away from their destination.

He'd stayed behind to monitor the island and keep an eye on the teleon for any news reports concerning their activity, hoping there wouldn't be any until Marigold's destruction. Then he'd contact the palace and lay out his demands.

Enidat stated who he'd come to visit, produced his

identification as required, received the mandatory four-hour dose of Clodec, and the guards let him through the minimum security gate of the halfway house. Told to wait in a foyer, he stood with hands in pockets until the lovely Borella appeared.

"Enidat, how nice to see you."

Her beautiful face reflected no such emotion, and he couldn't keep that disappointment from showing. "You look well."

"I'm sorry, I've offended you," she said. "Would you mind telling me how?"

The outer door opened and a Combrian officer in Zane's army walked in. He stood aside to let the soldier enter the lobby, and refocused on her. "You don't look pleased, that's all."

Borella exhaled a sigh. "I'm embarrassed is why. Or didn't you see me on the news?"

"Oh I saw you. Why did you do such a stupid thing? You only had ninety days to go, now a hundred more has been added to it."

"I know . . . it *was* stupid. It's just that it's so boring around here. When the warden told me of Universal Quest's offer I couldn't resist the excitement of being smuggled out. Anyway, I've learned my lesson and am lucky to be alive."

He nodded. "You are indeed, my sweet. You could have been killed by Prince Zane's soldiers."

"True, but that's not what I meant. Four other females were taken to the bunker with me, and Gram strangled one of them not long after we arrived. It's fortunate I'm not a masseuse because that's why he chose her to come to his sleep chamber. We were warned on the way there to be very obsequious to the king or be prepared to suffer his wrath. I don't know what she did to anger him but something really set him off. Anyway, how have you been doing?"

Before he could answer, an eerie whistling sound from above made him glance at the ceiling. A second later it flew away in a firestorm.

"Dammit to blazes . . . !" Vern slammed a fist on his desk and launched from his chair, stomach tied into a knot so tight it made his sides cramp. "According to this report over two hundred thousand residents are dead—annihilated by one of Nanzar's bombs. Connect me with the palace immediately, Sergeant!"

Captain Morris buzzed. "Daniel Smith is on the line, Prince Zane."

Very surprised to hear that, and grateful for the coincidence, PC picked up the receiver from his desk communicator. "What can I do for you, Doctor Smith?"

Free burst into the office, looking white as a night lapper. "Marigold has just been blasted into oblivion by an atomic bomb!"

"What?!"

"Everyone in the city is dead, PC—everyone!"

Reeling with shock, it took him a moment to remember Daniel was on the line. The receiver shook in his quivering hand, but he tried to sound calm. "I've been trying to find you, Doctor, but it looks like I'm too late. I think one of your old Mancombra colleagues at the asylum has just turned Marigold into a graveyard. Where are you?"

Arrogant laughter rang in his ear. "That would be my comrade Lathe, Prince Zane. You see, Gram Pillhigh wasn't wrong about the Mancombra threat after all. There are a dozen of us including myself. We coerced Doctor Nanzar into teaching us about how to create the doomsday weapon. Once that was accomplished we killed him and gave him to you. Quite generous of us, don't you think? The city of Juxbow is going to be hit by a thermonuclear device that will produce an explosion ten megatons greater than the fission bomb we dropped on Marigold. Then we'll drop another after that, and another after that unless you abdicate your position and transfer it to us. You'll be our guest at the palace, under lock and key of course. You have exactly one hour to announce to all of Combria that Daniel Smith and his eleven Mancombras have taken over your rule. If not, we'll force your hand soon afterwards when your subjects learn you could have stopped the destruction of Juxbow but failed to do so."

With no time to lose he had to act immediately. Hoping Free wouldn't have a heart attack from what he was about to see, PC set the receiver on his desk and entered it. The transmission voltage propelled him through Daniel Smith's earpiece a nanosecond later.

Instantly reacquiring his normal shape, he jammed the barrel of his service revolver beneath Smith's chin before the startled idiot could blink twice. "Can't thank you enough for calling me, Doctor, otherwise I wouldn't have been able to pay you this little visit. Where are the Mancombras?"

✝

Free stood with hands covering his mouth, staring at the empty space where PC had vanished. He'd been disintegrated, completely disembodied in a fraction of a second. Fear squeezed his bowels, mingling with the nausea that had been churning through them since hearing about Marigold. What kind of weapon could do that—totally vaporize someone without so much as putting a crack in a window pane? The office was on the fourth storey and the curtains were closed, so how had the assassin been able to take aim?

Cautiously making his way to one of the windows, he parted the curtains only enough to peer below. Seeing no one, he numbly walked to the chair he always used when taking meals in this office, and sank into it, weeping over the loss of his best friend.

I can't let anyone know he's dead—not even Vern or Morris for the time being. Combria must believe their righteous leader will bring whoever dropped that bomb on Marigold to justice, and total panic would break out if they knew how their prince was assassinated.

He prayed whoever took out PC wouldn't get to Vern because his experience and strategic mind would have to save the day. If Vern called seeking his commander's counsel, he'd lie and say Prince Zane had decided to defer to the general's judgment on all matters pursuant to capturing those responsible for the atomic bomb that obliterated the harbor city. Since he normally served as liaison between the two, General Yonker would have no reason to question his veracity.

The screens came to life and Voola immediately placed Daniel Smith's picture on the sensor tray. A few minutes later she had the data correlated and turned to Hammer. "He's on the same island where the transmitter located Nanzar."

He switched on his field communicator and relayed the information. Whatever he'd been told afterwards made his countenance plummet. She'd never seen that look on Hammer's face before—something was terribly wrong. Voola waited until he finished speaking to General Yonker's aide before asking about it.

"Marigold was destroyed by an immense explosion. Someone dropped an atomic bomb on it." He swallowed hard and sniffled. "I spoke with Arigot earlier today, and he told me he was going there to spend the evening with Queen Releen. I can only pray something detained him, otherwise my brother's dead."

Chisel stood at the helm of the carrier as they sailed back to the island. The mission had been a *smashing* success. He chuckled inside over the adjective, recalling how Shoehorn had rubbed it in Nanzar's face. Encountering no resistance, everything had been accomplished exactly as the brain trust calculated. They'd managed to leave the archipelago undetected and he hoped their return would be equally uneventful. If not, whatever warship they encountered would have to be destroyed.

How grateful he felt to have been selected by Dr. Smith to join his crew. Combria belonged to them now—all twelve of them—just as the genius had assured it one day would back at the asylum. Getting Prince Zane to surrender the throne would be a mere formality. If the fool didn't, he'd soon be overthrown because everyone on the planet would despise him for not preventing a multitude of deaths and the colossal destruction of private property.

Drawing a deep breath, he savored the ocean air, recalling Shoehorn's words when he'd been called to the doctor's office at the asylum to discuss his psych examine. It had been a subtle hint of what was to come.

"You far exceeded the intelligence quota, Chisel, but your social evaluation reveals tendencies of disdain for established authority, and a disturbing inability to feel true guilt over wrongdoing."

He'd cringed, fearing the position would surely be given to another. Dr. Smith had sensed his trepidation and smiled. "You look worried—don't be—I admire such traits, being I have them myself."

They'd be sailing all night and had agreed that each would spend two hours steering the ship while the other ten rested. His shift would end in twenty minutes.

"Look, Grandfather!" Togo pointed at an Urth crawling out of the ebbing tide on hands and knees, panting for breath. The man wore a uniform similar to the sailors that had come before. One side of his shirt was soaked with blood, and he looked barely alive.

Grandfather hurried to him and Togo followed.

"He's been shot," said the old chief as he knelt beside the Urth. "What's your name, Captain?"

"D-Denton . . . Baylor Denton."

Shoehorn had never seen anything so remarkable in his life. "How did you do that?!"

"It's just one of those weird dreams I told you about," Zane haughtily replied.

"This is no dream."

"No, Smith, it sure isn't. What you've done is create a nightmare." Zane pressed the barrel harder against his esophagus. "Where are we?"

"In uh, an underground stronghold beneath uh, beneath an uncharted island. Nanzar unwittingly selected it to test his bomb. We watched from here and uh, overtook the soldiers with him when he got ready to test it." He coughed for breath.

"So we're in the Lower East Combrian Sea. That means your Mancombras couldn't have flown that bomb all the way to Marigold from here. How'd they get hold of a whirly to carry it?" He jabbed the cold steel further into his throat. "Don't even think about lying to me, you piece of shit."

Almost hyperventilating, it was a struggle to speak. "We c-captured a m-mini carrier . . . the one everyone thought s-sank in a sea storm."

"That means they won't make it back here until

tomorrow," Zane calculated with a confident smirk. "I'll have this island completely secured by then. Give me that communicator . . . ."

✝

Aqua commandos by the dozens had landed on the beach, Clodec gas emitters mounted on their machineguns. Forty sailors were in Smith's underground compound, wearing gasmasks to keep from choking on a perpetual cloud of the drug. After issuing orders to Vern Yonker via communicator, PC had called Free and begged him not to tell anyone what he'd seen, promising to reveal all when he got back to the palace. His old pal had been beside himself with joyful relief to learn he hadn't been obliterated by some form of new weapon.

The CS Storm had sailed close enough to Opian to allow a hover whirly to reach the palace. He had Daniel 'Shoehorn' Smith aboard with him.

The power-mad psychiatrist had told him of a drug he'd invented that elevated the mental powers of the eleven Mancombras to such an extreme that no whirly or ship dared get within half a mile of them. Reconnaissance whirlys had verified the mini-carrier's position. The killers were twenty-three miles from their island headquarters.

PC was also aboard their vessel, but none of them could see him, hear him, or sense his presence through telepathy. He went to the helm. Having no idea how long he'd be there, he feared a gunshot would alert the others and they'd escape on shuttles or the stolen whirleys if he blew a hole through the bastard's head. So he pulled a Clodec hypo from his gun belt. The Mancombra didn't feel it when he stabbed the big male's arm, but that wouldn't negate the effect. Within minutes he'd injected the other ten. Each had been given a forty-hour dose. While thanking the unseen power for giving him time enough to neutralize them all, the carrier disappeared as his duality ended.

Picking up a communicator the captain of the Storm had given him, he turned to Smith. "I'm about to order the capture of your Mancombras, Doctor—be thinking of what you want for your last meal. All twelve of you are going to burn at high noon tomorrow, and the whole of Combria will be watching."

Smith shook his head, helplessly. "You've got me, and that I can do nothing about, but you'll never capture the others. That serum doesn't wear off. They're super beings, Prince Zane—no one can get close enough to hit them with a Clodec dart. You might as well face it, sooner or later they'll dethrone you. Spare my life and I'll convince them to be merciful to you when they do."

He grinned at the would-be dictator and turned on the communicator. "You've got it backwards, shit face. Your eleven Mancombra puppets are at *my* mercy."

Vern thanked Lieutenant Free and hung up. "Well, Sergeant, it looks like Combria's going to survive after all."

The noncom smiled broadly while wiping his brow. "So glad to hear that, Sir."

"Unfortunately the entire mid eastern seaboard has to be evacuated because of radioactive fallout coming from

Marigold . . . what used to be Marigold I should say. The weather's on our side though. Steady winds are blowing the bulk of it across the Upper East Combrian Sea. Makes me almost believe there really is a supreme being."

Chisel was utterly confounded, and worried. Try as he might he couldn't even knock a hat off any of the aqua commandos motoring towards the carrier on power shuttles.

"What's going on?!" cried Shovel, copper face aghast with anguish. "I don't have any powers!"

"Neither do I!" yelled Hoe, looking equally alarmed.

One of the sailors fired a tranquilizer dart into Miter's stomach, and the Mancombra slumped to his knees. Chisel ran towards the boarding intruder, preparing to wrap that rifle around his puny Urth neck—but when he got within arm's reach he felt something pierce his shoulder. Looking to his right, he saw a Combrian standing on a shuttle below, lowering the rifle that had just sedated him.

Though Togo rowed diligently, he knew the boat owed its swift motion to the arms of Grandfather and the other adults. They'd been heading towards a warship, but seeing sailors on an island, the chief had opted to speak with them instead. Several stood on the beach, watching their approach. All were armed.

"Ahoy there!" yelled Grandfather. "I'm the tribal chief of a band of Wanderers! I have a wounded Urth captain on my island and have come seeking help for him!"

One of the sailors motioned for them to continue to shore.

Baylor cracked his eyes open, and through blurred vision ascertained he'd been taken to a tent. He had to get word to General Yonker that a group of Mancombras with unnaturally strong powers of telekinesis and telepathy were planning to take over Combria.

After forcing Commander Dorph's suicide, the Mancombra named Chisel had boasted about how nothing could prevent him and his friends from taking over the entire planet. Immediately thereafter Baylor had felt a bullet go through him while he was being flung off the ship, the telekinetic power hurling him so high he feared smashing into the ocean would kill him. Instead, the plunge had revitalized him from shock, and he'd resurfaced on the port side of his ship. The bullet had only pierced muscle above his left hip, leaving his bowels intact. Fearing the Mancombras would scuttle the Battle Fish, he'd swam away from it, trying to avoid being killed by the explosion. They'd soon willed the missiles to launch, and seeing them circling backwards he'd submerged, diving deep as he could before his aching lungs had forced him to come up for air.

Debris floating everywhere, he'd swam to a thin plank of wood that had once been part of a tabletop, lashed himself to it with his belt, and stuffed his wounds with shards of cloth torn from a shirtsleeve with his teeth.

A female Wanderer entered the tent, followed by an aqua commando. "My men and I have come to take you home, Captain Denton."

Straining to raise his head he said, "How did you know my name?"

"The tribal chief told me. He also said you've lost a lot of blood."

"Listen—" he tried to rise but couldn't "—there's a group of Mancombras that are extremely powerful and *very* dangerous. You've got to warn General Yonker about them because they intend to take over Combria. They destroyed my ship through telekinesis and were fifteen hundred feet away when they did it."

The commando gave him a reassuring smile. "They've been captured, Captain—all eleven of them, along with their leader. What we need to do now is get you to sickbay."

He relaxed his neck and heaved a sigh of blissful relief.

FORTY THREE

POLKA SAT TO THE RIGHT of Drill and his sweetie. While they'd been in line to receive their Clodec injections, she'd found a good spot in the stands and laid down on the bench to reserve a place for them. Being old had its advantages, for no one dared rouse a poor frail woman from a much needed nap. Of course her snores had been fake. She still hadn't gotten to talk to Prince Zane about her new lab because the Marigold tragedy had understandably delayed his plans to meet with her. The eleven Mancombras and their duplicitous leader—her old colleague Daniel Smith—wouldn't be dropping any more bombs, thank The Spirit That Created All Things. The twelve of them where shackled to poles, awaiting execution by conflagration.

Such a death was far too merciful for those murdering reprobates. The death toll had reached two hundred and thirty thousand by the time all the murdered citizens had been accounted for.

†

Baylor pushed a button and the automated hospital bed raised his upper body to a reclining position. Remote in hand, he turned up the teleon volume, awaiting the execution— eager to watch those sadistic bastards go up in flames, especially Chisel. His makeshift bandages had kept him from bleeding to death in the ocean, but the entry and exit wounds got infected. The contaminated tissue had been surgically removed, and he'd get to convalesce at the palace in one of the VIP suites, courtesy of Prince Zane. A pretty Urth nurse told him he'd be taken there tomorrow.

Wearing his dress blues and medals, Vern secured his hat, preparing to march down the death walk ahead of PC and behind Captain Morris.

A private handed Morris the torch.

Shoehorn wept over the cruel injustice of it all. Why had fate so abundantly blessed his efforts from the asylum all the way to the very edge of power, only to yank glory from him at the last moment? The bitter smell of fuel oil assaulted his nostrils, forcing globs of mucus to form, adding salt to this horrible wound of unfairness. With his arms lashed to the pole pressing against his back, he couldn't wipe away the snot trickling over his trembling lips and dribbling down his chin. His Mancombras were all sobbing as well. He owed it to them to give a modicum of relief from the unbelievable misery that had befallen them due to that cursed devil PC Zane. He wasn't a Mancombra who looked like an Urth but a demon—an evil abomination of spirit that had somehow clothed itself in the illusion of a flesh and blood man.

His account of how Zane found him hadn't been believed by the Combrian officer who'd probed his mind. The fool had dismissed it as the delusions of a lunatic. Zane had claimed he'd been taken to the island by a secret sniper squad who'd discovered his location. The diabolical usurper had then warned the Combrian that information was top secret and disclosing it to anyone would land him in front of a firing squad.

"My fellow Mancombras," Shoehorn cried, unable to keep fright from quaking his voice, "in case you've forgotten your physiology training I'll remind you the pain will end once the burns turn to third degree. There won't be any nerve endings to feel anything at that stage."

He started to say more but a pride of rip howlers leapt from the bleachers, bounding towards him. While screaming in torment as they devoured his flesh, he could hear the spectators cheering, applauding, and laughing at his plight. *How ridiculous I must appear*—he thought desolately as one of the imaginary carnivores chewed off his face—*writhing in pain with no apparent source causing it.*

When the psychosomatic episode finally dissipated, drums pounded in his ears:

The death knell of ancient Combria.

Hammer was sitting beside Voola in the mess tent, eyes glued to the portable teleon he'd purchased to catch Gram's execution. The camera scanned the audience and tears began to flow when the lens scrolled past a Combrian brigadier general who looked like Arigot.

He closed his eyes. *I'm hallucinating, my love. I just thought I saw my half brother.*

No, I saw him too, she transmitted. *If not for him being a general, I would have sworn it was Arigot.*

Exhaling a mournful sigh, he rose from the table.

"Where are you going?"

"To call the palace. I haven't had the heart to confirm his death, but I just realized I can't let him rest in peace until I do . . . ."

†

On his feet cheering like everyone else as Morris, Vern, and PC marched through the gate, he felt someone nudge his shoulder. He turned to see Sergeant Brush standing there.

"Sorry to disturb you, Sir, but I thought you should know your brother thought you'd died at Marigold. Lieutenant Free sent me to find you after speaking with him when he called a few minutes ago. It seems General Hammer won't believe he's not being patronized."

Arigot frowned. "Why in blazes does Hammer think I was in Marigold when the bomb fell?"

"I don't know, Sir, you'll have to ask him."

Angry at having to miss the ignition, he followed the sergeant from the stands.

✝

"Yes it's really me dammit! Curse you, Hammer, you're causing me to miss the execution."

His brother's anger didn't spoil the elation of knowing he was alive. "You told me you were going to the halfway house to spend the evening with Queen Releen, how was I to know you'd changed your mind?"

A groan filled his ear. "I did spend the evening with Releen."

"You couldn't have, Arigot! That halfway house is near the heart of the city, right where the bomb hit."

"Yes, the one in Marigold is, but Releen wasn't sent there, you idiot! She's being detained at the new one Gram had constructed between here and University City."

Now Hammer was getting angry. "You told me Marigold, Arigot."

Another groan passed through the communicator. "All right, it is my fault. I didn't know you weren't smart enough to realize she'd be sent to a halfway house only forty-five miles from the palace rather than to the one in Marigold six hundred miles away. The name of the one she's staying in is Marigold Two. It never occurred to me you'd require the damn number to understand where I was going when I said Marigold Halfway House."

He laughed at the misunderstanding, extremely grateful there'd been one. "Forgive me, Arigot, this is the first I've heard about that halfway house. You'll never know how glad I am to learn you're alive. I love you, brother."

"Yeah?! Well run when next you see me, because I just might kill you!"

The communicator went dead. Hammer whooped for joy

in spite of being hung up on, and hurried for the mess tent, anxious to get back in front of the teleon. Something dawned on him along the way that made him frown. *When the blazes did Arigot get promoted to brigadier general?*

Releen wished she'd been at the halfway house when Gram burned, instead of locked up in the palace dungeon, then she'd have gotten to see the beast die on teleon. Watching the eleven Mancombras quivering on their poles as the flames danced higher, she couldn't help but think the mad king had been partially right: Combria nearly *had* been taken over by half-breeds. How ironic they'd been enticed to do so by the Urth dying alongside them. Gram had always been suspicious of that race too.

The evening she'd spent with Arigot two days ago had been wonderful until news arrived that Marigold had been destroyed by an atomic blast.

"I have to report to the palace immediately," he'd said.

"When will I see you again?" she'd asked.

"As soon as duty permits, I promise."

She'd been thrilled by the gleam in his eyes when he'd spoken those words, for the colonel had given her the unmistakable look of love. If Arigot hadn't been under the influence of Clodec he'd have known immediately she felt the same.

Finished with the post execution speech, PC headed for his office, dreading his arrival with every step he took. It was time to fulfill his promise to tell Free about the abilities he'd apparently inherited rather than been blessed with by The Spirit That Created All Things.

Fool—either way, the unseen power saw to it you received them! The words came as if telepathed by a Combrian or Mancombra even though originating within his own mind. Euphoria washed over him, for the thought was true. Savoring that glorious revelation, another manifested as he neared the door: he didn't have anything to worry about after all. For all Free knew he only had one power rather then three, so he'd naturally assume his so-called clairvoyance stemmed from it. Voola knew about two of them, but not the teleportation. When the secrets slipped from them, which they inevitably would via mind probes, it would appear to the populace as mere legend, since Voola's tale and Free's wouldn't coincide.

He'd promoted Arigot that morning for insisting his suspicion about Shovel and the other ten Mancombras warranted investigation. While handing over the stars he'd informed Arigot that his old captain had survived the destruction of the Battle Fish. That news had excited the Combrian more than his promotion. Then Arigot had inquired if he could ask a personal question.

He'd granted him permission and heard: "Free's been a lieutenant since you wore bars, Prince Zane, and he's your chief aide. Don't you think it's about time he moved up in rank?"

His reply had been curt. "Would you like to be busted to private, Brigadier General?"

"No, Sir, of course not."

"Then don't ever bring up the matter again."

With that fresh on his mind, he entered his office where

Free anxiously awaited an explanation. For several minutes he paced back and forth, pretending to be lost in thought.

"I didn't come here to watch you wear a hole in the floor, PC."

He drew to a halt. "I was just mulling over something Voola told me."

A scowl swallowed the look of anticipation on Free's face. "Dammit, don't stonewall me, I have a right to know. I thought you'd been killed when I saw you vanish."

Despite Free's protest, he proceeded. "While she was in the pyramid she read about a country on Earth called The United States of America. It was started by a revolution against an oppressor called King George the third. They governed themselves by elective democracy, claiming a document called The Constitution held supreme say. I'm thinking of paying her a visit tomorrow to hear more."

Free ejaculated a heated sigh. "What's that got to do with your gift you promised to explain to me?"

Shrugging his shoulders, he strolled to his desk and sat down. "All right, if you don't want to help me govern Combria I won't bother learning more about it."

As anticipated the statement excited Free. His brows lunged towards his hairline. "What are you talking about?"

"Oh no, I wouldn't dream of carrying on any further. You came here for an explanation and you shall have it. Back when I was six double-years I was talking to Harv on the communicator. Someone came into his office and he told me to hang on a minute. He set the receiver on his desk and started chatting with a professor. A few minutes later their voices trailed off and I heard his door close. Realizing he'd absent-mindedly forgotten I was still on the line, I fantasized about how funny it would be if I could fly through the wires like an energy wave, step out of his earpiece, and surprise the blazes out of him when he returned to his office. The next thing I knew I'd done just that. I was so shocked and frightened I immediately tried to wish myself back home, surprised all the more to find I'd succeeded.

"Well, I never said a word about it to Harv or anyone else, but as you can imagine, I was pretty enthralled at being able to do such a thing, and did a lot of experimenting. I can travel through airborne communication waves as well as cables, but only when another device is operating on the other end. If Daniel Smith had turned off his communicator before I'd gotten to his location, I'd have been drawn back through mine. That's why I had to let you see me do it— Smith might have hung up on me any second." He couldn't explain that he'd learned that fact by calling himself while being in two places at the same time, otherwise Free would know he had other talents and demand to be told about them. "I took out every commander opposed to me in the Urth Army by simply calling them. When they answered I was standing in front of them with a gun in my hand less than a second later. Always having the element of surprise, I got the drop on every one of them. After blowing them away, along with anyone unfortunate enough to be in the vicinity at the time, I entered their communicator and came out the other end from mine."

Free's hands were glued to the sides of his head, and his eyes were as wide as a spur sucker's. "So you did it all instead of your secret sniper team. You don't really have one, do you."

"That's something you'll never know, old friend."

Frowning again, Free lowered his arms. "I can't see how this amazing ability of yours helped you gather all the information you lied about receiving through intelligence reports."

He shot him a condescending frown. "Don't be dense, Free. If you can't see it, I can't tell you."

"You think I'm stupid, PC? You can't tell me because that's not how you did it. Flying through communication lines isn't the only fantastic talent you have, is it."

"Now see here," he cautioned, faking angry impatience, "I promised to explain what happened when you thought I'd been disintegrated, and I've done just that, now we're finished with the topic. Bring it up again and you'll find yourself wearing chevrons on your sleeves instead of bars on your shoulders, *Lieutenant.*"

Free rubbed his face and groaned, exasperation radiating from him like steam from a boiling kettle. "Will you at least tell me more about this democracy Voola spoke of? And just what did you mean about me helping you govern?"

FORTY FOUR

Eve of The Feast of the Annual Snow

CASCADING FROM DENSE CLOUDS HOVERING over the palace, white crystals looked like tiny ghosts flittering towards fallen companions who'd united to form cold downy mantels draping the multitudes of spires and donjons. The snowfall would continue until the setting of Life Giver tomorrow evening, whereupon it would stop, as it uncannily did each winter when making its first appearance. While prowling through Goralov's electronic archives, she'd learned the Earth pilgrims sent to Combria had been taught of an annual holiday called Christmas and its celebrants always hoped for snowfall on that day.

Voola had chuckled upon learning that a folk hero called Santa Claus magically distributed presents for all good little girls and boys by slipping down their chimneys on Christmas Eve. She'd laughed because the term had gotten corrupted to Sacka Cloths. Otherwise the legend remained pretty much intact. Earth children woke on Christmas morn to find toys awaiting them beneath a decorated tree. During their interplanetary flight the earthlings were taught about the holiday but under the name *The Feast of the Annual Snow*. Almost every inhabitant of Combria exchanged gifts with loved ones in the days leading up to it—presents that were forbidden to be opened until the morning after the first snow of the winter season.

The narrator, an Earth woman rather than Goralov, had explained the celebration stemmed from a religion but the earthlings traveling through space wouldn't be taught that, due to its origin not being considered mythical at the time of their launch from the space station. She'd said, "If God is real, then He'll manifest Himself in some way to the progeny we've sent to your planet that won't have been corrupted by our traditions and superstitions."

Doctor Goralov's instructions had always started from the moment she entered the main room from her sleeping quarters until exhaustion forced her back to them. Before retiring after each session, she'd spent at least two hours accessing the archives from a console by the bed. Prince Zane had developed an inordinate interest in a political structure she'd perused: a democracy called the United States. She'd given him a brief synopsis of the topic during their trip to Mount Opian that resulted in finding Gram.

It was one of the many sections of Earth history she'd selected to be preserved on a device Goralov had said Charley would give her at the end of her intense schooling. At the close of each segment of information the woman would say, "To record this topic, please press the *Save* button at the bottom of your screen." She'd left the pyramid with the history recorder inserted in one of the many inner pockets of the coveralls provided by Charley. The day after Daniel Smith and his eleven Mancombras were executed, Combria's splendid prince had flown to Mount Opian seeking to learn more. She'd shown him how to operate the device and had allowed him to take it back to the palace, reminding him it was only a loan.

The camera aboard a hover whirly quit transmitting

aerial views of the palace as one on the ground zoomed in on the promenade, where Prince Zane would soon be giving his first holiday speech as ruler of Combria. Lieutenant Free was addressing the crowd.

"Turn up the teleon, Hammer, I can barely hear it."

The brigadier general aimed the remote and settled back against a mass of pillows. Lying in an opulent bed in the palace honeymoon suite, they owed Drill a debt of gratitude that could never adequately be repaid. Three days ago, while she'd been inspecting the office complex still under construction at Fort Goralov, Hammer walked up carrying a package the driver of a supply wheeler had given him. It was marked as a holiday present for Hammer and her from Drill and Pliers, with an inscription that it wasn't to be opened until The Feast of the Annual Snow. Drill had drawn a face on the card with a winking eye, and upon seeing it, Voola had ripped the paper off immediately, suspecting what the box contained. She'd squealed with glee upon confirming it was indeed essence of valley fern, and a very generous supply. The sniper had left another note inside the box which read:

Shame on you for breaking tradition! Just kidding of course. We'd love to have you come to the palace and be our honored guests as we celebrate this upcoming holiday by being mated for life.

Hammer had given his new second in command the reins and they'd taken a long, leisurely drive to the palace, stopping at almost every inn along the way to make love. They'd gotten mated by Captain Morris that morning in a quick military ceremony in his office, and would be in attendance when Drill and Pliers exchanged vows tomorrow. Prince Zane had presented her a mating gift: the seven glimeralds she'd stolen from Gram. They'd soon be adorning a necklace at Hammer's request.

The magical douche not only worked, it *far* exceeded her expectations. Not wanting to take any chances of having to go long periods without sex when unable to find more, she planned to visit a botanist and learn how to make the stuff herself. Valley fern grew wild all around Mount Opian, so she wouldn't have any problem obtaining the main ingredient.

Hammer had promised to still love her after she grew fat. She'd awakened that morning to find an instinct, possessed by all non-Urth females, had risen from its lifelong dormancy to alert her she'd been impregnated.

In ten months a new Mancombra would enter the world.

At PC's insistence he'd gone with the demolition team to Daniel Smith's island and examined the bombs assembled by the Mancombras. Harv had shuddered with relief that Smith's plot failed. If they'd been deployed, each of the completed thermonuclear weapons would have successfully detonated. He'd carefully photographed each phase of their disassembly so Voola could pinpoint the location of any such apparatuses in the future.

Daniel Smith's formula had frightened Harv almost as much as the bombs. It had not only geometrically increased the telekinetic and telepathic strength of his Mancombras, but also enabled them to absorb and retain the intelligence of any mind they probed. Until their capture, Daniel Smith literally had the brainpower of eleven Nanzar's at his disposal. PC had told him Smith claimed the medication lasted for life, but thankfully that had been a lie. A probe of

Smith's mind revealed the active enzyme key to the serum required replenishment every twenty-four hours. A team of chemists had produced an antidote. Smith's formula and remaining serum were now locked away in a safe at the Army Command Center.

His son still refused to divulge how he'd really apprehended the psychiatrist. *Secret sniper team indeed, that was nothing but a load of sern shit.* Harv suspected Free knew, but the lieutenant wouldn't tell him either. He was one up on the aide though. PC intended to make Combria a democracy and appoint Free as its first president. No one else knew about it at the moment, he'd only confided those plans to Molly and him.

They'd moved back home a few days after Smith's execution, and learned a beautiful veterinarian named Stellar Allure had bought the house next door during their stay at the palace. Harv marveled at what a small world it was because she and Daniel Smith were apparently the only ones like PC in all of Combria, since no one else had tested positive. They'd befriended her and learned she had some secret plans of her own.

She was at their house now, lounging in the parlor, waiting to hear PC address the planet. "I wonder if we'll be able to have children."

Molly laughed and tilted her holiday drink towards the vivacious rare-breed. "Don't count your hickers before they hatch, Stellar. PC's only seen you one time, and here you are thinking you're to become his mate."

Her pretty lips spread with a knowing smile. "It's not the number of times a man sees you, but the way he sees you that matters. You could have parked a wheeler in his mouth when I first walked into his office."

"It was gaping that wide, huh?" Harv laughed while saying it.

She nodded and took a sip of her liquored mixture. "He tried to hide it all evening but I saw right through him. I left his apartment thinking I had no chance because of his dedication to duty, but the moment I found out my new neighbors were his adoptive parents I knew fate had deemed us to mate. Look at the oddity of my moving next door—I had no idea you lived here. It may take some time to convince him, I'll grant that. But I will . . . wait and see."

He took a pull of his hot spicy malk and winked at her. "PC invented stubbornness, Stellar. I wouldn't get my hopes up if I were you."

Her big blue eyes narrowed with an endearing squint. "You didn't see the way he looked at me, Harv. It was so cute how he tried to conceal his feelings. Has he always worn his hair so delightfully long?"

"You like it, huh. Well I sure don't."

"Oh I love it! What about you, Molly?"

"I think it makes him look feminine, and I've told him so at least a thousand times. I made him keep it close-cropped until he left home. When he was a small boy PC dreamed about an Urth who had supernatural strength. The Spirit That Created All Things warned the man never to cut his hair or wear a hat, because if he ever did his great strength would be taken from him. PC woke up convinced that if he mimicked the Urth he'd grow strong like the man in his dream. He cried and cried when I wouldn't let him grow it out, bless his heart. After he got promoted to colonel and had the right to choose his own hairstyle, it grew longer each time we saw him. By the time he made general it was the length he wears it now. Of course it never added one iota to his strength, but I know he superstitiously thinks not cutting it makes him invincible, though he'll never admit it."

Blancomet was a rugged desert continent composed of thousands of square miles of flat land running north and south between dormant volcanic mountain ranges. Its three million civilian residents resided in oasis towns strewn along the equator. Only one broadcasting system could reach them, as the others' frequencies weren't recognized by a satellite the Opian Broadcasting Corporation launched into space five double-years ago. Like the communication satellite which enabled people to call one another from any point on the globe, its creation had been ordered by the House of Pillhigh, who'd monopolized teleon broadcasting and communication services until Gram's father allowed the creation of other companies to prevent an uprising. PC—who wanted another built and launched as soon as possible so the audio-video signals of all the broadcasting companies would be bounced back to the planet—had made OBC a public company when dealing with all the Special Cases regarding proper ownership of assets, lands, houses, and enterprises.

After flipping through a dozen channels with the teleon screen showing nothing but scrambling white dots, Arigot finally found reception and set the remote down. Because of its isolated location on a northern peninsula—jutting into the Upper West Combrian Sea a thousand miles from Opian's west coast, and four hundred miles north of the nearest oasis city—Fort Haloon served as a military prison. Haloon was Combrian for *Wasteland.* He hadn't expected to run the place, PC deciding to reunite Releen with her children and exile them here had prompted his desire to be stationed at the most unpopular base on the planet.

"How fortuitous of you to request such a transfer," Vern

had said. "We've had a colonel presiding over it since we took out the two stone universal in command there early in the revolution. He hates the damn place and would love nothing more than to return to Opian. You'll ship out tomorrow. I'll contact the colonel and tell him to turn over the reigns to you after you get acclimated to your new command. I can't imagine why you'd want duty on Blancomet to begin with, but why Fort Haloon, Arigot?"

"Because I've fallen in love with Gram's widow and she's been exiled there," he'd answered unashamedly.

He sat beside her on a sofa in his parlor, waiting for PC to make his holiday address. A sergeant was watching over her kids at the base house she'd been granted. She and they were free to go wherever they pleased within the fenced in perimeter of the residential section, which included a commissary, school, gymnasium, and park built for the amusement of military brats. The supply ship that carried him from Opian had docked five days ago. They'd made love within two hours of his arrival and numerous times since. He'd relished every minute of time spent at what was colloquially called Fort Shit.

They were savoring mugs of hot malk spiked with dark sweetener and liquor, waiting for Prince Zane to appear on Duke Kaleen's massive teleon. The festive concoction had already made her a little giddy after only two sips. Polka gazed fondly at Drill and Pliers, sitting next to each other. Tomorrow they'd be mated in The Celebration Room of the palace, a favor she'd procured from Price Zane, who'd promised to attend. Tragically, Pliers had also lost her entire family before the abolishment of the Genocide Directive, so she was the closest thing either Mancombra had to being a relative.

Captain Morris had pulled some strings with SIS at her request, and they'd dispatched Specialist Ling back to the palace. No one could be more capable of teaching the mind probing technique than her protégé who'd mastered it. Construction of her laboratory and a new house by Palace Lake were well underway, and she couldn't believe the number of tibs the government deposited in her account every fourteen days. But what she'd really been blinking her eyes over was being awarded the Combrian Medal of Honor for Scientific Achievement. She'd made it clear in her acceptance speech, while weeping before an array of teleon cameras, that the award really belonged to her deceased mate, who'd spearheaded the research.

She took another nip from her glass and reached for a confection ball. Pliers had baked a mountain of them. Their main ingredients—soger, booter, kackanut, and schlokick—really *had* been brought by the Urths from outer space like the old myth alleged. Their proper names were sugar, butter, coconut, and chocolate, she'd been informed by Drill's friend Voola, whom she'd met that morning in Captain Morris's office because Drill had asked her to attend the impromptu mating of his former commander.

Voola had also told her that earthlings pronounced malk *milk,* which also went into to the making of confection balls. Serns were native to Combria but so similar to an Earth subspecies called Cattle from a species known as Bovine— exported with other livestock accompanying the Earth pilgrims—Voola speculated no one in modern times could be certain which one's malk, meat, or hide-item they were buying at the market.

Tossing Drill a sentimental smile she said, "It seems like an eternity since we were living at my farm last spring, doesn't it?"

"Yes, it really does." Drill scooped up a handful of sweets from the mound. "And yet only three seasons have passed since. Is that journal you told me about still there?"

"Mm hmm. I'm going to pay my old neighbors a visit after the holiday and fetch it while I'm down there. I don't have the heart to sell the place since it's where my mate died, so I'm planning to get the house refurbished and rent it out."

Drill grinned. "What are you going to do with your old wheeler?"

"That outdated piece of junk? The renters can do whatever they want with it. My mate would have found the price I paid for my new one obscene, rest his soul. I so wish we could have had children so a piece of him would still be around. He contracted the mum at puberty and it migrated from his salivary glands to his testicles, leaving him sterile. That's what inspired him to go into genetics as a matter of fact." Drill and Pliers were suddenly looking at her with deep sadness in their purple eyes, obviously feeling her loss, so she shifted to the present. "But my oh my I can't complain—living in the lap of luxury like this."

A guilty frown emanated from Pliers, the same expression she'd worn when first hearing her plans. "Are you sure you want to stay here?"

She nodded. "I've gotten spoiled to this apartment. You two will enjoy the lake house much more than I would—I'm too old for swimming and water sports. You kiddos get to live there rent free as my mating present. It'll be in my name of course but I've left it to Drill in my will. Like the two of you, I don't have any blood kin still living."

The pretty Mancombra sipped her festive malk and smiled. "I'll miss cooking for you, Ma'am."

"No you won't," said Drill with a cocky grin. "You'll be cooking for me now. She'll have to make her own meals for a change."

Polka let out a dry laugh. "Fat chance on that. The lab will have a kitchenette where Pliers can fix my lunch. I'll eat breakfast and dinner in The Great Dining Hall. Oh, here comes Prince Zane!"

Snowflakes landing on his long red hair, Pythagoras Copernicus Zane stepped up to the podium.

"Holiday Greetings to all citizens of Combria. This Feast of the Annual Snow will be the first in modern times to be celebrated without an oppressive dictator in power. Not long after the war ended I met with the head of the Opian Broadcasting Corporation and asked him to produce a documentary of an amazing event that befell a Combrian female named Voola. I'm very pleased to announce that four-hour documentary will air on OBC at noon tomorrow, and will be repeated tomorrow night and each night thereafter for the next forty days to ensure all who wish to see it may do so.

"In that presentation you'll learn that the large majority of myths about Urths are in fact based on reality. There really was a time when only one race lived on our small planet, a time before a colony of beings came here from a place called Earth, E-A-R-T-H, over eleven trillion miles away. They were sent here in the hope that the human race would survive on Combria in the event global war terminated it on Earth. Fellow citizens, that's what almost happened to us, and we must take every precaution to make certain that such an event never occurs.

"Voola learned of a country on Earth called The United States of America which was run by a government *of* the people, *by* the people, *for* the people. The inner workings of that government will be presented to you in the documentary. At the moment I serve as your sovereign, but I plan to make Combria a democracy divided into forty-eight political zones on Opian, and one each on Sorria and Blancomet for a total of fifty. The citizens will elect representatives from the zones they reside in, choosing the ones they feel will fight for their best interests in a congress where they'll vote on all matters pertinent to their constituents. The majority vote will become the law of the land if approved by a president elected by all residents of Combria, or vetoed if the president so chooses. Conversely, the president won't have the right to pass anything into law unless his proposal gains a majority vote in the congress.

"I've yet to decide on a time frame for the president to be in power, but there will be a limitation. Your first president will be appointed by me. After his term is up a majority vote by you, the people, will decide who'll reside in the palace as Commander-In-Chief. No one person—Urth, Combrian, or Mancombra—should have complete control over our planet because we're all fallible beings. Once such a government is installed I will serve as supreme overseer, using that overriding power only when necessary to avoid costly mistakes such a young government will inevitably make initially. That position will die with me, and the president and congress must then pick nine judges to serve on what will be called The Supreme Court, making the government of Combria three branches: executive, legislative, and judicial, with checks and balances for each. All the particulars will be hashed out and recorded in a document to be called The Constitution of Combria, patterned very closely to one called The Constitution of The United States, which you'll learn about in the documentary.

"My follow Combrians—and by that term I mean Urths and Mancombras as well—the only one capable of absolute equity in ruling all peoples is The Spirit That Created All

Things. And I swear to you by that holy name that for the duration of my life I'll do my best to serve you as prince of that unseen power: the omniscient, omnipresent, omnipotent deity being king and lord over us all.

"What you'll also learn in the documentary is that our standard of living is about to be greatly enhanced due to a technology an Earth scientist named Ivan Goralov blessed us with. It will not only enable us to prosper, it virtually makes it impossible for any known criminal to avoid capture. Indeed it was Goralov's devices given to Voola that enabled me to find Gram Pillhigh. And so to honor Doctor Goralov, from now on the tenth day after every second Feast of the Annual Snow will be a holiday to be called Goralov Day, also to be known as New Year's Day. No longer will a completion of our planet's orbit around Life Giver be called a double-year, because the term came from the earthlings whose planet circled their star twice in that number of days. Ten days from tomorrow will be recorded in our history as Year One. On the next Goralov Day it will be written as Year Two and so on. These devices I spoke of were built to last a thousand Earth years. By then our scientists should know how to replace them, perhaps even surpass their capabilities.

"Truly we stand at the threshold of a possible paradise, but it cannot be realized unless we all love one another and show that affection by treating everyone the way we'd like to be treated. So let us learn to love all others as we love ourselves, strive to live righteously—help the unfortunate, maimed, and handicapped—and walk humbly before that unseen power watching over all creation. The Spirit That Created All Things bless you all."

About the Author

Arley Owens, Jr. is a musician, composer, poet, artist, author, producer, and rancher who resides on his ranch in Midland County Texas with his lovely wife Cristi, also a native Texan. He's a member of the musical group TORN PAGE. http://www.tornpageband.com

Other books by Arley Owens, Jr.
  A Tale of the Mojave
  The Cyrus Syndrome
  A Texas Ghost Story
  Incident In Baltimore
  Death Ranch
  20 Miles to Justified

SHORTY MAE PRODUCTIONS
P.O. BOX 81102
MIDLAND, TEXAS 79708

www.ingramcontent.com/pod-product-compliance
Lightning Source LLC
Chambersburg PA
CBHW050753030726
47505CB00002B/522